ARE YOU
MY
HALLEY HART?

CLAIRE McCAULEY

JOFFE BOOKS

Joffe Books, London
www.joffebooks.com

First published in Great Britain in 2024

Cover art by The Brewster Project

ISBN: 978-1-83526-578-9

For my mother and my daughters:
Allison Claire, Genevieve Clara and Celestine Allison.

PROLOGUE

Wednesday, 19 February

From: Henry Inglis
Subject: Are You My Halley Hart?
To: Halley Hart

Dear Halley,

After my encounter, back in September, with a woman I only knew as Halley Hart, I couldn't get her out of my head. I had no idea whether I stood any chance of finding her, nor, of course, of everything that lay ahead. Now, five months on, the reality is that the distance between me and 'my' Halley — *you* — is further than ever.

I know you'll recall that today's my birthday. I also know you won't be in touch. Maybe that's why I've been able to think about little but those early days, and why I've found myself compiling all the emails that resulted from my search. I've attached a copy for you. You've seen some of it before of course — indeed, you wrote parts of it.

I hope this doesn't make you feel worse about everything — that's far from my intention.

Henry

FIVE MONTHS EARLIER

PART ONE

Saturday, 21 September
10.15 a.m. — Henry

Henry glanced into the window of the coffee shop, then paused. Every table was full, there was a queue at the counter, and he was in a hurry. Facing the day's task without caffeine felt especially unappealing, when standing in the drizzle.

The rain began falling harder and faster. Internally, Henry swore.

'*Oh shit*,' a woman said, with feeling, from behind. The sensation that she'd given voice to his thought was so strong that Henry glanced over his shoulder, catching sight of a tail of bright, streaming hair, flying out behind the woman as she shot into the café.

Taking refuge indoors was the only sensible response to sheeting rain so, ignoring his qualms about lateness, Henry pushed through the door, its bell jangling.

Surveying the inside, he pulled back his hood and ran a hand through his hair, wavering again. This place made far better drinks than the chains, but wasn't renowned for speed. And the queue stretched the entire length of the counter with five customers ahead of him — six, including the woman from outside, who now joined the end of the line.

With a wince of sympathy at how wet her hair and thin jacket were, he took his position in the queue. He'd give it a few minutes. The woman in front of him appeared to shiver and as she repositioned her shoulder bag and lifted her ponytail from her neck, droplets of water scattered and flew. He shifted backwards — but not nearly fast enough to avoid a fine misting of water across his face. He reached for the napkins on the counter. The movement seemed to alert the woman to his presence, and she spun around.

His first impression was that she appeared to be in her mid-twenties, not far from his own age of twenty-eight. His second, that in response to his damp face her own became dismayed. He tightened his fist around the napkin to conceal it.

'I didn't notice you there,' she said, reaching back to catch her ponytail between both hands. She had an American accent, and a throaty tone. 'I'm so sorry.' Her skin had a slightly pinched look, presumably from the sudden deluge, and several flecks of mascara had migrated to her cheekbones. It didn't detract from the impact of her eyes, which were large and grey within their round orbits.

'Not at all,' Henry murmured, finding himself suddenly much less despondent about the wait. He added, with a smile, 'My fault entirely for standing too close.'

That won him direct eye contact, and a mirroring smile with a flash of dimples. He opened his mouth to speak again as the door jangled. A couple entered, moaning about the rain, and the young woman rotated away.

Absurdly, Henry felt bereft at losing her attention. He couldn't stop watching as she nimbly twisted her hair, forming it into a crescent which she held against her head with one hand. She rooted inside her jeans pocket with the other, eventually drawing out a yellow pencil, which she thrust horizontally through the crescent. Somehow, pencil and hair remained perfectly in place.

Henry suppressed an urge to ask how she'd tamed gravity. His first question shouldn't in any way reference her appearance. *Do you come here often*, he considered before scoffing at himself. He eyed her again, wondering if introducing himself would be unwelcome. With her hair up he could see the outline of her shoulder blades through her jacket, and the slender gold chain around her neck. None of that hinted at her interest — or disinterest — in conversing with him.

She inclined her head to examine the chalkboard menu on the wall behind the counter. Her profile revealed full lips balancing out a decidedly firm chin. He cleared his throat.

Unsure if she was listening, Henry began anyway. 'I'm—'

'Latte with a double shot,' the young barista hollered at the same moment, drowning him out.

'That better be mine — with oat milk, right?' the customer at the front said with a scowl.

The barista frowned. 'Was it? I forgot. Hey,' he raised his voice again. 'Anyone wanting a double-shot cow's milk latte, to drink in?'

Without missing a beat, the young woman called, 'I'll take it.'

An instant later she was on her way to the till, and Henry snapped his jaw shut on a pointless protest.

She was asking how much she owed for the drink. Glancing around a taller man, he watched her press a bank card to the terminal then accept the proffered cup and saucer. She squeezed through to the only empty seat, where she sat down and disappeared entirely from Henry's view.

At the counter, the belligerent customer was kicking up a fuss about how long he'd already waited, and the barista seemed to respond by remaking his latte even more slowly.

Henry released a long stream of breath. There was nothing for it but to make a dash for Costa. Before he reached the door, he took a moment to look again for the young woman.

She was lost from his sight in the sea of bodies.

* * *

Radcliffe Square was surrounded on three sides by crenellated walls and varied university buildings, and on the fourth by a church with an ornate spire, but Halley's attention was on the imposing circular structure in the centre of the quadrangle. It was tiered like a wedding cake, with symmetrical columns reaching up to a domed roof.

Halley resumed her walk around the perimeter of the cobbled square, dodging people and the puddles which, like her damp hair, were reminders of earlier rainfall. Pausing to drink in the view of the Radcliffe Camera from another angle, she pulled her pencil free, releasing her ponytail to dry. Behind her, someone commented on the building's beauty at so high a volume that it cut straight through the general hum of sound. It was a fellow American, of course, and Halley winced. Until her arrival in Europe a few weeks earlier, she'd assumed their international reputation for loudness was overstated.

Another American piped up with a shrill question, and she glanced over. Both her compatriots were attached to a tour group, assembled in a semi-circle around a guide who was facing away from her.

His voice was authoritative yet kind, and Halley edged closer. He was explaining that the iconic landmark in the middle of the square, known as the Radcam, remained a working library, which she knew, and that it was connected to other sections of the Bodleian libraries by an underground tunnel, which she didn't.

Deciding she'd too quickly dismissed the idea of an organized tour, Halley lingered to ask about the route. If it went past the place she was most keen to see, she'd try to buy a ticket.

'Take a wander through the quad,' the guide broke off to say. As the group collapsed into smaller clumps he half-turned to call after them. 'We'll move on in five minutes.'

Halley seized her opportunity and stepped forward, looking up into his face — though not very far up, since he wasn't much above average, for a guy. 'Excuse me. Do you go past—'

Recognition flashed through every nerve in her body and she broke off, struck speechless.

The tour guide was the guy from the coffee shop.

The *cute* guy, over whom she'd shaken droplets of water, like some wet dog.

The cute guy who was now meeting her gaze, so she witnessed his moment of recognition.

'It's you,' he said blankly.

Heat spread up Halley's face.

'I beg your pardon,' he added quickly. 'That came out wrong. It's just I . . . I thought I'd never . . . well, uh . . . anyway. How can I help?'

Poised on the balls of her feet for escape, Halley opened her mouth to tell him that it didn't matter.

'Sincerely,' he said quickly. 'I'd like to help, if I can. Do you need directions?'

She searched his face, now devoid of its odd expression. His mouth had relaxed and his blue-green eyes were alert with interest. She eased her tightened arches, rebalancing her weight from toe to heel.

'I wondered about your route.' Her voice sounded stiff so she employed a trick of her mother's, to keep from sounding nervous, and smiled broadly. 'Particularly, whether it takes you past Halley's observatory.'

He blinked. His lashes were long, and a fraction lighter than his mid-brown hair and eyebrows.

'It's not what we'd think of as an observatory these days,' she added quickly. 'Just an old house in New College Lane. Edmond Halley — who predicted the return of the comet that came to be named after him — lived there in the early eighteenth century.' She had to stop to take a breath, a sure sign she'd been gabbling.

He nodded, and gestured toward the exit at the northeast corner of the square. 'It's over there, but we head inside the library to look around the Old Bod next, so don't pass it until the end of the tour.'

'So could I?'

His lips rippled, and then he was reflecting her smile back at her. It made his eyes crinkle into creases. 'Uh . . . *could you?*'

'Buy a ticket and join you for the rest of the tour?'

He hesitated. 'Unfortunately not,' he said eventually, sounding genuinely sorry. *Inside Oxford* is a private walking tour — it can only be pre-booked online. But on Broad Street there are several tours that depart on the hour, with tickets available direct from the guides. I can direct you—'

'Henry, is this the middle of the campus?' a man scurried over to ask.

Aware of taking a few seconds too long to cover her disappointment, Halley was grateful for the interruption, though the guide himself — Henry, she now knew — appeared confused, surveying the questioner with an air of surprise. After a short pause, he expelled a deep breath, then seemed to refocus.

'As I mentioned at the start,' he said mildly, 'the university's made up of over thirty colleges and numerous department buildings that are spread throughout the city — there isn't a campus, as such.'

His attention returned to her, and Halley smiled again. 'I understand. Thanks for your time.'

'No, *wait*,' he said instantly. 'Thinking about it, the rotten weather caused several no-shows.' He lowered his voice. 'As long as you wouldn't mind keeping quiet about it to the rest of the group, I could reassign one of those unused tickets to you — free of charge, of course.'

Halley didn't need to think twice. 'Really? That would be great!'

'Brilliant!' he said, as though she were the one doing him the favour. 'I'm Henry, by the way.'

'I heard,' she said. 'I'm Halley. Halley Hart.' She beamed at him, but multiple members of his group were assembling beside them, so she didn't add anything else.

He did a brief headcount then rounded up a few stragglers to sweep them all through into a smaller quadrangle, entirely enclosed by library buildings.

'People are working inside, so we have to respect that they need silence,' Henry said. 'We will only talk in the stairwells, and even then, need to keep our voices low.' His gaze travelled over them all, but paused on hers. Halley flushed, sure it was because she was American, and Americans, being loud, needed to be doubly warned about the sanctity of libraries.

Someone asked if students would really be inside the library on a weekend.

'It'll mainly be academics, today — and graduate students,' Henry said. 'The academic year doesn't begin for another week or two, so undergraduates aren't yet in residence.' He continued as he led them inside the grand main entrance, explaining that Oxford University had three terms, each only eight weeks long, which rendered them immensely intense, and that students didn't live in residential halls, but spread out through their colleges.

Halley hung back as everyone passed into the library, uncertain about not having paid for a ticket. But the whole group was ushered inside without challenge, and up a twisting staircase into a triple-height room of breathtaking beauty. Under a panelled ceiling, the full length of the walls were filled with leather-bound books in ancient oak cabinetry. A carved staircase and wraparound gallery offered access to the upper level of the collection. Only the far wall was empty of books, instead being taken up by a huge arched window, segmented by stone mullions, each set with a plethora of leaded-glass panes.

'It's stunning,' the American woman beside her cooed, at volume.

Halley glared at her, shooting her index finger to her lips for good measure.

* * *

1.09 p.m. — Henry

Viola would absolutely marmalize him if she found out about this. Her company didn't spend so much on advertising their *expert-led cultural tours to all corners of the UK* for him to turn around and give away a freebie. And he didn't even want to imagine her reaction to hearing that he'd done so in response to a pretty young woman's eyes lighting up at a library tour. She'd probably call him a creep.

Not that sharing a love of libraries was the only reason for his impulsive offer, he admitted to himself, leading his group down the final staircase. The biggest was an instinct that he couldn't let Halley Hart slip through his fingers again, not after the serendipity of this second encounter. He intended to take the opportunity to ask what she was doing in Oxford — and how long she could stay. Then there was the fact that despite knowing so little about her, he already liked her. It was more than merely the way she looked — he flicked his eyes to her, at the back of the group — though that was certainly part of it. He shook his head at himself, and glumly reflected that Viola might be right to call him a creep.

Henry was recalled to the job in hand when one of his group stumbled, then shrieked. After going to help, he launched into his final section of spiel about the history of the place. Halley remained at the back, and Henry silently chided himself. He wanted her beside him, where he could indulge his curiosity, but by asking her not to mention joining them for free, he'd made her feel self-conscious.

He wondered if he was correct to visualize her name spelled like the comet, and if so, if it explained her interest in Edmond Halley's observatory, of all things. It certainly wasn't a place that appeared on any list of the ten best sights in Oxford. It didn't even feature on *Unofficial Oxford's Forty-Two Nerdiest Things To See* list, alongside the sweetshop that the real Alice in Wonderland used to visit, Tolkien's grave and Einstein's blackboard.

Ushering everyone through an exit leading onto a court-yard, Henry saw Rupert Peters, his boss at his proper job, hurrying toward him.

'Henry! Glad I bumped into you. There's an issue with the tutorial schedule—'

'I warned you I'd be rather busy today,' Henry said.

Rupert looked at him blankly. He was a good boss, aside from forgetting everything he considered irrelevant — from the unwritten rules of polite discourse, to what day of the week it was — though his memory was prodigious for everything he deemed important. Since he was a medieval history professor of significant renown, this basically meant every event that befell humanity between the fourth and sixteenth centuries.

'How about I drop by your office later?' Henry suggested, returning to his group before Rupert could object. They'd emerged, blinking and slightly dazed, to congregate past where he waited, which conveniently positioned him near Halley Hart. He directed everyone onto Broad Street, then right for the Bridge of Sighs, before falling into step beside Halley. 'Your observatory's the next stop after that.'

Her mouth quirked in a way he couldn't begin to interpret. 'More precisely, my eleven times great-grandfather's observatory.' He glanced at her uncertainly, and she laughed. 'Edmond Halley is an ancestor of mine, via one of his granddaughters. Because they lost the Halley surname through marriage, a tradition built up of using Halley as a Christian name for the eldest daught— Hey, should you do something about that?'

His eyes shifted in the direction she was pointing, to discover his family of Norwegians had gone left, rather than right, to make a beeline for a bookshop. He waved his thanks to Halley as he scarpered toward them.

By the time he caught up with his group again, they were gaping up at the striking covered skyway that connected two parts of Hertford College above New College Lane. His attention was drawn, yet again, to Halley, neck craned and observing it in motionless absorption. He'd already noticed how purposefully she moved, and this sudden stillness had a purpose all of its own.

'Ghost!' a French teenager sniggered and Henry was obliged to look away from Halley to the figure, surrounded by swirling black, that could be seen rushing through the bridge, before disappearing from sight at the other end.

'That was someone wearing an academic gown, in a bit of hurry.' He added more quietly, recalling what had kept him busy the day before, 'Probably late to an SCR meeting, discussing Hertford's incoming freshers.'

'Freshers are freshmen?' an amused voice said from behind him, as he guided the group along the lane. 'But what's SCR?'

He glanced back at Halley. 'Senior Common Room: the college's academic staff — with graduate and undergrad students known respectively as the middle and junior common rooms. And also a physical space — generally a series of interconnected recreation rooms.'

'Are you a member of Hertford's SCR, or a different one?'

He darted a sidelong look at her. 'Another college's. How on earth could you tell?'

'That guy who stopped you outside the library knew you, and he was the type of professor who only knows other academics. Besides, I don't get the vibe that the tour-guiding gig is who you really are.'

'You're observant,' he said.

'I get told that a lot,' Halley said, half laughing. Her eyes widened. 'Oh, this is it . . .' she breathed.

The three-storey house was set back from the street, and partially screened behind wrought-iron railings and mature foliage. Before he could suggest that she would get a better view if she moved down to look through the gate, she pointed up at a rectangular structure jutting up from the slate roof, her eyes shining. 'That was his observatory. It was built for him specially. And look at this—' He followed the arc of her gaze sideward, to a stone plaque on the gate post. It was engraved *Edmond Halley, 1656–1742*. Above the words, the comet was depicted as a golden ball with a multi-stranded tail.

Halley traced her fingers over it and Henry recalled himself to duty, turning to gather the group back together. He raised his voice to project over the distant wail of a siren. 'This was the home and workplace of the astronomer and mathematician who was first to calculate the orbit of the periodic comet that came to be named after him.'

'We saw it in the eighties, didn't we hon?' a man said to his wife.

'I was in grade school,' said an American woman in her forties. 'I don't remember seeing it, only the project we did about it.' She brightened perceptibly. 'You're meant to get to see it once in your lifetime, and maybe it's not that I forgot, but I really didn't see it. Which means I'm guaranteed to live until at least . . . at least . . .'

Henry recalled that Halley's Comet was visible from Earth every seventy-six or so years, but was hazy on when in the eighties it had last appeared, so couldn't help with the calculation.

'2061,' Halley supplied. She had got a proper camera out of her bag, and unclipped the lens cover. She didn't tell the rest of the group about her link to the comet, so Henry didn't mention it either, but did his best to answer the rest of the questions.

Halley photographed the sign then backed up, probably to get some of the entire property. But other members of the group kept stepping into shot, so she lowered her camera, no doubt biding her time.

Henry needed to walk the group back into Radcliffe Square but he was convinced Halley would remain behind to get her pictures. He was tempted to stay, dispensing with the formality of accompanying the group to the tour's end point. But, visualizing his sister's exasperated reaction, he knew he must follow protocol. Viola had rescued him when, after being awarded his doctorate, he was rejected from academic posts left, right and centre. She had hired him as a guide for the national cultural expedition company she helped run. It had kept him in full employment until last year when he began his current role as a junior research fellow at St Jude's College, Oxford. The downside was that when short-staffed, Viola begged him to step in and conduct tours, and he didn't like to refuse, though it wasn't an ideal way to use his weekends.

He directed the group back the way they'd come, and as everyone else began retracing their footsteps Halley just watched them, remaining where she was.

'I need a moment,' he called after the departing group. 'Turn left at the end, and you'll be back in Radcliffe Square. I'll catch up shortly.' He glanced at Halley, and lowered his voice. 'It was nice to meet you, Halley Hart.'

'You too,' she said. 'Thanks for letting me tag along.' But she was already looking through the camera's viewfinder at the house. Castigating himself silently for thinking she'd, what — fall into his arms once they were alone? — he turned to trudge away.

'Henry—'

He swung back instantly. 'Yes?'

'Would you have time to take my photo? My mom would love one of me here.'

'Not a problem,' he said, striding over and accepting her camera. It had an intimidating number of dials and buttons. 'I'm afraid I haven't taken photos with anything but a smartphone for a long time.'

'Just point, and click the red button.' She sidestepped until she stood adjacent to the sign. Grateful beyond belief to be able to look at her without pretending not to, he centred the house within the viewfinder, clicked once, and then a few more times for good measure.

'Would you take a few close-ups — just me and the sign? Twist that same button to the left to zoom in.'

Henry twisted, and the lens lengthened. He trained it on Halley's face. Her large grey eyes were screwed up slightly against the sun, which was also highlighting the palest streaks in her fair hair, so they shone. Her smile was broad, so her dimples had deepened to the point that they would be more accurately described as pleats bracketing her wide mouth, and they weren't quite symmetrical, with the one on the right more pronounced. Her slender gold necklace had a tiny charm shaped like a five-armed starfish hanging from one side of it, but if there were other charms they were concealed beneath the crew neck of her top. Combined with her easy intelligence and careful way of examining and interacting with the world around her, she was irresistible.

He clicked the button several times, then lowered the camera and blurted, 'What are you doing this evening?'

Her brows twitched up. 'Finding someplace for dinner . . .'

'Any interest in eating with a local?' he asked on a rushed, single breath. 'Though no problem if—'

'If you can make 7 p.m., that sounds cool,' Halley said.

Henry's heart soared, and he ransacked his brain for quiet options with decent food, that would be easy for her to find . . . He had it. 'How about we meet at the Hope and Anchor? It's a pub on Nor—'

'Yoo-hoo, Henry?' someone called from far behind him. 'Are you coming?' Several members of his tour group were waiting at the bend in the street.

'Go,' Halley said, her eyes sparkling as she accepted her camera back. 'I'll see you at seven, at the Hope and Anchor.'

* * *

5.56 p.m. — Halley

The teenage boy behind the reception desk grunted when she returned to the cheap hotel she'd stayed at last night, in a janky room she'd been glad to check out of early that morning.

'I left my backpack in your luggage store,' she began.

He jerked his head toward a narrow doorway and mumbled a string of vowels.

'I know it's in there,' Halley said. 'The thing is, I've made dinner plans, but I'm not sure where the pub is — the Hope and Anchor? If it's nearby I'll return for my bag afterwards, but if it's on the other side of the city I'll have to collect it now.'

He cast her a gormless look.

'You could look up the location for me,' she suggested.

He grunted something she thought was *no need for that*, and pressed a grubby finger to the laminated Oxford map, Scotch-taped to the reception desk.

Halley bent closer to read the tiny street name. 'Globe Road — that's where it is?' At his nod, she considered. When Henry had suggested the Hope and Anchor, she'd had a vague sense of recollection, and thought they may have passed it during the tour. But Globe Road appeared to instead be north of the city centre. Unfortunately, as her hotel was way to the south, it left her little choice but to turn up to dinner with luggage.

She sighed as she poked her head through the doorway, identified her mid-sized backpack and heaved it over one shoulder, rearranging the strap of her camera's shoulder bag across the other.

'Thanks,' she called back at the boy, who didn't even bother responding with a grunt. It served her right, she knew, for booking the cheapest room in the city, though that was less a choice and more a necessity, forced on her by the depletion of her funds after three weeks in Europe.

She hoped the pub wasn't expensive, then stood, stock-still in the middle of the sidewalk, panicking in case it was. Maybe she shouldn't go. Henry lived in Oxford, and she was leaving soon.

Halley resumed walking, weighing the matter over and over. She'd squeezed in a lot, in her short time in Oxford, but only managed to visit one of the multiple museums after the tour ended. Another museum stayed open late on Saturdays, and it was illogical to miss out on that for the sake of an evening with a near-stranger. However cute he was. Or courteous he was — but in an understated way, not like he was showing off about having good manners. And whether or not he listened intently when others spoke, and spoke eloquently without ever being glib.

Realizing she had been walking aimlessly, she decided to at least head in the right direction, and paused to ask a local for directions to Globe Road. She could scope the pub out before making up her mind. Maybe even head inside a little early, and check she could afford the prices on the menu.

* * *

7.04 p.m. — Henry

Henry careered up the narrow street, came to an abrupt stop beside the kerb, and swung a leg off his bike. As he fastened it to a half-empty rack, he glanced over at the Hope and Anchor, confirming that Halley wasn't waiting for him outside. His second tour group of the day had been particularly garrulous, and afterwards he'd run to college to chat to Rupert. It had left him little time to return home to shower, and even with cycling back, he was a few minutes late.

He unclipped his cycle helmet and carried it under his arm, hastening past the coffee shop at which he'd first seen Halley, earlier in the day. He'd chosen this pub partly because it was on the same road, so it would be easy for her to find, though he hadn't had time to explain that properly before the interruption.

He ducked under the low lintel and surveyed the small space: Halley hadn't arrived yet.

'What can I get you?' the barman said. Henry forestalled ordering, explaining that he was waiting for someone who hadn't been here before, and might need to pop outside to keep an eye out for her.

His phone buzzed, and he experienced a pang of dread in case it was Halley, cancelling on him. But, of course, they hadn't got around to exchanging numbers, and the alert was for a new voice note. It would be Viola, since uninterrupted vocal utterances were his sister's favourite mode of communication. She'd want an update on today's tours, and to update him on their parents, whom she'd gone to see. Henry didn't need to listen to it to know that Dad's hip looked like it was painful, but he insisted it felt fine, or that Mum's next appointment at the memory clinic still hadn't come through.

The door opened and Henry raised his eyes expectantly. But it was a couple of strangers. He strode to a small table in the far corner and slid into the chair that faced the entrance. Hanging his cycle helmet from its arm, he told himself to calm down. He knew so little about Halley that he absolutely shouldn't feel so desperate to see her again.

He went out and checked both ways along the street, as well as outside the coffee shop. There was no sign of Halley. On his return to his table he listened to Viola's message, for something to do. All was as he had predicted, and he stowed his phone in his jacket pocket. Then he pulled it back out and checked his email then scrolled through the day's news. None of it was an effective distraction from the question that was rapidly overtaking his attention . . . was Halley even coming?

He sprung up again to look outside, this time pacing the entire length of North Parade — the street on which the Hope and Anchor and the coffee shop were situated. He had expressly stated that address to Halley — or at least he'd started to, before being interrupted. But if Halley hadn't heard it all, she only needed to google, or ask anyone, and she'd be given this address.

Something niggled in the back of Henry's consciousness as he went back into the pub.

'Cheer up,' the barman said. 'Either that, or drown your sorrows . . .'

Henry ignored the heavy hint. 'This is the only Hope and Anchor in Oxford, isn't it?'

'Nah mate. It confuses everyone — especially with being so close by. They're bigger and all, but we were named first.'

Henry was already racing to snatch up his cycle helmet. 'Where is it?'

'Globe Road.'

Henry sprinted out. He'd never been along Globe Road, which explained why he hadn't been aware of a pub with the exact same name. It was under half a mile away — only two to three minutes, on his bike. He'd be there before half seven, he thought, reaching the bike rack, which was entirely empty.

Henry stared around, in case he'd forgotten which rack he'd leaned his bike against. But there was only one. He must have been so stressed by arriving late that he hadn't locked it properly, and then so distracted by whether Halley would arrive that he hadn't noticed when it was stolen, despite coming outside regularly. Worst of all, he thought, starting to run again, he now wouldn't be there by half past.

Dusk was falling and he was breathing hard as he turned into Globe Road and spied the other Hope and Anchor, a red-brick Victorian building. He leapt up the step to push through the front door, and gazed around wildly.

Halley wasn't in sight, but as the barman at the last place had pointed out, this was a bigger establishment, and Henry continued around the back of the bar and then into another room, filled with diners. Still no Halley. Finally he went to the bar.

'I was meant to be meeting someone here. Halley Hart. She's blonde, American, about five foot seven — have you seen her?'

The barman said that he hadn't so laconically that Henry asked if he could check with the other staff. A bar manager came over, confirmed that she also hadn't noticed anyone of that description, then went to confer with the waiters. 'Unfortunately not,' she said, on her return. 'It's been a busy start to the night.'

Henry had lost his appetite, but wanted to hang around, in case Halley was extremely late, rather than having been and gone — or never turned up. So he ordered a sandwich and cup of tea, which he took over to nurse at the sole empty table, against one wall.

Staring into the mug, he tried to come to terms with being down one bicycle — and one Halley Hart.

* * *

7.53 p.m. — Halley

A tumult of emotion plagued Halley as she neared the railway station. After she got to the quaint pub half an hour ahead of schedule, she'd wanted to stay, and even sat at a table. But then her rational self took over, and she'd listed all the reasons this was a dumb idea.

But she'd hated the thought of standing Henry up, so waited, her eyes fixed on the door, until 7.14, when he still wasn't there, and she'd slumped back, annoyed. Maybe he had a succession of girls from tours turning up here, only for him to never show at all. At that, she sprung up, seized her backpack, and left swiftly. She paused only to queue at a food truck, paying with the last of her British cash for a falafel wrap that she could barely taste, on her mile-long trudge to the railway station.

Inside, she scoured the departure board for an earlier train to London, and saw one listed for 8.35, leaving her only forty minutes to wait, as long as her e-ticket allowed changes. She stomped to the information desk, groping at her side for her camera bag, to get her phone from the front pocket.

'I wanted to ask if I can hop on the earlier train to London,' she said, smiling perfunctorily at the station employee. She glanced down. Her backpack was slung properly over both shoulders, to lighten the load while she walked. But she didn't have her camera bag.

'That's fine, love — I don't need to check your ticket,' the woman said. 'Everyone's got to get on the 8.35, because that's the last. The later one's cancelled.'

'I don't . . . I don't have my bag,' Halley said. Her voice reverberated curiously in her skull.

The woman clicked her tongue. 'Thieves operate in here, though we do our best to—'

Halley shook her head vehemently. It hadn't been stolen. It was a mile back, at the Hope and Anchor, under the table she'd left in such a hurry. And the last train was leaving in thirty-nine minutes. She broke into a run, darting around people and suitcases and bicycles, then out the double doors into the darkening evening, down the steps, and back the way she'd come.

Elite female runners could complete a mile in under five minutes. Unfortunately, preferring Pilates and yoga, she was far from elite, even without a heavy backpack. She'd been nearly five minutes already, she calculated as she slowed to cross a road, and was around halfway. That meant ten minutes to get there, five to find her camera bag, and fifteen to get back and onto the right platform. It was doable *if* she found her bag quickly. Panting, she increased her speed.

By the time she reached the Hope and Anchor Halley could only breathe in short, tearing gasps, and felt too exhausted even to push the front door open. Thankfully a group of giggling women exited, and she slipped through. Her eyes darted between the bar and her table from earlier, unsure whether to start looking herself, or ask if it had been handed in. Since the table, against the far wall, was empty, she tried there first, dropping to her knees and scrabbling under the long tablecloth.

Her hands alighted on the waxed canvas, and she drew her bag out, unfastening it shakily. Her camera was inside, with all its accessories, and her phone and sunglasses were in the front. She put those alongside her wallet in her jacket pocket, then squashed her camera bag into her backpack before heaving the whole thing onto her shoulders.

Outside, rain had started up again, and she shivered. The evening's ordeal wouldn't end until she made it onto that train. She sucked in a deep breath, readying herself for another run.

Her eyes alighted on a black taxi, which rounded the corner before pulling up in front of the pub. Even as she made a dash for it, she saw a figure, lit by the warm glow of a street lamp, who'd already held an arm out to hail the cab.

A figure she recognized, even from behind, and in different clothes to earlier. It was the shape of his broad shoulders, and his hair: close-cropped at the back and sides, neatly blended to a longer length up top, where it was textured and slightly wavy. Henry had been waiting for her, and without stopping to think, she hollered his name.

He froze, then rotated slowly toward her, his eyebrows sky high.

All of a sudden, the bottom dropped out of her stomach, like she was in free fall.

'You came,' she breathed, pacing forward to bridge the distance between them.

'Forgive me,' he said. 'There's two Hope and Anchors, and I went to the other. I've only been in Oxford for a year, I hadn't realized.'

Under the illuminating street lamp she could make out faint freckles on his fair skin, and glints of stubble along his defined jaw. An unexpected longing burned through her lungs, but logic reasserted itself, yammering a protest.

'I need that taxi,' she said. 'My train's cancelled and the last one leaves in fifteen minutes.'

Henry locked eyes with her. 'My bicycle's been stolen.'

'Will one of you just get in!' the cab driver yelled.

Henry's slanted blue-green eyes tightened, like he was thinking hard. Then he moved aside, opening the cab door. 'Take it,' he said.

It was too late to tell him that her desperation for the taxi had waned, replaced by a sudden desire to remain in his presence. Instead, even as she told herself she must have lost her mind, she rose onto tiptoes, leaned in and pressed her lips to his cheek. When he didn't resist, she turned her head minutely and brushed her lips against his. His lips were warm, and he'd been drinking something she couldn't identify, because his breath was woody and mellow and also slightly sweet.

His hands grasped hers and he leaned closer.

The cab driver blared his horn, and she flinched.

'Thanks, Henry,' she said breathlessly, tearing her hands from his and sliding into the cab, before slamming the door. The impatient driver screeched away before she'd even got her backpack off and seat belt on. Her eyes stinging, she didn't dare look back.

PART TWO

Wednesday, 2 October
Henry

Noise drifted up from the quadrangle and through the window of Henry's college office, where he sat thinking of the woman he'd promised himself to stop thinking of. Eleven days on from being struck speechless by the heated collision of Halley's lips, he was still seeing stars.

Every time he closed his eyes a series of images flashed: Halley's hair held up with a pencil . . . Halley appearing to him at the Radcam . . . the glow of a street lamp haloed around Halley when she kissed him. Seconds later she'd left to get the train somewhere, and he'd been left behind, rigid with shock and regretting not jumping into the taxi beside her, to confess he'd fallen for her and beg for her phone number. Now, all he knew was her name, and all he had were her sunglasses, which had fallen onto the kerb.

He'd found several Halley Harts in the USA, but it was immediately evident from their profile pictures that none of them were *his* Halley. And when he expanded his search to the rest of the world, it was more of the same. If his Halley had a digital footprint, he'd come up blank with finding it.

The only idea he had left was emailing HalleyHart@ every single domain name he could come up with, which was entirely too extreme.

Shoving to his feet, he glanced through the dormer window that jutted from the sloping ceiling of his eaves office. Down in the old quad the college porters were supervising a strict one-in one-out system for the cars queuing behind the gate. As each was admitted, some of the waiting third-years, who'd returned a day earlier, sprinted over to greet the new student, and offer help unloading.

Henry paced to the far side of his office, where the ceiling was higher with no risk of banging his head, and he rested a hand on the bulging old plaster of the wall behind him. From this angle he could see straight out across the gables, chimneys and spires of Oxford's skyline, a view that never failed to relax him.

Well, until Halley fled in that taxi, which had displaced his ability to relax, with this pent-up jittering.

Pushing off from the wall, he returned to his desk and flipped to the middle of his leather-bound journal, which was part-filled with his neat, slanted handwriting. He'd kept the log of daily developments in his historical research since his Ph.D., often filling a full page with reflections on papers he was reading, analysis of problems he'd noticed, or hunches on locations for the old documents he sought. Never before had he used it for anything personal, but now there were several pages devoted to Halley. He turned to a fresh page, determined to do some proper work.

He was investigating a possible extension of his first research paper, which had recently been accepted for publication in an academic journal. The focus of that was a sketchbook from 1806, which had lain unexamined in the St Jude's library until Henry had unearthed it soon after his arrival. He'd spent the previous year laboriously decoding the writing beneath the drawings, discovering diary entries by a girl named Louisa Sedgwick, in which she quoted letters from her brother, Lawrence, who was a young British naval officer, at that time away at sea. Over the summer, Henry had invested many hours into scouring his college's records, but had found nothing else related to the Sedgwick family.

He glanced at the time on his phone, then got up, grabbed his academic gown from its hook on the back of the door, and exited his tiny office. His office was on the top floor, and he tramped down the four storey staircase, pushed outside and went under the archway into the old quad. He slowed to a lope over the cobblestones and shoved first one arm, then the other, into the wide sleeves of his gown. The black fabric caught the breeze so it billowed out behind him as he passed an overfull Volvo, where two parents appeared to be playing car Jenga, attempting to dislodge boxes without pulling the rest of the pile over. Their black-haired daughter was trilling at the third years about how *oxciting* it was to arrive at Oxford.

Henry spared her a smile as he rushed on, through the covered passage and out the other side into East Quad. He was headed to a building on the far side of the square, diagonally across from him, but he couldn't cut across the grass without breaking five hundred years of tradition, and risking a penalty rumoured to be the miscreant's choice of beheading, defenestration from the Dean's office, or a £250 fine. He continued down one edge at a jog, then round to pass the old cloisters, where he stopped short just in time to avoid a collision with a man, who was elderly, but by no means frail. Professor Geoffrey Hogshaw, frequently referred to behind his back as Hogshoo, due to the loud snoring that regularly emanated from his office, was a fellow historian, but beyond their subject they shared little in common.

Henry gave him a cautious nod, which Hogshoo barely deigned to return, instead scowling at a rake-thin boy who wandered past them, almost buckling under the weight of a shoe box, and glancing all around him as if he were lost.

'God help us if there's a war,' Hogshoo said with marked disgust.

Henry intervened quickly, asking the boy his staircase number and directing him, before nodding once more at

Hogshoo and continuing on to enter the Senior Common Room.

Ruth, the college's rosy-cheeked young chaplain, who was also in charge of student welfare, was beside the coffee machine. As he sidled over she noticed him, and rooted in the pocket of her floral dress, which she'd layered over her clerical shirt and collar.

'Kwame said he put it at the far end of the bike shed,' she said, proffering a small key, 'in hope that none of the new arrivals inadvertently lock theirs to it.'

'Perfect,' he said, accepting the key to the lock of the bike he'd bought from Ruth's husband, who lived with her in the chaplaincy accommodation on the college site. Kwame owned a second-hand cycle shop. He was also a friend. Henry liked Ruth, too, despite feeling somewhat restrained by her vocation when she turned up to the pub in her dog collar. 'Thanks for the key — and to Kwame for delivering the bike.'

'It's no problem. We know the start of Michaelmas is manic for all you tutors.'

'The *rest* of Michaelmas term will be manic for me, too,' he said in an undertone. 'Did you hear that Hogshoo pulled out on tutorial teaching? Forced by a medical situation, he claimed. And he refuses to ask either of his senior doctoral students to cover him. Both are too close to submitting their theses, apparently. Rupert can't understand why he's being so obstructive.'

'Mmm,' Ruth said, because she was too diplomatic to point out what everyone but Rupert knew, that Geoffrey Hogshaw clearly held a grudge against the decade-younger Rupert, for being catapulted above him as St Jude's Senior History Tutor when the previous incumbent retired. 'So Rupert's taking on double teaching, and you're having to do extra too?'

'Exactly,' Henry said on a sigh. 'The only advantage being that I'll get most of my contracted teaching hours out of the way this term, freeing the rest of the year for my research. That's not going great, so maybe it's just as well.'

'Is that what's keeping you up half the night?' Ruth asked.

He met her eyes, silently questioning how she could possibly know of his trouble sleeping.

'I've noticed you leaving college after midnight three times this week, and Kwame said he sees you arrive at dawn most days. Those hours don't leave much time for shuteye.'

'Well, I've had to plan a full set of tutorials for the first years that were just foisted on me.' It was an effort to speak mildly, and he suspected Ruth had clocked his defensiveness. He scratched his head, thinking hard. He never liked to lie, and he certainly wasn't going to do so to a friend — and minister of religion. But neither did he want to take Ruth into his confidence about Halley in the middle of a room crowded with colleagues. He lowered his voice, and chose his words carefully. 'But it's not just that, you're right. I've been struggling to sleep — struggling to do much of anything — for worrying about . . . something I'm desperate to find.'

Ruth's diplomacy kicked in, and she didn't pry further. 'My experience with issues that intrude every time you try to think about something else, is that drowning them out — with work, or booze, or worrying about worrying about them — is never as effective as confronting them head-on.'

As Henry considered that, one of the college bigwigs announced it was time to make their way through to the conference table in the next room. Ruth grabbed her coffee and rushed forward.

Henry caught up with her. 'How would I do that, though? When I can't find something, it's impossible to face it head-on.'

Ruth paused. 'It's hard to advise without knowing the details, but — have you searched until you've exhausted every possibility?'

He recalled the list of email domain names. 'No . . .'

Ruth brightened. 'I'd start there.'

* * *

From: Henry Inglis
Subject: Are You My Halley Hart?
To: Halley Hart, Halley Hart, Halley A. Hart, Halley B. Hart, etc ...

Dear Halley,

Are you my Halley Hart?

Not that I mean to imply ownership in any way, I'm just specifically seeking the Halley Hart who I encountered during her/your visit to Oxford on Saturday, 21 September.

If you are Halley — my Halley — then hopefully you know why I'm going to these lengths to find you.

If you're a different Halley, please accept my profuse apologies.

With very best wishes,
Henry

* * *

Delivery to the following recipients failed permanently: [Halley X. Hart] [Halley Q. Hart] Reason: User unknown.

* * *

From: Halley S. Hart
Subject: Automatic reply Are You My Halley Hart?
To: Henry Inglis

Greetings from purgatory!

I'm currently offline, due to vacationing at an all-inclusive wellness retreat that's sprung a digital detox on me.

If your message requires a response, I'll be in touch as soon as I've stolen my phone back from the lockbox, or otherwise once I'm released ...

If it's urgent, you're very welcome to parachute into the Arizona desert to rescue me.

Sincerely,

Halley S. Hart

* * *

Friday, 4 October

From: Halley HART
Subject: Bad news, Good news!!!
To: Henry Inglis

Dear Henry,

The BAD news is that I'm not the Halley Hart you're after. Actually I'm not Halley Hart at all. I'm Halley diMaggio, but my hair salon is called Halley Hair Art . . . Halley H-ART, geddit?

Anyway, you should be so lucky for sending this to me, because the GOOD news is that I know how you can find her! You see last year Foof, my Teacup Pomeranian, was snatched from the salon. I know, totally traumatic! But also kinda lucky because obvs I put her adorable photo straight on my socials, hash-tagging it #SnatchAlert #FindMyFoof and before I knew it my post was high-key trending! Jeanine from *Real Housewives* even shared it, and that brought my salon more new clients than all the times I've run a referral discount put together!

Soooo I really think you should post a photo on your socials and tag it #AreYouMyHalleyHart. If you're hot then you can @ my salon and then you never know . . . Jeanine might share it! No offence, but if you're not hot then maybe skip the photo.

Good luck!

Halley diMaggio

* * *

From: Halley P. Hart
Subject: Are You My Halley Hart?
To: Henry Inglis

Well bless your heart, Mr Inglis. I hate to have to tell you but I'm the wrong Halley Hart.

I read your email aloud at chair yoga this morning to see if any of the girls might know the right one, but they all said I'm the only Halley Hart they have ever rightly heard of.

My friend Marcia thinks you sound real charming, and I'm to say that if you don't find your Halley Hart you'd be most welcome to correspond with her instead. She might be madder than a wet hen, but in my seventy-three years I've never tasted better devilled eggs than Marcia's.

Cordially yours,
Mrs Halley Priscilla Hart

* * *

Sunday, 6 October

From: Halley S. Hart
Subject: Are You My Halley Hart?
To: Henry Inglis

Dear Henry,

Sorry not to reply properly sooner, I've been away for something that my relative, Edie, optimistically called a vacation, as you should know from my auto-reply.

'Your' Halley Hart made a big impression, huh?

Before I reveal anything about myself I'd like you to confirm a few basics. Like, what's your general state of solvency, do you have a police record, and are you definitely single?

By the way, how many Halley Harts have written you back? I thought ours was a pretty rare name.

Sincerely, Halley

* * *

From: Henry Inglis
Subject: Are You My Halley Hart?
To: Halley S. Hart

Dear Halley,

I did indeed get your auto-response. I hope you ended up having a restful trip, and thank you for taking the time to reply now you've got your phone back.

So far, I've had two other Halley Harts confirm they are not the intended recipient.

Turning to your other questions. Of course I'm single, my last relationship was short-lived and ended ten months ago. Unfortunately the outstanding balance on my student loans is far in excess of my bank balance, so I have little claim on solvency. In better news, I have no police record. Well, not unless they recorded that my bicycle was stolen last month, when I reported it. Though if you're Halley — *my* Halley — I briefly mentioned that before the kiss.

Dare I hope that you are indeed my Halley?

Very best wishes,

Henry

* * *

Monday, 7 October

From: Halley C. Hart
Subject: Are You My Halley Hart?
To: Henry Inglis

It's not me, I've never even been to Oxford. Good luck in your quest!

Halley Ciara Hart

* * *

Tuesday, 8 October

From: Halley A. Hart
Subject: Are You My Halley Hart?
To: Henry Inglis
Roses are red and violets are blue,

Of course I'm your Halley, and I love you!

Halley

* * *

From: Henry Inglis
Subject: Are You My Halley Hart?
To: Halley A. Hart
Dear Halley,

Thank you for the speedy reply. And the declaration of love.

I must admit to being somewhat taken aback, having heard, several days ago, from another Halley Hart who I thought was the one I'm seeking.

Sorry to put you on the spot, but may I ask — what was the object that you inadvertently left in my possession?

All best wishes,

Henry

* * *

Wednesday, 9 October

From: Halley S. Hart
Subject: Are You My Halley Hart?
To: Henry Inglis

Hi Henry,

How are you today?

Your student loans don't count against you, by the way. I know all too well that despite being priceless, education is expensive. Have you replaced your stolen bike, and may I ask with what?

As for whether I'm your Halley . . . didn't someone smart say famously that every correspondence benefits from a healthy dose of mystery?

Sincerely, Halley

* * *

From: Henry Inglis
Subject: Are You My Halley Hart?
To: Halley S. Hart

Dear Halley,

I'm afraid the Oxford Dictionary of Quotation contains no entries for the keywords *mystery*, *correspondence* and *healthy*. So it hasn't yet become famous, and anyway, I'm not convinced that the originator could have intended the mystery to be the identity of one of the individuals engaged in corresponding?

I've replaced my bike with another battered old bicycle — which is more expensive, in Oxford, than a new one, since it's less likely to be stolen.

As for how I am doing today . . . to be honest, I'm feeling rather discombobulated, after receiving a reply from another Halley. She's claiming to be the one I met, in which case my suspicion that you're such is wrong. I've asked her to confirm what the object was that Halley inadvertently left in my possession, and I need to ask you the same question.

Very best wishes,
Henry

* * *

Henry reluctantly switched his mobile off as he entered the dining hall. Never, when sending the email, did he consider the possibility that two Halley Harts would claim to be his, and he was impatient for answers from each. But hall etiquette stated no mobile phones. He navigated through the rows of trestle tables, rapidly filling with hungry students, to reach high table, which was set perpendicular to the others.

'Good news, Henry,' Rupert called, as Henry reached an empty seat two-thirds of the way down. 'Did you hear me?' Rupert added, in a bellow down the length of the table, loud enough to silence the general hubbub. 'I'm pleased for that breakthrough on the hunt for—'

'I heard!' Henry called back, frantically trying to recall how his boss could know anything about his search for Halley. He'd bumped into Rupert during the tour, but Halley hadn't even been at his side, and he certainly hadn't introduced them.

Rupert opened his mouth again, and Henry added, 'Can we discuss this later?'

'A bit hush-hush, you reckon?' Rupert asked amiably. 'Let's sit a little more privately then.' With that he rose to his feet and moved towards the far end of the table. The convention was to fill high table strictly from right to left without leaving gaps, so there was a general rustling of indignation. Rupert ignored it — or more likely, wasn't even aware of it, and Henry tried to look suitably apologetic as he trailed after the older man. They settled into new places, with a clear eight empty chairs between them and their colleagues, as a quavering undergraduate stood up to stammer out grace in Latin. The first time Henry had witnessed this, he'd wondered if it was some sort of punishment, before learning it was bestowed as a dubious reward on second years who'd attained the highest marks in recent examinations.

Rupert's amber eyes were lively with conspiracy, and he spoke in a hoarse whisper. 'This is very cloak and dagger. What have you discovered?'

Henry laid his hands flat on the oak table top, scarred with centuries of wear, as if a stable foundation might steady his breathing. 'Forgive me, Rupert, but I fail to see what your interest could be in my search for the woman I fell for. Let alone how you even—'

'Woman?' Rupert said, so loudly that several heads turned in their direction. 'What's it got to do with a woman?'

Henry studied Rupert, staring at him with the same confusion.

'I put it in your pigeon hole this morning,' Rupert said. 'I thought you'd follow it up immediately.'

The steward arrived with the soup course, and placed bowls in front of them.

'Thanks,' Henry said, before returning his attention to his boss. 'I haven't seen any note. I was busy marking my first years' essays, then taking their tutorial. What was it regarding?'

'That sketchbook you unearthed last year,' Rupert said, in a low, confiding tone. 'Belonging to the Sedgwick family. I thought you'd want to know . . .'

When Henry was applying for his current position, he'd asked a friend who attended some of Rupert Peter's lectures what the man behind the impressive reputation was really like. *Peters by name, peters by nature* had been the reply, and Henry always recalled it at times like these, when Rupert's attempt at an explanation petered out so quickly it was rendered nonsensical.

Rupert lowered his head, with its resplendent crop of salt-and-pepper hair, over his bowl, as he brought his spoon up to his lips. When he went in for a second scoop without elucidating, Henry intervened.

'Sorry, you thought I'd like to know what?'

Rupert frowned, then his face cleared. 'Ah, yes. Well, I came across a mention, in records from 1952, that this college transferred Sedgwick family papers to the Bodleian.'

Henry almost dropped his heavy silver spoon in his surprise. 'You're serious?'

'Entirely,' Rupert assured him. 'I can only surmise that the sketchbook was inadvertently separated from the rest, before the donation took place.' He frowned again. 'Speaking of searching, what was it you thought I was referring to?'

'No matter,' Henry said, with unfeigned excitement. He'd checked the Bod's online catalogue for the name Sedgwick, but when nothing related to the family in question leaped out at him, his attention remained on St Jude's archives. With a definitive place to look, and knowing the year of donation, that would change.

'What did you make of your . . .' Rupert said, gesticulating with his spoon.

'First years?' Henry guessed, with a grimace.

'Oh dear. What was the issue?'

Henry pursed his lips, recollecting the tutorial where his pair of students' essays, and the wider reading that he'd set them, were discussed. 'Both submitted essays showed promise, so I had high hopes. They weren't dashed by the young lady, who is . . . uh . . . enthusiastic.' When she'd bounced into his office, he'd recognized her as the one trilling about her *ox-citement* on arrivals day. While they awaited the other student, she gasped about the view from his window, proclaimed the sloped ceiling *ox-quaint*, and begged him for a selfie to mark her first *ox-tute*. 'But the young man arrived late, then didn't say a single word for the entire hour, except for muttering *exactly* after everything his tute-partner said. When I asked him direct questions, he shuffled his feet and went dumb.'

'He could be shy.' Rupert was always quick to defend young people, whom he liked almost without exception.

'But generally that also shows up with a lack of confidence in their written work, don't you think? Whereas his essay took a firm stance and defended it to the hilt. But he then couldn't — or wouldn't — add a single thought on the matter verbally.'

'Best run it through the plagiarism detection software,' Rupert said with a sigh.

Henry already had, and no cheating had been identified. Before he could say so, the steward returned to his side.

'Phone call for you, Henry. Apparently, it's an urgent matter.'

'Excuse me,' Henry murmured to Rupert, switching on his mobile. He had missed no calls while it was off. Viola would have tried that first if there were any emergency with their parents. Which left . . . could Halley be calling? While his full name was in his email address, he hadn't included any contact information, or even his college or occupation in any of the emails. His Halley alone knew he was an academic. A quick online search would lead her to St Jude's website.

'Do you know who it is?' he asked, shuffling his chair back to bound to his feet.

'The porter didn't say. Just that it's a lady.'

Henry's heart sped up, and he scraped his chair across the parquet flooring in his rush to stand up. 'Sorry — I have to take a call,' he said to Rupert, before striding out.

He raced up to his office, because it was the only location in college where privacy was guaranteed, lifted the receiver from the landline, and pressed the button that connected him to the porter's lodge at the college gates. As well as dealing with incoming visitors, parcels and security, the porters manned the phone for general enquiries. 'Henry Inglis here, could I be connected to my incoming call?'

'Righty-ho, Henry,' a porter said.

His pulse thudded in his ears as there was a click, and then a female voice, with some sort of accent, said, 'Is that Henry?'

Every millimetre of his body contracted in a spasm of surprise and delight, his hands knotting around the receiver, his back hunching over his desk. His Halley had found him.

'Henry Inglis, I mean,' she said. 'Or, I guess . . . *Dr* Henry Inglis? My name's Halley Hart.'

All the blood drained from Henry's head, and he sat down in a hurry. This woman's voice wasn't right, and her accent wasn't American. Somehow, a different Halley had found him.

'Are you there?' Not-his Halley demanded.

'Yes,' he said, dry-mouthed.

'Good. I got an email that purported to be from Henry Inglis, of Oxford, looking for someone called Halley Hart, spelt exactly like I spell it in my email address. It seems to be a pretty sophisticated romance scam, because there's no way any fraudster would bother with as weirdly specific a name as Halley Hart rather than Sarah Smith or something, so presumably they've programmed a bot to change the name to match each email address.'

Henry dropped his head into his hands. 'Oh God . . .'

'It must be a shock,' she said. 'But when I saw that you're a uni lecturer, I was determined to pass on the intelligence. I thought, shit, what'll happen if this email explodes into his students' inboxes? I'd searched for Henry Inglis in Oxford, you see, because there was no way a scammer like that would use his real name — the smart ones scrape enough identifying information on a real individual to pose as him, and he seems pretty smart, because he didn't fall for me immediately claiming to be his Halley and in love with him. He's probably learned from being ambushed by a scambaiter before.'

Henry latched onto the last thing she said. 'Scambaiter? I've never heard—'

'It means I feign interest in obvious scams, to purposefully waste fraudsters' time, hopefully limiting how much fraud they're getting away with elsewhere. Basically, I scam the scammers. Have you heard of the "hey mom" scam, where they pose as someone's kid, pretending their phone was stolen so they're on a new number, and need money transferred for an urgent bill? That one's my specialty. I keep the pretence up for hours with my favourite ruse, that I'm this bougie parent, replying like, *Darling, I think we should get you a new phone too*, and spamming them with links for different options.'

'Thanks for the explanation,' Henry said, stalling. 'I'd never come across the profession of scambaiting before.'

Running back through what she'd said, he realized she must be the one who sent the *roses are red* reply. He hadn't had another email from her after challenging her on what Halley left in his possession.

'I can't go so far as to claim it's my *profession*, but I'm working towards getting licensed as a private investigator here in Queensland, and when that happens it kind of will be. For now I'm night receptionist at an office block. My boss doesn't give a crap what I do as long as I look busy. So I listen to true crime podcasts and email, text and call scammers.'

The mention of Queensland helped Henry to identify her accent. 'You're making an international call, from work, in Australia, uh . . .' For one ludicrous moment, he hadn't been able to recall her name. 'Halley?'

'It's Halley-Anne, actually. Hyphenated. I dropped the Anne for my email address so I can immediately pick out who really knows me, and who's faking. And yeah, calling from Brisbane, Australia. As I said, my boss wants me to appear busy. Y'know, part of me wishes you had been the scammer, so I'd a chance of wheedling out where the Halley Hart romance scam is heading. I guess I'll have to report back on it to my friends in the scambaiting community instead — see if any of them have any ideas on its purpose.'

'It wasn't a scam,' Henry blurted.

'What?'

He took a deep breath. 'The email wasn't a scam. I met an American called Halley Hart, and couldn't get her out of my head. Then I wrote the email and . . . and sent it to Halley Hart at every domain name I could come up with, as well as various versions with a middle initial. It wasn't a scam and I'm not a scammer, just genuinely looking for my Halley.'

There was silence. Then Halley-Anne swore. 'In my defence, you wrote the sketchiest non-scamming email I've ever set eyes on! And, seriously, so I have this right . . . Your Halley Hart left such an impression that you're doing the email equivalent of cold-calling every Halley Hart in the phone book?'

'Correct,' Henry said, wondering if he sounded as idiotic as he felt. 'And there's no need to apologize. I'm the one who should say sorry for sending you the unsolicited correspondence in the first place.'

'Did it work?' Halley-Anne asked. 'Have you found her yet?'

'I don't know,' he said heavily. 'Someone's been messaging, but so far she's refused to divulge if she's my Halley or not. I was hopeful that it was her, maybe feeling shy or something, until I got your email. Then I asked her the same question, about the object, and she hasn't replied.'

'Then it's not her,' Halley-Anne said immediately. Henry couldn't disagree. 'By the way, what *was* the object? And are you certain it was inadvertent and not some kind of clue as to how to find her?'

'Her sunglasses. They fell from her pocket as she left.'

'Describe them to me!'

Henry hesitated.

'I'm a trainee PI, Henry,' she urged. 'I'll help you search — no charge, but you've got to write me a reference when I start my business. Now come on, full description of the sunnies — and the case, if they were in one.'

Henry made a swift decision that he had little to lose by taking her up on the offer, and caught them up. 'The sunglasses are light blue plastic, and shaped like cat eyes. The case is black, I don't know if it's artificial leather or the real stuff. Both are marked only with a logo that says Doe Eyes, which I've never heard of before, though I don't know much about fashion.'

'I know masses about fashion, and I haven't either,' Halley-Anne said speculatively. 'I wonder if it's a small independent brand that can help us pinpoint her location . . . Email me a picture of them, and your mobile number, and I'll do some research and get back to you. Bye!'

Henry stood, holding the receiver and blinking. After talking so volubly, Halley-Anne had instantly ended the call.

* * *

Halley took a rough headcount as she accepted papers from students traipsing past her into the lecture theatre. When everyone was in, she leafed through the pile, confirming her initial impression.

She raised her voice above the hubbub. 'Listen up! Some of you sneaked by me without submitting your problem sheet.'

'Didn't seem any point,' said a brave soul at the end of a row. 'When Jacob hasn't uploaded any of our grades for the work we've done already.'

'They'll be marked within five days in future,' Halley said grimly, 'and the . . . blip with your outstanding assignments will be investigated.' As lead teaching assistant for the large introductory astronomy course, she'd had no choice but to attend the lecture in Jacob's place, after he'd quit on the spot. She'd put a hundred bucks on him not having marked a single one of their papers, and if she couldn't draft someone else quickly, she'd be stuck marking all of those, too. And in double-quick time, since Jacob had been assigned to Professor Tung's lectures, and he happened to be her own doctoral thesis advisor. If there was a single professor in the astronomy department whom she wanted to keep happy, it was Tung.

'Unfortunately, personal circumstances mean Jacob is no longer assigned to this section, and you'll meet your new TA soon. I'm covering until then, and from now on, please upload your assignments to the portal when they're due. If you've been too sick to do the assignment, email me your excuse and I'll pass it along to Professor Tung for consideration. If you need help with the assignment, visit me in my office, or email me for support. If you dispute the marking on an assignment — who wants to venture a guess? — yes, let me know via email. I'm Halley Hart, and my email address is now up on the screen, and also on the portal.'

Professor Tung arrived, followed by a keen TA from another section. Halley breathed a sigh of gratitude, and went over to confer.

'I can take over,' the TA said. 'I helped design the assignment this lecture will feed into.'

Halley glanced at Professor Tung to gauge his attitude. Having been messed around for the first few weeks of the quarter, he might insist on Halley, since he knew her best.

'That's fine,' he said.

'You're sure?' Halley asked.

'It doesn't help any of us if you keel over from exhaustion — go!'

'I'm going!' Halley gathered her things and made a quick exit.

Pacing down the corridor, she realized she had a whole four hours until she needed to be anywhere. That was long enough to head home for a nap. Stepping out of the building's exit, she was blocked by a couple of cheerleaders trying to gain entry. Tall, burly cheerleaders — both young men squeezed into female cheerleading outfits, crop tops and all.

'Fraternity initiation ritual?' she asked, barring their way in.

'No,' the one with the hairiest stomach said with a shrug. 'We're here for the freshman party. High-school stereotypes theme.' He held out a crumpled flyer.

'You're at the wrong building. Show me that flyer, and I'll work out where you belong.'

She suppressed an urge to snark about them winning places at one of the most competitive schools in the country when they couldn't read door signs or a simple map. Dependence on phone navigation was the problem, and she didn't have time to resolve that for them, so she just pulled up the address they needed on her own phone, and showed it to them.

The one who'd parted his hair into stubby pigtails took her handset. 'The address said it was right off Campus Drive, and that's where we are.'

'But see how it loops around in almost a whole circle?' she said with forced patience. 'You need the opposite end.'

'Oh.' He glanced at her ID hanging from her lanyard. 'Thank you, Halley Hart.'

'Let me look at that.' His friend jostled to see her phone screen. 'You've got a text, by the way.'

'It says *call me*,' Stubby pigtails said. 'And, hey, no way — it's from Halley Hart. But that's you! How are you texting yourself?'

Halley held her hand out, and he put her phone in her palm.

'Don't be a doofus,' Hairy stomach said to his friend, as they wandered away. 'She has to know someone else with the exact same name. Probably she's, like, an identical twin.'

By the time Halley stopped gaping, they were too far away for her to quiz them on whether they were actually dumb enough to think any parent would give twins the same names, and she headed toward home. She set a steady pace for the mile walk to her apartment, drinking in the view of the wide, blue Californian skies, and not recalling the text message until she was almost off campus.

She tapped her phone to call the messenger back. 'What's up?' she asked, wedging it under her chin. She screwed up her face, struggling to follow the fast, high-pitched diatribe that came down the line. 'Can you repeat that, Mom?'

'*I know you're pulling crazy hours, Junior, but it would only have taken a few minutes to tell me about Henry!*'

'I have no idea what you're talking about.'

'You had a memorable encounter with a man called Henry when you were in Oxford.'

Halley nearly tripped over the empty sidewalk. 'How the hell could you know that?'

'So I'm right,' her mom said, with satisfaction. 'And I know it because, in the course of contacting all the Halley Harts in the world, searching for you, he emailed *me*. What does he look like, by the way? I couldn't find a picture of him online, but he's a British Henry — is it crazy that I'm picturing Henry Cavill?'

He's contacting all the Halley Harts in the world . . . How would someone even go about that? Her head spinning, she resumed an unsteady walk.

Mom's voice rose again. 'Why have you gone quiet? Is he a creep? Was that kiss he mentioned non-consensual? Did he maul you—'

'There was absolutely no mauling,' Halley put in, her cheeks ablaze. 'And he wasn't a creep.'

'So, you're interested in him, too?'

Too. Halley swallowed heavily. 'That's irrelevant.'

'Aha,' Mom said, as if Halley had answered in the affirmative. 'And is he cute?'

'Also irrelevant.'

'So he's better than cute! Is he *a snack*, like you used to say about that boy who lived two doors over?'

'I haven't talked like that since I was in high school — Mom, stop laughing!'

Halley passed someone she vaguely knew, but she fixed her eyes on the sky in the distance, rather than returning their wave.

'I'm sending you Henry's email address right now.'

He's contacting all the Halley Harts in the world, Halley thought again. Reaching an empty bench, she sunk onto it, and opened her mail app. There was nothing in her Stanford account. She switched to her lesser-used personal one, and her mouth went dry. 'You don't need to do that.'

'You've got nothing to lose by replying to him.'

'I meant, you don't need to forward anything because I just found his email in my spam.' Her eyes were moving rapidly as she read. When she reached the end she sat in silence, then something Mom said earlier came back to her. Figuring she must have missed it, she reread his email, but no, there was absolutely no mention of it. 'Mom, I don't get how you knew about . . . the kiss thing?'

'He let it slip in one of his replies,' Mom said airily.

'Replies?' Halley echoed faintly. 'Mom, are you saying Henry emailed all the Halley Harts in the world and you *wrote him back*?'

'Exactly! I didn't know for sure that it was you he was looking for, but the date seemed to fit, so I thought I'd strike up a conversation to check he's not sketchy. I couldn't ask a lot of the basics, since that risked putting him on to me, if those were things you already knew, but he's employed, educated and not a criminal. Unfortunately there was no way to check he's not in a cult, since cult members are programmed not to recognize themselves as such, so you'll need to look out for any red flags there. But,' she said triumphantly, 'I confirmed he owns a pushbike, and heard no mention of motorcycles at all.'

'Motorcycles and cults are what freak *you* out, Mom. Personally, I'm bothered by people who reply to emails that weren't intended for them!'

Mom wasn't listening. 'I'll forward you all his messages so you can take over the conversation from your own email address. Just tell him you changed it or something, and then he'll never know that it wasn't you from the start. Oh, and what was it you inadvertently left in his possession? Is that how you lost your sunglasses?'

Stunned into disbelief, Halley couldn't say a word.

'He got my auto-reply about that digital-detox retreat Aunt Edie dragged me along to,' Mom continued. 'So I'll tell you about it, in case he ever asks for the details — Halley? Are you still there?'

'I am. But I'm . . . Mom, *you pretended to be me*?'

'I never lied,' Mom said quickly. 'I only said I *might* be the Halley Hart he was looking for. Honey — are you really mad at me? I didn't mean to overstep, I was just acting instinctually, to check he wasn't a stalker.'

'*Acting instinctually*,' Halley spluttered. 'You catfished him! What's wrong with you?' She felt so numb with shock that it was an effort to keep a hold on her phone. 'Don't send me those emails. And don't call me back. I need to think.'

PART THREE

From: Halley Hart
Subject: The Halley Hart you're looking for is me
To: Henry Inglis

Dear Henry,

I have to make a confession. The Halley Hart who has been messaging you isn't the one you encountered in Oxford. *That* Halley is a forty-nine-year-old who should know far better than to string someone along in response to an email clearly not intended for her. She's also my kooky mom, whose name I share, since it's passed down in family tradition. But I told you about that already.

If it's not already clear, the Halley Hart you were looking for is her daughter, and that is me. (Or should that be, *is I*? I've never written an apology to a British academic before, and it's got me flustered about my prose.)

I'm sorry about Mom not being upfront about who she was. By the way, she's not actually mentally unhinged, but I wouldn't blame you for assuming so.

I should say that she's told me a little about you, but I didn't let her forward me all the emails. It feels too much like eavesdropping. So I've only read your first one, which I found in my spam after she confessed.

Henry, can I ask why you went to the effort of tracking me down? At first I was influenced by Mom's assumption about your motivation, but then I worried all night that you're mad at me? Or just wanting to return my sunglasses?

Again, I'm truly sorry,
Halley

* * *

Tuesday, 15 October

From: Henry Inglis
Subject: The Halley Hart you're looking for is me
To: Halley Hart
Dear Halley,

I suspect a grammarian would insist that a pronoun following a linking verb should be in the subject case and hence 'that is I'. Though I believe that 'that is me' is entirely valid as a stylistic choice. But to be frank, I find it hard to give a fig either way — I'm just so glad that you replied.

I'm very sorry, however, that you stayed up all night worrying that I may be mad with you. This is very far from the case. And while I'd be happy to reunite you with your sunglasses, doing so wasn't on my mind when I set out to find you. I wanted to make contact simply because I haven't been able to stop thinking about you. In a good way.

Perhaps though, you don't recall our . . . far from standard encounters in the same way I do, in which case I should apologize again. Especially with what I let slip to your mother.

49

Halley, there are so many things I want to know about you, but it seems unfair to barrage you with questions before I know even whether you're single, let alone if you share my interest in corresponding. If you do, I'd love to hear . . . well, in all honesty I'd love to hear anything and everything about you. I'll start with what I've wondered for over three weeks now — where are you?

All best wishes, Henry

* * *

Wednesday, 16 October

From: Halley Hart
Subject: In a Good Way
To: Henry Inglis
Hi Henry,

Far from standard encounters — you like an understatement, huh? I shook water all over you like a wet dog, joined your tour group without paying, stood you up, then I demanded your cab and . . . did what I did next.

And after all of that, instead of being mad, you went to these efforts to find me. Because you've been thinking about me, in a good way. (I'm smiling as I type this.) (Because, despite my embarrassment over kissing a near-stranger like that, I've been thinking about you in a good way too.)

And *yes*, I'm single and *yes*, want to correspond with you!

Don't worry about anything you told Mom. It's her own fault for writing you back. I feel like I should say sorry again for that, but I've noticed that we keep saying sorry to each other, Henry, so maybe we should both agree to stop apologizing?

Right now, I'm in the apartment in Palo Alto, California that I rent with my friend Angelie, while I finish up my Astronomy Ph.D. here at Stanford University, where I'm also a senior TA. But I was born and raised in Chicago, and stayed local for undergrad at Northwestern, and I guess I miss it. Usually I get back there for the summer, but I was too busy this year, first working the summer session here, then travelling around Europe, from the base of a London Airbnb my aunt and her husband rented. It was right at the end of that when I went to Oxford.

In case you wondered, I was rushing for the last train so that I could get back to Aunt Edie, ready for our flight early the next morning. Once I was on the airplane, I realized there would have been a bus from Oxford to Heathrow, if I'd missed that last train, but then again, I don't know how Aunt Edie would have reacted. She's a lot like Mom, only, believe it or not, even more extra. Also, yes, eldest daughter in the family is Halley, younger daughter is Edie, after *Edmond* Halley. Their maternal grandmother, however, was an eldest daughter named Mary, so the jury's out on whether this is a genuine longstanding tradition, or something my great-grandmother came up with.

By the way, you don't need to feel bad that I was up worrying all night before my first email. It was because I was working — I use Stanford's telescope to gather my thesis data, which I can obviously only do when it's dark. (And the sky is cloudless. And there's not a full moon. And there are no darned fireworks. Which rules out a lot of nights. But that was a perfect, clear and dark one.)

Now over to you, for the same question. I mean, I know you live and work in Oxford, but I want specifics. Like, what's your subject and what was your journey to becoming an academic/tour guide, and, and, *and* . . . I think you know the feeling.

Halley

* * *

Thursday, 17 October

From: Henry Inglis
Subject: In a Good Way
To: Halley Hart

Dear Halley,

I can't begin to tell you how delighted I was with your email, and, in all honesty, how relieved, too. In the spirit of your excellent suggestion that we stop apologizing to each other, I won't say how sorry I am to have contributed to you feeling embarrassed when recalling that kiss, because, as we both know, you merely *initiated* it. I could have stepped back rather than joining in. For what it's worth, I haven't regretted joining in for a moment. Which reminds me to ask if you'd mind passing a message onto your mother, that there are no hard feelings?

My subject is History. I got my BA, masters and doctorate in London, and then, as it so often goes, found myself overqualified and underemployed, with only bits of occasional lecturing work. My sister, Viola, sprang to my rescue, hiring me as a specialist guide at the large cultural tours company she helps run. A year ago I secured this five-year early career fellowship in modern history, and I occasionally still conduct tours when Viola's short-staffed.

Where I live currently is a small Victorian terraced house in the far north of the city, which I share with Julian Dent, who owns it. We've been friends since undergrad, and he now holds a junior research fellowship in Classics, so when I arrived in Oxford it was ideal to move into his spare bedroom. As it happens, though, it's close to running its course, so I'm currently house hunting. Or viewing overpriced shoe boxes, as these things go in Oxford.

The place I work in is mostly in my office in college, but my college is also much more than just the place I work. It's central and small and, being founded under a Tudor, it's neither modern nor one of the truly ancient ones. College is also where I take most of my meals, at hall, which refers to the physical location, as well as the meal itself. Or, some evenings, at formal hall, which is in the same location, but the food's fancier.

Tell me more about Angelie? And what made you choose Stanford for grad school? And I'd love to hear about your astronomy work. Though, on the latter point, I hope I don't cause offence by admitting I'm not sure how much I'll understand. That doesn't mean I'm not interested, and I'll do my best to follow.

Halley, we seem to have an awful lot in common, but our memories of our encounters differ. I recall wanting rather desperately to strike up a conversation with you at the coffee shop. When we chanced on each other again, I was so pleased that I insisted on you joining the tour. And I've been unable to forgive myself for ruining our dinner plans by accidentally choosing a venue that shared a name with another pub. All this is to say that I've never been happier to hear that you've been thinking about me in a good way too.

All best wishes, Henry

* * *

Friday, 18 October

From: Halley Hart
Subject: In a Good Way
To: Henry Inglis

Hi Henry,

Telling my mom there's no hard feelings would be a hard no! She raised me on her own after my dad died (I was so young I don't remember him, so that's much sadder for her than it is for me), and I'm her only child, so we've always been super close. But her emailing you like she did was so intrusive, when she could have forwarded me your email, or told you straight up that it might be me you were looking for, or like, stayed the hell out of it like a normal human being. She needs to learn that it wasn't OK, and if she gets even one sniff of *no hard feelings* she'll decide she was right all along.

I ended up at Stanford because I didn't get a fully-funded offer from any of the universities with access to a dark sky observatory, for cutting-edge deep-sky astronomy. But Stanford was a top school offering full course funding and a part-time TA role, so I came here happily enough.

It turned out Stanford were interested in me because of the work I'd done on my home telescope, back in Chicago, to mitigate against light pollution. During the earlier part of my Ph.D. I turned that work into an algorithm, to upgrade the software on other optical telescopes used in areas with too much light pollution. You can imagine the problem like static on a TV, and my work as getting the picture slightly clearer. Then for the past year I've been collecting data to prove it works, which is why I pull so many all-nighters up at Stanford's observatory, in the hills a mile or so from campus.

If my advisor agrees that I have enough data, in our next meeting in late November, I can switch my focus to writing up, then submit my thesis in the summer and start job hunting. Ideally I'd like to stay in academic research, like you, but astronomy isn't a well-funded field, so openings are pretty sparse.

In my spare time I . . . hahaha! I think I've forgotten what spare time even is.

Angelie and I met our first week here, moved in together our second year, and now she's my best friend. Last year we decided we'd had enough of life on the farm (Stanford's nickname!) and moved to a subsidized off-campus apartment. She's Filipina-American, her family having moved here when she was a few years old. Her hair is currently blue ombre and she has an absolutely stellar brain, which she uses minimally for her computer science Ph.D. (so she's about a year behind me, I think) and maximally in pursuit of founding a successful tech start-up. She's increased her chances by helping found nearly as many start-ups as there are days in the week, each with a different team of students, who all think she's devoted solely to their idea. Somehow she manages to stagger the meetings to keep any of them from figuring out what she's up to.

I noticed you mentioned that your period is modern history, but you also described Tudor times as though that's not that old. So tell me, by modern do you mean you actually study *modern* history, or, like, events that happened centuries before my country was even discovered by Europeans?!

I've gotta go supervise a lab, so final questions for now — tell me about Julian, and also, do you have any other family, besides Viola?

Halley

* * *

55

From: Henry Inglis
Subject: In a Good Way
To: Halley Hart
Dear Halley,

Having spent my doctoral research years virtually chained to a desk within a dusty library archive
room, it's fascinating to hear how different yours have
been. Though, at a guess, the reality of overnight stargazing is perhaps less romantic than it sounds?

Angelie sounds great! Julian's defining feature
is his kind-heartedness. He's bumbling and talka-
tive, but he never says a bad word about anyone,
which means he's quite rightfully universally pop-
ular. He'll always be a friend, but it's time to move
on to a new place.

Aside from me and Viola, who's three years
older, there's our parents. They started a family
much later in life than your mother, so Mum's in
her early seventies and Dad nearly eighty. Mum was
a professional musician until she got married, and
Dad retired from the Royal Air Force when I was
ten. Mum's in the early stages of dementia, and he
insists on caring for her himself — and on remaining in their house, with three flights of stairs — in a
village in Hampshire. The level of support they need
increased after he broke his hip earlier this year, but
thankfully Viola lives in a town near them.

As it happens, I'm genuinely 'modern' by most
definitions, specializing in post-1790 British and
European history. But your point is entirely proved
by the fact that modern history is officially defined
by Oxford as everything after the fall of the Western
Roman Empire, in the fifth century.

I'm sure it's no coincidence that my father left
home for long periods of time during his military

career, and my Ph.D. was on the effect of service in the Napoleonic Wars on soldier's families. Last year I concentrated on a young naval officer, after coming across his sister's sketchbook, and I'm currently searching for more papers from the same source. Or I will be, once I finish planning my teaching for the term — I was stuck with an increased load at short notice.

Halley, I'm so sorry to hear about your father. And of course I don't want you to pass along any message that you disagree with, but I hope very much that this whole episode hasn't had a lasting effect on your relationship with your mother. Her approach was unconventional, but I was, to her, a stranger searching for her daughter, so her protectiveness is understandable. And I can't help but wonder, with my email sitting unnoticed in your spam folder for several weeks, whether we would have connected at all without her intervention?

All best wishes,
Henry

* * *

Sunday, 20 October
Henry

As Henry manoeuvred his battered new bike through the front gate, one hand on the seat and the other between the handles, Julian hailed him from the other side of their street.

'Where are you off to?' Julian added, hopping off his bike.

'Looking at a flat,' Henry admitted, wishing he'd left a few minutes earlier, and avoided this.

Julian's face fell. Henry put on his cycle helmet, seeking a hasty change of subject. Where Julian had been was evident from his muddy tracksuit, so that wouldn't do, and neither would asking about his friend's plans for later in the day, which risked opening up the topic they were both avoiding.

Henry sought refuge in continuing their conversation from a few days earlier, when he'd been marking his first years' essays in advance of their second tutorial. 'Thanks for recommending that AI detection tool. My fresher's essays passed with a high degree of originality, so either he's paying an essay mill an awful lot of money, or, more likely, it's his own work and he's too terrified of me to speak.'

'Tutees need time and tact, so you can't force it,' Julian said, already returning to earnest good humour. 'But I've also found that wearing comedy socks can do wonders for lightening the mood.'

'I'll consider it,' Henry assured him, sitting astride his bike. 'See you later!'

Cycling down the main road, Henry's thoughts drifted to Halley. It was the middle of the night in California, but that seemed to find her taking observations at a telescope more often than sleeping. He held out his left hand to indicate, briefly checked over his shoulder, then swung into the side street. As he locked his bike to a lamppost outside the block of flats, his phone rang. He pulled it out, wondering if it could be Halley — he was expecting another email from her, as they'd fallen into a pattern of replying a day after hearing from the other, but a call would be even better. But, of course, he'd never given her his number. And this one was withheld, so probably whichever junior estate agent was stuck working a Sunday, checking he was coming.

'Henry? Halley-Anne here! You never know what — I've got a really strong lead to the location of your Halley!'

* * *

Monday, 21 October

> *From: Halley Hart*
> *Subject: Sorry!*
> *To: Henry Inglis*

Dear Henry,

Sorry not to write you back yesterday. I really wanted to, but left it until after my assignment marking, so I had something to look forward to, then was so exhausted having been up all night and the marking dragging on for ages that I thought I'd nap first. The next thing I knew, it was five this morning . . .

Astronomic observations alone in an observatory are probably not that different from researching in old archives — patience, commitment, and the ability to concentrate hard for long periods of time being essential. But I can't deny that I enjoy stargazing, and I think it's got the potential to be romantic, with the right person . . .

I'm sorry to hear about your parents' struggles to stay independent. And I'm curious about Viola staying living close to them. Do you think she planned that, or chose to support them? I guess I ask because I sometimes feel guilty about moving so far away from my mom — and other times, I feel like she deserves space from parenting. She's in no way infirm or bored — she's a senior nurse, running triage in one of the busiest emergency rooms in Chicago. (Her experiences there are why she might have pried into any links you have to cults or motorcycles. She's paranoid about me getting involved with either, as her most physically traumatized patients are bikers and most emotionally traumatized was a cult escapee.) Don't get me wrong, she's still in my bad books.

Where are you writing me from? Like literally, where do you sit? I keep trying to picture your day-to-day life in my mind's eye, and failing. I'm currently in my workspace in the astronomy faculty, which is a small cubicle with two tables pushed together to make a large L-shape desk, and a few powerful computers. I should be crunching data, but instead I'm writing you, and before that I was thinking about you and before *that* I figured out that the distance between Stanford and Oxford is 5321 miles. :(

Halley

* * *

Tuesday, 22 October

From: Henry Inglis
Subject: Volunteering!
To: Halley Hart
Dear Halley,

I'd like to volunteer for the role of joint-stargazer, in service of discovering whether it can be romantic . . . Well, as long as you're open to the possibility of filling it with a complete beginner.

Halley, I'm glad you caught up on some much needed sleep. And even if you hadn't sensibly suggested we stop apologizing, there really is no reason for you to be sorry for not replying because you were busy, or sleeping, or any other reason.

I spent the past hour in the SCR, which in my college is located in a series of interconnected rooms, one of which has antique wing-backed chairs and an open fireplace, conversing with my boss, Rupert Peters, who you correctly pegged as the 'type of academic who only knows other academics'. Then your email arrived, and since I prefer to be alone to read your words, I relocated to my office. It's a small room tucked up in the eaves of one of the oldest buildings in the college. The most pleasant thing about it are the views across Oxford's rooftops.

From the little I know of your mother, she strikes me as wanting you to pursue all your dreams

— unless they involve cults/motorbikes — not limit yourself to opportunities in close proximity to Chicago for her sake. (I'm cautious to add this, but most of all, I imagine she'd like to hear from you.)

Viola always tells me that she likes Hampshire, and since she often works from home, has more space there than if she moved to London. But I suspect there's an element of staying near Mum and Dad to support them — though if she said that to Dad, he'd tell her he doesn't need any support at all — which isn't true.

I saw two flats over the weekend. One had a sudden price increase, to well over my budget, though the other was surprisingly cheap — but sharing with a drummer . . . So back to the drawing board.

Halley, writing to you is so much better than the weeks of wondering about you, and receiving your replies is even better again. The next step seems to me to be exchanging phone numbers, so mine's attached. I won't be offended if you think it's too soon, but for my part, I'd love to hear from you if texting is of any interest. Or calling. Or video chat.

All best wishes, Henry

* * *

Halley

'You're back early,' Halley heard, unlocking the front door. Angelie was tilting her chair on its back legs, to peer into their entryway from the kitchen. 'Everyone's still here.'

'So I see,' Halley said, strolling in. She recognized most of the people huddled around the table. It was one of the first groups Angelie had got together, to design some sort of wellbeing app.

'Hi, everyone,' she said. She recalled most of their names, but never risked using them: making a mistake could expose how badly Angelie was cheating.

'Hi, Halley,' they all chorused, except for one guy, who was funnelling peanuts into his mouth instead. He was newer to the group, Halley thought, certain she'd have recalled him if he'd been around much. He was built like a linebacker, and had curly hair.

'Well?' Angelie asked, with an enquiring glance. 'It's not even eleven. Didn't you say you'd be at the observatory most of the night, again?'

Halley leaned against their refrigerator door, careful not to dislodge the magnetic dry-wipe board, on which they listed all essentials: groceries to pick up, Wi-Fi password and Angelie's detailed plan to survive a zombie apocalypse. 'Weather forecast was wrong,' Halley said lightly. 'Cloud cover. So it was pointless.'

Her final sentence was true. Tonight, it had proven to be entirely pointless to take her observations. All she could think about were those twelve simple digits, now burned into her mind, that made up Henry's phone number. So she'd packed up, locked up, and driven home.

'Woohoo, Halley?' Angelie sang. 'You were a million miles away! I was asking if you wanted to help us finish the latest draft of our feasibility study?'

'Nowhere near a million,' Halley murmured. 'Only five thousand, three hundred and twenty-one.'

Angelie's attention was back on her laptop. 'What?'

'Nothing. Have fun — I'm turning in.'

In her room, with the sturdy door locked behind her, and the window closed for good measure, Halley replaced her grey hoodie with a cream knit and gazed rather despairingly at herself in the mirror. It was evident that she wasn't getting enough sleep, and she slicked on mascara, tinted moisturizer, and lip balm, as though it were morning.

Before she could talk herself out of it, she input Henry's number into video chat, and clicked to connect. It rang once, twice, three times, before her face minimized to a small window in the corner.

Rather than Henry's face appearing, the rest of the screen was dark, and a man said, 'Hullo?'

'Henry?' The questioning tone was nerves. She'd recognized his voice even from one word. 'It's Halley.' Her throat was dry, and she swallowed several times, then licked her lips. 'Halley Hart. We've been writing each other.'

'*Halley!*' There was a rustling sound. Hearing his voice again, everything flooded back, and she sunk onto her desk chair under the weight of memory. 'Sorry, let me switch the light on.'

Before she'd absorbed the meaning of that, he appeared on her screen. He was wearing a light green T-shirt, which brought out the green in his heavy lidded eyes. His mid-brown hair was slightly longer than when she'd seen him before, and not so neatly combed.

Henry seemed to be leaning back against some sort of wood panelling, though she thought he must be sitting rather than standing, as between his shoulders and the wood there was an upholstered chair back, with blue and white stripes. He sat up straighter and the stripes slipped, so it was actually a cushion, she thought. A rectangular one, like a pillow . . .

No, not like a pillow but *actually* a pillow, and behind it wasn't panelling, but a headboard. Henry was propped up on his elbows *in bed*.

'Oh my God,' she breathed. 'I woke you up! I didn't even think about the time difference!' Nearly eleven p.m. in California, and the UK was eight hours ahead — so it was before seven on Wednesday morning, for Henry.

'I can't think of a better way to be woken,' he said, smiling as he rubbed his eyes. 'And I'd usually be up now. I had an . . . interrupted night, that's all, but I'm bloody ecstatic to hear your voice. Just give me a second—' As he returned to full view, Halley identified the small object as a pair of tortoiseshell-rimmed glasses, which he slid on his face. 'And now I can see you properly. Halley, you're every bit as lovely as I remembered.'

She was caught off-guard by the sensation that swept over her skin. If this was any other man, she might be tempted to deflect the compliment coyly: *You'd say that to any girl who kissed you in the street.* But this was Henry.

'I was thinking the same about you,' she said. To her ears it sounded too simple, in comparison to his own declaration, but he must have sensed her sincerity because his face pinked slightly. Cautious of embarrassing him further, Halley lowered her eyelids over her delight at making him blush so easily. 'I really like your emails,' she blurted.

His smile widened. 'And I yours. Though this is even better.'

'But not as good as actually being together.'

His smile dropped. 'Indeed not.'

'I wish I could take you up on your offer, and teach you to stargaze,' Halley said. 'I mean, I know you were kidding around, but—'

'Say the word, and I'll book annual leave, Halley,' he breathed, with toe-curling intensity.

'Seriously? It's a long flight.'

He made a scoffing sound. 'I'd walk the five thousand, three hundred and twenty-one miles, if I had to.' He was smiling so much that his eyes crinkled in the way she especially liked. 'Have I remembered that correctly?'

'Every single stinking one of them,' she said, wondering if he'd want to come for Christmas, or if he'd been joking. She changed the subject. 'I leaned into my crazy stalker tendencies earlier.'

'You're in good company,' Henry said. 'I turned my research skills to finding all the Halley Harts in the world, remember?'

'Not in a stalker-ish way,' she quickly objected. 'And my mom catfished you.'

That made him chuckle. 'It wasn't quite catfishing. Anyway, tell me what you did?'

'I manually changed my IP address to a British one, to get dating apps to show me men in Oxford. I wanted to see if I'd match with you on any of them.'

'I haven't been on anything like that since I moved here. With teaching undergraduates, the risks outweigh the benefits.'

'I quit them last year,' Halley said softly. 'I'd got too busy.'

His smile returned, softer this time, but then the picture on her screen shook, before changing, so she saw the top of his head, then his chest. Then she was looking down on him, and realized he'd propped his phone up high. He bent out of sight, leaving her a view of floorboards beside his bed.

'Henry?'

'Sorry . . . getting decent,' he said. 'Jeans seem more appropriate than pants.'

'Jeans *are* pants, oh, you say pants for . . .'

'Boxers,' he said, waggling his eyebrows as he returned into shot. 'Or briefs, drawers, or, erm . . . tighty-whities — all pants. Jeans are jeans. Or *trousers*. Like George Bernard Shaw said, England and America are two countries separated by a common language.'

'Was he British or American?'

'Irish, believe it or not,' Henry said, presumably picking up his phone, because she was suddenly at his level again. She beckoned him with her finger, and after a few seconds he leaned so close into the camera that she could see that he hadn't shaved.

'I want to see more,' she breathed.

His eyes widened. 'Er . . .' he began.

She grinned. 'Of your *room*, Henry. Give me a tour!'

'You absolute minx,' he said, laughing along with her. 'You totally had me there.'

'Serves you right for all the underwear talk — damn, that's a lot of books!'

He swung the camera back on himself, from the wall of stuffed bookshelves, and shrugged. 'It's human nature to have some form of addiction. I decided early to make mine books.'

'I like books too, and I *love* music, but my addiction's coffee.'

'Can I see?'

'Sure,' she said lightly, as she kicked her pyjamas under her bed, then rotated her phone toward the bookcase. The bottom shelf was populated by vinyl LPs. Above it was a shelf of non-fiction, mostly related to science, and another of fiction. 'What do these say about me?'

'The spines are cracked, so you're a reader rather than a collector.'

'Rather than an addict,' she corrected drily.

'Book addicts are both readers and collectors. When I move up the pay scale, I want a reading copy and display copy of everything. Do you want to see the rest of my house?' She nodded vociferously, as he corrected himself. 'Well, Julian's, strictly speaking.'

'Is he still sleeping?'

'No, he leaves for the river at the crack of dawn, year round. He's into rowing.'

'How—' Halley cut off her observation. That sounded hideous! 'Is that an interest you share?' she asked cautiously.

'Good God, no,' he said, sounding genuinely appalled. 'Living with a rower's bad enough. He talks about it so much, it's as if rowing's the opposite of Fight Club.'

'Oh — it's like CrossFit! My old roommate was a CrossFitter, and never shut up about it.'

Henry swung his phone in a final slow arc around his room and she caught sight of him in a wall mirror. He really was wearing jeans. But his feet were bare, which felt, some-how, weirdly personal.

'I can't give you a tour around our whole apartment this time. Angelie's got one of her app development teams here.'

'This time,' Henry said.

She couldn't see him, only the landing of the upper floor of his house, but she could hear that he was happy. 'Implying there'll be a next time, yes,' she said.

On her screen, the door at the opposite end of the landing came into focus, then got larger.

Abruptly, it swung open.

A woman wearing something black and lacy, with legs that went on forever, sashayed out. 'Henry, darling,' she said. She had an accent, but it was different again from Henry's.

'Bloody hell, Gabrielle!' Henry said. His tone was startled, but not shocked. Like, he didn't know she'd been in there, but also like a barely-dressed woman wandering around his house calling him darling was nothing unusual. 'I thought you'd left.'

'Really?' she said, with a quizzical glance. 'So soon, after last night? No, I was in the bath. Would you make me a coffee—'

Her heart hammering, Halley cancelled the call, then switched off her phone for good measure.

PART FOUR

Wednesday, 23 October

Text messages between Henry and Halley:

> *Halley, I'm so sorry about that, but it WASN'T*
> *what it looked like. Can we talk? Henry.*

> *Halley, please can I call you back?*

> *Halley, I know it's the middle of the night there,*
> *but let me know when you're awake. Anytime.*
> *ANYTIME. Please.*

> > *Henry, if it really wasn't what it looks like, then*
> > *explain.*

* * *

From: Henry Inglis
Subject: Explanation
To: Halley Hart

Thank you for replying, Halley. I hope you're OK, and got some sleep?

That was Gabrielle. She's Julian's . . . girlfriend I suppose, though I haven't heard them define it. I thought she'd left with him, shortly before you called.

But she isn't just Julian's girlfriend or whatever. She's my colleague, from the history department. Also, I dated her during my first few months in Oxford. It was short-lived, never serious and fizzled out over ten months ago. Which might make what just happened seem worse. I don't know.

Them getting together is why I'm moving out. Not because I have any lingering feelings for her — I'd feel like a spare wheel whoever Julian got serious with.

Finally, please let me know any questions. I'll answer anything. And if you need corroboration, I'm sure Julian would be prepared to talk to you on the phone.

Very best, Henry

* * *

From: Halley Hart
Subject: Questions . . .
To: Henry Inglis

1. Why did she call you darling? And walk around in what was barely more than underwear?
2. At the start of our call you said you hadn't had much sleep?
3. Wait — you told Julian about me?

* * *

From: Henry Inglis

Subject: Answers
To: Halley Hart
Dear Halley,

Thanks for giving me the opportunity to explain further.

1. She's French. She talks like that to everyone. And she doesn't seem to do embarrassment. But I do, and was, at seeing her . . . scantily clad like that.

2. I avoided hearing Julian and Gabrielle by blasting music through my headphones all night . . . To be clear, I wouldn't have wanted to have listened to Julian . . . entertaining anyone.

3. Yes. I hope that's OK. Gabrielle finally clocked my phone, and asked bemusedly if I was filming her. I was stammering that I'd actually been on FaceTime with the woman I'm involved with as Julian got home. It was an exceedingly awkward conversation all round, and once she left I told Julian the whole story. I know it was awkward for you too, and only hope this hasn't changed anything.

Very best, Henry

* * *

Thursday, 24 October

From: Halley Hart
Subject: Good answers . . .
To: Henry Inglis

It was an unfortunately timed incident. You don't have anything to be sorry for, and I should have thought it all through before I overreacted like that. There was always going to be a logical explanation, and I'm a logical person. Except where you're concerned, when logic flies out the window and I can only FEEL. Right from that senseless kiss, onwards.

I was really enjoying our vid-chat, until then. Wanna try again this weekend?

* * *

From: Henry Inglis
Subject: Yes please!
To: Halley Hart

What about Saturday, noon your time, eight p.m. mine? I can't wait.

And our kiss may have been senseless, Halley, but I'll never regret that it happened.

I hope you're having a good week,
Henry

* * *

Friday, 25 October

From: Halley Hart
Subject: It's a date
To: Henry Inglis

Crazy-busy week, rather than *good*, but the department just hired another TA, so once she's trained, my schedule should let up a little.

Looking forward to Saturday.

* * *

Text messages between Mom and Halley:

How long will you ignore me? (To the tune of The Waterboys' 'How Long Will I Love You'.)
Love Mom

I'm not ignoring you, Mom. I just need a little space.

* * *

Saturday, 26 October
Henry

It's a date.

The three words from Halley's subject line echoed in Henry's head all night. Despite reminding himself, in stern management of his own expectations, that it was probably a turn of phrase, he'd gone to a lot more effort for a video call than ever before.

He pushed into the Hope and Anchor on North Parade and navigated his way to the bar, unsurprised that it was busy.

The barman waved a hand. 'The back room's ready for you, Henry. What do you want to drink? It's on the house.'

Given that Henry had paid £60 for exclusive use of the back room, he readily accepted a pint. Carrying it carefully through the throng, he heard someone call his name, and, glancing over, saw Kwame and Ruth round the far side.

He picked his way over, and Kwame clapped him on the back. His name may have hailed from Ghana, where his father was born, but his accent was pure Bristolian. 'Aw-reet, mate?'

'Great. And you both?'

'Any news on whatever you're searching for?' Ruth asked, her eyes fixed on him rather too intuitively. He avoided meeting them. As yet unsure if the disaster caused by bloody Gabrielle was entirely resolved, he didn't feel like talking about Halley.

'Kind of — thanks for the advice. Now, my biggest problem is the amount of time house hunting takes up.'

Kwame's eyebrows shot up. 'You wouldn't be interested in—'

'Kwame,' Ruth said on a sigh.

'What? It was your idea to rent it out.'

'Not to *Henry*,' Ruth said.

'Why?' Kwame said, at the same moment as Henry said, '*What?*

Ruth rolled her eyes despairingly. 'Where Kwame lived before we got married. Instead of selling it on, he's been shelling out several hundred a month on maintenance, while it sits totally empty.'

'Because it's the best location in Oxford! Completely peaceful, stunning views, and only ten minutes from the city centre. We'll be glad of it if you ever switch to a role without accommodation.'

'I'm never living there, my love,' Ruth trilled.

'She can't see past the composting toilet,' Kwame said, returning his attention rather mournfully to Henry. 'But there's gas for cooking, solar panels for leccy, even a power shower.'

'Sorry,' Henry said. 'I'm not following. You used to live where?'

'A houseboat, on the canal,' Kwame confirmed. 'I was years on a waiting list to get that mooring — I'm not giving it up. So I thought I'd keep it as a man cave, for when Ruth's writing sermons, or gets a crying student over. But I've barely used it, so she suggested renting it to someone desperate.'

Ruth hissed at her husband, 'You realize you're implying—'

Henry cut in, amused. 'He's right — I am desperate. What's the internet connectivity like?'

'Superfast broadband.'

Henry smiled. 'Sounds perfect. I'll call you to arrange to see it?'

He moved off before they could ask what he was up to, retreating into the small private room with its reserved sign on the door. Inside, he arranged his pint and laptop on a table in front of the open fireplace, before adding a log to the fire and seating himself. He sucked in a deep breath and touched Halley's name.

She sprang onto his screen an instant later. She must be in the dark, he thought, as only the blue light from her phone illuminated her face. It emphasized her grey eyes which now looked enormous, and threw the contours of her face into sharp relief, like her bones were pressing through her skin.

'Did I wake you?' he asked, wondering if she'd been up all night.

'Not at all. I have a habit of working with the blinds closed.'

'I've interrupted you then — I could call back?'

'No, this is good,' she said. 'Well, as long as you're not calling to announce that my overreaction to Gabrielle scared you off.' She let out a rather breathy laugh, then cut it off abruptly.

It took him a few beats to realize she was nervous. 'Your reaction was proportionate to what happened, Halley.'

Her wide mouth twitched. 'Your roommate getting together with your ex. Isn't that against some sort of bro code?'

He shrugged. 'I told Julian that if they can find happiness together, more power to them. And *ex* is too strong. We went on fewer dates than I can count on both hands.'

Halley fiddled with her hair. 'And you said it fizzled out?'

'It did.' Henry sipped his beer, thinking hard. He'd never put his unease into words before, or even fully formed them into a thought. 'I wasn't really feeling it. I thought she wasn't either. Then she immediately turned her attention to Julian. It took months for him to get over his nerves and respond, but . . . I don't know. It was odd.' Henry shook his head. He absolutely didn't want to waste any more time on this. He motioned around him. 'This is the Hope and Anchor I intended to direct you to.'

Halley's eyes widened. 'We're having a do-over?' She sounded delighted, and he sent the message from his draft folder.

'Click on the link in the email you just received.'

She did so, then grinned. 'A log fire video. So we both get one to enjoy! What's that you're drinking? I'll grab something similar.'

'Locally brewed bitter.'

She pulled a face, before disappearing, and returning with a bottled IPA. 'Closest I've got. By the way, what were you drinking while you waited for me, that night?'

He thought back. He'd ordered a sandwich, and something to wash it down with. 'Just Earl Grey tea.'

'Huh,' Halley said, leaning back on her desk chair, and looking at him through her lashes.

There was a significance to this that he was entirely missing. 'It's a black tea, flavoured with oil of bergamot orange.'

Halley straightened, and slapped her desk with both hands. 'Citrus! There was like, a smokiness, combined with something sweet and fragrant.'

Henry furrowed his brow. 'I'm not following.'

Halley blushed rather becomingly. 'Ever since we . . . since I kissed you, I've been trying to figure out what you . . . smelled like.'

'What my *breath* smelled like?' Henry asked, appalled.

'In a good way!' Halley chewed on her lower lip.

'Oh . . .' Henry was feeling rather helpless.

Explosive giggles took over Halley entirely. 'Sorry! The look on your face!'

Henry had to place his mug down, then put his face in his hands and laughed.

When they'd recovered, the lingering tension had broken. Henry planted his elbow on the table, propped his chin in his palm, and smiled into his laptop, wishing harder than he'd ever wished for anything that he could see her again in person. 'Tell me how your work's going, Halley.'

She caught him up on her research and explained her TA responsibilities, then asked about his own. He explained the subjects he was tutoring this term and described his students, including the first year who was presenting such a conundrum of silence.

'And your research? You mentioned a lead on the records you're after.'

'Haven't achieved any forward progress on that,' he admitted. 'They should be logged on the Bod's archive database, but I can't find them there. It probably means a transcription error, and I need to try a load of possible typos and misspellings. Halley — I'm intrigued why a Northwestern University alumna, and current Stanford Ph.D. student, is wearing a hoodie that says *University of Illinois at Chicago*.'

She glanced down at her torso. 'I guess I find it fun to confuse people. This was Mom's, from when I was a baby and she went back to school to complete her nursing training.' Before he could ask if she'd like his college scarf, she added: 'So now your buddy knows about me, right? I feel kinda bad I haven't told anyone about you, yet.'

The *yet* seemed to be left dangling, and he considered scooping it up, and asking when she might tell someone, or what she would say. Caution won out. 'Your mother knew I existed before anyone on my side.'

Her smile faded. 'She doesn't know we're . . .' She waved her finger between them. 'I still haven't spoken to her.'

'I don't like seeing you look sad,' Henry said, because it was true, and because he didn't want to say the wrong thing and risk making the situation worse. 'Is there anything I can do to help, sweetheart?' Her eyes blazed and he added hastily, 'I should have checked if you mind—'

'Henry,' she snapped with mock annoyance. 'I know we've fallen off the no-apologies wagon pretty badly, but if you say sorry for *that* then I'll be really pissed.'

He smiled. 'Sweetheart works?'

'Unless in your head you're imagining it written sweet-h-a-r-t, and it's a pun. I hate puns.'

'Furthest thing from my mind.'

Her mouth regained its bracket of dimples. 'Then it's the nicest thing I've been called in ages. Angelie's given me a nickname so bad it's unrepeatable, Mom calls me *Junior*, and the guys in the cubicles either side of mine call me Hal.'

'Then we share a nickname! Viola calls *me* Hal, on occasion.'

'Shouldn't it be Hen?'

'I suppose Hen's a bit avian. Historically, Hal's derived from Harry, which Henrys are also often called. Prince Harry was christened Henry, but it also goes back centuries — before he ascended the throne of England, Henry V was called Harry or Hal.'

'Thanks for the history lesson, Prince Hal. D'you have any other nicknames?'

He thought for a moment. 'Viola called me Eggy for a while.'

'Like egghead, because you were a book addict?'

'Eggy like a boiled egg,' he said wryly. 'When I was small my hair was white-blond, and my eyebrows were so pale they were invisible. So apparently I looked just like one. Don't laugh! She saw it as performing her sisterly duty, to stop me getting arrogant.'

'Well, good job, Viola,' Halley said, still smiling.

Henry seized the moment. 'Uh . . .' He filled his lungs. 'In light of the debacle earlier in the week, it feels important to ensure that you know that I'm not, uh . . . *corresponding* with anyone else, in this way. I mean, obviously I do write a lot of other emails,' he added, suddenly flustered. 'And one of the Halley Harts phoned a few times, wanting to help me find you. By *corresponding*, I mean that I'm not romantically involved with anyone else, on any level.'

She was either completely still, or the internet connection had frozen. 'Halley?'

'I'm here,' she said. 'Just . . . is what you're saying, that you want our correspondence to be *exclusive*?'

He scrutinized her face, but her expression gave nothing away. It was tempting to leave it there, and pick up the conversation at some later date. But she'd been hurt by that mix-up with Gabrielle, which made him determined to be honest.

'Yes,' he said bluntly. 'I know on some level that must sound ridiculous, with so much yet to learn about each other, and the vast distance between us, and having only met once. But . . . that's what I'd like. Of course, you may not, which is totally . . .'

'I do, though! Except, we don't have to keep calling it *correspondence*, do we?'

He beamed at her. 'We can call it whatever you want.'

She sucked her cheeks in, thinking. 'This,' she said eventually, pointing at him, then at herself — 'feels like a date. So let's do more of it.'

'More dating, through a screen,' Henry said, grinning. 'Exclusively,' he added, trying not to sound smug. From the way Halley narrowed her eyes at him, he wasn't entirely sure he'd succeeded.

'Sure,' she said. 'Though I'm not sure yet how the logistics work, with both our schedules.'

'I won't remain as busy as right now.' Henry wondered if it was too soon to ask what she was doing for Christmas. 'I can take leave once it gets to mid-December.'

'That's when your term ends?' Halley's gaze moved to one side. She was consulting a calendar, he guessed.

'That's a little earlier. Then there's ten days of interviews — prospective candidates for admission next year. Afterwards I'll have at least two weeks of freedom.' He tightened his hands under the table.

Her forehead wrinkled as she made a few rapid calculations. 'I'm committed to a symposium here until the eighteenth of December, but I can swing a break afterwards. How would you feel about celebrating the holidays in California?'

He thudded his fists on his knees, then moved his hands to his keyboard and bashed on a random stream of keys. 'I hope you meant that — I've just booked a ticket.'

He was hoping for a smile, but her reaction was quite different. 'You're serious,' she said unsteadily. 'You'll come?'

'I'll be there,' he said, trying to transmit maximal sincerity through the screen. 'I can't wait.'

'Me either,' she breathed.

'And until then, we've got these video calls, and texts.'

'I still want to email,' Halley put in. 'I love our emails.'

'Me too. So that's agreed? Exclusively dating. Still emailing. Christmas in California. And as for all the other logistics, well, we've got one and four-fifths of a pair of doctoral degrees between us.'

Her eyes lit up. 'Exactly. If anyone can figure this whole thing out, it's us.'

* * *

Sunday, 27 October

From: Henry Inglis
Subject: Now we're dating . . .
To: Halley Hart
Dear Halley,

Now we're dating, I hope it's OK to ask when your birthday is? Mine's February 19, when I'll be twenty-nine.

And may I have your address, so I can return your sunglasses? I'd give you mine, except I'm viewing a potential new place in a few days, so hopefully I'll be moving.

Henry

* * *

Monday, 28 October

From: Halley Hart
Subject: Now we're OFFICIALLY dating . . .
To: Henry Inglis

Henry!! Our birthdays are the same week! And Valentine's too! I'll turn twenty-eight on Feb 13.

I want to organize our next date. The sky's at its darkest right now so I'm pulling a lot of late nights, so how about a week on Saturday?

Address attached. In exchange, you need to tell me *alllll* about the potential new place once you see it!

Your Halley

* * *

Tuesday, 29 October

From: Henry Inglis
Subject: Now we're OFFICIALLY and exclusively dating . . .
To: Halley Hart
Dear Halley,

A date a week on Saturday sounds great. Same time as before?

Of course I'll let you know how the viewing goes!

Hope your week's going well? Sorry to keep this brief — insanely busy today.

Henry

* * *

Thursday, 31 October

From: Halley Hart
Subject: Now we're OFFICIALLY and exclusively dating AND I'M YOUR SWEETHEART . . .
To: Henry Inglis

Henry, never apologize for being busy. I know what it's like! Between TA stuff and a couple all-nighters, I didn't even get time to write you

80

yesterday. Tonight is two days before a new moon, so the conditions are perfect for astronomy, but there's no point in going up to the telescope. It's Halloween, and fireworks are the bane of astronomers. The darn things should be banned.

Next Saturday, same time as before, for . . . wait for it . . . a movie date! Here's a link to instructions for a system setup, so we can watch a movie and see each other at the same time.

Your Halley

* * *

Friday, 1 November

From: Henry Inglis
Subject: Now we're OFFICIALLY and exclusively dating AND I'M YOUR SWEETHEART and my flight to San Francisco is reserved . . .
To: Halley Hart
Dear Halley,

I've reserved a flight for December 19, from London Heathrow to San Francisco International, and I'll buy it on payday.

I'm sorry to hear fireworks ruined a good stargazing night. Halloween isn't such a big deal here, so I hadn't properly clicked that it was yesterday, until my third years arrived for their tute as Marie Antoinette and a traffic cone. The costume was a marked improvement for the traffic cone, who usually attends in grubby pyjamas.

The viewing went well, but I haven't yet committed to the new place. I wanted to check first: what would you think if I lived on a narrowboat on Oxford's canal? Photos are attached . . .

I'm about to take a tutorial with my first year — Mr Exactly, I find myself calling him internally, as he says little beyond *exactly*. His tute-partner, Ms Oxcited, emailed to say she has *ox-freshers flu*. It could be an entirely silent hour . . . we'll see.

A film date sounds fantastic and I'll do my best with that setup you suggest.

Henry

* * *

Saturday, 2 November

From: Halley Hart
Subject: Now we're OFFICIALLY and exclusively *dating AND I'M YOUR SWEETHEART, and* my flight to San Francisco is reserved *AND I'M WEARING YOUR SCARF* . . .
To: Henry Inglis
Hi Henry,

I don't know if I'm more excited that you've reserved your flight or about those photos! For what it's worth, the boat looks like a cool place to live. And my favourite photo's the one with you in it.

Also, my sunglasses arrived this morning. Thanks so much! And, even more for the college scarf, which I adore.

Between the scarf and the photos, I'm feeling really close to you, Henry. I just wish you were physically closer. Like, right here next to me. December feels like a long time to wait.

Halloween isn't such a big deal in Britain? Wow! I should move there.

How was the tutorial?

Your Halley

* * *

Sunday, 3 November

From: Henry Inglis
Subject: Now we're OFFICIALLY and exclusively *dating AND I'M YOUR SWEETHEART* and my flight to San Francisco is reserved *AND I'M WEARING YOUR SCARF and* yes, you should move here . . .
To: Halley Hart
Dear Halley,

Are you well?

I have to admit that we have fireworks here on Bonfire Night, which is upcoming. But I really don't think you should let that stop you from your excellent plan of moving here . . .

Funnily enough, Mr Exactly came alive in his solo tute. So at least I've been able to confirm that the strong written work he submits is his own. I'm hoping that now he's started talking, he'll continue. Fingers crossed!

I'm glad the photos and parcel weren't unwelcome. Could I have a photo of you too? Either that, or permission to miss half the film, taking screenshots of you . . .

Henry

* * *

Monday, 4 November

From: Halley Hart
Subject: Now we're OFFICIALLY and exclusively *dating AND I'M YOUR SWEETHEART* and my flight to San Francisco is reserved *AND I'M WEARING YOUR SCARF and* yes, you should move here *AND I'VE TOLD ANGELIE ABOUT US* . . .
To: Henry Inglis
Hi Henry,

No, I'm not well. I have a hangover. And it's your fault, because I told Angelie everything, and she opened a bottle of wine to celebrate and somehow we finished the whole thing. She wanted to know if you say *fanks*, *babes*, (because that's how everyone talks on British Love Island, which she's obsessed with) (I said I didn't think so?) and also how many x's you do when you write me. Apparently in the UK everyone does kisses to everyone in messages. I told her I have seen no sign of any numbers of x.

I've attached the pictures you took of me in Oxford so now you can concentrate on the movie! Oh, and as well as following the system setup for our date, you need to buy popcorn and a bag of M&M's, since it's what we'd be eating if you were really coming for a movie date at my place.

Gotta run to take a class,

Your Halley

* * *

Tuesday, 5 November

From: Henry Inglis
Subject: Now we're OFFICIALLY and exclusively dating AND I'M YOUR SWEETHEART and my flight to San Francisco is reserved AND I'M WEARING YOUR SCARF and yes, you should move here . . . AND I'VE TOLD ANGELIE ABOUT US and you're so beautiful . . .
To: Halley Hart

Dear Halley,

I hope the hangover has passed?

Thank you for the photos. You're so beautiful. I should have said that before now. I had noticed.

People do like to x at the end of messages here, but it's not a habit of mine. You, however, can always have as many as you want.

By the way, both M&M's *and* popcorn?

Henry

xxxxxxxxxxxxxxxxxxxxxxxxxxxxxxxxxxxxxxxxxxxx
xxxxxxxxxxxxxxxxxxxxxxxxxxxxxxxxxxxxxxxxxxxx

* * *

Wednesday, 6 November

From: Halley Hart
Subject: Now we're OFFICIALLY and exclusively *dating AND I'M YOUR SWEETHEART and* my flight to San Francisco is reserved *AND I'M WEARING YOUR SCARF and* yes, you should move here . . . *AND I'VE TOLD ANGELIE ABOUT US and* you're so beautiful *AND ONLY THREE DAYS TO GO . . .*
To: Henry Inglis

Yes, Henry, M&M's *and* popcorn. You mix them up in a bowl together. Please don't tell me if you don't like chocolate, because I don't date haters.

Thank you for sending all the kisses!

Three days! I CAN'T WAIT!

Your Halley

* * *

Thursday, 7 November

From: Henry Inglis
Subject: Now we're OFFICIALLY and exclusively *dating AND I'M YOUR SWEETHEART and* my flight to San Francisco is reserved *AND I'M WEARING YOUR SCARF and* yes, you should move here . . . *AND I'VE TOLD ANGELIE ABOUT US and*

you're so beautiful *AND ONLY THREE DAYS TO GO and* have I mentioned how much I love chocolate . . .

To: Halley Hart

Dear Halley,

Just a quick one to say that I can't wait to talk to you 'in person' tomorrow.

Dad's unfortunately had another fall. Nothing awful, apparently, but they're checking him out in hospital. So I'm off down to Hampshire, and I'm not sure how much opportunity I'll have for checking my messages, but I'll definitely be there for our date, one way or another.

Henry xxx

* * *

Saturday, 9 November
Halley

'You made it,' Halley breathed, the instant he appeared on their TV.

'Of course,' Henry said. His eyes swept over her to Angelie, beside her on the couch. 'This is Angelie, I take it?'

'When I told her about this, she insisted—' Halley cut herself off. 'How's your dad?'

'Absolutely fine,' Henry said. 'He was released from hospital earlier, complaining that he didn't need to be admitted in the first place. You look so worried, sweetheart — I shouldn't even have mentioned it.'

Angelie stabbed at the Bluetooth keyboard Halley had connected to their TV and the phone she'd propped above it, which was filming them. Henry's face was instantly obscured by a mute symbol. '*Sweetheart!*' she said, pretending to swoon. 'In that accent! It's even better than *babes*.'

'Give that here!' Halley hissed, reaching for the keyboard. Angelie snatched it up from their coffee table and hopped up onto the back of their couch, lifting it beyond Halley's reach.

'And I can't believe he's actually *so cute!*'

'Would I be so obsessed if he wasn't cute?'

'Erm . . .' Henry said, going pink. Halley stared at Angelie, who had unmuted just in time for him to hear that.

'Oops,' Angelie said, totally unapologetically, seating herself once more.

'Sorry to make you witness a murder, Henry,' Halley said, grabbing back the keyboard and raising a cushion in one swift motion. Pummelling her friend with it, she raised her voice. 'And that she hasn't left the apartment yet. She bullied me into this.'

'I pointed out ' Angelie wrestled the cushion from Halley and chucked it to the other side of the room, before gazing into the screen — 'that to keep your virtual date as authentic as possible, I should meet you at the start, like if you were actually coming over. So this is highly altruistic of me. Plus, I knew that you'd like to meet me, right, Henry?'

'Careful what you say, Henry,' Halley said. 'There are two options, and I'll be pissed if you go for the wrong one.' Henry must have stood up, because his chest came into view, then he moved aside leaving only a couple of armchairs in sight. 'What are you doing?'

'Gathering reinforcements.' His voice echoed from further away. '*Viola* — would you like to come and meet Halley and her friend Angelie?'

'Oh my God,' Angelie jabbed Halley with her elbow. 'He lives with another woman?'

'Viola's his *sister*,' Halley breathed. 'I'm gonna barf.'

Angelie gave her a critical once-over. 'Just as well you didn't wear that slutty dress I tried to lend you. You look lovely. You *are* lovely. She'll love you.'

A few heart-stopping seconds later, Henry reoccupied the same armchair. A woman with corkscrew curls seated herself in the one beside him, waving tentatively. Her colouring was darker than Henry's, and her freckles much more obvious. If Halley hadn't already known that she was a few years older than Henry, she'd have had trouble deciding the order of their births.

'Viola, this is Halley,' Henry said.

Halley gave the screen a tentative wave.

'Who I'm dating,' Henry added, with no sign of any tension. His mouth twisted with suppressed humour. 'Exclusively.'

'Hi, Halley,' Viola said, smiling between her and Henry. 'He's very keen on you!'

Halley's pulse sped, until she could barely hear the rest of the introductions above its thrum in her ears.

'It's lovely to meet you both,' Viola was saying, when Halley managed to concentrate again. 'Or — can we call it that, over a screen?'

'Sure, when they call it dating, over a screen,' Angelie said, tapping Halley's foot with her own. 'Don't you, Bu—' she continued, as Halley thudded her foot onto Angelie's smaller one. 'Shit, uh . . . *Halley*.'

The near-miss at her excruciating nickname getting out had somehow broken Halley out of her meet-the-family induced panic. 'It's good to meet you too, Viola. Are you visiting Oxford?'

'No, Henry's staying with me,' she said.

'Once we got Dad settled back in, there wasn't time for me to get home,' he explained. 'Plus, her TV's newer than Julian's, so the set up was easier.'

'And you said your dad's OK,' Halley said, wanting Viola to know that she'd asked after him.

Viola shot her brother a look of long-suffering exasperation, which would have immediately clarified which of them was the eldest. 'That's the second fall on those stairs this year. If he breaks the other hip, it could—' She broke off, turning back to the screen. 'Sorry. Henry's right, in that Dad got lucky, this time. What beautiful names you two have, by the way.'

Angelie grinned. 'It was how we first bonded, at this women in STEM mixer in our first week on campus. We had to go round in a circle and say something unique about ourselves, and Halley said she shares a name with her mom.'

'And Angelie said,' Halley put in, 'that she could beat that — she shares both her parents' names.'

'Dad's called Angelo and Mom's Lina. They put the first half of both names together to make mine — it's a Filipino thing. For my next brother down, they reshuffled the combination, and christened him Linelo. We just comfort ourselves that it could be much worse.' She was giggling again. 'Our youngest brother was born after we'd moved over here. They thought their American kid deserved something really special, so they smooshed together the best family they could think of, and called him Jejomar.'

Henry and Viola both looked baffled. 'I couldn't figure it out either,' Halley said. 'Jejomar is named for Jesus, Joseph *and* Mary.'

Henry snickered, and Viola's eyes went very round.

Halley took the opportunity to whisper to Angelie, 'D'you think she likes me?'

'What?' Angelie said at full volume.

'*What* what?' Henry asked, blinking.

'She was asking what . . .' Halley couldn't think of an excuse.

'What you two have found you have in common,' Angelie said smoothly.

'Ah,' Henry said. 'Lots of things. But most recently, that our birthdays are only a week apart.' His eyes flicked towards Halley. 'Though she's an Aquarius and I'm Pisces. I'll have to do our charts to know if that's a problem.'

Horror flooded Halley. But Viola's reaction — swivelling to stare at her brother — gave her pause, and then the wicked glint in his eyes confirmed it.

'The look on Halley's face!' Angelie said, cackling. 'Good one, Henry! Y'know, she once walked out ten minutes into a date with a guy who confused her being an astronomer with an astrologer and asked what it meant that he was on the cusp of Libra and Scorpio.'

'Not only that!' Halley said. 'He made almost constant puns, and didn't believe in the moon landings. I showed him an astro photo of the equipment left up there by Apollo 11, and he mansplained how photos can be faked.'

'Let me guess, you'd taken the photo yourself?' Henry said. 'Exactly!'

'Henry once dumped a girl for leaving a red-wine stain on the cover of a book,' Viola said slyly.

'There was a coaster *right there* and she actively chose to put her glass down on *A Tale of Two Cities*,' he grumbled, which only made the women laugh harder. 'Viola, you're meant to be reinforcements, and instead you're giving them ammunition.' His voice was amused, rather than truculent, and it hit Halley that Mom would approve. She always said you could tell a lot about a man from his reaction to being laughed at by a group of women.

A faint chirp sounded, and Viola brought a phone into view, then sighed resignedly. 'I'd better drop by the parentals. Mum says Dad's writing a strongly-worded complaint about the paramedics taking him to hospital against his wishes.'

'Thanks, Vi,' Henry murmured. 'I'll take over later.'

'Too right you will,' she said as she exited. Halley looked meaningfully at Angelie.

'I'm late to . . . something,' Angelie said, leaping up. 'Great to meet you, Henry!'

'So,' Henry said, once they were alone. His smile was very different to the one he'd given the others.

'You told your sister about me!'

'I did,' he said. 'She works with a lot of travel agencies and airlines, so I asked her help booking my flight at Christmas, and she wangled the whole story out of me. Including how we met, so I got a ticking off for that freebie — don't worry, she's not pissed off at you about it.'

Halley tucked her legs up under her. 'And how was the rest of your week?'

'Good — oh, except that Mr Exactly went silent again, with his tute-partner back. I think I'll ask Rupert for permission to conduct two tutorials for the final few weeks of term, and see them separately. What about you?'

She reached out to get the card from the shelf under the coffee table. 'It's Mom's birthday in a few weeks, and I'm preparing the card. Look at this . . .'

The aged birthday card displayed a cartoon kitten holding flowers, under a banner declaring *birthday wishes, especially for you*. 'Mom gave this to me when I turned five. Ten months later, when it was her birthday, I got it out, added a message to her, and gave it back to her. I guess I thought birthday cards were one single card, being exchanged back and forward — and that's what we did — and still do.' She opened it, tilting to give Henry a good view. Every bit of it was covered with *Happy birthday, Junior, lots of love, Mom* in a variety of sizes and colours interspersed with *Love you, Mommy, from Halley*, and other variations on that theme.

'We've so little space left, we're now on the back cover, and both keeping our writing very small.'

Henry was grinning, and moving his head to read it from every angle. 'That's adorable.'

She put it away. 'You ready for this movie? We have to click on it at exactly the same moment, or we'll be out of sync — it might take a few tries. Ready? Three . . . two . . . one . . .' Her TV switched to show two windows, side by side. One displayed the starts of the title sequence and the other the live feed of Henry. He held up a thumb. 'Turn your volume up.' She increased her sound too, listening intently to both audio feeds. 'Hey, we're perfectly in sync on the first try!'

'Not a surprise to me,' Henry said. 'There's never been anything wrong with our timing. We managed to meet three times in the day we were in the same city, after all.'

'It's the distance thing we need to improve,' Halley said. 'Christmas will be a good start . . .'

There was a beat or two of weighty silence, and Halley could read the same anticipation on his face that she felt.

She cleared her throat. 'Have you seen *Interstellar* before?'

'Never,' he said. He looked happy and relaxed.

'It's the best,' she promised. 'There's even a never-ending bookshelf for you. The plot's quite . . . mind-bendy though.' She added, hopefully, 'I'd be happy to pause it, every now and then, to explain the physics.'

'Would you? I'd love that.' He threw a piece of popcorn high into the air. He missed it, laughed, then tried again and caught the next piece between his teeth.

'Seriously? No one ever takes me up on that kind of offer. Especially not on dates.'

On one side of her screen, Henry's mouth turned up at the edges. 'Well, you've never dated me before.'

PART FIVE

Monday, 11 November
Halley

He's very keen on you! Recalling Henry's sister's words, Halley indulged in a shiver of pleasure, then pushed it from her mind to refocus on the data set she had open: she couldn't afford to get sidetracked from her mission to get all her data analysis into a presentable format in time for her late November meeting with her advisor. Her raw data comprised millions of ultra-high resolution images of the night sky, taken at particular arcs and depths, that she stored compressed in data shards in the cloud. With each of these now too big to easily manipulate on her personal computer, she was stuck working at her powerful desktop within her cubicle. In this room she was the only woman.

She knitted some unprocessed images together in a time lapse, checked her spreadsheet on a secondary screen for the correct grid reference, then renamed the file and dropped it into place on the master document. It would all ultimately resemble a jigsaw of the section of the night sky she'd focused on. Then she returned the new shard to the cloud and selected more unprocessed images. As they downloaded, a faint sound intruded through her noise-cancelling head-phones, and then something hit her shoulder.

She pulled her headphones off, grabbed the offending item — a blue stress ball — and shot to her feet in one swift motion. 'Whose is this?' she said mildly, into the appalled silence.

'Mine,' one of the guys in a cubicle over by the door admitted. Before she could chuck it back at him, he added, 'Shit, Hal, are you OK? I'm really sorry, I meant to throw it at Jacob.'

Halley lowered her arm. 'I know you didn't do it on purpose.' Now he'd apologized she couldn't do what any of the guys would have done, and fired it right back at his head. Rather than responding with raucous applause, as they would for each other, there would be injurious silence, and later, someone would question why she hadn't accepted his apology.

'You're not hurt?' he added.

Hurt. From a stress ball at fifteen metres.

'I'm fine. Catch.' She sent the stress ball arcing toward him. He fumbled it, of course.

'I did yell *incoming*,' she heard him mutter. 'Why did she have to make such a big thing of it?'

She bit her lower lip to stop herself retorting that she'd been wearing headphones, had she not been *she'd* have caught the missile. If she got into that, she'd end up pointing out to the whole lot of them that treating her so carefully felt exclusionary. Instead, she checked the time. Discovering it was early evening, she reflexively rotated her shoulders, and glanced through the window behind her. The cloudless sky was rapidly darkening: a perfect night for sky-gazing, if only she didn't have so much data wrangling and undergrad marking to do. She was tempted to head up to the telescope anyway, but that would be nuts. Instead, she switched to a different interface and more straightforward task, marking problem sheets.

After working through half of them she got to one with answers so far from correct that she couldn't even decipher how the student had reached them. Deciding this meant that sleep was now the priority, she switched everything off, stretched, then rose, scooping up her belongings.

As she left the building and began to walk, her thoughts returned to Henry, as so often happened when she wasn't actively concentrating elsewhere. On this beautiful evening, with the stars appearing overhead, her longing to see him was stronger than ever. If it wasn't the middle of the night on his bit of the planet, she'd have phoned him.

Halfway home she found herself behind a couple, walking arm in arm. She semi-recognized them, and wondered how, until a split second later, when she realized that they reminded her of herself and Henry. The woman had a thick, fair ponytail, and the guy was a little darker, and three inches taller.

The woman half-turned, and the illusion was instantly broken, but Halley kept her eyes on them. She wasn't close enough to hear what the woman said, but the meaning was evidenced by the man's reaction, pulling off his sweater and smiling as the woman put it on over her thin dress.

Halley averted her eyes and plodded on.

* * *

Tuesday, 12 November

> *From: Henry Inglis*
> *Subject: My first American football match . . .*
> *To: Halley Hart*
> Dear Halley,
>
> Are you free Saturday at the same time? And, unfortunately, at similar — still separate — places.
>
> I had a visitor in my office today. Mr Exactly, asking if he could speak to me. I managed not to say, 'I really bloody wish you would.' He implored me not to go ahead with solo tutorials because — I think you'll like this — he's in love with Ms

Oxcited . . . In her presence it's almost impossible for him to think, let alone formulate complex sentences, so he puts all his energy into hinting that he likes her by agreeing vociferously with everything she says.

Yesterday I met my friend Kwame — who owns the boat — and arranged to rent it for an initial six months. On my way home I passed a pub that shows American sport. They were advertising that the San Francisco 49ers were playing, and I thought of you. I even went in for a pint, and tried to follow the match.

Is it too early to start counting down to Christmas?

Henry xxx

* * *

Wednesday, 13 November

From: Halley Hart
Subject: Your first American football GAME
To: Henry Inglis
Yes! Same time, same place for me. You, on the other hand, seem to be in a different location every time we vid-chat. Where do I get to see next?

And no — It's never too early to count down to Christmas — it's my favourite holiday anyway, and I have a feeling this one will be the best ever.

When do you move on to the boat?

I absolutely love the update on your students! (From now on, I need regular updates — I'm massively over-invested in this situation!)

Henry, I get that you don't follow *American sport* and also that San Francisco is the nearest major city to where I currently live. But if you wanna date me then you've got to understand that we're

Chicago Bears fans all the way. And while we're at it, we support the Cubs not the White Sox, and the Bulls are the best basketball team on the planet.

How's your dad doing?

Your Halley

P.S. What's our soccer team? I'll order their baseball cap for my collection.

* * *

Thursday, 14 November

From: Henry Inglis
Subject: Match, not game, noted!
To: Halley Hart

Dear Halley,

I'm moving to the boat next week — Kwame's got belongings there to shift out first. And Dad's fine, don't waste a moment worrying about him.

I gather that thinking of you because of the 49ers was something of an insult? Please forgive my cultural faux pas! The nearest Premiership footie team to where I grew up is Southampton FC, but I don't really watch sport so I'm a nominal supporter at best. My father used to take me along to watch Hampshire County Cricket Club on occasion, but I shouldn't think they produce much in the line of baseball caps. There might be beanies?

There was an SCR working lunch earlier. I attempted to radiate invisibility, so as not to get landed with any extra tasks, and thankfully succeeded, though it got dicey when an issue with a staircase near my office was reported. Apparently the housekeepers have repeatedly found straw and hay scattered around inside there, and fear it's the start of an elaborate prank, similar to one a decade ago, when apparently the MCR carpet was sown with grass seed and watered until it grew. Hogshoo volunteered me to investigate, but it was decided instead to inform students resident on that staircase that it has to stop, or daily spot-checks on their rooms will become mandatory.

I've never been the biggest Christmas fan, but this year I'm looking forward to it more than words can express. And to keep us going in the meantime, there's our date to look forward to. See you Saturday!

Henry xxx

* * *

Friday, 15 November

Voice note from Viola to Henry:

Henry, It's me. The appointment's come through for Dad's hip operation at long bloody last. But the date's rather awkward so we need to work out a plan. Call me!

* * *

Saturday, 16 November
Halley

She knew when she'd been dreaming about Henry, for the simple reason that she always dreamt about Henry. And she knew when Angelie was having one of her groups over for a breakfast meeting when she was awoken by raised voices.

Halley squashed her spare pillow over her face and ears, blocking the intrusion out. She'd give Angelie hell for having people here at the crack of dawn. Except, Angelie wouldn't do that — their agreement was that meetings began no earlier than 9.30, so Halley had overslept. Which meant that she only had two hours or so until her next date with Henry.

She sat bolt upright, smiling with anticipation.

'Listen up,' Angelie bellowed in another room. 'If this decision was easy, we'd have made it already. Let's break for ten, run through the options *calmly*, then take another vote.'

Halley hastily dressed, keen to make the most of their break, so she didn't have to make coffee to a soundtrack of arguing.

Passing several of the group in the hallway, she recognized them as members of the mobile game team, and the concept art all over the breakfast bar in the kitchen confirmed it. Then she second-guessed herself, because the curly-haired guy built like a linebacker was sitting beside Angelie, and he was from her wellbeing app team.

Halley caught Angelie's eye, and jerked her head toward the hallway.

'What's going on?' she hissed, once they'd shooed the others back into the kitchen. 'We agreed, if you ever merge a couple of your teams, you'd tell me how you explained their existence to each other, so I could back up that story.'

'I didn't, though.'

Halley scrutinized her. 'Don't try to tell me that guy's not from wellbeing.'

Angelie sucked in her cheeks, which Halley had seen her do hundreds of times when thinking hard in an attempt to cover her tracks with one group or another.

'Just the truth, thanks,' Halley said, letting her voice grow louder.

'Shh! And don't be like that. He's a psychology Master's student, and his input on the mental wellbeing app's been so on point that I decided to loop him in on this one too — we're struggling with getting the game sticky enough.'

'Sticky, in that context . . . oh *addictive* enough? So he's dedicating his time to both the improvement of mental wellbeing, and purposely addicting people to their phones?'

'*Sticky*,' Angelie emphasized severely. 'He's helping us with a positive reinforcement offer. He's already come up with a potentially transformational reward for the gamer who enables push notifications.'

'So he knows you're working on multiple projects?'

'He knows I'm working on two, and he's sworn to silence.'

Halley watched through the glass in the door as the linebacker wandered to their refrigerator, removed a pint of yoghurt, and dug into it with a spoon. 'That's mine!'

'I'll replace it,' Angelie said rapidly. 'He can't help it. He plays football and he's from Texas.'

Halley gaped at her, then strode into the kitchen. 'Hey, you! You shouldn't steal people's food.'

'I was hungry, and Angelie said to help myself.'

Halley glared back at Angelie, being intercepted by a girl who looked like she was about to combust. She wondered why, of all the fifty or so people involved in her groups, it was this one she chose to double-up on time with.

'What's your name?' Halley demanded.

'Ben,' he said in that southern drawl. He pronounced it *Bin*, which was apt.

'The bottom half of the refrigerator is Angelie's food. Eat as much as you like of that, but leave my stuff alone, Bin.'

Angelie scurried in. 'How about I bring you coffee in your room, Bu— uh, *Halley*?'

Halley ground out a thank you and returned to her bedroom, where her phone was chiming with an incoming call. The astronomy department's number flashed on her screen, and she eyed it with distaste: there was either a severe emergency, or someone had forgotten it was a weekend. 'Yes?' Listening hard, she slipped on a hoodie and grabbed her keys, then remembered that her car wasn't outside. 'I don't have wheels today. It'll take me a while to get there . . .'

She waved at Angelie, mouthed *emergency*, and left the flat, pressing Henry's contact on her phone.

He answered within one ring. 'Halley, everything all right?'

'Yeah. No.' She took a breath, even as she set a steady pace. '*I'm* fine, but the fire alarm went off at the observatory. Seems to have only been from a campfire started by some idiot immediately outside, and the fire service are already packing up to leave. But I want to check over all the equipment myself. I'll probably be late for our video call, but you know I'd rather be hanging out with you, right?'

'Of course,' he said. 'Actually, I got held up myself, and I was going to have to rush to get to the . . .'

When he didn't continue, her forehead creased. 'You're out and about? I thought we could at least chat while I was on the way, but—'

'We can,' Henry said. 'Now that I can saunter back, rather than legging it.'

'I'm legging it,' Halley admitted, jamming her phone between her shoulder and chin. 'So you'll have to do most of the talking. In the worst possible timing, I dropped my car into the shop yesterday.'

'Did I know you have a car? I don't think you've mentioned it before.'

'Seriously? I don't use it for going between the apartment and campus, but it's thirty minutes to walk to the observatory — usually in the dark — so I brought it down from Chicago for my second year. Do you have a car?'

'No, though I borrow Viola's periodically. What's the problem with yours?'

'Needs new brake pads. Usually I do anything like that myself but I don't have time right now, and brake issues can't be delayed, of course. Where are you walking? I want to picture you.'

'Down Banbury Road — I'm about to pass North Parade. Where we first saw each other.'

'I dream about that all the time,' she admitted suddenly. 'Not like daydreams — well those too, sometimes — but proper dreams. A few nights ago, instead of what actually happened, in my dream you jumped into the taxi beside me, demanded that I kiss you again, and then . . . things progressed.'

'Hmm? When you say *progress* — shit,' he hissed suddenly. 'I'm so sorry — are you OK?' he added, in a rather strangled yell.

'Henry?'

'I stepped into the road without looking both ways. Made a cyclist do a rather abrupt emergency stop. Listen, it's not that I don't want to hear about how things . . . culminate in your dream, but it leaves me rather unable to focus—'

'On the road,' Halley said, her lips twitching.

'On absolutely anything,' he corrected, with wry self-consciousness.

'Then I'll wait to tell you sometime when it doesn't risk your life and limb,' she said, checking no one was in earshot. 'Because keeping you alive is the only way to figure out some-day if my dream's as good as reality.'

Henry's mock groan cheered her up considerably.

* * *

Text messages between Halley and Henry:

> *Sorry, it's taking an age to check everything. You OK to stay up late, or shall we move our date to tomorrow? x*

>> *If it's really all right, sweetheart, then let's say tomorrow? Hope all your equipment's undam-aged? xxx*

> *Everything fine so far, but I'm not taking any chances. 'Til tomorrow, usual time. x*

* * *

Sunday, 17 November
Henry

Henry scanned around, appraising the place. It was . . . fine. He tried again, imagining what Viola would say if she were beside him, and his eyes alighted on the teetering crates of books in one corner. He straightened them before opening his laptop and staring at Halley's photo outside the Halley observatory in Oxford, which he'd added to her contact. He wished he'd stayed at her side, shortly after taking it, for long enough to confirm the location of the Hope and Anchor. Or even better, that he'd blown off bidding his tour group farewell, cancelled on conducting the later tour, and spent the entire rest of the day with her.

Aware he was delaying the chat because of what was weighing on him, he muttered, 'Chicken,' and double-clicked to initiate the call.

Halley was already smiling when she appeared on his screen, but a split second later she gave the biggest grin and her eyes lit up.

'You've moved into the boat already!'

'Yup — surprise!' he said, trying to match her level of excitement. 'Kwame emptied it earlier than planned, so I got the keys Friday night and spent the weekend shifting everything in. I haven't unpacked much yet.'

She leaned in, so her face overtook his entire screen. 'Henry, what's wrong?'

'How do you . . .' He shook his head. It didn't matter how she could tell.

'I'm freaking out here. Is it . . . is your father OK?'

'He is. It's good news for him, actually. The hip surgery he's needed for over two years has finally been scheduled.' Halley opened her mouth, but he pressed on. 'Unfortunately, for the twentieth of December. Mum will need someone staying with her during his admission. And while he should be discharged in time for Christmas, they'll then need at least two weeks of intensive support at home. We're trying to line up carers to assist with all that, but with Mum so confused and Dad instantly cantankerous at even the mention of support, there's no guarantee that it won't all end up on Vi's shoulders if I'm . . . if I'm away.'

'You're saying . . . you can't come here for Christmas?'

Henry compressed his lips hard enough that it was painful. 'Unfortunately so.' He sucked in a deep breath. 'If I stay,

I can take it in shifts with Viola. We've agreed we'll do every other day, or similar. I didn't want to talk through all the details until I'd told you.'

He'd been dreading making Halley's face fall, but she looked contemplative, rather than devastated. He supposed that should make him feel a little less wretched, but instead he was beginning to worry. Maybe she wasn't experiencing the desperation to be together that he was.

'If you won't be busy supporting your parents, like, every minute of every day, what if I come there, instead? I could get on with some dissertation writing every other day, while you're with your parents.'

Henry couldn't move.

'Umm . . . Henry?'

'I . . . you . . . you'd seriously come here, to . . . to stay on a boat and see me every other day?'

Her eyebrows rose. 'It's the practical solution — and infinitely preferable to not seeing you for *any* days. If you . . . well, if you'd like that?'

'If I'd like that,' he repeated, dazed. 'I'd bloody love it!' He'd recognized her brilliance very shortly after meeting her, but sometimes, he mused, it still took him by surprise. 'You're amazing, Halley. Coming up with that plan instantly, under the auspices of practicality.'

She shrugged, but was smiling again. 'It's decided, then? I'll book a flight.'

'I can look into transferring mine to you—'

'Don't be dumb. Save it for coming out here as soon after that as you can manage. Now quit making me think someone's dying, and give me the grand tour!'

He transferred the call onto his mobile and swept it around as he walked into the bedroom, where he'd made up the bed. 'We'll start at the front — the bow.'

'What size is that bed? It's hard to figure out the scale.'

'It's a standard double,' he said, as blandly as he could. He resolved to pull out the sofa, later in the tour, to show her that it became a small-double guest bed. 'I more often use the door in the stern to exit and enter the boat, but there's also one here to a little covered deck,' he said, unlocking it and stepping out. He panned in a circle, showing her the canal, with neighbouring boats, and the towpath and then the exterior of the boat. 'Narrow boats have names, and despite getting hers from the owner before Kwame, it happens to remind me of you. Want to venture a guess?'

'It couldn't be called Halley. Nothing has my name — except Mom and the comet.'

'My email unearthed another dozen or so Halley Harts,' Henry pointed out.

'Just as well I knew my name wasn't unique from birth. Oh God, it's not a pun on Hart is it? *The Heartbreaker* or something.'

'Nooo. Give up?' He lowered his phone, until it displayed the words rendered in swirling letters just above the water line: *Blue Moon.*

* * *

Monday, 18 November

Text messages between Halley and Mom:

> *I was just thinking that it's nearly your big birthday, Mom. What would you like? Aside from our card, of course. x*

>> *Only the card. And a phone call with my daughter, if she can make time.*

>> *And what's with the x? Have you done as you threatened age 15, and changed your name? I'm not calling you Xena!*

> *Of course I can make time for a phone call, Mom. I miss you. (Ignore the x — clumsy thumbs.)*

105

I miss you too, Junior. Talk soon and take care!

* * *

Tuesday, 19 November

> *From: Halley Hart*
> *Subject: Once in a Blue Moon*
> *To: Henry Inglis*
> Hey Henry,
>
> What have you done about the tutorials for your student — will you let him stay in one with the girl, only parroting *exactly*?
>
> Hope you're starting to feel at home in the Blue Moon. Such a cool name — though the astronomical phenomenon isn't as cool as people think. It's nothing to do with the colour, only that a set of moon phases takes 29.5 days, which means twelve lunar cycles in 354 days. So every 2.5 years a thirteenth full moon is observed within a calendar year, and that's named a blue moon. (It's always seemed odd to me that the idiom is *once in a blue moon*, when there's one so regularly.) (It should be *once in a Halley's Comet*, since that's genuinely about once in a lifetime.)
>
> I've arranged to call Mom on her birthday next week.
>
> Can you do same time, same place Saturday for next date?
>
> Your Halley

* * *

Wednesday, 20 November

> *From: Henry Inglis*
> *Subject: Once in a Halley's Comet*

To: Halley Hart

Morning, Halley,

I'm pleased to hear about the phone call with your mother!

I've entirely finished unpacking the galley (full admission: wrote *kitchen* and had to backspace), and moved onto books. There aren't nearly enough shelves, but Kwame said I could put more up, so I've added that to my ever-expanding list of things to do once term ends.

I went back to consult Rupert on the issue of the tutorials, and he declared, 'Well, all's fair in love and war, as they say,' before petering out, as he does. I chose to interpret that as assent for the two of them to remain in a tutorial together . . . I must be going soft.

On my end, I told Viola our new Christmas plan and she offered to do extra days with the parentals while you're here, if I pick up the slack in the weeks before and after your visit. To show willing, I'd like to offer to go down to stay with them this weekend, so she can have one completely free from them. (Feel a bit bad typing that — I should have offered sooner . . .) Anyway, if so, I can't make our date on Saturday, but the thought of waiting another week after that is unpleasant. Do you have any other free time next week at all?

Once in a blue moon will never pass my lips again — only the infinitely superior *once in a Halley's Comet*.

Henry xxx

* * *

Thursday, 21 November

From: Halley Hart
Subject: Thanksgiving?

To: Henry Inglis
Hey Henry,

As an only child, and lately a pretty lousy daughter, I'm not best placed to advise on the situation with Viola taking more responsibility for your parents. But you seem to be describing feeling a little guilty about it, so of course you should go down this weekend! As for a midweek date — wanna celebrate Thanksgiving with me on Thursday?

I've been looking at options for flights. There's plenty of availability so I thought I'd wait a couple weeks before booking, in case your father's operation changes date or anything? (I've heard all about cancellations in the NHS, because Mom's really interested in different countries' health systems.) (She doesn't talk about NHS cancellations in any insulting kind of way — she's actually really keen on 'socialized medicine'.)

Your Halley x

* * *

Friday, 22 November

From: Henry Inglis
Subject: Thinking about you constantly, as ever . . .
To: Halley Hart
Dear Halley,

Would you believe, Ms Oxcited and Mr Exactly arrived at my office for their tute earlier *hand in hand*. I don't know what happened so suddenly, but unfortunately he's so in love that he still only speaks to echo everything she says with *exactly*, though now with an awed smile. So this development has left him a lot happier (and presumably her too), but not really me.

I totally understand with the flight. And virtual Thanksgiving dinner date sounds amazing — I'm there!

Sorry to keep this short — I'm on the train and arriving soon. Apologies in advance if I don't get time to message much — I'll be thinking about you constantly, as ever.

Henry xxx

* * *

Sunday, 24 November

From: Halley Hart
Subject: On a practical note . . .
To: Henry Inglis
Henry!!

I was so excited at the update on your students that I screamed a little, and Angelie sprinted into my bedroom with a fire extinguisher! She thought an intruder (possibly zombified) had climbed in my window, not that there was a fire, but she'd previously identified the extinguisher as a good weapon.

I'm also a little envious of them. They get to hold hands, and we don't. Not until Christmas. Is it weird that it's one of the many things I'm actively looking forward to? I don't think I've ever particularly been into holding hands before.

I hope your weekend with your parents has gone OK. I didn't email yesterday so that you didn't feel any pressure to write me back.

I'm busy getting my data tidy for the astronomy symposium here in a few weeks. I get to present my work — as long as my advisor signs off on my analysis at our meeting on Wednesday — which is great visibility prior to applying for jobs in academic astronomy. On a practical note, this gave me an idea. . . what if I told him I'd be especially interested in meeting professors from any European astronomy programmes who might have an opening upcoming? Or is it too soon for me and you to be planning for the future?

I'm constantly thinking about you, too.

Your Halley

* * *

Monday, 25 November

From: Henry Inglis
Subject: It's absolutely not too soon!
To: Halley Hart
Dear Halley,

I'm still grinning — and I read your email eleven hours ago! From my perspective, it is absolutely not too soon. But also, please feel no pressure to do so if it were just an idea. And either way, good luck at the meeting with your advisor!

Emergency SCR meeting earlier, and I feared having to investigate if there's a straw prank, after all. It turned out to be something quite different — the bursar saw a shadow moving up the outside of one of our buildings. There's a historic feud with a neighbouring college which we were hopeful had died out, but if it's been reignited it could be one of their undergrads climbing over — or one of ours heading over there. Unfortunately Hogshoo volunteered me again, this time successfully, and I've been deputized to identify the climber if at all possible.

What are we doing for Thanksgiving? My oven's too small for a turkey but I could roast a chicken or make turkey soup.

I can't wait to hold your hand, Halley.

Henry xxx

* * *

Tuesday, 26 November

From: Halley Hart
Subject: Thanksgiving dinner-date
To: Henry Inglis

Hey Henry,

I hope the identification of a climber doesn't mean any climbing yourself? Please be careful!

You don't need anything fancy for Thanksgiving, just your favourite comfort food. That's what Mom and I always did, when it was just the two of us. We only ate the traditional stuff when we went to Aunt Edie's in Florida for the Thanksgiving week-end. (Which we managed occasionally, when other nurses were kind enough to swap shifts with Mom.) (So since I turned 18, Mom has worked most holidays, after swapping with single moms.)

I'm definitely asking about jobs in Europe tomorrow, Henry. I mean, there's no guarantees. Academic astronomy is poorly funded, so there are never many jobs, and my dull thesis topic won't set the world on fire. But I wanna try to be close to you, and not just at Christmas.

Your Halley

* * *

Wednesday, 27 November
Halley

'Halley, come in,' Professor Tung said, as she hovered in his doorway.

He was bald with a thick neck and small features, so he resembled a thumb with a face drawn on it. Some students nicknamed him Professor Thumb as a result, though Halley had never done so. This was the human being whose opinion of her and her work would have the biggest effect on her future.

She sat on the other side of his desk, and smiled, to keep from looking as nervous as she felt.

'I've examined your data analysis, and I have to say, I've always had high hopes for you, Halley.' He laughed. 'High hopes, get it?'

High hopes for her because she was an astronomer named after a comet. He absolutely loved terrible gags.

'Good one,' she lied.

'But about your data . . .' He pulled an apologetic face. 'I'm afraid you've missed something . . .'

PART SIX

Thursday, 28 November
Henry

Henry crouched in front of the small oven, examining the dish inside. The parmesan had darkened, so he lifted the lasagne out with folded tea towels, adding oven gloves to the mental list of essential items to buy before Halley arrived. He wondered, setting the dish on the table that bisected the galley and the living area, if she'd booked her flight yet. He wanted a date to put in his diary, and to begin a daily countdown.

His laptop buzzed, and he glanced at the time. Halley was ten minutes early, but he was ready, and he slid onto the bench on the galley side, accepting the call.

Halley was cross-legged on the floor of her living room, with a pile of junk food in front of her.

'I misinterpreted comfort food,' he said. 'Pasta sprang to mind, not crisps and biscuits.'

'This is mostly candy,' she said, without a smile. Her voice had a different quality to usual. 'I was going to make macaroni and cheese but ran out of time.' She reached for something. A napkin . . . no — a tissue.

'You're unwell? Should we—'

She jerked her head. 'Don't suggest a rain check. I might just wimp out and take you up on it. I've fucked up.'

His stomach lurched. He kept his tone calm, his volume soft. 'What happened?'

She compressed her lips, her eyes watering.

Surreptitiously he opened his email, and reread her recent messages, hunting for clues. 'Should I attempt a guess?'

She raised a shoulder. *Go ahead.*

'Is it . . . related to your mother?'

She shook her head.

'Then, the meeting with your advisor?'

Her jaw clenched. *Yes.*

Henry's tension dissipated a little, and he released a long, slow breath. Halley hadn't suffered a bereavement or been diagnosed with a terrible disease or met someone else. This was about her Ph.D. Though that didn't mean it wasn't earth-shattering. He sought the softest words with which to frame the likeliest scenario.

'Has your advisor . . . revised the timeline on when you'll be PhDone?'

'Kinda,' she croaked. 'Henry, he saw an error with one of the shards in my data set. I don't know when it happened, or how, but it's corrupted. I've got to patch it, as best I can, by collecting more data. It means I can't take part in the symposium, and worse, sets me back on writing up.' Sniffing, she half-turned, holding balled tissues to her eyes. 'I'm missing data over thirty-two days. He says I've still got a shot at finishing on time — if I virtually live up here at the telescope between now and mid-January. Which means I can't . . . come to Oxford.'

Henry's heart kicked his ribs, as the woman rapidly coming to mean everything to him buried her face in her arms. He knew how awful she felt, having had to deliver similar news to her. And rather than wallowing with him, she'd conjured a practical solution. But he couldn't think of one. 'Halley, I don't know what to say . . .'

She glanced up at that, and blew her nose before she spoke. 'I've spent all night figuring out if I can both collect this data and get to Oxford. But the only dates that aren't vital for me to be here are literally dawn on the 23rd to dusk on the 28th. The travel knocks out at least twelve hours each way, which would leave us four days together, some of which you'd be busy supporting your parents. I don't think either of us have got the money to travel that kind of distance for two to three days together? I certainly don't — especially since Professor Tung also recommended I quit my TA role in January, to throw all my efforts into writing up. I'll be majorly broke, but I think he's right. And I also won't be ready to present at the symposium ' She picked up one of the packets, unwrapping it resignedly — 'so that sucks. Professor Tung said he'll recommend me to the organizing committees of symposiums taking place next year, but there's no guarantees.' She threw a sweet into her mouth. 'Sugar helps. Vodka would be better.'

'Didn't know you like vodka.'

'I don't. I just want to get wasted. Ideally, with you. Hey, what's that expression for?'

He debated saying it, then succumbed, fixing his eyes on her intently. 'The first time I see you again, sweetheart, I intend to be absolutely and entirely sober.'

She flushed. 'That's . . . a better idea than mine.'

He smiled at her, and an edge of her mouth tilted upwards.

'So, can I come to California in February, when you've completed your nights at the observatory, and Dad's recovered from his op?'

Her eyes lit up. 'Our birthdays, and Valentine's — we could be together for all of that! But . . . are you allowed to take vacation in term time?'

'Not technically, but my double teaching load this term means I won't have any next. I think Rupert would let me disappear for a week.'

'A week's not long enough!' Halley insisted around another mouthful of sweets. 'Not if we're waiting more than two whole months.' She unwrapped a bar of chocolate. 'Hang on . . . now I'm quitting as TA, I'm not continually tethered to Stanford. I could come to Oxford for a couple weeks, as long as I make some time to write while you're at work.'

'You could easily get guest status at the Bod,' Henry said. 'Or work here on the Blue Moon — whatever you prefer.'

She smiled properly, at last. 'Then it's a deal.' She twisted up her hair and secured it with a pencil. He wanted to let it loose again. 'And I feel a little better. And it's Thanksgiving — your first?'

'Yup,' Henry said, eyeing his lasagne. He'd lost his appetite, but heaped a serving on his plate anyway.

'Henry, do you ever just eat, like, a salad?'

He stared significantly at her pile of sweets, and she laughed. 'That was a genuine question.'

He considered his diet. 'College does meat-free Mondays, and I'll usually have veggie chilli. Does that count?'

'What? How would that count?'

'It's a plate of plants,' he said, enjoying her laughter.

'Hot, with sour cream and nachos and cheese!'

'Compared with sweets, it's a salad,'

'*Sweets*,' she said, in an over-emphasized imitation of his accent. 'Which is at least traditional for me at Thanksgiving. Mom and I ate them while obsessing over the *Gilmore Girls* — because they too loved candy and shared a name.'

'They were friends of yours?'

She scrunched her face up in confusion.

'The Gilmore girls you mentioned?'

'The *Gilmore Girls* is a TV show from the noughties — Mom and I binged the reruns. We even kept a cupboard filled with Mallomars and Red Vines so we could eat along when Lorelai and Rory had them. Henry?'

'Yes, Halley?'

'How much of that did you follow?'

'I remember the noughties. I'm hazy about everything else.'

'Lorelai is the Mom's name. And she called her daughter Lorelai too, only she went by Rory. Hey — we should watch a Thanksgiving episode together!'

Comfort viewing, and comfort eating, because he wasn't there to comfort Halley himself. Nor was he seeing her at Christmas, so it wasn't only Halley who needed comforting. He wondered if he had any chocolate in the cupboard.

* * *

Text messages between Halley and Henry:

> *Night 1 of 33 at observatory is done! And at about 2 a.m. I realized I'll have to mail you a Christmas gift. How do I do that at the Blue Moon? Your Halley x*

> > *Royal Mail don't service houseboats, so I get my post delivered to St Jude's. The best Oxford advice I ever received was to make friends with the porters, and it's paying off now — they inform me about any parcels immediately. Hoping for good weather for your observations, sweetheart. Henry xxx*

* * *

Tuesday, 3 December
Halley

Halley stared into the bathroom mirror. She looked as tired and drained as she felt, and there wasn't anything miraculous enough in her make-up bag to hide the signs from Mom's scrutiny, but she made her best attempt, then wandered back into her bedroom. The kitchen was both full and silent, which meant Angelie had the quietest of her groups over, who were developing something to do with cyberattack detection. Ironically enough, Angelie's noisiest group, who did little but argue, were working on a productivity platform.

Her bed would be visible in the background, so she made it to Mom-standard, hospital corners and all, then dimmed the lighting before sitting at her desk. She shoved aside the stacks of assignments. She'd mark them later, as well as texting Henry back and doing some laundry, she promised herself, initiating the video call.

As it connected, she put a party horn between her lips.

'Jun—' Mom began.

Halley blew hard, so the horn unrolled and blared, making Mom wince. 'Happy 50th, Mom!'

'Those things should be banned,' Mom said, as she had every birthday since Halley first woke her with one, aged around seven.

'At least I don't subject you to it at five in the morning anymore. You don't look in your fifties, by the way.'

'Thank you,' Mom said drily. Her hair was fading beautifully to silver-blonde, and she'd worn it bobbed to just above her shoulders for as long as Halley could remember. 'Did you know Aunt Edie's visiting?'

'Hi, Junior,' Aunt Edie said, appearing over Mom's shoulder. 'You look terrible! Doesn't she look terrible, Halley?'

'She looks *exhausted*, not terrible,' Mom said. Aunt Edie was the only person Halley knew who made Mom seem diplomatic. 'Edie, go away. The call's my gift from Halley.'

Aunt Edie rolled her eyes. 'So dramatic. Bye, Halley!'

'Bye, Aunt Edie,' Halley said. She loved her aunt a lot — especially when only subjected to her in small doses.

'So why are you tired?' Mom asked once Edie had shut the door behind her.

'Can't we focus on you, on your birthday?' Mom raised an eyebrow, and Halley relented, briefly explaining about the corrupted data shard, and the nights she had to work for the next six weeks, if she was going to complete her Ph.D. on schedule. 'It'll be easier once the quarter's over, and I can sleep daytimes.'

Mom frowned. 'Are there financial implications if your Ph.D. extends into another year?'

'My basic stipend would carry over — it's more the opportunity cost, of another year unable to earn. But it shouldn't come to that. It's six weeks extra to squash in, not six months. So not a disaster, aside from ruining Chri—' Halley broke off, furious with herself.

'*Christmas*? What had you planned?'

'Huh?' Playing dumb might work, since Mom knew she was tired.

'You were saying, it's ruined your Christmas plans, were you not? What had you planned?'

'It doesn't matter,' Halley ground out. 'It's not happening anyway.'

Mom stared at her. Halley stared back, unblinking. *Mom cannot read my mind*, she chanted internally.

'Aha!' Mom said. 'Christmas with Henry was on the cards!'

Halley slumped back in her desk chair. 'How the hell d'you do that?'

'I figured it was going well with him, when you went quiet for all those weeks. Then you gave yourself away ending a text with a kiss. That's very British. I was hoping,' Mom added, 'that you were so exhausted because he's visiting . . .'

Halley's face heated. 'Well, he's not,' she said shortly. 'We haven't seen each other again. And we can't until February. Mom, I know it's your birthday and I want to play nice, but you've got to swear you'll never talk to him again — in any format — without express permission from me.'

'I swear,' Mom said immediately. 'Which means anything you tell me is safe. I won't tell anyone — except maybe Edie, if we open champagne later. Come on, pretend I know nothing, and fill me in from the very start . . .'

* * *

Wednesday, 4 December

119

From: Halley Hart
Subject: Clear Skies
To: Henry Inglis
Hey Henry,

Sorry I didn't reply yesterday. Between Mom's birthday call and my body clock readjusting to staying up half the night, this week's been a mess. Aside from my one piece of good news — clear skies so far!

I was hoping an email rather than text might make up for being tardy, but now I gotta run and take a class, so it's not long and newsy like I planned.

Hope you're OK? And that you know I miss you.

Your Halley

* * *

Saturday, 7 December

Text message from Halley to Henry:

Henry, I'm hoping you're just crazy-busy and there's not been some emergency, with your parents or something. Can you drop me a line to confirm you're OK? x

* * *

Sunday, 8 December
Halley

Halley woke with an ache in her jaw, and massaged it gingerly. She must have been grinding her teeth in her sleep, worried about Henry even during her few hours of unconsciousness.

She grabbed her phone from the nightstand, but there were no new messages, and she vowed to call him after a cup of coffee.

There was a bang on her door. 'Halley?'

She considered pretending to be asleep, but Angelie sounded panicked. 'I'm awake.'

Angelie rushed inside. 'You have to help me get rid of Ben! We overslept and now my robotics team are about to arrive, and he can't know!'

'Ben?'

'Texan. Football player. Hot as a barn burner, as he would put it.'

'Bin the human trashcan,' Halley said, groaning. 'I thought a lot of my food's been disappearing. When did you two graduate from being co-workers?'

'We didn't. We're co-workers with benefits,' Angelie said icily. 'Here's what I need you to do. I'm going back in my room to get dressed — I'll be loud enough to make sure I wake him, but I'll act all unconcerned. Like it's fine for him to hang out a while. But I've just programmed our doorbell to go off in five minutes. I'll go out to "see who it is", while you go into my room and tell him that my boyfriend has turned up to surprise me, so Ben must leave quietly. I'll go in the kitchen and talk as if I'm with a guy who's the strong but silent type. Then, and only then, you make sure Ben tiptoes through the hall and out the front door. Now get up!'

Halley dazedly felt for the flip-flops she wore like slippers. 'You'd rather the guy you're sleeping with think you've got a jealous boyfriend, than that you're involved in more than two businesses?'

'Exactly! Come on!'

Halley's phone chimed. She snatched it up, her heart thumping: *Incoming voice call, Henry Inglis.*

'Henry?'

'Hi,' Henry croaked. 'I've got flu.' He coughed, and didn't stop.

'You sound terrible!' She didn't think he could even hear her over the cacophony of coughing, but she jabbed to mute the call anyway. 'Henry's sick, you'll have to handle it yourself.'

'Properly sick?' Angelie asked with suspicion.

Halley held the phone towards her, and Angelie cocked her head, listening as he hacked. 'Eww.'

'Exactly.'

As Angelie retreated from her room, Halley unmuted the call, and sank back onto her side, her head on her pillow. 'Babe, I've been so worried about you.'

* * *

Monday, 9 December

> *From: Halley Hart*
> *Subject: Rest up!*
> *To: Henry Inglis*
> Hey Henry,
>
> It's even worse not being with you when you're sick. I want to feed you chicken noodle soup and make sure you're taking enough Tylenol. I want to check if you have everything you need, and if you're doing any better, but I don't want you to write me back, because you need to rest, so ignore my questions, and sleep! And don't rush back to work too soon.
>
> Mostly clear skies over the weekend, but a minor irritation marred my morning. I'm used to a lot of different spellings and pronunciations of my name, but today a student wrote *dear Holly Heart* — two mistakes — despite sending it to my email address where my name was obviously spelled correctly . . .
>
> Your Halley

* * *

Tuesday, 10 December

> *From: Henry Inglis*

Subject: Doing better
To: Halley Hart

I'm doing a bit better, and no offence but personally I'm glad you're not here, Holly Heart. I wouldn't want to infect you.

Julian's dropped stuff off at the door a few times, and other people have offered but I haven't needed to take them up on it. Hogshoo was forced to step in to assist Rupert with end of term and interviews, so no worries about work. I'm even hoping this might get me out of pursuing the climber.

It was lovely to hear your voice the other day, sweetheart.

Henry xxx

* * *

Wednesday, 11 December

Text messages between Halley and Mom:

How are your Christmas plans shaping up, Junior? You don't have to be at the observatory 23rd-28th, right?

> *Haven't even thought about it. Angelie's going to the Philippines, so I'll gate-crash some other friend's lunch.*

How about you come home instead?

> *Sorry, Mom, I can't really afford it.*

I'll send you a ticket as your Christmas gift. Junior, please? I'm not working this Christmas, and Edie's going to Tahiti. It'd be nice not to be alone.

If it means that much to you, of course I'll come.

* * *

Friday, 13 December
Henry

Henry was sitting up in bed, fighting guilt. He'd binged the
first series of *Gilmore Girls* over the prior two days, and managed multiple brief phone calls with Halley, which surely
meant he was capable of a bit of work. Reluctantly, he slid
his tortoiseshell-rimmed glasses on then navigated to the
Bodleian's manuscripts and archives webpage, and clicked
into the search box. It had come to him in the middle of
the night that two separate errors, like in the email Halley
received, was an avenue to explore for the Sedgwick papers.

His phone buzzed with a withheld number. Grateful for
the interruption, he answered.

'Henry!' It was a familiar voice, but not Halley's.

'Halley-Anne,' he said, a few seconds later. 'Uh . . .' His
brain was on go-slow how to ask politely what the hell she
wanted. The last time she called she said she thought his Halley
was in Chicago, where her sunglasses were made. He'd had to
apologize profusely for forgetting to update her that his Halley
had found him in the meantime. 'How are you?'

'Still fighting the good fight against the scammers. I'm
currently messaging Brad Pitt, who wants to date me but is
temporarily cash strapped, so I need to send him Amazon
vouchers. And even better, I've started a podcast! It's called
Romancing the Scam, subtitle *They'll Tug at Your Heartstrings to
Tug Open Your Purse-Strings*. My aim is to smash the fraudsters
and blast onto the Aussie podcast top one hundred.'

'Sounds great.'

'It will be. And I had the best idea — to have one of
my introductory episodes about the time I called a scam
wrong — it's good to show some foibles along with your

successes, listeners find you more sympathetic. So I thought you could come on as my guest! Get this — I wrote you the best intro . . . *Joining me tonight direct from Oxford University, it's renowned historian, Professor Henry Inglis!*'

'Junior research fellow of zero renown, actually.'

'Creative licence,' Halley-Anne said. 'And then you could do a snappy turn, on the history of romance scams, before I lead our discussion into why I thought you were a love scammer.'

'I'm afraid,' Henry said cautiously, 'that it doesn't really sound like my kind of thing.'

'I thought you'd say that.' Halley-Anne's enthusiasm continued unabated. 'So back-up plan: scrap you being there as a guest, and I just read out your email, then analyse it for the listeners, identifying all the elements that sounded so scammy. I'll change the names so you don't need to worry about privacy.'

'But . . . aren't you releasing the podcast in your own name?'

'Sure . . . Well, at least the version I use publicly: Halley Hart. You know I reserve the *hyphen Anne* for friends and governmental communications.'

Henry dropped his head back onto the pillow. 'So, you could keep my name out of it, but not Halley's — *my* Halley's. Since I sent it to all the women with a certain name — and that name's plastered all over your podcast.'

'Strewth,' she said eventually. 'You're right.' Her voice perked up. 'And you don't think she'd be OK with this whole thing getting out there with her name on it?'

'I suspect not.'

'Well could you ask her? Because if she didn't mind, it would be the simplest thing. She could even come on the pod! Get back to me in January will you? Bye!'

As ever, she cut the call off without waiting for him to return the farewell.

Rubbing his forehead, Henry returned his attention to his laptop. He input a donation date that was a decade out, then tried various misspellings of Sedgwick.

Sedgewick . . . Segwik . . . Segwick . . . Cedgwick—

Suddenly his screen flashed: 1 result found. He scrolled down.

Miscellaneous papers of Cedgwick family, donated 1962. Archive box 13995.

* * *

Saturday, 14 December

From: Henry Inglis
Subject: Breakthrough!
To: Halley Hart

I might have found the Sedgwick papers, thanks to inspiration from you!

I'll go to the library to request the archive box on Monday, and if it contains what I hope it does, I'll have a few days to start cataloguing it before I'm due in Hampshire to help during Dad's op. I'll be at the hospital with him, and Viola at their place with Mum, settling in the live-in carer.

It's a full moon so you won't be at the telescope this week, I think. Time for a movie date?

Sweetheart — that flu wiped me out during the week I was planning on posting your Christmas present, so I'll have it couriered now instead.

Henry xxx

* * *

Sunday, 15 December

From: Halley Hart
Subject: Breakthrough!
To: Henry Inglis

That's awesome!! Let me know how it goes at the library!

Sorry, I wish I had time for any kind of date but I'm hideously busy finishing off senior TA admin, ready for doing a handover. Almost busy enough to distract me from how depressed I am that I'm not packing to come see you, as I should be. I'll continue calling whenever I can.

Henry, I'm heading to Chicago for a few days over the holidays, so you'd be better sending a gift there, rather than here. But I haven't sent you anything either. It was on my to-do list, but then things got so crazy I lost the list . . . So how about we wait until our birthdays to exchange gifts? (But Mom's address is attached in case you hate that idea.) (I'd seriously prefer it, though — the only thing I want for Christmas is to see you, and that's impossible.)

Your Halley

* * *

Monday, 16 December
Henry

Henry hurried up the wide steps of the Weston Library. It was one of the few genuinely modern buildings in central Oxford, yet it housed some of the most ancient of the Bodleian's collections, including manuscripts, maps, and some of the archives. More of the archives were stacked in the labyrinthine tunnels under the streets, or within depositories outside the city.

Being so close to Christmas, there was no queue at the service desk for archive requests, and the librarian behind it gave him her attention immediately.

'Name?' she asked.

'Henry Inglis.' He showed his Reader card, with its staff privileges.

'Not yours — the item you'd like to examine.'

'Right,' he said, feeling like an idiot. 'It's archive box 13995.'

She typed as he spoke. 'Miscellaneous papers of the Cedgwick family, donated in 1962?'

'That's it,' Henry said, 'Except that I suspect it was donated in 1952 by St Jude's, and contains the Sedgwick — with an S — family papers. There were two entry errors when it was catalogued.'

'Two entry errors!' The librarian bristled as though he'd said something obscene. 'We librarians are certainly not in the business of slinging around papers of historical interest without cataloguing them properly.'

'I understand that,' he said quickly. 'Obviously, it would have been some sort of accident. And I could be incorrect entirely. I'll know once I see inside, if someone could arrange access to that box for me.'

The librarian released a resigned sigh. '*Someone* would be me. But it's in long-term storage — it'll take some time.'

'I can wait.'

'Some time meaning *days*,' she said, typing again. 'I'll email you once it's available.'

He thanked her and retreated, as she muttered, '*Two entry errors!*' sounding scandalized.

PART SEVEN

Friday, 20 December

Text messages between Henry and Halley:

Dad's out of surgery. All went well. xxx

> *I'm so pleased to hear that! (Librarian still not been in touch?) x*

Literally just got notification that the archive box is now available! But they're closed 24 Dec–2 Jan, so I won't get to check it out before 3 Jan, unless Rupert can work some magic. I'll call him shortly. How are you? xxx

> *That's exciting, though! I'm regretting agreeing to go to Chicago . . . I'm so tired, and Prof T wants to do interim checks on new analysis on Monday, before I fly.*

At least you'll be reassured that you're on track, sweetheart. xxx

*** *** ***

Sunday, 22 December

From: Henry Inglis
Subject: Good news!
To: Halley Hart
Dear Halley,

All's going well here. The carer's great with Mum, and Dad's doing so well the hospital's discharging him shortly. *And*, Rupert had the archive box transferred to St Jude's library, which is open 24/7. I'll check it out tomorrow, as Vi's happy for me to return to Oxford for Christmas. She's being mysterious about why, but wants a week away from the parentals over New Year instead. (I'm guessing she's met someone . . .)

Let me know when you'll be free for Christmas virtual dates. That's my biggest priority, Halley — we've both had so little free time lately. Aside from that I'll be studying these papers, if they are indeed about my Sedgwick's, and going to Ruth and Kwame for Christmas lunch.

I hope the prep for meeting with your advisor's going well. Good luck and safe travels for tomorrow, if I don't get to speak to you beforehand.

Henry xxx

*** *** ***

From: Halley Hart
Subject: Good news!
To: Henry Inglis
Babe, all that's awesome to hear! Especially that your parents will be reunited for Xmas! And I'm so excited for what could be in the box!

Data prep's all done, but I'm a little nervous about the meeting.

I have to rush to the airport afterwards so if I don't update you immediately, I will once I'm in Chicago.

Your Halley

* * *

Henry braked Viola's car at St Jude's vast gates. When she'd offered to lend it to him he'd been concerned about where to park, until he recalled that with college so sparsely populated at this time of year, space should be available on site. It had made it significantly easier to give in to her insistence that he return to Oxford. Short of emergencies, he should take a break until the twenty-eighth, she'd said, when they'd swap over, and he'd stay with their parents while she buggered off for a week with a friend.

The duty-porter waved from the lodge beside the gates, before they began to open and Henry navigated through. He wondered what was behind Viola's reticence about her burgeoning relationship. She'd never refused to tell him details before, so perhaps this was more serious than usual. Or she didn't want to make him feel even worse about all his plans with Halley crumbling into nothing.

Halley. He was desperate to see her, through a screen at least, after several weeks of rushed phone calls and short messages, but she was travelling today. Hopefully tomorrow, then. For now, there was an archive box to explore.

* * *

Note on Halley's laptop:

Hi Henry,

131

I'm writing this from 30,000 feet over Nevada, on my way to Chicago. Because, on the rare occasions I have ten minutes free, I email or call you, and now I have a whole couple hours but no internet connection. Maybe I'll send this once I'm at Mom's.

I wonder if you know the right drink to order on an aircraft? With the altitude there's a microclimate drier than any desert on the planet. This numbs our tongues to the point that it's like losing a third of our taste buds. And the background noise affects our inner ear, causing us to taste umami better than salt or sugar. All this means tomato juice is the best option, so I've ordered a Bloody Mary. (There's no improvement from the vodka.) (Except in the way it improves any unpleasant experience.)

I can hardly believe I'm writing this, but it didn't go well with my advisor . . . no, it went AMAZING. Because of it, I've got a Christmas gift for you after all, though I wouldn't know how to wrap it. But telling you in email is anti-climactic so I'll wait until we vid-chat on Christmas Day.

Your Halley x

* * *

Henry

Henry's phone buzzed insistently. He glanced at it, hoping for Halley, fearing it to be Vi. Seeing his sister's name, he grimaced and strode into hall, which was otherwise empty.

'What's happened?'

'Don't worry, only updating you that it's all good. Dad started giving the carer gyp — *I'm perfectly able to fend for myself, thank you, Madam* — but then she showed him a photo of her son, and he was delighted.'

'Sorry, of her son?'

'Turns out he recently joined the RAF! Dad's loving it, passing on career advice and listening to anecdotes the boy's told his mum. Which means the stress is off for us, and an emergency dire enough for you to have to rush back is unlikely. Were your papers the right thing, by the way?'

'I'm about to check them.'

'Well have fun! And don't worry about things here. Not until the twenty-eighth, at least.'

'Where are you off to then, by the way?' Henry asked lightly. 'I forgot to ask earlier.'

'Hmm? Sorry, got to run — postie at the door!'

* * *

Halley

Halley emerged into the domestic arrivals hall at O'Hare. She didn't look out for Mom, because her mom tended to call when she reached the pick-up point, where cars could wait for fifteen minutes. Until Halley heard from her, she'd get a coffee and—

'*Junior!*' someone was yelling. '*Halley Junior!*'

Halley spun and saw Mom a short distance away, her hands on her hips.

'*Here, Mom*,' Halley called back, hastening toward her. 'Why've you bothered parking?'

The older woman didn't answer as she scurried the last few steps, flinging her arms around her daughter. 'Love you, honey.'

Halley hugged her back. 'I love you too.'

'You brought the bare minimum again,' Mom noted, releasing her and grabbing the handle of her small suitcase. 'You've brought your passport, though, in case someone breaks into your apartment, with you and Angelie both away?'

'I have,' Halley said, squinting at her with confusion. Angelie had made exactly the same point, several times. Before she could figure out what was going on, Mom was on the move.

'Come along — we're in a hurry.'

Halley had to speed up to catch her. 'Why are you being weird?'

'I'm a woman of mystery.' With that, Mom refused to say another word until they reached her car and she flung open the trunk. Another suitcase was in there.

'Wha—' Halley began, as Mom hauled it out, re-locked her car and turned for the tram that transported passengers between terminals.

Hurry, Halley!'

'Say that quickly three times,' Halley muttered, but her confusion was rapidly lifting. Mom had sprung a similar surprise before. When Halley was ten they'd come to the airport to collect Aunt Edie for a visit. Only, once they'd arrived, Mom had produced luggage and tickets, and announced that instead they were going to meet her sister at Disney World.

'Presumably it's not Disney again,' she hollered. 'So where *are* we going?' She raised her voice further. 'Mom, I'm not walking another step until you tell me.'

'Bye then!' Mom called back.

'That won't work — I'm not a kid anymore!'

'Have a nice Christmas on your own in Chicago!' Mom waved, and disappeared around the corner.

* * *

Henry

Henry had taken the heavy archive box through to the confines of the oldest part of St Jude's library. He'd verified that the number was correct, and noted that despite being handled and moved over the past few days, the box remained dusty. More than that, he couldn't tell until he opened it. Instead of doing so, he'd been staring at it, because someone was speaking vehemently in the quad outside, her voice reverberating through the single-paned glass. Wanting silence, to concentrate fully, he waited for her to move on.

'Of course it's a mess!' she added. 'What would you expect?'

Abruptly, Henry stood up, seized the box, and returned to the library's modern extension. He'd recognized the voice as one of his undergraduates — Ms Oxcited, as he'd dubbed her — and it didn't seem right to listen in. He considered going outside to check on her, and enquire why she hadn't left college for Christmas festivities with her family, but dismissed it as a welfare matter. He'd mention her to Ruth, instead.

He eyed the box again. He wasn't sure where the trepidation he was experiencing had come from. If this wasn't what he was looking for, he'd resume his search. Or if it was, but the contents were too degraded to read, or too dull to be of much use, he'd find a new research focus, no big deal.

But it *was* a big deal as, deep in his psyche, he'd linked the two searches, for the Sedgwick papers and Halley, and desperately wanted them both to be successful.

He put on his reading glasses, then unclipped the box's lid. It was stiff, and he averted his eyes from the contents until he'd swung it all the way back to rest on its hinges.

Inside, it was full almost to the brim, of sheaves of folded yellowing paper, most of which were tied in bundles with cords or ribbons. *Letters.*

* * *

Halley

Halley increased her pace to a sprint, leaped, and made it into the tram an instant before the doors closed behind her.

'Well done,' Mom said, as it pulled off.

Bent almost double, her hands splayed on her knees, Halley gasped, 'I'm gonna . . . kill you.'

'Oh I wouldn't advise that,' Mom said warmly. 'Not if you want to spend Christmas with Henry.'

All the air disappeared from Halley's lungs, like she'd been transported into orbit. 'What?' she asked, after finally managing a full lung-inflating inhalation. 'The . . . Hell?'

'You look nauseated. Oh Lord, Halley — don't say you finished with him and failed to let me kno—'

'Explain what's going on, Mom! Properly, from the start.'

Mom scanned her from head to foot. 'Well, I told Edie about you and Henry — back when there was a you and Henry . . .'

'We're still together,' Halley said, to stop Mom harping on about it.

Mom beamed. 'I *thought* so. Anyway, Edie said it was such a shame that you weren't seeing each other over Christmas, even for a few days, and I said, who's got the money to buy a trans-Atlantic flight for just a few days, and she said I *do* . . . so then I persuaded you to take a break and she bought you a return ticket to the UK.'

The tram slowed, and Halley grabbed a pole just in time to steady herself for the lurching stop.

Mom placed Halley's small suitcase on top of the slightly larger one, and exited onto the platform. 'I mean it that you need to hurry, Junior. Your plane leaves in two hours.'

Halley scrambled after her. 'Mom, how can I just fly to . . .'

'London Heathrow,' Mom put in, without letting up on the pace she'd set.

'Exactly! See I don't even know where I'm going or when I'm coming ba—'

'Leaving noon on the twenty-eighth, which, with the time difference, arrives direct into San Francisco mid-afternoon the same day. Even allowing for a delay, you'll be at the telescope by dark. Any other concerns you need me to alleviate?'

Halley tried in vain to re-centre herself. She was going to England. Going to see Henry. To be with Henry. Her shock was dissipating, but in its place was a knot of so many entangled emotions that she couldn't have put names to half of them. She moved her focus back to the practical. 'I haven't packed the right—'

'I raided your closet,' Mom said, gesturing towards the lower of the stacked suitcases as she continued the speed-walk.

If she did this, she'd get to the UK in, what, ten hours or so. With the time zone six hours ahead of her present location, she'd arrive at Henry's boat on the afternoon of Christmas Eve.

'I'm scared,' Halley blurted.

'Oh, kiddo. Of course you are. You want to go though, right?'

Before Halley could even consider her answer, she was nodding vociferously. 'Of course. But, Mom, Henry's busy with his family. His dad had sur—'

'I've been monitoring that situation. For a while it looked like you'd be joining them in Hampshire, but now it's confirmed that he's in Oxford while you're there — no, *not* by Henry — your arrival's a surprise to him too. And yes I do recall my ban on communications, thank you. Someone else passed on intel, but I'm sworn to secrecy on the details.'

Someone else could only be Viola. But Mom didn't even know Henry had a sister. . . Angelie, however, had met Viola over video call that time.

'So you told Angelie about this surprise, to make sure I brought my passport, and she turned double-agent and contacted Henry's sister for updates on his Christmas plans?'

'As I said: sworn to secrecy.'

Halley let it drop, since something else was niggling. 'Mom, you said you didn't want to be alone at Christmas?'

'And you fell for it — honestly, Halley! I've been on the rota to work all along.' She pulled her phone from her capacious purse, muttering about forwarding Halley her e-ticket.

Numbly, Halley confirmed that the email was in her inbox, and clicked to download the boarding pass, as Mom gave her a final squeeze. 'I love you.'

Halley took her cases. 'Me too, Mom. Merry Christmas.'

* * *

Text messages between Halley and Aunt Edie:

THANK YOU, Aunt Edie. Best Christmas gift ever!!

The surprise really worked — you didn't guess??

It was a MASSIVE surprise!

> *Do you want a hotel room in Oxford? We'll be on our flight to Tahiti when you arrive, so I'll book it now if you do.*

Thanks, but I have a place to stay.

> *That's what your Mom thought, but as I told her, Halley needs to be careful. Men aren't light bulbs — you can't unscrew them.*

I think it'll be OK. Have a great time in the South Pacific!

* * *

Note on Halley's laptop:

> *Oh my God, Henry.*
> *Oh. My. God.*
> *I'm on my way! I can tell you the news in person!*
> *I'm so excited now that it's hard to keep still, but I was half-frozen with shock at O'Hare. It only hit me that it would be smart to call and let you know I'm coming when the plane was taking off, at which point I had of course lost connection to the world beyond this metal cylinder, so now I have no choice but to perpetuate the surprise.*
> *I'll send you this, and my previous note, once we're together. How weird, to be there to witness you opening and reading one of my emails! Maybe I'll suggest you take a walk alone, to reply. Scratch that. We'll have four days together — there's no time for doing anything alone. (Aside from if you need to be with your family, of course.) (Also, bathroom breaks.)*

By the way, I've switched to Virgin Marys because of what you said one time. That when you meet me again you want to be absolutely and entirely sober. I agree. Oh God. Your Halley x

* * *

Tuesday, 24 December

Voice note from Viola for Henry:

Hal, call me as soon as you wake up. It's nothing to worry about — the parentals are fine. I've found something out that you need to know — I'll explain when you call.

* * *

Halley

Halley steered a luggage trolley toward the green *nothing to declare* sign, as anticipation slithered up her spine: Henry could be waiting for her.

After a nap at the start of the long flight, she'd changed her phone to GMT and drunk two black coffees. Getting accustomed to the new time zone as quickly as possible would minimize jet lag and ensure she'd be alert during Henry's waking hours. During the long period in a cramped seat afterwards, she'd busied herself by replaying the information Mom had relayed, including her confidence that Henry was in Oxford for Christmas. She was certain Mom and Angelie had been conspiring, and pretty sure Angelie had made contact with Viola. As she mulled it over, Halley wondered if Viola knew she was coming, and if so, if she'd alert Henry, so he could meet her at the airport.

By the time the plane bumped to a landing, Halley had talked herself into the likelihood of Viola figuring out why Angelie cared about Henry's Christmas plans. And when she switched airplane mode off on her phone and there was no message from him, her suspicion deepened. Henry hadn't contacted her 'in Chicago' because he knew she wasn't there, and was instead waiting at Heathrow to surprise her.

Clearing customs amid a small crowd, Halley hung back before the final corner to rub her front teeth and push her hair behind her ears. She hoped she'd done a good enough job of washing up in the bathrooms beside security. She didn't want to smell skanky when she ran into Henry's arms.

She took a firm grip of the trolley to stop her hands trembling, fixed a smile on her face, then rounded the corner.

* * *

Voice note from Henry for Viola:

Vi, I'll make it by the skin of my teeth! I can't thank you enough for the heads-up, and I swear, I'll be there to take over with Mum and Dad by the evening of the twenty-eighth, as agreed! Thanks again and Merry Christmas!

* * *

Halley

Halley paced into her second arrivals hall in twelve hours, scouring every face of those waiting beyond the retractable barriers: there were a myriad of anxious relatives, exuberant children and bored taxi drivers, but no Henry. Reaching the end of the line she paused and glanced back.

Someone touched her shoulder, and she whirled: 'Henry!'

But a stranger had brushed her — a woman, muttering an apology, with a baby strapped to her chest and other kids trailing behind.

Halley rose onto her tiptoes to survey the concourse. Henry wasn't the kind of person to arrive late for anything, *let alone* to meet someone from a trans-Atlantic flight, and *doubly* let alone to meet her. But he might not have had much notice, and if traffic in the UK was anything like Chicago's on Christmas Eve, anyone could be late.

Then again, maybe she was wrong and Viola had preserved the surprise, in which case Henry was pottering around on his boat, oblivious to her arrival. She gritted her teeth, calculating whether to wait, or get the express train to Paddington, where she could change to the line for Oxford. Ideally she'd call Viola to check, but she couldn't ask for her contact details, with Mom on shift at the hospital and Edie en-route to Tahiti.

Worst of all, she decided, would be another mix-up like the Hope and Anchor, when she hadn't waited long enough for Henry to show. So she'd head for a food outlet and watch for him, while figuring out a Plan B.

* * *

Text message from Halley to Henry:

Sorry to be cryptic but would you let me know where you are right this minute? Like, your precise location? Halley x

* * *

From: Halley Hart
Subject: URGENT
To: Henry Inglis
Hi Henry, you've turned your phone off so I guess you're in the library and might still see email . . . hopefully, anyway!

Don't freak out at all the missed calls from me. Nothing's wrong, except transportation strikes and bad weather and . . . ugh. I'm not sure what you know already but I'll explain everything when you call me. Urgently. Please.

Your Halley x

* * *

Halley

Halley rested her head against the coach window, looking up at the sky. The view was distorted by the kamikaze hailstones hurling themselves at the glass, but it wouldn't have mattered anyway — no stars were visible through the thick cloud. The coach swung around a corner, and she recognized the street name and got her bearings. Oxford's bus station was close, and she pulled her coat on in preparation for disembarking.

She checked her phone again, but there were no texts and the only new email was about holiday closures in Stanford's astronomy department. Pressing Henry's contact, she listened intently: straight to voicemail, again. Her thumb hovered over the number for St Jude's she'd found online. But the friendly porter she'd spoken to twice already was adamant Henry wasn't on site, and had already promised to inform him to contact Halley Hart immediately, if he turned up.

Disembarking, her face was stinging within seconds, as the hail pelted her skin. It wasn't quite seven in the evening but was as dark as midnight in California, and she had to stop twice to seek directions to the towpath. Once on it, she became distracted by her suitcases which were awkward along the track, and stepped into a puddle so deep the frigid water sloshed up her calves.

'Shit,' she hissed, because it was preferable to crying. That would have to wait until she was dry and warm inside, recounting the misery of getting to Oxford in the midst of a rail strike on Christmas Eve. A cab driver had quoted her three hundred pounds, and all the earlier buses had been booked up, leaving her waiting several hours.

But Henry was in Oxford, and not at St Jude's. Which meant he was on his houseboat, having switched his phone off for a reason that would be perfectly logical once he explained, and the look on his face when she knocked at the door would prove this all worth it. Though perhaps not until she'd cried. And taken a shower. And he'd warmed her up in front of his log burner.

'Fifth boat along,' she murmured. Henry had described the Blue Moon's location several times, but the gaps between the boats were longer than she expected, so it seemed an eon before she reached the fifth. She directed her phone torch at the boat. It was sixty feet long and painted in yellow and navy. But unlike the four houseboats she'd passed, every window, porthole and hatch was black. There were no lights on inside at all. And chains were locked across the small decks at either end.

Refusing to accept that it was as empty and shut-up as it appeared, Halley left her luggage on the towpath and scrambled onto the open area in the back — no, *stern* of the boat. The deck was slippery underfoot as tentatively she tried the handle on the door. It didn't budge, so she leaned in to stare through the small window beside it, tilting her phone torch to illuminate the interior. Everything appeared neat and tidy, but Henry wasn't there. She angled her phone more acutely, and spied a photo of herself, outside Halley's observatory, in a frame on the table.

It triggered the tears that had been building up through exhaustion and stress and the stinging, freezing hail. Her silent tears fell, warming her cheeks, until a sob tore free from her throat, recalling her to herself. Dashing away her tears with the backs of her hands, she screwed her eyes shut and breathed slow and deep.

Her biggest fear was that Henry was hurt. This weather and a bike were a terrible combination. But the coach driver had commented that it had been sunny at lunchtime, when he drove out of Oxford, so an emergency with Henry's parents was far more likely. If he'd rushed back to Hampshire she could do nothing but seek some place dry and warm, and wait until he switched his phone on.

She didn't have keys for the boat, and it was locked up pretty securely. Attempting a break-in risked getting arrested. Which left only one other place she could head for.

After climbing back onto the towpath she took a few seconds to plan. In case Henry had broken his phone, she printed a message on a page of her notebook, then tore out the sodden sheet, placed it in the clear plastic bag she'd needed for her liquids in the airport, and forced it through the padlock's shackle. Then, fighting a wave of fatigue, she curled her numb hands over each suitcase handle, bowed her head against the hail, and slogged on.

* * *

Handwritten note from Halley:

> *7.05 P.M., 24 DEC.*
> *SURPRISE, I'M IN OXFORD!*
> *MY CELL PHONE BATTERY GETTING LOW.*
> *I'M GONNA GO ST JUDE'S.*
> *YOUR HH x*

* * *

Text messages between Halley and Mom:

> *Get in touch when you're off shift! I've arrived safe in Oxford, but Henry's not here . . .*

> > *Just leaving the hospital. What? Why? Have you called him??*

> *Of course! His phone's off. Did Angelie give you his sister's number? I need it.*

> > *Do you have someplace safe to wait??*

> *I'm with Henry's friends, who live at his college. Ruth's a Reverend in the Church of England (that's like Episcopalian — NOT a cult), Kwame owns Henry's boat. I'm about to have a shower and nap in their guest suite. Do you have Viola's number or not?*

I can neither confirm nor deny anything. As I said, I'm sworn to secrecy.

Mom, that's insane — I have to find Henry!

Mom??

* * *

Henry

Henry's phone, stowed within his backpack, gave another buzz. He ignored it. When he'd been able to turn it back on he'd seen multiple missed calls from Halley, as well as a cryptic text asking for his location. As impossible as it seemed, she must have somehow got an inkling of where he was. He didn't want to lie to her but was determined to preserve some semblance of surprise, so hadn't replied. Anyway, it was unnecessary, when he'd be seeing her so very soon.

The air was so cold that every exhale was visible, but he refused to slow down. His heart thrummed as he identified the correct house. Steep steps led up to the entrance, and he took them two at a time, his feet crunching into the thin layers of freshly fallen snow.

The front door was red, with a huge wreath encircling a wrought-iron knocker. There was also a doorbell. He hesitated. Before he decided which to opt for, swift footsteps sounded from inside. Then the door opened and bright light spilled out, outlining the figure of a woman, a few inches shorter than him, with fair hair.

'*Halley*,' he said. For a split second, before his eyes had adjusted to the light, he thought he was correct. Then he registered that this woman's hair wasn't long, but bobbed above the shoulder. And her eyes, although a familiar grey, were set into a face that was twenty-two years older than his Halley's.

'Yes,' the woman said. The voice was husky, like her daughter's. 'But not the Halley you meant. I'm afraid she isn't here in Chicago, Henry.'

PART EIGHT

Text messages from Mom to Halley:

> *Junior, you'll want to call the house when you wake from your nap. Henry's here, looking a little dazed. Apparently he learned this morning that an airplane ticket he hadn't been able to use would expire at the end of the year, so rebooked immediately to come surprise you.*

> *By the way, I assumed my ban on speaking to him without your express permission was temporarily lifted, because I didn't think I'd have much success miming this series of events.*

* * *

Henry

As he dialled Viola, Henry couldn't take his eyes off the framed photographs of his Halley Hart, at a dozen different ages, that were set along the mantle. One showed her unwrapping a telescope, on a birthday in her mid-teens. Her face displayed the kind of delighted smile that fully exposed her lopsided pleats of dimples. It was the expression he'd been envisioning as her reaction to his arrival. He swallowed back the constriction in his throat, as Viola answered.

'I thought you'd be too loved-up to bother checking in. Tell Halley *hi* from me.'

'I can't,' he said bleakly. 'She's asleep.'

Viola laughed. 'Knackering each other out so quickly was—'

'Nothing like that.' Henry interrupted more because he didn't want to think about what might have been, than any real fear that Halley's mother could hear. She was in the kitchen, on the other side of double doors, having gone to see if she had *the fixings for hot tea with milk*. 'Halley's asleep in Oxford.'

'You rebooked for Halley to come over, rather than you going there? I told you the carers and I can cope fine with the parentals.'

'No,' Henry said, much more patiently than he felt. 'I'm in Chicago. Halley landed in Heathrow about the time I was getting on my plane there, I think. I've only had the story second-hand, but it seems it took her a long while to get to Oxford, with the rail strike. Finding my boat empty, and that I hadn't replied to any of her messages, she thankfully threw herself on the mercy of St Jude's porters. They passed her on to the chaplain, who's looking after her now.'

There was a long silence.

'Vi?'

'Still here,' Viola said. 'Just . . . Halley's in England and you're in America. That's properly fucked up. What are you going to do? Where even are you?'

'At her mother's place. She's kindly waved away my apology for turning up uninvited, insisting that I'm welcome to make myself at home for as long as it takes to find a flight back. Though Halley might be able to get here faster than I can there . . . I was hoping you could advise on which is most feasible?'

'Hang on . . . Right, which option would you prefer?'

'I just want to salvage something from this disaster, so a few days together in either location. But I'd be happier rushing back home than her returning here.' The rattle of crockery came through the double doors. He didn't want Halley's mother to think that he'd rather have Halley to himself on a boat, than under her roof. 'Halley's journey was more onerous than mine, and it sounds like she's shattered.'

'And you were due to arrive back on the afternoon of the twenty-eighth . . .'

He confirmed the timings and his flight number, then re-examined the photos. He was surrounded by every version of Halley . . . except the living, breathing woman. 'So near, and so bloody far.'

'What's that?'

'Doesn't matter. Found anything? I'd like to check with Halley, if at all possible, before I rebook.'

'Don't think that'll be the problem . . .' Viola said apologetically.

'What will be?'

'Transferring you to another flight.' He could hear her fingers flying over her keyboard. 'There're scant few departing tonight and tomorrow, and they're already overbooked.'

Halley's mother re-entered her living room, bearing an iPad in one hand, and a mug in the other, both held out in front of her like trophies. 'Tea, and Halley Junior on Facetime, Henry — oh am I interrupting?'

'It's my sister,' Henry said. 'Advising on flight options. Vi? Halley's awake and on another line — I'm putting you on speaker.'

'Tell her I say hi,' Viola said. 'And what a nightmare this is — I'll do whatever I can to help.'

While his sister's voice echoed out from his handset, Halley's mother passed Henry the mug, emblazoned with *No such thing as bossy — only a boss,* and propped the tablet on the coffee table. His Halley was sitting in an armchair with her feet tucked up under her. She was wearing something voluminous, fluffy and lilac, and, thank God, she was smiling at him.

'Hey, Henry,' she breathed, and then louder, 'Thanks, Viola. I can just about hear you. This might sound crazy, but were you contacted by—'

'Hi, Viola,' Halley's mother sang, lowering herself onto the sofa beside him.

With her voice so similar to her daughter's, it would soon get confusing. 'As well as Halley, via video call, you're hearing her mother. Ms Hart, meet — well sort of — Viola.'

'As I've already told Henry, please call me Halley,' Halley's mother said. Henry had no recollection of that, but then again, the depths of his shock in the few minutes after his arrival had rendered it rather a blur.

Halley rolled her eyes. 'What's that drink you've given Henry? Y'know he doesn't like coffee, right?'

'It's tea,' Henry assured her, smiling into the tablet as he brought the mug up to his mouth.

'I didn't think I had any,' her mother said. 'But then I found a tub of iced-tea mix at the back of the pantry. I figured, tea is tea, so it'd work for hot tea just fine.'

Henry manfully went ahead with his sip, swallowing speedily to avoid tasting the concoction for too long. It was vaguely lemony, and curdled. As he'd feared, *iced-tea mix* was not, indeed, tea.

'Really?' His Halley sounded dubious. 'It's OK, Henry?'

'It's . . . uh . . .' He never liked to be impolite, and especially wanted to make a good impression on Halley's mother, but had no intention of having more of the stuff pressed on him. 'I'm stupidly fussy about tea, so this isn't quite my thing.' Halley glared at her mother, and Henry hastily placed the mug down out of sight of the iPad's camera. 'I gather that you were able to surprise me because of a gift from your aunt?'

'*Attempt* to surprise you,' Halley corrected. 'It was so generous of her, and it's ended up such a massive fail.'

'It's sort of my fault that Henry's not in Oxford,' Viola said, sounding guilty. 'My airline contact alerted me that the ticket he hadn't been able to use is only valid for rebooking this calendar year. I told him it was use it or lose it, and surely four days together was enough to go ahead and use it.'

'It was my stupid decision to keep it a surprise from Halley,' Henry said.

Viola spoke up again. 'Hey, Halley?'

'Yes?' both Halleys said together.

'I mean, uh . . . Halley-who's-dating-my-brother. Can you ping me a copy of your ticket, so I can look into rebooking your return?' She spelled out her email address, then confirmed it had arrived in her inbox. 'Damn — it's not flexible. You can only come home on the flight already booked.'

'I feared that might be the case,' Halley's mother said. 'I'm sure it never crossed Edie's mind that you'd want to cut the trip short.'

'She was right,' Halley said. Henry glanced at the screen and found her gaze on his. 'I wouldn't. Except for this balls-up, I wouldn't.'

I love you, Halley Hart, Henry thought at her. His urge to say it aloud was so overwhelming that he knew it was real. This wasn't an emotion stemming from jet lag or tiredness or the ridiculous situation. He loved Halley, and he wanted nothing more than to tell her so.

But only in person, and without half their relatives as witnesses. He made a vow to himself as he smiled at her. She caught him, and shot a confused look. He only shrugged.

'It has to be Henry returning then,' Halley's mother continued.

Viola sighed. 'Then 6.05 a.m. on the twenty-seventh is the soonest available seat.'

Halley looked utterly appalled. 'With the flight time plus time change, we'd only have, like, twelve hours together before my flight home. There has to be something else!'

'Theoretically, one of you buying a whole new ticket, but even if you can afford it, I'm not seeing any availability,' Viola said. 'Shall I transfer Henry to the flight on the twenty-seventh?'

'Yes, Vi — thanks,' Henry said. It was hard to be sure on the tablet screen, but he had a horrible feeling that Halley was crying. 'Give my love to Mum and Dad.'

'Bye, Viola, bye everyone,' Halley said thickly. 'My phone battery's low, so I'm going for now.'

She was *definitely* crying, and she disappeared from the screen.

* * *

Text messages between Henry and Kwame:

> *Thanks so much, Kwame. Really appreciate you and Ruth looking after Halley.*

>> *Looking after her isn't a problem, mate. But Ruth gave me hell for not telling her that you have a girl-friend. I didn't want to say in front of said girlfriend that you'd never told me!*

> *She referred to herself as my girlfriend?*

>> *What? Isn't she?*

> *She certainly is. I've just never heard her say it.*

> *Has she said anything else about me?*

>> *Mate, you've got it bad for Hallee.*

> *It's Halley. Like the comet. And, I know.*

* * *

Halley

Henry was at Mom's house.

Henry was at Mom's house on Christmas Eve, and Halley was a quarter of the way around the planet, wearing a stranger's dressing gown and unable to do a single thing to rectify the situation.

151

After getting out her charger and finding a US to UK converter in the depths of the suitcase Mom had packed, she'd plugged her phone in and set to checking Viola's working. She searched available flights either way across the Atlantic on Skyscanner, then, in increasing desperation, triple-checked via each airline's website. At one point she'd found an empty seat on a plane to JFK from Paris. After hopping onto a connecting flight to Chicago Midway, she'd make it into Henry's arms late on Christmas Day. But, try as she might, she couldn't find a way to get to France for the midnight departure. By the end of an hour, she had ascertained that Viola was correct. There was no availability at all before the twenty-seventh.

Henry was at Mom's house on Christmas Eve, and Halley had never felt more sorry for herself. She didn't even want to call back, and have to witness him on Mom's couch, highlighting what could have been. Instead, she returned to rummaging through what Mom had packed for her. As well as warm clothing from her closet in Chicago, that she didn't need in California, and the cosmetics bag she'd left there at some point, there were brand new multipacks of panties and socks, like Mom had bought every summer for her to take to sleepaway camp. As she refolded it all, she wasn't quite smiling, but she found that she could finally face talking to Henry again.

He was in the back bedroom, she saw instantly when he answered, which Mom kept nice for guests.

'Good morn — no, *Good evening*, sweetheart,' he corrected, putting on his glasses.

'You should be used to figuring out the time difference by now,' she said, trying — and failing — to keep her tone light.

'May I remind you that the first time we ever vid-chatted, you got it wrong and woke me up.'

'I didn't get it wrong! I just didn't think about it because I was excited that you suggested it.'

'Yeah yeah, that's your excuse.' He waggled his eyebrows. 'You were actually desperate to see me in my boxers.'

'You wish . . .' She found herself smiling, grateful for whatever combination of instinct and good sense Henry used to figure out what kind of a funk she was in and respond appropriately. His earlier cautious sympathy had helped her avoid collapsing into sobs, and this cheery verbal sparring, which acknowledged her grouchiness while refusing to play along, was just what she needed now.

'I wish you were here . . .' he said softly. 'Or that I was there.'

Henry was at Mom's house on Christmas Eve. She considered it from a new angle. 'You flew over three thousand miles to surprise me at Christmas,' she said. 'I think — no, *I know*, it's the most romantic thing anyone will ever do for me.'

Henry's expression was intense as he shook his head. 'No it's not. I've only just got started.'

Oh God.

Halley swallowed, then rolled onto her stomach. 'Twelve hours isn't enough. But we can make it count.'

Henry moved around on her phone screen, shifting to mirror her positioning 'Absolutely, we can.'

'So no sleeping,' Halley breathed. 'Or at least . . .'

Henry finished her thought. 'Not solo . . .' There was a sound in the background and he sat up abruptly and swung around, so she could only see his back. 'Just chatting to her, actually,' he called, in a very different tone of voice.

'What's going on there?' Halley said.

'Come on in,' Henry added, before he was in sight again as he lifted his phone. 'Halley, your mother knocked on the door and suggested that we call you back.'

'I didn't realize you were already talking,' Mom said, coming into view in the background. 'I didn't interrupt anything, did I?'

'Yes you did!' Halley said. 'I was telling Henry that I missed at least two meals. When Ruth realized, she offered me supper of beans on toast, egg and soldiers, or Welsh rabbit.'

'I hope you didn't choose rabbit,' Mom said, looking repulsed. 'You could catch ringworm, mycobacteriosis or several different types of parasite.'

'Of course I won't choose rabbit! I'm thinking egg and soldiers, even though I don't know what constitutes the soldier, because beans on bread is weird—'

'But safe at least,' Mom said. 'What if the soldiers are that Scottish sheep intestine thing — haggis?'

'Eww, I didn't think of that.' Before she spiralled into complete panic, Halley recalled with relief that she had an expert at hand. She narrowed her eyes at him. 'Babe?'

He started to laugh. 'Welsh rabbit, or rarebit, is delicious, and certainly won't transmit disease. It's cheese and ale sauce grilled on top of bread. I have a feeling the name was originally derogatory, implying that the closest thing to meat that the Welsh could afford was cheese.'

Deciding that cheese and ale sauce sounded much better than beans on toast, Halley resolved to request that.

'And the soldiers, Henry?' Mom asked, sounding amused. She liked him — Halley could tell.

'Toast cut up into fingers for dipping into an egg.'

'So I was barely being offered a choice,' Halley said. 'Toast, with cheese, beans, or a fried egg.'

'No, never fried,' Henry said. 'Not with soldiers. They're served on the side of an egg cup, for dipping into a soft boiled egg.'

Halley flicked her eyes behind him to Mom, who looked as blank as Halley felt. 'In England there are cups for eggs?'

'Oh come on,' Henry said. '*You're* winding me up now.'

'Really, I've never heard of egg cups,' Mom said.

Henry looked astonished. 'What a shame. I'll send you some.'

Mom's mouth twitched, but she thanked him before explaining she was working Christmas Day, so he'd be alone from six in the morning until seven in the evening. 'Once I'm back, we'll order food and—'

'Don't get proper pizza,' Halley said instantly. 'I want to be the one to introduce him to it. Same for Chicago-style hot dogs and Italian beef sandwiches.'

'So what — I should order him *bad* pizza? I can't starve the man!'

Henry cleared his throat, but Halley ignored him. 'You could cook something, once you're back from work . . .'

'Or *I* could cook,' Henry said firmly, looking at Mom. 'I don't want to put you to any trouble, and I'll have plenty of time.'

'But you've never cooked for *me* yet.' Halley had tried to pitch her objection humorously, but her voice wobbled, and Mom and Henry's heads both snapped toward her.

'We'll figure something out,' Mom said. 'Halley, I presume you're able to stay with this minister and her husband tonight?'

'For as long as I want. They're very hospitable. You don't need to worry about anything this end.' Halley purposely let that hang, because she couldn't say: *focus on looking after Henry — well, but not too well.* 'So, she's not being too much of a lunatic?' she added, once Mom had exited.

'Not at all. She's been very gracious about the fact that I've turned up at her doorstep uninvited.'

'Don't be a bonehead — you didn't need an invitation!'

'Funnily enough, that's how your mother replied. Word for word, except that she called me a knucklehead.' Thankfully, he seemed to be amused rather than insulted. 'Halley, obviously I'd far rather you were here, but I have a feeling that getting to know your mother, and seeing where you grew up, will help me get to know you better even in your absence.'

Halley pondered on that. She didn't have the same sense, but, of course, she'd already been to Oxford, and rather than being in the company of Henry's family, she was with Ruth and Kwame. Right now, she longed for time on her own in a small room. Well, small boat. Because, short of being transported to be beside Henry, she wanted to be surrounded by the space he inhabited; getting to know him, even in his absence, like he'd described.

'Does Kwame have a spare set of keys for the Blue Moon?'

'Of course. You want to see it?'

'I want to stay in it, if you don't mind? So I'm already there, when you arrive back. If I go right after the Christmas lunch Ruth seems so excited about, then by the time it's morning in Chicago and Mom leaves for work, we can keep each other company.'

'For my part, that's absolutely fine. But logistically it might be tricky. I shut everything down before I left, so to get heat and light and hot water you'd need to crank it all back on again.'

'I mean, I'm pretty practically minded. Could you email me instructions?'

He tilted his head, considering. 'Of course. And please, once you're on board, make yourself at home.'

* * *

Text messages between Halley and Mom:

Don't show Henry naked baby photos. Or any video where I'm 1/ singing 2/ dancing 3/ when I did a science experiment in the Junior High talent show, and got booed. Please encourage watching football: lots and lots of football.

> *Understood. Do I have permission to show him your bedroom?*

If he wants to. But it's kinda boring since I packed most of my childhood stuff away.

> *Oh he'll want to. Anything to do with 'his Halley' gets the man's rapt attention. I worried he might give himself an aneurysm from staring so hard at your photos.*

Why 'the man'? You like him, right?

> *If I didn't like him, I wouldn't have set the two of you up.*

You didn't set us up! We met without any involvement from you whatsoever!!

You didn't get together until I told you he was searching for you.

Mom I very almost didn't write him back because I was so freaked out at you catfishing him! Seriously, if you try to claim the credit for me and Henry, I'll have no choice but to end it . . .

Idle threat, Junior . . . You're all in with Henry.

I'm not dignifying that with an answer.

That's fine. It wasn't a question. And for what it's worth, he's also all in.

How can you tell? Is he talking about me? What's he saying?

Oh come on. That man's as giddy for you as a goat on roller skates.

* * *

Wednesday, 25 December

Text messages between Kwame and Henry:

Happy Christmas, mate. Your comet wants to move into the Blue Moon. Presumably that's all right by you?

Happy Christmas to you too. And, absolutely.

Good, cos I already handed over the keys. Problem is, she rushed off there before I could talk her through everything. Should I follow immediately, or pop by later?

157

Don't worry about going along there at all. The water tank's pretty full, and I've explained how to sort out everything else in an email.

Some of it's fiddly, though. Sure she'll be all right?

Yeah, I'm certain. Halley says she's got it, which means she'll get it done. Thanks again for having her!

It was no hassle. Your girl's sound. By the way, Ruth says you'd better not let this one go — Halley's perfect for you. I said I reckoned you already knew that.

Was Halley privy to any of that conversation?

Yeah, and she ran screaming. (Why would we discuss that in front of her?!)

* * *

Henry

Halley was wearing a red jumper over her jeans, had gold tinsel in her hair, and was sitting cross-legged on his sofa in the Blue Moon, cradling a mug in her hands.

'Merry Christmas, sweetheart. You found the cafetière OK then?'

'I did,' she said, with one of her dimple-flashing smiles. 'I also found wine, but not any glasses — so this is wine in a mug.'

'I'm a bit short on that kind of thing. Though I've got acrylic tumblers if you'd prefer.'

'I saw.' Her crinkled nose made it clear what she thought about those.

'I know that life on the boat's much more . . . rudimentary than you're used to,' he said, with a sinking feeling. 'And it must be chilly after being empty for a few days. I'll organize you returning to Ruth and Kwame's—'

'Shut up, Henry,' she said, her nose crinkling again, this time in laughter. 'I adore the boat. Why wouldn't I? Look!' She turned her phone around, displaying the wood burner to him, which she'd lit, so heat would be radiating out of it. She did a slow sweep of the stern end of the Blue Moon, explaining everything she liked, from the swans that had glided past, to how quickly it warmed up and how ingenious all the storage was.

'How've you found the set-up? You've got water and power and Wi-Fi and all that?'

'Actually, I didn't get round to connecting to your Wi-Fi yet. If the call suddenly drops, my data plan's out, and I'll call you back. The rest was all straightforward.'

She'd probably sorted it all faster than he did, despite it being her first time, Henry reflected, smiling at her for being brilliant. 'Before your mother left for work she pointed out a *minor maintenance job*, heavily hinting I should do it by informing me you'd have done so if you were here.'

'Sounds like Mom,' Halley said, grinning. 'But I want all your attention, so please don't bother. Unless it's super simple?'

'Replacing a broken light fitting in the bathroom.'

Halley flinched, almost spilling her mug of wine. 'That involves the mains electric! Oh my God, she'd risk electrocuting you! Don't you dare—'

'I won't,' Henry promised quickly.

Halley hadn't included his bedroom in her mini tour of her favourite things. Perhaps she hadn't yet explored there. Or she had, and it didn't meet with her approval. He'd tidied, after booking his ticket, but he hadn't done a thorough job of it and changed his sheets.

'I left in a hurry,' he said. 'I hope there are no glaring omissions . . .'

'Henry, I told you I adore it here, and I mean it. I have everything I need. Except—'

'Proper glasses,' he supplied wryly.

'No, you fool! On the scale of my immediate wants and needs, glassware is so far down the list as to be redundant. I need *you* here with me. Have you found the wine at that end, by the way?'

He glanced at the time. It wasn't quite eleven, but his body clock was so confused anyway, it couldn't matter. He carried his phone to the kitchen, listening to Halley as she described where to find the chilled white, and a corkscrew and glass. He ignored the final instruction, reaching instead for a mug, and pouring it in. Her mouth twisted with amusement, but she only asked what they should toast to.

'Making the most of twelve hours together?'

Halley raised her mug. 'Absolutely. And to the Blue Moon, because I love her.'

The video chat window went black. Halley's data had run out.

Henry raised his own mug of wine. 'And here's to you, my Halley Hart,' he said, longingly, into the silence. 'Because *I* love *you*.'

Out of the silence, there came a sharp intake of breath.

'Did you mean that,' Halley said. Only it couldn't be Halley, because she was in Oxford, and their connection had dropped. He shot a look around, wondering dazedly if her mother had arrived home hours early. But he was as alone as ever.

'Did . . . Do . . . Do you . . .' Halley stammered.

Henry's throat constricted. There was no doubt about it; her voice was definitely emanating from his phone.

'Shit,' he heard her add. 'Shit, shit, shit.'

PART NINE

Halley

Halley's heart was beating nearly out of her chest. 'My video cut out from this lousy cellular connection, and I badly need to see your face right now.'

'My video went too.' Henry sounded strained. 'Actually I thought . . .'

'You thought?' she prompted, when he didn't complete the sentence.

'Halley, would you do me a favour, and call back once you've connected to Wi-Fi?'

'Sure,' she breathed. An instant later, there was a click and the call dropped entirely. She scrambled to her feet, rushing to the low cupboard in the galley and plugging in the router. She slowed on her return to retrieve her phone, scooping it up and continuing on, with a compulsion she didn't pause to decipher, to pass through the short corridor and into Henry's bedroom.

Sitting on the edge of his bed, her fingers trembled as she selected his network, then pressed in *MyHalleyHart*, which she'd discovered, in his email about Blue Moon practicalities, was his Wi-Fi password.

She swiped on his name. If she had any expectation, it was for Henry to answer immediately. But two rings went by, and then another.

The fourth ring was cut off early, and Henry appeared on her screen.

'Did you mean it?' Her subconscious must have been formulating the question, because the words she was previously struggling to find suddenly flew from her tongue. 'Do you love me?'

'Yes,' he said instantly. 'Though I didn't . . . well, I was hoping to tell you once we were together in person. I thought the call had dropped entirely, you see. And I know I've only ever seen you for one day but . . .'

He was flustered, and pink-cheeked, and especially cute, so she watched as he rambled on, all but apologizing for telling her he loved her.

'Got that out of your system?' she asked mildly, when he trailed off. 'Because I need you to shut up and listen, Henry Inglis. I also had something to say in person.'

He went entirely still.

'On a practical note, I love you too — but that wasn't my big reveal.'

He made a jolting motion, but didn't speak, and she continued.

'When I talked to my thesis advisor about applying for jobs in Europe, he didn't only wreck our Christmas plans by insisting I get more data. He made two other recommendations that seemed pretty unlikely to come off — especially when I was down on myself for missing that data corruption. In our meeting right before I left, he had updates on them both. One, was that I apply to present my results at an astrophysics symposium in January, in Chicago. My application was successful, so I'll be attending that. And the second . . . well the second was that I start making contacts in European departments, beginning by capitalizing on the fact that I can write my thesis up anywhere. He offered to ask his various European astronomer contacts if their institutions would accept me as a visiting student for the rest of the academic year. And, well . . . I've had an invitation from a university.'

'Where? Where is it in Europe?' Henry asked hoarsely.

Her mouth was dry. 'Not Oxford. Astronomy's only a small department and—' She broke off at the look on his face. 'I think it's the next best option, for us. It's Southampton?' It was the largest city in Hampshire, where Henry's family lived, and only sixty miles from Oxford.

'Sorry, could you repeat that?' Henry spoke with infinite politeness, but his eyes bored through her, even via their cameras and screens.

'The headlines are, I love you too, and I'm coming to England.' Something struck her. 'If you want me to?'

'That question is superfluous,' he said, grinning like a loon. 'How soon can you come, and how long can you stay?'

'I'll be there once the symposium ends, in late January. And I can stay through the end of the summer term. I'm hoping to submit my thesis by the end of June.'

'Six months,' Henry said, looking so satisfied he was on the verge of smug. 'You'll be down the road from my parents for half a year! We'll be together every weekend, at the absolute least.'

'I can make it to Oxford a lot, as long as I write while I'm here.'

'And I'll come to you. I'll buy a car to make it easier — we can share it.'

'I'd like to offer to go halves, but I'll be pretty broke,' she warned.

'The boat's cheap. I can afford it.'

She scooched back on his bed and rested her head on one of his striped pillows. It smelled of Henry.

Henry blinked. 'You're in my bed.'

'Is that OK?' He'd made a point of telling her that the couch unfolded into a guest bed several times in earlier calls. 'Should I sleep on the sofa bed?'

The vertical lines appeared between his brows. 'It's up to you.'

She rose onto her elbows. 'Henry, stop being enigmatic. If you don't want me in your bed, you can say so. And, like, explain *why*, because it seems kinda weird.'

His face coloured. 'That's not it. I just wanted to avoid pressuring you to sleep there, if you'd rather not.'

'You're not even here! How would I feel pressured?'

He laughed wryly. 'I don't know. I seem to have over-thought it.'

She flopped back onto his pillow. 'I wish you *were* here.'

He instantly sobered. 'Me too. Halley?'

'Yeah?'

'Please sleep in my bed?'

Her toes curled involuntarily, and she lifted her chin. 'Have you ever imagined me here?'

'Many, many times.'

She pinned his eyes with her own. 'Tell me about it.'

* * *

From: Henry Inglis
Subject: Happy Christmas!
To: Halley Hart

It's still just about Christmas Day here. Your mother's home from work and we ordered Chinese food. Afterwards she was keen for us to watch an American football *match* but I couldn't concentrate for thinking about you, so I exaggerated my jet lag to escape.

You know what keeps coming into my mind? You, right at this moment, asleep in my bed. And how I'll soon be there with you. And that when we have to part again, it'll only be for a month, after which you'll be nearby for half a year. Half a year, Halley! Also, I can't stop replaying the moment you announced: *on a practical note, I love you too*. At some point you'll need to explain how that could ever be a mere practicality.

All of the above means that, despite us being apart, it's the best Christmas of my life so far.

All my love, Henry xxx

* * *

Thursday, 26 December

From: Halley Hart
Subject: Happy Boxing Day!
To: Henry Inglis

What a perfect email to wake up to. I almost called you right away, but it's three a.m. there and I need you to store up sleep so we don't have to waste any of our twelve hours together.

I learned at lunch yesterday that today's called Boxing Day, though not from Ruth or Kwame, but another of their guests . . . I wonder if you can guess? I was going to mention it when you called, but what we ended up talking about was (much) better.

Mom misses me watching football with her — I'm sure she'd really appreciate you hanging out with her for the game today!

Love, your Halley

* * *

Henry

'Halley's bedroom,' her mother had announced, as she threw the door open. 'Since she was three years old.'

But most of the remnants of childhood had been removed, leaving it much like any other adult-child's former bedroom, in stasis between their infrequent visits. The equivalent space in his own parents' house was still always referred to as *Henry's room*, though Viola's former bedroom became *the study* when she bought her flat and emptied it out.

165

The biggest indication of Halley's long occupation of this room were the wooden letters spelling out her name, on the wall behind the bed. But he could also see her presence in the transparent stars on the ceiling, and the globe on the top of the dresser. He strolled over and spun it. Small red gems had been affixed to various locations, and they winked under the overhead light. There were also tinier gold gems, in a wider variety of places, and he leaned in, examining them.

His phone buzzed and he swiped to accept the video call. 'Good afternoon, beautiful.' Halley was out on the Blue Moon's covered bow deck, swaddled in green merino wool which he recognized from his wardrobe. 'Nice jumper.'

'*Jumper*,' she repeated, grinning. 'It's soft. Can I steal it?'

'It's not stealing if you stop to ask,' he said lightly, because *what's mine is yours* was perhaps coming on a little too strong.

'Hey — you're in my room! Did you notice the stars on the ceiling? They're laid out in real constellations.'

'I was busy trying to decode the globe. Oxford's gold and Chicago's red?'

'Red was places I'd been and gold where I wanted to go. I updated it through my teens, but Oxford was one of the first I marked out, when I was like, twelve.'

He knew she'd wanted to visit Oxford because of her link to Edmond Halley, and it wasn't like Henry had lived there himself back then. But her longstanding attraction to where he now lived and worked made him feel even more that the two of them were meant to be. 'What were the other original places you marked in gold?'

She sucked in her cheeks, thinking. 'London, Saint Helena and Antarctica.'

'Saint Helena? As in, the Atlantic island where Napoleon was exiled?'

'I don't know much about Napoleon, but it sounds like the same place. Edmond Halley had an observatory built there in the 1670s.'

'Don't tell me he made it to Antarctica, too,' Henry said, rotating the globe to look at the vast continent on the bottom of the planet. 'I didn't think it was discovered by Europeans until the nineteenth century.'

'It wasn't,' Halley said, laughing at him. 'No, Antarctica's nothing to do with treading my ancestor's footprints. That one's all mine. I read about how it's one of the best places on the planet for astronomy when I was a kid, and became obsessed. I sort of still am — I'd have pursued my Ph.D. at any of the universities with access to Antarctica telescopes if I'd got an offer.'

'It amazes me that you were so ambitious, so young. I don't recall even knowing what a historian was.'

She shrugged, and retreated back inside the Blue Moon. 'Sometimes I think my career trajectory's just nominative determinism — you know, people subconsciously gravitating to the kind of work that reflects their name? Comet by name, astronomer by occupation.'

'I'm sure there's more to it,' Henry said, carrying his phone through to the guest bedroom where he'd been sleeping. 'Oh, what was that about someone you met at Christmas lunch?'

Halley's pensive mood seemed to lift suddenly, and the pleats in her cheeks reappeared. 'Your *freshers*! You've always been discreet and not used their real names, but I recognized Ms Oxcited and Mr Exactly when a girl called Olivia announced how *oxcited* she was that it's Christmas, and a boy called Dexter murmured "Exactly," in agreement! When they heard I'm your girlfriend, she insisted on regaling me with English festive traditions, and I'm sure I'm meant to feed back to you how much history she knows.'

'That sounds tedious—' Henry began.

'Not at all — they're sweet kids. And it didn't go on long, anyway. They made excuses and left even before dessert was served.'

'Teenagers don't appreciate Christmas pudding.'

'Neither do American twenty-seven-year-olds,' Halley said, pulling an exaggeratedly sickened face. 'You eat that stuff? It nearly choked me. Trifle, on the other hand, is divine.'

'Trifle's great too,' Henry agreed, his mind on his students. 'You didn't happen to hear why they're both still in residence, did you? It's unusual for undergraduates not to have homes to go to over Christmas.'

'Nope, sorry. I assumed you knew they were still in Oxford, to be honest.'

'I realized vaguely that Olivia was, but I was too focused on the letters in the archive box to follow up — what is it?'

Her eyes were wide. 'Letters? Last I heard of the box, you were off to look inside it. But then you were in Chicago, and never once mentioned it, so I figured it had been empty. I didn't want to ask and remind you of the disappointment.'

'Ah,' Henry said. 'No, far from a disappointment. There are hundreds of Lawrence Sedgwick's letters inside, from the latter part of his Naval service. I think it's everything he wrote to his family in those three years, though I've only examined them briefly — I'm looking forward to plunging in properly.'

Halley had become very still. 'You weren't tempted to work on those over Christmas, instead of flying to surprise me?'

'I didn't give it a second thought,' he admitted, wondering why that irritated her. Then her chin jerked triumphantly, and he knew it hadn't.

* * *

Friday, 27 December

Text messages between Henry and Halley:

Heading for the airport — see you in about eleven hours! xxx

Remember I have to leave twelve hours after that, so hurry if you possibly can!

Sorry, Halley, I've arrived to find our time together might end up an hour or two shorter. There's a weather delay. xxx

*I know, I'm tracking O'Hare flights online. I
can't see a new departure time?*

*They haven't announced one yet. I'll keep you
updated. xxx*

* * *

Halley

Halley flipped through books. She'd imposed a rule that she
couldn't check her phone again until she entirely emptied
each crate of Henry's books, checked them over, and set
any that were damp to air beside the stove. Rising to her
feet, she yawned. She hadn't been able to sleep the night
before, instead turning over and over the knowledge that it
was her final night alone in Henry's bed. It hadn't felt real
that he'd be with her by around ten tonight, but that hadn't
prevented it hurting when she heard about the heavy snowfall
in Chicago, and it hit her that he wouldn't be.

She caught her phone up. No updates, and it was almost
noon. That meant it was almost 6 a.m. in Chicago. The
time Henry should be leaving, but he didn't even have a new
departure time.

In desperate need of distraction, she wandered into the
little corridor between the bedroom and living area, which
ran between several large cupboards Henry used as closets,
on one side, and a shower room on the other. On both walls,
and the individual doors, there was the framing for bookcases. Kwame had begun to build it, and Henry hadn't yet
had time to complete it, but it would look really cool when
he did. A book-lined corridor, with the doors to the shower
and closets hidden, unless you knew precisely where to push.
And Henry badly needed the shelf space.

She went through the bedroom to the steps that led
up to the bow. Henry had shown her, when he was right
here and she watching on a screen, that the horizontal treads

flipped up for storage. Inside were the tools Kwame had left for him to use. And up on the roof, wrapped in a tarpaulin, there was wood, pre-cut into the right lengths to finish the bookcases. She whistled as she rummaged through the tools.

* * *

Text messages between Henry and Halley:

Good news here! They've cleared the runway. xxx

And it only took two and a half hours . . .

Sorry, sarcasm was unhelpful. At least I'm on the Blue Moon — you've got to hang out in a jam-packed airport. How long's the backlog?

Not sure, but someone's saying that international flights will be prioritized for take-off slots. xxx

* * *

Henry

'Update on flight 2987.'

Henry straightened, instantly alert despite his long wait.

'For operational reasons caused by the inclement weather conditions, this flight has been re-routed via JFK Airport. Please watch the departure boards for a gate announcement.'

He leaned back again, deciding he must have misheard the flight number: a plane-load of people going to Britain wouldn't be taken to New York instead. It made no sense.

The tannoy crackled again, but the forthcoming announcement wasn't a repeat of the one that had drawn his attention, only a brief explanation that a Korean Air flight had been cancelled and passengers should contact their airline.

That was the second outright cancellation of a long-haul flight, though plenty had also taken off. He frowned, then got to his feet and strode to the departure board. The last time he'd checked there were only three gate numbers displayed. Now, many more were listed, as well as the two cancellations. And one single *re-routed* — *gate 54*, beside his flight number.

'That must be a mistake,' he muttered. His phone rang as he began walking. He was unsurprised to see it was Halley calling.

'You've gotta go to gate 54,' she said instantly.

'I know. I'm on my way—'

'And there's something weird going on. They're re-routing your plane through New York.'

'I saw. I don't—'

'Have you asked why?'

'I haven't had a chance. I will when I reach the gate.'

'And then let me know immediately? And I'll tell you if I figure out what's going on from this end. I've got alerts set—' she broke off to yawn, and he seized the moment.

'Sweetheart? I appreciate the offer, but there are constant announcements here, and I'm keeping an eye on the website for alerts, too. You don't need to be glued to your phone.'

'I'm not. I'm . . . well, you'll see when you arrive. But it's not going to take all day, and I've got to stay busy somehow. I couldn't sleep last night, and when I'm tired and bored I start to panic.'

'How about you try to nap? Or you'll be exhausted by the time I arrive.'

There were a few beats of silence. 'But then I won't know when to expect you.'

'I'll message you updates — no, I'll *email* you updates, so your phone doesn't keep beeping alerts.'

'I guess so, then. I just want as many hours with you as possible.'

'I know. Me too.' A huge sign for Gate 54 came into sight. A lot of passengers must have been closer than him when it was announced, as it was already busy, and he slowed his pace. 'I love you.'

'That's good to hear,' she said, in an altogether different tone of voice. 'I love you too.'

Stowing his phone away as he reached the gate, Henry avoided the scrum, instead finding himself a vantage point up against a wall, where he stood with his backpack resting on his feet. He had a decent view of the boarding desk, on which two landline phones were ringing. A member of the airline's ground staff was attempting to placate a man who was shouting that he deserved an explanation, and gesticulating wildly.

'I don't have any more information than you do, sir,' she said, before snatching up one of the phones. 'Yes? . . . I'm afraid I don't have any more information than you do.'

More passengers arrived, including several families, whose children were already crying, and three middle-aged men, wearing matching blue and orange tops and caps, who staggered up singing off-key about bearing down. Halley's mother's television seemed to be permanently stuck on American football games, but it was the Bears match that she'd all but forced him to watch, thanks to which Henry recognized the blue and orange as their colours. He thought the singing might be an attempt at their fight song and hoped fervently that American football fans weren't as commonly drunk and disorderly as footie fans travelling home from matches. The last thing he needed was the flight to be grounded while they were arrested.

* * *

From: Henry Inglis
Subject: Update: about to take off from O'Hare!
To: Halley Hart
Hopefully you're asleep, Halley, but just letting you know that I'm on the plane, and we're due to take off imminently. We've had no explanation yet for the New York thing, but there's a lot of speculation that we won't even be getting off, just picking up some passengers who were delayed there by the same storm. If that's the case, I think by the time I race through arrivals and drive to Oxford, we'll

have nine or so hours together. Then I'll drop you back at Heathrow and go on to my parents.

Funny thing . . . I'm sitting beside Brian from Bedford, who's a massive Chicago Bears fan. He and his friends fly over for almost all their matches.

Getting glared at by cabin crew so need to switch phone off now.

All my love, Henry xxx

* * *

From: Henry Inglis
Subject: Update: arrived in New York
To: Halley Hart

I'm hoping you're still asleep, but wanted to keep you updated, as promised.

Just after we took off, the mystery was solved about the stop in New York. Unfortunately the crew have been working too long, because of the delay at O'Hare, so we were deplaned here.

I've been telling Brian from Bedford all about you. It was a mistake though to reveal that you're a Bears fan, and let slip that I couldn't follow much of the game I saw with your mother, as he decided to tutor me in the basics. When I see you I'm to say: 'Man, what a game yesterday. The Monsters of Midway really are who we thought they were.'

Apparently our new aircraft will be departing around an hour from now. If that's correct, we'll get 6-7 hours together, Halley. Far from enough, but we'll make it count.

All my love, Henry xxx

* * *

Henry

Hell is other people, Henry thought, and there were thousands of them blocking his route to get home to Halley, the one person he wanted. He gritted his teeth, dodging a child in a tutu riding on a suitcase, and her parents, filming her on their knees. A group of pilots walked three abreast and he had to virtually smash himself against the concourse wall to get past without slowing. His flight had flashed up on the departure board alongside another one, as though they'd been amalgamated. If that was the case, they'd be overbooked. Unsure how airlines determined which passengers to bump, he was determined to get to the gate quickly, though unfortunately it was in the opposite direction from where he'd been waiting.

Reaching his gate, where the queue was only mid-length, he joined the line, resting his hands on his thighs and bending over slightly to catch his breath.

'Hiya, mate,' he heard, and glanced up. It was Brian from Bedford, immediately ahead of him in the queue, alongside his friends.

Henry clenched a fist. 'Da Bears,' he said, as Brian had instructed. He immediately regretted it, feeling like an idiot. But Brian appreciated it, and hooted, before launching into a description of one of the game highlights, which at least provided a distraction from Henry's writhing nerves.

As they neared the front of the queue he could see that there were two uniformed ground staff behind the counter. Brian and his friends stepped up to the one on the right, and he strained to hear what was being said, but couldn't catch much. The family on the left, however, ended their conversation looking relieved, and as they moved to one side, Henry paced forward.

The eyes of the employee grazed over him. 'Boarding pass?'

He proffered his phone, and she glanced between that and her computer screen. 'We're overbooked so we're asking everyone who can to wait for the next flight, later today. You'd be recompensed generously, with—'

'I'm sorry, that's impossible. My elderly father's had an operation so I've got to get home urgently.' It was true, to some extent. Viola would kill him if he wasn't there to take over, as promised. But it was Halley he'd miss if he wasn't on this one.

The computer pinged, and the woman's mouth twisted. 'Bad luck, sir. That was an alert that the flight's now full. Overfull, actually.'

He followed her gaze to Brian and his friends.

'No, I can't get all three of you on,' the male employee was warning. 'I've got two seats remaining, and I suggest you quickly decide between yourselves who's coming and who's staying, or we'll have to offer them to the next in line.'

Henry swallowed. The next in line was him. If the three of them would rather wait together than separate—

'Rock, paper, scissors for it?' one of Brian's friends said.

Brian laughed, and hupped three times. He produced scissors at the same moment his friend came up with paper. 'All right!' he hollered.

Henry's heart sank into his boots, and he turned away, blinking rapidly. He wasn't going to see Halley at all, and he had no idea how to break it to her.

'Henry?' Brian called. 'You made it on the plane?'

He glanced back and shook his head briefly.

Brian released a long growl. 'You swear your girl's a genuine Bears fan?'

'Lifelong,' Henry assured him. He held his breath.

'Hey?' Brian called to his friends, whose round of rock, paper scissors had descended into good-humoured scuffles. 'I'll wait for the next flight with whichever of you loses. Lover boy's taking my seat.'

* * *

From: Henry Inglis
Subject: Update: waiting at gate at JFK!
To: Halley Hart

Thanks to Brian from Bedford and you, for being a Bears fan, I've got a seat on this plane! My best guess is that we'll be landing about 5 a.m. Halley, we're not going to have very long together and I'm really sorry about that. But I refuse to be devastated,

175

because in about a month we'll be together for half a year. *Half a year!*

I'm guessing no replies means you're still sleeping, and I hate to wake you only to say I won't be there until the morning. I'll be in touch when I land.

All my love, Henry xxx

* * *

Halley

Something was drumming as Halley half-woke. It was hail again, landing on the Blue Moon's roof, she thought blearily.

Then she sat up, her head spinning. She had no idea where her phone was, to check for updates, but could see it was dark outside. She'd overslept, and Henry must be on his way.

And the drumming was getting louder.

'Hello!' a man with an English accent called. 'Are you in?'

She was on her feet a split second later, narrowly avoiding a tangle with the bed covers. She sprinted into the corridor, vaulted over the tools she'd left out and raced past the log burner, which was only warm.

'Henry?' she called, as she leaped up the steps to the door in the stern, which she kept bolted closed on his instruction.

'Yes,' came the muffled reply from the other side. She wrestled with the stiff bolt, finally thudding it across as he added, 'We're here to see him.'

Her stomach lurched as the door sprang open. A man with thinning, sandy hair leaned into view. 'Is the old boy in? We were out for a stroll and thought we'd pop in to say hullo.'

We, Halley thought, straining to see behind him. 'He's not here,' she said. 'He's . . . well he's on his way, I guess. I need to check my phone.'

'Sorry to trouble you with questions,' the man said, looking at her anxiously as he entered. 'But I hope you don't mind me asking . . . y'know . . . who you are?'

A pale woman with shiny black hair came in behind him, and scoffed. 'Don't be preposterous, Julian darling. This must be Henry's American.'

* * *

Henry

His phone rang as he boarded the plane, and he answered quickly. 'Halley? You got my emails?'

'I did. I'm sorry I slept so long. And that you've sat in airports for hours to only get a few hours closer to home.'

'At least that's about to change. I'm boarding in New York.'

'*Finally*,' she breathed. 'What's your ETA?'

'Touching down just before 6 a.m.,' he admitted, making his way up the aisle to his seat toward the back. 'I've only got hand luggage, so I can hopefully disembark and make it through to the car park by about half past.'

'That decides it then. *Julian* — you're right. I need to go to Heathrow early.'

'Halley? Julian's there?'

'And Gabrielle,' she said significantly. 'They popped in to see you, and found me.'

His mouth fell open. Halley and Gabrielle, on the same small boat. For the first time in days, he wasn't desperate to be aboard the Blue Moon. 'How . . . uhh . . .'

'Later,' she said, then louder, 'Julian reckons there's no point you coming back here, when I'm meant to be at Heathrow shortly after nine ready for my own flight.'

'He's right,' Henry said, clamping his mobile between his shoulder and his chin as he reached to open the overhead locker just before his row. It was overfull already, and he slammed it shut. 'I should have thought of that. You'll have to check our terminals, and meet me at mine. There's no link between arrivals and departures beyond security, so wait in the arrivals hall.'

'Obviously.' He could almost hear her eyes rolling.

At the next locker along, a couple were stowing their stuff. 'The trains don't run that early, though, and I don't want you subjected to another long coach trip. Please order a taxi, Halley, and I'll pay you back.'

'That's not necessary,' she said. Before he could argue, she added, 'Julian already offered to drive me.'

'Seriously?' The couple shifted into Henry's row, and he sidestepped to the next overhead locker, which now only had a tiny gap left. 'Tell him I owe him one.'

'Will do. And have a good flight, babe. I love you.'

It was the first time she'd said it first, and, despite everything, he felt heady with happiness. 'I love you too,' he said, pushing at the bags until he created a little more space, then wedging his backpack in. 'And I can't wait to see you soon.'

Carrying only his phone and book, he paused at his row. His was the middle seat of a row of three, and the man and woman were sitting either side of it. His assumption that they were a couple must be wrong.

'Excuse me please,' he said to the woman, who was in the aisle seat with an iPad and water bottle and snacks piled on her lap.

Rather than moving her legs to one side, she scowled. 'We book an aisle and a window so we can share three seats for the price of two.'

'No one ever chooses the middle one, unless they can help it,' the man by the window said.

So they were a couple after all.

'I suppose I couldn't help it,' Henry ground out, his happiness already draining away. 'Full plane, and all that. Would either of you like to swap with me?'

'No,' they said together. The woman stood and moved into the aisle, and Henry shifted into his seat. The man put his wrist on the armrest to Henry's right. The woman put her elbow on the armrest on his left. Then they both took their shoes and socks off. Henry pinched the bridge of his nose, wondering if this flight could possibly get any worse.

'Good evening, ladies and gentlemen,' a voice said through the speakers. 'This is your Captain speaking. Unfortunately air traffic control has us waiting for a take-off slot, so we'll taxi out to the runway but we're anticipating a delay after that.'

Henry thudded the back of his skull against his headrest.

* * *

Saturday, 28 December

From: Halley Hart
Subject: FOUR HOURS!!!
To: Henry Inglis

I'm sorry for sleeping through all your email updates. It sounds like a hellish journey, and I hope you're catching up on some sleep now.

Gabrielle's a peach by the way. By which I mean the exact opposite. She kept calling me *the American* as if it was a curse word, and crinkling her nose like I smell. Also, I don't want to be all *why do people who speak other languages speak other languages*, but she kept saying things to Julian in French, then laughing. When he asked if I understood (I think to try to stop her — he's a very nice man) and I said 'No, being American, I learned Spanish,' she stage-whispered something about *les americaines* and imbeciles. You'll never know how badly I wanted to snap back that I hadn't recognized her with her clothes on. (I only managed to suppress it by biting my lip so hard I drew blood.) (Just as well you'll be able to kiss me better in a couple hours!!!)

Anyway, Julian wanted the whole story, and then he made coffee while I read your emails, and then I updated him all over again and he came up with the Heathrow plan. I'd have probably accepted the ride anyway but when I saw how pissed Gabrielle was about it I definitely had to.

They've left again now but Julian's coming back with his car to collect me later. Unless Gabrielle makes him cancel, in which case I'll jump in a cab.

But I have a feeling he won't stand for that. He seemed pretty mad at her as they left.

FOUR HOURS and we'll be together! Which means only two for me to pack and clean and do some more of a project I hope you'll approve of.

I love you! (Despite your taste in ex-girlfriends.) Your Halley

* * *

Texts messages from Halley to Henry:

Well I made it to Heathrow and I'm sitting in your terminal. Julian drove me and was super-nice. He offered to wait with me, but I sent him home. ONE HOUR until you land!

Ugh. Your ETA just changed. Looks like you'll be here closer to 7 than 6. I hate airlines. And Chicago snow. And Oxford rain/sleet/hail. But I love you. Please hurry if you can.

You're now arriving at 7.39. And 739 is a cool number. It's a prime where if we take a digit from the end, it's 73 — also a prime. Take another digit away, and 7's a prime too. Maybe I'm nuts, but you arriving at 7.39 would be perfect, so I've called it as correct, and I'm brushing my teeth. Because you're arriving at 7.39 and I CAN'T WAIT!

I jinxed it by calling it. It's now showing 8.03 . . .

I can't believe that yesterday we were sweet summer children who thought twelve hours together was too short. Do you know what I'd give for twelve hours with you now? At least a kidney. Hurry, hurry, hurry. And call me the second you see this!

* * *

Halley

Halley bounced her leg and gnawed her sore lower lip, her eyes cemented to the arrivals board. She'd paced out the route to the terminal bus, investigated the duration of that journey and called her airline to check the latest possible time that she could arrive for her flight. Apparently it was a peak departure time, so there were long queues through security, and if she got to her terminal less than two and a half hours before her flight was leaving, she may well miss it.

And she couldn't miss it. If she didn't collect the final week of her data now, it would set her back another month, ruling her out of the symposium in Chicago and significantly delaying her arrival in Southampton. Which meant the last terminal bus she could catch was one departing at 9.30.

Henry's flight status had been labelled *delayed* all morning, and its arrival time had constantly been put back. Until the past hour, when it had only displayed 8.43. Her eyes shot to the clock on the top right of the huge screen — it was 8.42.

And then her phone chimed. *Henry.*

Her heart rocketed in her chest as she fumbled to answer.

'Halley?' he said.

'I'm here!'

'We've just landed — still taxiing in. We were really delayed leaving and I didn't know how long you could wait.'

'I'm here,' she choked out again. 'But I can only stay for forty-seven more minutes, Henry.'

'I'll get there.' His voice was deep and determined. It sounded like a vow. 'We'll see each other.'

She wiped her nose with the edge of her sleeve. 'I'm at the meet and greet right beside the exit from customs.'

'I'll be there as soon as I can.'

* * *

Text messages between Henry and Halley:

They're letting us disembark now. I'm readying myself to run. xxx

> *Forty minutes exactly.*

Almost at PP ctrl. xxx

> *Thirty-three minutes.*

Queues at the e-gates, but I'm in the shortest one.

> *Twenty-nine minutes.*

The email you sent while I was in the air just loaded in my inbox.

> *Maybe don't bother with that right now. Twenty-eight minutes!*

WTF . . . Gabrielle!! I didn't exactly think the two of you'd get on, but I had no idea she'd be that unpleasant. I can't believe I ever dated her.

> *Ha. Twenty-six minutes!*

Seriously, I can understand it making you question my judgement. And as for her looking at you like you smell — you might like to know that her perfume made my eyes water.

> *I do like knowing that! But I shouldn't have made that dig about your judgement because everyone's got that one ex they regret — I'll tell you about mine someday. Twenty-four minutes!*

E-gate had error. Had to move queue.

> *Twenty-three minutes. How long's the new queue?*

Medium. But once I'm through here, it's plain sailing.

Twenty-one minutes.

Henry??? How's it going? Only seventeen minutes?

Almost through! Then I'll sprint until you're in my arms. xxx

I like the sound of that. But there's only thirteen minutes.

Henry, there's only seven minutes. (Don't slow down to reply.)

* * *

Halley

'Six,' Halley hissed, stacking her smallest suitcase on top of the other one, and manoeuvring them around the tall man who'd just stood in front of her, without removing her gaze from the crowds of strangers streaming through the customs exit.

'Five,' she muttered, putting both hands on her hips, her elbows bent at acute angles, to block the tall man's attempt to move in front of her again. He could easily see over her head, dammit.

'Four. Come on, come on, Henry.' She was aware of glances from the people either side of her, probably wondering why the crazy American was talking to herself. She didn't care. Maybe they'd give her more space. She checked over her shoulder. When the double doors opened, she could just about see the bus stop, beyond. The 9.30 bus hadn't arrived yet, and there was a crowd waiting. That was OK — she'd monitored it all morning, and there was always enough space for everyone to cram in.

The countdown timer on her phone chimed. *Only three minutes.* She scanned everyone who'd come through customs in the past thirty seconds, in case she'd missed him, then snapped her eyes back to those rounding the corner. Fear and stress and longing were strangling her oesophagus, but she had to keep breathing; If Henry appeared now, she was claiming a 180 second kiss.

Her phone pinged for two minutes, and she stared at the screen in disbelief. Minutes had never gone by so quickly before. She checked behind her: the bus was pulling up. She surveyed the corner again, where a couple appeared, holding hands. She glared at them as her phone chimed one minute.

Come on, come on, come on, Henry . . .

Reluctantly she ceded her place at the very front of the meet and greet area to the tall man, as she scrabbled to call Henry, desperate to at least speak to him while they were under the same roof.

It rang and rang. He didn't answer. There was a beep for his voicemail.

'Henry?' she said, staggering backwards, dragging her cases and still looking for him in the face of everyone who made it round the corner. 'I gotta go. I love you.' She couldn't hear anything but the whoosh of air, like she was falling, and she only knew she'd made it to the other side of the double doors because it was instantly colder.

She turned and leaped on the bus, instantly pivoting to stare through the bus door, which was open behind her. Across the sidewalk, through the double doors and beyond a sea of bodies, a figure dashed round the corner from customs, sprinting so fast she knew it was him.

'Henry!' she yelled.

Three loud beeps emanated through the bus . . . a warning that the doors were closing. She screamed again at the top of her lungs. 'Henry, over here!'

His head jerked, and she thought he might have heard her, in the split second before the doors closed and the bus pulled off, and they were separated again.

'Americans are so loud,' she heard someone behind her hiss, as a solitary tear streaked down her cheek.

PART TEN

From: Henry Inglis
Subject: Gutted
To: Halley Hart

Halley, I'm so gutted I missed you.

I stupidly dropped my phone, and it smashed. I almost left it and kept running, but it raised a customs officer's suspicions, and he insisted on checking my bag. I finally got into the arrivals hall at exactly half past, so we must have only just missed each other. I even thought I heard your voice, calling me, but perhaps it was wishful thinking . . .

And I didn't have my laptop with me, so I couldn't even let you know until I just reached my parents' place. I'm so sorry. I hope you're not too upset.

I love you, and you love me, and we'll be together in about a month, for *half a year*.

All my love, Henry xxx

* * *

From: Halley Hart
Subject: Cursed
To: Henry Inglis

Henry, it feels like I'm cursed to eternally being driven away from you. That's what happened — I was on the terminal bus just outside when I saw you, and yelled.

I'm glad you heard me, but I wish you saw me, if only for a second, like I saw you.

I really, really like the way you look. I mean, I knew that already, because I've met you and I have your photo and I see you on my screen all the time. But now I'm in love with you, I was overwhelmed by it. Even really briefly, at a distance. (What's it going to be like in a month, when you meet me at the airport and we know we'll be together for *half a year*?) (I hope it's OK to assume you'll come meet me. If you're too busy or something, I can go straight to Southampton, and get to Oxford the following weekend.)

Please don't be worried about me being upset. I'm not gonna cry the whole way to California. Instead, I'll spend the flight finalizing my transfer forms for Stanford and enrolment forms for Southampton. And by the way, I haven't forgotten that we're spending a week together, for our birthdays and Valentine's. Can we please still do that — I don't wanna keep being apart from you for big celebrations?

Please say hi to Viola for me, and I hope your parents are both doing as well as can be hoped.

Love, your Halley

* * *

Sunday, 29 December

From: Henry Inglis
Subject: Yes and yes and yes
To: Halley Hart

Dear Halley,

Since you mentioned a curse, I should admit to something similar, when I was stopped by that customs officer just metres from where I knew you were waiting. That thing about Halley's comet only being seen once in a lifetime flashed into my mind, and I panicked that the one day on which I saw you, nearly four months ago, would be the only one, ever.

So I wish I'd seen you too — at any distance and however briefly. Or maybe it'd be a new kind of misery, watching you leave in a vehicle again, and it growing smaller and smaller on the horizon. The first time, I wished very hard for another taxi to pull up, so I could leap in going, 'Follow that car!' This time, I suspect I'd have raced around to your terminal and bought a cheap ticket anywhere, so I could hang out with you through security. It would have made me late for my parents, so Viola would have had my guts for garters. Fair enough trade, for an hour at your side.

I can't answer what it'll be like when we're together again at last, but I dream of it often. And it's yes and yes to your other questions — you're mine-all-mine for that week in mid-February, and I can't imagine anything that could prevent me being there to collect you, beyond you not telling me the date and time. Which is a hint to let me know, as soon as you've booked your ticket.

Dad's good — the check-up went well, and he's back home now. Mum's been especially confused, unfortunately, so Viola's been working on Dad to downsize, and release the funds to keep the carers on long-term, but he hasn't agreed yet. I only saw her briefly before she left to visit her 'old friend' Aron, in Iceland. Yes, you read that right — *Iceland*! I've never heard of this Aron before, and she only went to Iceland once, accompanying a tour group last summer.

Are you doing anything to mark the New Year? I'll be here in Hampshire, with plenty of time and a new phone . . .

All my love, Henry xxx

* * *

Monday, 30 December

> *From: Halley Hart*
> *Subject: Also yes!*
> *To: Henry Inglis*
> This is a quick one, because jet lag's screwed up my biorhythms and I slept when I should be getting ready to go up to the observatory. I have to be there tomorrow night, too, but I'm totally up for seeing in your new year, eight hours before mine. I'll vid-call you shortly before.
>
> If you contact Viola, tell her I say New Year with the northern lights sounds awesome — actually, scratch that. DO NOT contact Viola — leave her to enjoy her Viking fun!
>
> Love, your Halley

* * *

Tuesday, 31 December
Halley

Halley scrolled through the accommodation that was available in Southampton. There were minimal photos, and everything was expensive.

'Honey, I'm *home*!'

She hastily minimized the page, before springing to her feet and pacing into the hallway. 'I wasn't expecting you for a few hours.'

Angelie reached up to throw her arms around Halley. 'Flight got in early.'

'Some people have all the luck.'

'You got a bad delay returning from England?'

Halley paused. With everything that had happened afterwards, she'd forgotten that Mom told Angelie about the trip, to ensure Halley had her passport. At some point, she'd have to figure out at which point Angelie had contacted Viola, and how she'd avoided letting Viola know that Halley was coming for Christmas, but now wasn't the time.

'Worse than that,' Halley said. 'Henry flew to Chicago while I was headed there.'

'Wait, what? You didn't see Henry after all?'

'Except for a glimpse from the transit bus,' Halley confirmed morosely, collapsing onto their couch and explaining the calamitous events. 'I can't figure out if it was worse for him, not seeing me, or for me to get a reminder of how cute he is just as the bus pulled away. Seriously, he's *so, so* cute.'

'Good to know you've finally noticed.'

'It's nearly four months since we met, and people look different in real life compared to flat on a screen.'

'So, fly back there,' Angelie said. 'You've only got two weeks' worth of data to collect, right? And if your aunt paid for that flight, at least you haven't blown through all your savings pointlessly.'

'Yeah, I can afford a new ticket,' Halley said with caution. She didn't want to confess she was moving to the UK until Angelie had at least caught up on some sleep, having experienced the terrible combination of bad news and jet lag herself. 'But I can't visit in January. I've been accepted to give a presentation at that symposium in Chicago.'

'You have?' Angelie shrieked. She unzipped her suitcase, which was so huge that she practically had to dive inside to fish around at the bottom. 'I brought something we can celebrate with . . .' She popped up again, bearing a bottle of Filipino rum triumphantly. 'We'll have to drink it all today, because my diet starts tomorrow. I ate so much lechon, the top button on my jeans won't close.' She glared at Halley. 'Earth to Halley . . .'

'What?'

'You're meant to tell me I look fine as I am, and the voice in my head insisting I need to be the thinnest woman in the room is toxic,' Angelie called, disappearing into the kitchen. She returned a moment later with two tumblers.

'You're stunning as you are,' Halley assured her. 'And despite your concerns about fitting into your *size two* jeans, you remain the thinnest woman in this room, at least. I'd really worry more about the fact that you're hearing voices.'

Angelie poured the rum, and passed one glass to Halley. 'It sounds just like my mother's. *What you mean you're getting tattooed — you want to look like a jailbird, huh? You want to look like a prostitute?*'

'You got a tattoo?'

'I was going to get a tiny one, and cover it with my watch strap, but the voice is too strong. Hey, what did your mom make of Henry?'

'She already liked him, but she's even keener now. Apparently he's clean and polite, and expressed apt horror at both motorbikes and cults. It helps with—' Halley broke off rather than explain that it meant Mom was enthusiastic about her only child's plan to move to Europe. She gulped more rum instead. 'I've made plans with Henry. Can we hang out in an hour or two?'

'Sure,' Angelie said, topping both their glasses up before Halley made for her bedroom, rum in hand. She sipped it as she raked through her wardrobe for something to wear. Henry liked seeing her in his sweater before, or . . . she had a better idea, and pulled off her T-shirt and sports bra, replacing them with a push-up bra and a sequin crop top.

'Experiment to test if Henry's an abs or cleavage man,' she murmured, grinning at herself in the mirror, and added red lipstick, aware that rum on an empty stomach was making her bold.

She manipulated her mouse, calling him from her desktop.

'Halley!'

'Hey, handsome.'

His blue-green eyes sharpened, and he leaned closer to his camera. From the angle, she guessed he'd borrowed a tablet. 'Well you're a sight for sore eyes. I didn't know we were dressing up.'

'This old thing?' She wiggled so the gold sequins sparkled. 'We're celebrating a brand new year, at least half of which we'll be spending together.'

'That's worth celebrating properly,' he agreed, pushing one hand through his hair. It took a little effort to figure out the trajectory of someone's gaze through a camera and a couple of screens. She scrutinized him from under her lashes as she repositioned on the desk chair, tucking her legs under her.

'Aha!' she said.

'Pardon?'

'Nothing.' He was mostly looking at her lips, but his eyes had flicked to her cleavage then moved down to her abs, before speeding back to her face. He was trying to be polite, and failing in a flattering kind of way. He also wasn't betraying any particular preference — he must like both abs and cleavage.

'What are you drinking?' he asked.

'Strong rum.'

He lifted a crystal tumbler filled with a yellow concoction. 'Dad made me a snowball — it's not dissimilar to the eggnog I had with your mother — and warned me not to drink it too quickly in case it went to my head.'

She sipped her drink. 'This rum's going to my head. Your dad wouldn't approve.'

'Is it now,' Henry said, smiling. 'I couldn't have guessed.'

'Really?'

He laughed. 'It's four minutes to midnight, beautiful. Do you know the words of "Auld Lang Syne"?'

'Never heard of it. We don't do that in America.'

He raised one eyebrow. 'Don't believe you.'

'Fine, fine! I lied. I'm good at a fair few things, but singing isn't one of them OK?'

'Kissing, however, is,' Henry said, his eyes lingering on her lips again. 'But we're over five thousand miles apart. So let's toast in the new year.'

Halley was dubious. 'I'm not usually superstitious, but when we drank to making the most of twelve hours together, we didn't even get twelve seconds.'

'And then you drank to the Blue Moon, and I drank to you, but neither the boat nor you disappeared from the face of the planet.'

'I still don't think we should do toasts until we're together in person to clink glasses.'

'Or mugs,' Henry said, so solemnly that she knew he was amused. 'But fair enough. There's one minute to go . . . shall we just say Happy New Year?'

'And make a joint resolution, never to surprise each other again?'

'No surprises takes it too far,' Henry said firmly.

'Very good point. How about no surprises involving trans-Atlantic travel? We have to inform the other first, so we can workshop the logistics?'

He nodded. 'It's a resolution — and it's time — happy new year!'

She blew him a kiss. 'And to you. I love you so much, Henry.'

'I'll never tire of hearing that.'

'What about if I sang it to the tune of "I Know a Song That Will Get on Your Nerves"?'

'Then I do get to hear you sing?'

'Absolutely not,' she said promptly. 'Where are you, anyway?'

'This is my room in my parents' house. Brief tour . . . chess trophies, childhood books, dinosaur duvet cover . . .'

'Seriously? Let me see!'

He winked at her. 'Joking, Halley.'

'Oh. Rum makes me stupid.'

'That's impossible.' Parallel lines appeared on his brow. 'Don't you need to drive to the observatory once it's dark?'

'I'll have sobered up by then, but I'll walk anyway. I never drive if I've drunk even a drop — Emergency Room nurse's kid, remember?'

Angelie hammered on her door. 'Want a top up?'

'Not really,' Halley called back. 'But you can say hi to Henry.' She switched the call to her laptop and carried it through to the lounge, tilting the screen before leaning back on the couch beside Angelie, who was writing on small wooden blocks.

'Hi, Angelie,' Henry said, with a wave.

'Hey, Henry. I'm making drunk Jenga for later. You know it? Well, there's intrusive or funny or weird questions written on each of the blocks. If the stack falls while it's your turn to place one, you chug your drink, then pick up a block and answer it. But I've run out of ideas for questions.'

'I've got one,' Henry said immediately. 'What's the nickname you call your best friend?'

Halley stiffened, as Angelie stared at the screen for a moment, then collapsed into laughter. 'You know I've got one for Halley that she hates with a passion?'

'I do. I've never been able to work it out though.'

'I could tell you,' Angelie said, with a sly expression, as Halley squeaked a protest. 'But then I'd get to ask you *two*, and you'd have to answer honestly.'

'N*ooooo*,' Halley insisted, but Henry looked intrigued.

'Deal,' he said.

'I don't consent to this,' Halley said loudly. Angelie whacked her with a cushion, but Henry's eyes softened.

'If I've overstepped—'

'You haven't,' Halley said, relenting. 'But get it over with quickly, Angelie.'

'So you know how my name was made by my parents smooshing both theirs together?' Angelie asked, bouncing up and down a little in her glee. 'I nickname my friends by smooshing their parents' together too. Halley's dad went by

Buddy, and her mom's obviously also Halley, so she's *Buddha*. You can imagine the looks she gets, as a skinny white girl, when I yell *Buddha* at her in public!'

Halley retreated behind her glass as Henry laughed — though not as hard as Angelie, who was endlessly entertained by her own humour when she was drinking.

'My turn to ask a question,' Angelie slurred. 'And you both have to answer honestly.'

'That wasn't the deal!' Halley protested. 'Only that Henry had to.'

'I changed it. But I'll only ask things I've written on blocks already.' She made a show of rummaging, before pulling one free. 'What's the thing you like least about your current crush?'

'It doesn't really say that,' Halley said, snatching at the block. 'Henry, you don't need to answer.'

'It does though,' Angelie said.

Halley checked it, and groaned. 'We're still not answering.'

'Henry will. He made the deal,' Angelie said.

Henry was looking between them. 'I'd much rather not.'

He hadn't said there was nothing he didn't like about her. She wondered what it could be — or if she wasn't even who he considered his current crush. 'How about we both answer it at the same time, off the top of our heads. And neither of us will take offence.'

'Exactly,' Angelie said, leaning back as if getting out of the way of a lit firework. 'It's only a bit of fun! Three, two . . .'

'He's pretty ignorant about sports,' Halley blurted.

'She's really obsessed with sport,' Henry said, at exactly the same moment.

She stared at him and, also in tandem, they burst out laughing.

Angelie's mutter that they were sickening was interrupted by the doorbell, and she stumbled off to see who it was, re-entering with a curly-haired linebacker.

Halley rolled her eyes, and mouthed 'Bin! The one who steals my food!' at the screen. Henry nodded quickly.

'Well we've got work to do,' Angelie said, towing Ben toward her bedroom.

Halley snorted. '*Work*? That's what they're calling it these days?' It must have come out louder than she'd intended, because Angelie dropped Ben's hand and returned to the couch.

'Someone in this apartment has to get some bedroom action,' Angelie said.

Ben grinned, and Halley glowered at him, avoiding catching sight of Henry. 'So go get some.'

'Not until I've asked Henry's second question,' Angelie said. 'Ooh, it's a fun one. What sentence would you use to indicate you were being held hostage? Y'know, it should sound completely innocuous to the kidnapper, but obviously wrong to us. Well, to Halley, since I've only met you twice.'

Henry pursed his lips, thinking.

'Off the top of your head again,' Halley said, wanting it over, and him to herself once more.

He smiled at her. 'To be clear, this is the opposite of what I really want, to alert you that there's a bloke with a gun to my head.'

Halley winced at the mental picture. 'I get it, babe.'

'Halley, I don't want you to move over here next month, after all,' Henry said.

Silence descended.

'Shit,' Halley murmured.

'What?' Angelie said. 'What the hell does that mean? Halley?'

* * *

Wednesday, 1 January

Text messages between Halley and Henry:

> *Henry it was an accident. If it's anyone's fault it's mine — I should have given you a heads-up she didn't know yet.*

> *Not thinking it through more carefully is on me. Is she still refusing to communicate with you?*

195

Yes and no. She hasn't spoken to me, but slamming doors is some sort of communication, right?

Ugh. Poor Angelie.

Ben was still here when I got back from the observatory, so at least she has someone to hug her.

Oh Halley, I'm sorry. I wish I could hug you right now.

I know you do. And sure, Angelie took it harder than I expected, but again — my fault, not yours. She's mad I didn't tell her I was even applying for visiting studentships — but I didn't tell anyone, because I didn't think I'd get one! And she's even madder that I didn't tell her as soon as I got the offer — but I wanted to tell you and Mom first. I'll get all that through to her, when she calms down.

I hope so. xxx

* * *

Thursday, 2 January
Henry

Henry shouldered his bag as he headed out of Oxford railway station towards the nearby canal. Dad was doing well, and the carer had urged Henry to get back to Oxford. Wanting to check on the Blue Moon, and make a start on the Sedgwick letters, Henry had agreed, promising to return for the weekend, when Viola would be back and they'd try together to persuade Dad to downsize.

It was only as Henry reached the towpath that it clicked quite why he wanted to be at the Blue Moon. Kwame had been keeping an eye on it, and reported no problems that were evident from the outside, at least. It was that Halley had been there, sleeping in his bed and cooking in the galley, and he wanted to feel close to her even more than usual, after dropping her in it with Angelie. It was embarrassing to admit, even to himself, that he'd been so thoughtless because he was distracted by how especially delectable Halley was looking.

He shook his head in a vain attempt to clear it as he neared the boat. Angelie would surely forgive Halley soon, and then he'd be able to forgive himself. In the meantime, he needed to manage his own expectations: Halley had been aboard the Blue Moon for less than three days — there probably wouldn't be any sign of her occupancy. His hand alighted on the chain padlocked across the decked area at the stern. There was something caught in the lock — a plastic bag, with paper inside. He smiled, recognizing the note from Halley's description of her harried arrival. She'd forgotten to remove it — or more likely, purposely left it for him.

Cheered already, he released the chain and stepped on, before unlocking the back door and ducking as he entered. The temperature felt even colder than outside, and the galley appeared just as he'd left it. On the other side of the dining table-come-desk, the only change he could identify was moved boxes, which were no longer pushed flat against one wall. He puzzled on that as he pressed on, into the short corridor toward the bedroom — and halted.

The bookcases lining the walls were three-quarters complete, and filled with an assortment of his books. And there was a folded sheet of paper on the shelf at his eyeline. He squinted to read it, too impatient to get out his glasses.

* * *

Handwritten note from Halley:

> *4 A.M., 28 DEC.*
> *SURPRISE! I GOT BORED AND WORKED ON THESE. A FEW CRATES I HAD ABSORBED SOME DAMP, SO I PRIORITIZED SHELVING THE BOOKS FROM THOSE. FINISH THEM READY FOR MY RETURN, OK?*

ABOUT TO LEAVE FOR THE AIRPORT
WITH JULIAN AND I'M BESIDE MYSELF AT
SEEING YOU IN TWO HOURS!!
  I LOVE YOU
  YOUR HH x

* * *

Friday, 3 January

From: Henry Inglis
Subject: Love letter
To: Halley Hart
Dearest Halley,

'Can you humbly request whether Miss Mallory will write to me, dear sister? For I have often thought you noticed that my feelings for her were much deeper than that for your other friends, and it is true. Please tell her, if you think she would not be insulted, that I love her for her beauty and wit. And for her kindness to you when I am so often absent.' Second Lieutenant Lawrence Sedgwick, 1809.

The above is a quote from the earliest dated of the Sedgwick letters, from the archive I discovered. It was written by Lawrence to his sister, Louisa, about her close friend, Miss Mallory. His sister was presumably successful, because there's a whole sheaf of letters from Lawrence to Miss Mallory — I'll work on decoding the first of those tomorrow.

Lawrence Sedgwick would have written the above in the cramped Lieutenant's cabin, amidst conditions so bleak they're unimaginable to us. Paper was incredibly expensive, so his handwriting was purposely tiny, and for the above paragraph alone, he'd used the code his sister had devised, to keep the request from prying eyes. It hit me as I left the library that he went to all that effort, inspired by his love for Miss Mallory, and yet I've never written a love letter to you.

To (mis)quote Lt. Sedgwick: Halley, I love you for your beauty and wit. I love you for leaving proof you've been here, and the promise of your return. For the bookcases and for sleeping in my bed, which left traces of your scent on my pillows. I love you for kissing me when I was a stranger, and flying around the planet to surprise me, and your upcoming half-year visit to be near me. I love you whatever you wear — clothes from random universities, my jumper, skimpy sparkling things — and, at some point in the future, I'll love you when you're wearing nothing at all.

And I'll love you booking your flight. I need to know when we'll finally be reunited.

All my love, Henry xxx

* * *

Saturday, 4 January

From: Halley Hart
Subject: Love letters, plural.
To: Henry Inglis

I love your letter and I love hearing about Lawrence's and most of all, I love you. But don't you know, Henry — you've been writing me love letters all along!

A couple practical things, before I forget . . . I think my scent on your pillow must be from my perfumed shampoo. I don't want to repel you, so I'll switch brands if it makes your eyes water? Also, thanks for the reminder — I booked my flight for the twenty-seventh, so there's officially now only twenty-three days to go! Finally, can I stay with you on the Blue Moon through to at least your birthday? I don't want to commit to a rental in Southampton before checking out options in person. I'll be able to do my writing remotely, and for events I need to attend at the university it looks like the train only takes ninety minutes.

Love, your Halley

* * *

Sunday, 5 January

From: Henry Inglis
Subject: 22 days . . .
To: Halley Hart

Sweetheart, it never ceases to amaze me how romantic you can be under the guise of getting practical. Thank you for booking the flight — and I can't think of anything better then you staying with me. And, not that I don't want you here constantly, because I very much do, but Vi insists I tell you that she lives twenty minutes from Southampton, and you're welcome to crash on her sofa whenever you need to in those first few weeks. You'd need wheels, though, so I'll speed up on the search for a reliable car.

Viola and I are here with our parents. Dad's pretended to be offended that we've ganged up on him to suggest downsizing, but we saw him watching one of the carers getting Mum smiling by playing a recording of one of her old violin performances. Maybe he's quietly considering the benefits of keeping care on full-time, so we're going to stop pushing for now.

I've finished transcribing the first letter from Lawrence Sedgwick to Miss Mallory. He thanks her for her own letter and tells her a couple of shipboard anecdotes I suspect he's highly sanitized. Then he hints rather charmingly to preferring her letter to any he's received from his family, and even to the one when the Admiralty commended him for valour in a sea battle. And while he signed off to his sister with the valediction '*yours, etc . . . L*', Miss Mallory got '*Always remaining your most humble and affectionate servant, Laurie.*'

Lots of work ahead with these letters — I think I might get a book out of them. But I'll spend every waking moment I'm not in the library finishing those shelves, so all the crates are unpacked ready for your arrival. Hope your nights are going all right at the telescope, and that Angelie's coming around?

Oh, and I can't imagine anything about you repelling me in any way. Including your shampoo.

Always remaining your most humble and affectionate servant, Henry xxx

* * *

Monday, 6 January

From: Halley Hart
Subject: 21!
To: Henry Inglis

That's very nice of Viola! Please tell her I look forward to a night or two on her couch, getting the tea about Aron!

I'm pleased to hear that you'll finish those shelves, as a humble and obedient servant should. Seriously though, with my belongings to squeeze in as well, to begin with, space will be at a premium.

How would you feel about waiting for me to help you choose a car when I arrive? I'm good at recognizing bargains that I can cheaply repair/upgrade — I sold both my prior cars for nearly twice what I bought them for.

Lawrence sounds like such a babe — I can't wait to hear if his stealth-brag about his commendation for valour impressed Miss Mallory! And you've got to keep it up with the cute valedictions — I'd like a new one in every email!

Data collection's going good, aside from cloud cover last night. Which reminded me to compare the weather — apparently Oxford has an average of 165 rainy days each year? (Actually, of all types of precipitation, but that's almost all rain.) Chicago has an average of 127 days a year, and Palo Alto only 61. I'd have guessed Oxford's rainy days to be much higher than that, since it's been wet every day I've spent there. I'm starting to think it's personal, and Oxford hates me.

Angelie's thawing a bit. She left a note on the refrigerator offering to replace my smoothie that she'd 'accidentally drunk'. (Bet it was actually Bin, on purpose, grr . . .) (I've replied telling her not to worry about it, as a peace offering.)

Love, your Halley

* * *

Tuesday, 7 January

From: Henry Inglis
Subject: 20 . . .
To: Halley Hart
Dear Halley,

I'm so pleased to hear that the data collection is progressing to plan, and that things are improving with Angelie. I'd be delighted to wait until you can advise on a car, and don't worry about fitting your belongings in — I've already removed the crates you unloaded and moved the full ones to my office in college. So once I've finished the shelves there'll be plenty of empty ones for you.

Viola called to say Aron's arrived for a return visit, and she wants to bring him to guest night at St Jude's, tomorrow. I asked what he's like and she only took the piss, saying he's six foot four, blond and bearded, and shovels snow for a living. I'll report back with the reality!

Rupert goes on sabbatical in a few days. Hogshoo will step in as senior history tutor for the term, but I guess Rupert doesn't trust him to do the role properly, as he's asked me to alert him, on the quiet, if any issues arise with our undergraduate historians. I agreed, on the proviso that I can take a week off work entirely in the middle of February . . .

I've deciphered the next Sedgwick letters, including Lawrence's second to Miss Mallory. I gathered that she'd asked him for more details of the sea battle, so I suppose she was impressed. I already knew about it from the Naval records — the ship he served on got blocked between two larger French vessels, and he led a small force to fight their way aboard one of those. They succeeded in taking it as a prize, which both enabled their own ship to escape, and earned them a fair wedge in prize money. It's probably why Lawrence feels he's in a position to pursue Miss Mallory — he's got some money behind him. Anyway, Lawrence goes on to ask if she would consider telling her father that they're corresponding. I think, if she agrees, she'd be acknowledging him as her suitor. He ends that he would be most obliged if she would let him know her decision on the matter, and *'Yours to command, Laurie'*.

Only twenty days until you're in my arms . . . And Halley, Oxford could never hate you. Oxford loves you, as do I.

Yours to Command, Henry xxx

* * *

Wednesday, 8 January
Henry

Aron was six foot four with a bushy blond beard.

He wrenched Henry's hand and boomed, 'Nice dress!'

'It's more commonly called an academic gown,' Henry said mildly, nursing his right hand in an attempt to restore the blood flow, as he directed them up to high table. 'What is it you do in Iceland, Aron?'

'I have a glacier excursion company with two friends,' he explained, beaming beneath the beard. 'Gunner deals with bookings and Ingrid manages the office, and I focus on everything outdoors. It's easier to hire guides than people who can undertake the track maintenance, so it generally falls to me to shovel snow.'

'I told you,' Viola muttered to Henry. 'Why wouldn't you believe me?'

'It sounded like you were just listing stereotypes,' Henry murmured back, as he pulled her chair out. Aron took the place opposite Viola so Henry sat beside her, and introduced Rupert when he came over to join them. He'd had a neat haircut for the first time since Henry had known him.

'My sister again, Viola,' Henry said, with heavy emphasis on *again*, in an attempt to remind Rupert that they'd met before. 'And this is Aron, her . . .'

'Icelander,' Viola finished smoothly.

'I'm pleased to meet a relative of Henry's at last,' Rupert said affably to Viola, like he had on at least two prior occasions. 'And Iceland, how . . .' he petered out as the space on Henry's left was taken by another early career research fellow: a physicist who'd been appointed the previous term.

Rupert had launched into a series of questions about one of the Icelandic sagas. Henry opened his mouth to steer the conversation away, but saw Aron nodding enthusiastically.

'My mother works at a museum dedicated to Njáls saga, so I know something on the matter.'

Viola groaned softly, and from the surprised look that came over Aron's face, Henry suspected she'd kicked him. But it was too late for any diversions — the conversation now in his favourite sphere, Rupert would do his best to keep it there.

Soup was served, and Henry's attention drifted again. The colleague to his left had been joined by a couple of guests, who seemed from their conversation to be from her department.

'So you're saying,' Rupert said, ignoring his soup and instead using his spoon to punctuate his words. 'That it's believed to form a cross shape? Do they know anything about the patina?'

'A little,' Aron said. 'Except . . . how to explain it in English. Ah no need.' Aron got his phone out and Rupert craned his head over it, as Aron found a photo.

Viola widened her eyes at Henry, conveying an enquiry about his opinion of Aron.

He leaned closer to her. 'If you like him, I like him. *Do* you like him?'

She widened her eyes again, this time enigmatically, as the waiter returned and asked Rupert if his soup was to his liking. Rupert stared down as though he'd just noticed that the soup existed, and Henry capitalized on his distraction to chip into the conversation.

'Aron, Viola's never told me how you two met?'

Aron launched into an explanation of Viola accompanying several groups of tourists to the glacier, over the course of a few days, and how pleased he'd been when she'd finally accepted his invitation to go for a beer. Viola flushed, which Henry noted with amusement. He never saw much of that side of her.

She steered the conversation to the difference between Aron's company, and the larger one that she worked for. 'I organize more complex travel itineraries than anything else at this point,' she added rather glumly. 'Apparently I've got a knack for them — not that your situation at Christmas went to prove that, Henry.'

Rupert perked up and re-entered the conversation. 'I've been meaning to ask about your trip, Henry. How did you find Chicago?'

'It seemed a great city, though extremely cold.'

Rupert nodded slowly, as though Henry has offered something more interesting than a comment on the weather. 'I've been trying to book my upcoming trip to America. I'm speaking at several different universities before stopping off in . . .' he petered out, before restarting. 'I was complaining about the complexity earlier, and our bursar said it was a travel agent I needed, rather than trying to do it all alone.'

'I'm not really a travel agent,' Viola said quickly. 'But I could recommend someone good.'

While the main course was served, Henry found his attention drawn by the group on his left again, as a word they'd repeated filtered into his consciousness . . . *astronomy*. He listened intently. The man was a year post an Astronomy Ph.D., Henry gathered, and not having much luck on the job market.

'I can't survive on this part-time lectureship,' he said, stabbing his steak with his fork.

'You're not looking further afield?' the female guest asked. 'There's a bit of funding in America.'

'I can't. My fiancé's career isn't portable — you know he's a junior doctor? I'm hopeful something in Italy might work out as a stopgap, so at least we could fly back and forth cheaply. But it's doing grunt work, rather than focusing on my own project, and without my own projects I won't get the recognition that I need to ever get a junior professorship.'

Losing his appetite, Henry introduced himself to the four of them. 'I heard mention of astronomy. My girlfriend's just finishing up an Astronomy Ph.D. at Stanford, though she's heading to the UK, with visiting student status, to write up.'

'Why would she do that?' the male guest asked, looking scandalized. 'She should stay there, sucking up to her American contacts for all she's worth. Surely she knows that's far and away her best chance of an academic job?'

PART ELEVEN

Henry

However repeatedly Henry swallowed, he couldn't dislodge the lump from his throat, and the more the guy went on about the shitty astronomy funding in the UK, the worse it got.

Viola nudged him, and he realized she'd been listening. 'Halley's coming to write up, not pledging her soul never to go back to America.'

Henry tried to summon a smile. 'I know.'

'So what's upset you?' Viola hissed. 'Dreading passing the bad news on?'

He shot his sister a look. 'Oh come on. She already knows.' Halley would have to be naive in the extreme to have missed the basics of the astronomy job market, and Halley was far from naive. 'I wish she'd felt she could tell me how slim her chances are of being able to stay.'

'She obviously didn't want you getting all wounded like this, and telling her not to sacrifice any career opportunities for you. But she's not pursuing a job over here *for you*, is she? She's doing it for *herself*, because she's in love with you, and wants to be with you.'

Viola made it sound reasonable, but it didn't feel that way. Not when Halley was the one making all the sacrifices — not just the job thing, but moving over to write up, and falling out with her best friend in the process. But he thanked Viola and made an effort to be visibly more present, as he silently formulated a plan.

When dinner was over, everyone at high table was ushered upstairs to the SCR for port, and Henry sidestepped Viola and Aron to engage Rupert.

'I wondered whether you might do me a favour, while you're in America?'

* * *

Thursday, 9 January

> *From: Halley A. Hart*
> *Subject: HNY!*
> *To: Henry Inglis*
> Happy new year! Did you talk to your Halley about my scambaiting podcast? You said you'd come back to me about it in January!
> Halley-Anne

* * *

Friday, 10 January
Halley

'Hi Junior.'

'Anything up, Mom?' Halley jabbed her phone screen to switch it to speaker, then placed it on the table. 'I've just got to the observatory.'

'Only checking in,' Mom said, too casually.

Halley squinted into the telescope lens, then back at her phone. 'You don't do that without an ulterior motive, though. Not when you know I'm busy.'

'I want to find out how you're doing, that's all.'

Halley didn't buy that for a moment. Mom hadn't been blessed with subtlety as a character trait — a condition that was perhaps catching, since it was shared by a lot of Chicagoans. But it was hard to dent Mom's self-confidence, so playing along might be the best way to figure out what was up.

'I'm as good as I can be. Between collecting the final data and writing my presentation for the symposium, I'm not getting much sleep.' She purposely didn't mention Henry. If Mom wanted to pry into her relationship, she'd have to be direct.

'Do you have plans for selling your car — I could ask at the hospital if anyone's after one for their teenager?'

Halley drew back from the telescope, content with its positioning, then connected her laptop and enabled the start sequence for her algorithm. 'Cool. I'd appreciate that.' When it booted up, she clicked the programme that took the astro-photographs she needed.

'Oh,' Mom said, sounding slightly disquieted. 'Good. And what's your timeline on job applications?'

'The process is so laborious that it's generally OK to start applying during the final semester of writing up. I'll prepare my résumé as soon as I've got time, ready to submit whenever suitable vacancies arise.' Silently, she predicted Mom's next question.

'Out of interest, what constitutes suitable?'

Halley had been correct, but she felt no triumph. Mom had made so many sacrifices to raise her, it was natural she'd become upset when it sank in that her only child was planning a future on another continent. 'Post-doctoral fellowships,' she said carefully, 'at universities as close as possible to Oxford. They're thin on the ground, and of course I can't stay in the UK long-term without a visa, so at some point I may have to start applying back here too.'

Mom let out a whoosh of breath.

'Mom? I'm sorry. It's not that I don't want to be close to you. I'll be back to visit so often, I promise. And you can come stay with me! And then long-term, like *long* long-term, I'm sure coming back here will be an option, but Henry's tied into his fellowship for three more years so—'

'Halley Hart,' Mom snapped. 'You don't need to persuade me of why you should pursue your chosen career path in any location that you see fit. I'm not pining for you to stay in America — though I'll hold you to your promise to make me welcome whenever I visit you. However long I may choose to stay.'

Halley reassessed rapidly. 'Well played, Mom. But what's with the questioning then? I know it seems crazy to head for a country with more light pollution and less funding. But like I said, it's not *long* long-term. And . . . well,' she said, with more defiance, 'You like to claim that you got Henry and me together. I've fallen for him now . . . it's either be close to him, or be miserable.'

'You don't have to justify your life choices to me, Junior. Or — not professional and romantic choices. I retain the right to stage an intervention if you—'

Halley chimed in, saying in time with her mother: 'Buy a motorcycle or join a cult.'

'Mom,' she added. 'If you're good with me job hunting in Europe, then what is it you actually want right now?'

'I got a vague idea,' Mom said, 'That the plan might have changed. That's all.'

Halley frowned. 'Changed in what way? And where did you get this idea from?'

Mom was silent. 'I can't tell you how I know,' she said. 'But I promise I'm not in touch with Henry. And you shouldn't tell him that you know — you'll have to find a subtler way of handling it.'

'God help me, Mom — you're gossiping directly with Viola now? You need to quit that before there's some crazy miscommunication that messes everything up.'

'Listen,' Mom hissed. 'Henry asked his boss to look out for jobs he could apply for in America.'

'Bullshit,' Halley ground out. 'He'd have told me.'

'I assumed so. But, it seems, he hasn't. Presumably he thinks you'd talk him out of it?'

'I would. It's crazy — he loves Oxford! And he just found these amazing old letters which could be a major deal. And most of all, his parents are elderly, and need a lot of support right now.'

'All good reasons he shouldn't be leaving Oxford. So what are you going to do about it?'

'I don't know,' Halley said on a sigh. 'But I'm on it.'

'Remember, though — you have to be subtle!'

'I can do subtle!'

'While, I remember,' Mom added. 'I'd already booked another wellness retreat for that week you're in town for the symposium, and I haven't been able to move it.'

Halley frowned. 'I won't see you before I fly to England?'

'Sorry, kid. But as we've established, I'll be visiting regularly. I could come for your birthday?'

That was the week Henry had scored off work. 'I'll . . . still be settling in. Later in February would be better.' She ended the call and put her hands on her hips, breathing heavily. It wasn't even dawn in the UK; Henry would be fast asleep. So, she'd finish her work, catch a couple hours sleep in the morning, and figure out a subtle approach after that.

* * *

Saturday, 11 January

Text messages between Halley and Henry:

Henry, what the hell were you thinking???

> *Sorry — what was I thinking about what, sweetheart?*

Don't play dumb. You know what you did.

> *This isn't about bloody Gabrielle again is it? I took Julian a bottle of whisky, to thank him for driving you to the airport, and literally saw her in passing. That's all. I didn't even stop and say hello, since she was so rude to you.*

211

Oh. Good job. On the whisky and ignoring, I mean. But it's not that. Think again.

> *Has Halley-Anne contacted you about the podcast? If she said I promised anything, she's exaggerating. I agreed to think about it so she didn't unilaterally go reading out my email.*

Isn't that the Australian? You said she was a trainee detective, not a podcaster. And no, she hasn't contacted me.

> *I'm scouring my conscience, but not coming up with much else.*

Your conscience doesn't recall your attempts to leave Oxford for a job at an American university?

> *Ah. That. 'Attempts' is too strong. It's an exploration of whether any suitable jobs are upcoming, after it came to my attention that there wouldn't be many enticing options for you over here.*

But why wouldn't you talk to me first? I had to hear via Mom, who got it from Viola. I've had a hunch since Christmas that they're talking behind our back, and I'm sure of it now. But you can't tell Viola we know, because I promised to be subtle.

> *I didn't even realize Viola overheard. It was just a spur of the moment enquiry, when I was feeling guilty at everything you're giving up.*

That's so stupid. I need you here so I can be mad at you. Really, really mad.

> *Would the phone do? I'm in the library but I'll finish the letter I'm on, then call you on the way home.*

No, it's not the same. But make it a video chat, and then OK.

You have time?

Yeah, no stargazing for three days — full moon.

Then it's a date!

Jeez, Henry, no it's not! It's an appointment for you to get a ticking off. 4 P.M. your time, and don't be tardy.

Sorry. Yes. 4 P.M., for a bollocking.

Remember not to say anything to Viola! (By the way, if I had you here I wouldn't JUST be mad at you). (But I would be mad at you FIRST.)

* * *

Henry

As he left the library, Henry turned up his collar and shoved his hands deep in his pockets. It wasn't much above zero, and windy with it. On a whim, he headed around the quad towards the rear of the college. He'd be hard-pressed to make it back to the boat by four, so he'd leave through the lesser-used back gate, and call Halley from the pub on the corner.

Ruth bustled past, but she was engaged in conversation with the organ scholar so for once didn't stop him to declare emphatically how much she liked Halley, as if he needed heavy hints not to let her slip through his fingers. He returned her wave, and ducked through to the narrow passage, where he almost collided with a couple of students heaving something along between them.

'Sorry,' he said, halting. It was his freshers, Dexter and Olivia, and his vague concern about them having had to stay in residence throughout Christmas flooded back. Now he'd promised Rupert to keep an eye on the undergraduate historians, he had a duty to follow it up. 'Hello, you two. How was your break?'

They stared at him, then each other, and then down at the obstacle they were carrying. It was a large wicker hamper, which their strain suggested was exceedingly heavy.

'Do you need some help?'

'No,' Olivia said. 'It's fine. We're just . . . going to Port Meadow for a picnic.'

Henry blinked. 'In this weather? You'll freeze.'

'We've got thermals on,' she said.

'Exactly,' Dexter added.

'Hmm.' Henry opened the back gate, and held it for them as they followed with their burden.

'We've got it,' Olivia said, panting.

'It's fine,' Henry said, retaining his grip on the icy wrought-iron. He couldn't believe it was only food in the basket, and considered what they could be feeling guilty about, before twigging. 'Is that a whole keg of beer?'

Their eyes snapped to his. 'We're going to a party,' Olivia said.

'Well, be careful,' Henry said, making sure the gate closed behind them. There was no more he could reasonably say — they were adults, after all. He watched for a moment as they lumbered down the street, then swung away to stride for the pub, where a blast of warmth welcomed him. It was half-empty, as he'd hoped, being too early for the Saturday night peak.

He requested the excellent craft beer on tap, paid and settled at an alcove table in the furthest corner from the bar. He gulped a mouthful of beer, set up his laptop and inserted his ear buds, then commenced the video call.

Halley was on a bench, in the sunshine, glowering at him. 'I don't get where this came from, all of a sudden,' she said immediately. 'We had a plan — *have* a plan I thought we were both excited for. Don't you want me to move over?'

'You know I do.' He laid both hands flat on the table. 'Please come, as planned?'

Her mouth seemed a smidgen less severe. 'What about your job thing?'

'You're making the first sacrifice — the second should be mine.'

Halley made a scoffing sound. 'Not-perfectly-optimal job application conditions isn't a—'

'Plus, Angelie being furious with you. And is your mother upset, too? Something must have motivated her and Viola to discuss it like that.'

'Mom's fine with me moving. And she'll tell Viola that you've changed your mind, so she stops panicking.'

'All I've done at this point is ask Rupert to let me know, while he's visiting US history departments, if there's anything coming up that could suit me. The answer might well be no. I don't have a big enough publication record for anyone to want me, yet.'

'Because that's the whole point of early career fellowships — time to publish, to build up an academic résumé. When it ends, you'll be competitive for junior professorships. Right now, you'd get another post-doctoral role *at best*, and have potential employers wonder, for the rest of your career, why you hadn't been able to hack it at Oxford.'

'That's putting it a bit strongly,' he protested. It was, but really only a bit.

Her chin jerked. 'Leaving those Sedgwick letters for someone else to work on would kill you. And I don't believe you'd really be prepared to move thousands of miles from your parents right now.'

'You're right,' he said. 'As usual. I . . . missed the wood for the trees, when I heard how tough the astronomy job market is. I know I can't leave. But picture it, Halley. We're on the cusp of half a year together. We're so . . . in sync already, I can only imagine how entwined we'll be by then: we'll be desperate to stay together.'

Her gaze was fierce. 'I refuse to believe we can't figure it out. But not with you jacking-in Oxford. I refuse to accept that sacrifice.'

'I don't want to be sacrificed to, either,' he said, much more gently than he felt. 'And if you can't find a good job on this side of the pond—'

'Then we'll find a compromise, instead.' She smiled at last. When he smiled back, he was even granted a flash of dimples. 'The first step is my visiting studentship. But I'm only coming if you tell Rupert you were having a mad moment, and actually intend to see out your contract in Oxford.'

'Fair enough. I'll contact him, I promise.' He drank more lager, and her large eyes narrowed, though she was still smiling.

'Do you deserve beer, during *a bollocking*?'

'It's a longstanding British tradition!'

She laughed, and stretched out her neck. 'Thank God I get to sleep this weekend. And next week I've only got two more nights collecting data. It's the end of an era. Oh — how was the library?'

'I finished a few more letters, including one to Miss Mallory in which Lawrence described the sunset and said he would love to show it to her, if only she could somehow be beside him.'

Halley gave a wan sigh. 'If I could suddenly somehow be beside you, what would you want us to do?' She lowered her voice. 'Clearly, not anything dirty — we're both in public.'

Wishing he didn't feel his face heat whenever she surprised him with a comment like that, Henry tried to focus on the question. 'I'd have to think. Would you be here for the evening?'

'You'd want to do something that lasts longer? Then sure.' She spread her arms expansively. 'And there's no budgetary constraints, but we have to obey the laws of the universe — no magical abilities.'

'Then I'd want to stargaze with you. Somewhere really dark, like you love.'

'Snap! Maybe we could fly to Antarctica? It's late-summer there now, so that's possible, with a very experienced pilot.'

He leaned back in his seat. 'Tell me what we'd get up to.'

'It's mainly radio telescopes down there, so I'd teach you to use one, to see into deep space. Antarctica's amazing for that. It's the only place on the planet with a great view of the southern hole — this patch of clean sky, without many stars.'

'That's why the Antarctic's perfect for astronomy?'

'Partly. It's also the geographic conditions. It's a huge landmass — literally a polar desert — so it doesn't have disruptive weather patterns. And it's at a really high altitude, which means it's dry. Dark, cold and dry is pretty much stargazing perfection. So yeah, we could go there. Unless you have a better idea?'

'I do. Because if you're already beside me, I don't want us getting anywhere near another bloody aeroplane — they have it in for us. So how about we stargaze in the darkest sky site in mainland UK?'

'Somewhere in Scotland, right?' Halley ventured. 'Northerly, with minimal light pollution . . .'

Henry opened a new window, and typed the query. 'The Cairngorms,' he confirmed, as it flashed onto his screen. 'Our largest national park.'

'That would work. We could take binoculars — you can see a lot of the night sky through a decent pair.' Her gaze shifted to one side, as she found the website. 'This park looks great. Will we take a train?'

'I'll borrow Viola's car.' She owed him one, after all. God knows why she'd taken it on herself to eavesdrop on his conversation with Rupert, let alone snitch to Halley's mother. 'And I'm choosing us somewhere to stay . . .' He scrolled through options. Hotel or B&B, or . . . secluded cabins. He clicked on the latter, and found one with not only an open fire, but a hot tub outside on the decking, and beside it, something even more perfect. 'What do you think of this? Link coming through.'

'It's even more romantic than the Blue Moon. And—' Her eyes shone suddenly. 'There's a telescope on the deck — I love it! Ugh, I wish I *was* beside you, and we could go right now.'

'It's only sixteen days, sweetheart. We'll make it.'

* * *

Sunday, 12 January

> *From: Henry Inglis*
> *Subject: Update on career trajectory*
> *To: Rupert Peters*
> Dear Rupert,
>
> I hope you've had a good flight?
>
> I spoke too hastily on the job situation. I'm happy at Oxford and don't intend to seek a new position, so please don't bother making any enquiries on my behalf.
>
> Best, Henry

* * *

Monday, 13 January

> *From: Rupert Peters*
> *Subject: Update on career trajectory*
> *To: Henry Inglis*
> Pleased to hear it!
>
> Rupert

* * *

From: Henry Inglis
Subject: 14 days . . .
To: Halley Hart
Dear Halley,

I've informed Rupert that I'm happy at Oxford, as promised.

Miss Mallory must have let Lawrence know that she's told her father they're corresponding, because he's bidding her send his compliments to her mama and papa. And he's using a new valediction to close his letters to her — see below!

Only fourteen days until you arrive, and I think tomorrow's your last at the telescope? Any chance you've got time for a date, soon after?

I have the pleasure to remain your ever-loving and devoted beau, Henry xxx

* * *

Tuesday, 14 January

From: Halley Hart
Subject: 13 days . . .
To: Henry Inglis
Good Evening, Devoted Beau,

I'm seeing my advisor tomorrow morning, for him to sign-off on my new data — or insist I collect a little more. Don't panic though — worst case scenario I'd have to miss the symposium, but it shouldn't delay the visiting studentship. Let's have a date right after — 8 p.m. your time, to celebrate/ commiserate?

And I think there'll be something else to celebrate, stemming from a major breakthrough with Angelie! She's written on the refrigerator that she's heard about a potential new roommate, and he's coming to see the apartment later. I hadn't dared even raise the idea of someone taking over my lease, but not having to make rent here would go a long way to alleviating my biggest problem — being broke in England.

Love, your Halley

* * *

Halley

'Need for now,' Halley muttered, dropping the pile of underwear back in the drawer. 'Storage . . .' She threw her swimwear into a cardboard box labelled *CHICAGO*. 'And England.' She added Henry's sweater to her crammed suitcase.

Then she reconsidered the bathing suits. Southampton was a port city so there must be beaches nearby. But in February, in the Atlantic . . . she shuddered at how cold it would be. No, with space at a premium she needed to prioritize winter clothing — and *skimpy sparkling* things.

The doorbell rang and she rushed through to the hallway.

The guy on the other side of the door had the good fortune of being tall and exceptionally handsome. He'd enhanced this accident of genetics with a great haircut, white teeth and buff muscles, and Halley beamed.

'Would you mind taking your shoes off? The apartment's fantastic and Angelie's the best roommate ever. I'm only leaving to be with my boyfriend in Britain.'

He bent to remove his shoes without complaint, as Angelie exited her bedroom. She glanced at her prospective roommate, and squeaked.

'Come through and tell us about yourself, and then she'll show you around the place,' Halley said, pointing the way into the living room.

As he headed in, Angelie mouthed, 'Oh my God. He's like, exactly my type.'

Halley murmured something noncommittal — if she looked too enthusiastic, Angelie might find something to dislike about him just for the fun of it. Better to be cautious until she'd ascertained whether he studied something that would be helpful to one of Angelie's start-ups. The chances of that were pretty high, between the sheer variety of her fledgling businesses and the STEM specialisms of the majority of Stanford students.

In the living room, he stood in his socked feet in the centre of their cream rug, his shoulders back and spine straight, as though he was caught in a spotlight on stage. 'I'm Dan Elfman,' he said, enunciating every syllable. 'I'm twenty-three years old and in my second year in the graduate programme of the Theatre and Performance Studies department.'

Halley intervened quickly. 'People are so much more than just their subject, don't you think, Dan? What are your hobbies and interests?'

'Well, I founded a new ensemble last quarter, and we've got our first recital next week.'

'What kind of music?' Angelie asked.

A terrible suspicion dawned on Halley. 'Does it matter if you share a taste in music, though?'

Angelie rounded on her. 'I've heard you state that every roommate you've ever had has listened to great music — whether they like it or not.'

'I can't help having excellent taste in music,' Halley shot back. 'If I didn't, I'd wear headphones. Like Dan will, if you don't like Dan's. Right, Dan?'

Their heads swivelled toward him in tandem. 'Sure,' he said, with the utmost confidence. 'Except when I'm practising piano.'

Halley pressed her fingers to her temples, and Angelie breathed so heavily her nostrils flared. Dan seemed oblivious to the appalled silence, as he smiled between the two of them.

'Piano,' Angelie repeated.

'I'm happy to have it in my bedroom — that's more convenient when I get up early to practise. Though — don't worry — not too early! I sing as I play, so I wait until about seven, after my cup of hot water with lemon.' He smiled again. 'This is fun! What else can I tell you about myself? My vocal part is tenor and my range is up to A4. Anything else you can think of?'

Angelie looked at Halley. 'What else can we think of, Halley?' Never had a question sounded so much like a threat.

'I've got nothing,' Halley said, sinking lower into the couch.

'But I do,' Angelie said. 'I don't think we've established what genres of music it is that you play and sing, Dan?'

'*And* I dance,' he said. 'Tap, and jazz.' He splayed his hands and shook them. *'Jazz hands,'* he warbled. Angelie snatched up a cushion and smashed her face into it. 'But I mainly sing show tunes. Musicals are my passion.'

* * *

Wednesday, 15 January
Henry

'An actor sounds ideal, though,' Henry said, planting his elbows on his office desk. The only illumination came from his laptop screen, as the overhead light bulb had blown as he switched it on. 'He'd be great at covering for her, when she gets herself in a pickle with all those start-ups she cheats on.'

'Henry, he's literally specializing in the development of musical theatre,' Halley said. 'And Angelie hates musicals. *And* jazz hands, which she finds creepy almost to the point of a phobia.'

Henry scratched his jaw, wondering if it would be too unsympathetic to enquire into the logistics of a phobia of jazz hands. Was it any deliberate movement of raised hands, or only when accompanied by a musical performance? 'Is she aware of anyone else actively looking for a place, instead?'

'Not yet,' Halley said, heaving out a sigh. 'But we're telling Dan no, anyway. I mean, I don't mind musical theatre, but I wouldn't want to live with him either. Though maybe that was the puns. At the end he started singing "Piano

Man ", but with the words changed to Piano *Dan*. Angelie had sprinted to her bathroom and locked the door by that stage, so I interrupted to inform him she was sick. Then he pouted and went, "*Don't you want to listen to the rest of the song? It's my danthem! Get it? My anthem because I'm Dan!*" Henry,' she added darkly. 'Are you *laughing*?'

'No,' Henry said, working harder than he ever had to maintain a straight face, as he pictured Dan, singing at two blisteringly clever, and utterly unimpressed, women. 'It's bad luck — I know you're worried about money.'

She slumped on her sofa. 'I shouldn't have gone on about that. Don't freak out about sacrifices again! The main cause was giving up my TA role, and that was to get PhDone this year, and nothing to do with our relationship.'

All the hours she'd spent corresponding with him, back in the autumn, couldn't have helped that situation, but he didn't say so, instead leading them into smoother waters. 'I'm so chuffed to hear your advisor's pleased with your data.'

Halley's mouth turned up a little at the edges. '*Chuffed*. And yeah, Professor Tung's approval means a lot. Hey, I've been meaning to ask about Halley-Anne. What was the podcast thing?'

He grimaced, explaining briefly about the scambaiting podcast, and her plan to have one of them as a guest — or to read out the email he'd sent to every Halley Hart in the world. 'She hadn't thought through that while she could change my name, yours would be obvious, given it's the same as hers.'

Halley's expression was more contemplative than concerned. 'I mean, she could have gone ahead and featured the email without asking permission. It's nice of her to check. And she was trying to help you find me, right? We kinda owe her one.'

'You want us to *go on her podcast*?'

'Not especially, but we could consider it, so give her my number?'

'Halley, she's suggesting I do a *snappy turn on the history of romance scams*,' he spluttered.

'I won't commit you to anything, I promise,' Halley said, when she'd stopped laughing.

Henry wanted to protest, but he wasn't even sure why it bothered him so much, and his attention was suddenly seized by something in the darkness beyond his dormer window. A bird, heading for the glass, or no, he thought, rising. They were pale shoes, scrabbling to find purchase, below denim-clad legs. An instant later the idiot had gone, but he'd distinctly seen him or her scramble to one side — so they hadn't fallen, at least.

'Sorry, sweetheart — duty calls,' he said, pushing his feet into his trainers. 'The climber's at it again, and made it onto the roof. I'll call you back in half an hour!'

Without waiting for a reply, he opened the window, held onto the frame, and leaped out.

PART TWELVE

Halley

Henry had distinctly said half an hour before he jumped out of the window.

Henry had distinctly said half an hour before he jumped out of the window, *thirty-five minutes ago*.

Halley paced into her bedroom, keeping her laptop open. Henry had forgotten to cancel the call, so an almost entirely static image of his oddly-shaped college office remained on her screen. She had confirmation that it was live, and hadn't frozen, every sixty seconds, when the slender minute-hand moved on the clock hanging on the far wall, between an exposed wooden beam and the slope of the ceiling. She stared at the open window. At least if there'd been a drape at it, she could watch to check it didn't flutter, and perhaps soothe her anxiety over whether it was windy out. Though rain or frost would be even worse.

Henry's office was built into the roof, but he'd never specified how many floors were below him, and she couldn't quite recall from her visit to St Jude's. Screwing her eyes shut, she saw the building in her mind's eye, and counted the sets of windows . . . but the mental image wasn't clear enough for her to be sure, beyond that the building was at least four storeys high, and possibly five.

She collapsed onto her bed, thinking hard. There was a calculation for measuring the lethal dose of any given substance, called median lethal dose, or LD50. Somewhere, she'd once come across the LD50 for falls from heights, which was forty-eight feet. At that distance, there's a fifty percent chance of survival — or of lethal injury. And an average storey was maybe ten to twelve feet . . .

She buried her head in her pillow.

'Uh, Halley?'

She sat bolt upright.

Henry was in his desk chair, his head tilted. 'Do you feel all right?'

'No! I thought you were dead . . .'

'Why?' he asked, looking bemused.

'Because you climbed out of a four or five storey window, in the dark, when it's probably windy or rainy or frosty, and you didn't come in again for thirty-six minutes!'

'There's a fire escape leading down from the roof — I wasn't shinning drainpipes.'

'Oh.' Her pulse slowing, she scrubbed at her face. 'I didn't know. What happened?'

'Unfortunately the miscreant *was* shinning drainpipes — and hopping between windows, and then he scarpered round the side of the building. By the time I sprinted round there, he was gone, and I had to report it all to the bursar before I could get back to you. Halley, you've gone as pale as anything. You really thought I'd jump out of a window?'

The adrenaline was wearing off, and she felt exhausted. 'Can we please change the subject?'

'Of course,' he said, glancing around. 'It looks like the packing's going well. How many of those boxes are for the UK?'

'Literally none. Shipping's too expensive, so I'm only bringing my essentials,' she said, glad of something practical to focus on. She explained that Mom would bring more of her stuff, in late February, and described her system: two large suitcases and one small, to take on the plane, and everything else in boxes, ready for the drive to Mom's.

Henry looked confused. 'Drive?'

'Hadn't I mentioned? I'm setting out on Sunday for Chicago.'

Henry spluttered, coughed, then cleared his throat. 'You're driving all the way from California to Chicago? That's three-quarters of the way across a continent!'

She compressed her lips. 'I've done it before, and can assure you it's a lot safer than jumping out of windows.'

'I'll take your word for it.' Henry sounded dubious, and she eyed him sceptically. If he tried to mansplain the perils of road-trips, she'd . . . well she didn't know what she'd do, but it wouldn't be pretty. But he let it drop, pulling something from a desk drawer. 'I've got a copy of Lawrence's next letter to Miss Mallory, and it finally reveals her name.'

'I've been wondering about that! What is it?'

'Christobel. He's written a few lines of verse, and rhymed it with *heart swell.*'

Despite her lingering annoyance, Halley couldn't help but laugh. 'My dearest Christobel, how you make my heart swell?'

Henry grinned. 'Not far off. It's *my heart does swell, for my Christobel.*'

'Cute! Though the swelling thing — could that be him hinting, like . . . euphemistically, how another part of his body reacts to her?'

Henry laughed, but he also, faintly, coloured. She didn't feel guilty. He had made her think he was *dead.*

'It's unlikely that a gentleman of the period would dare hint at such to a young lady. Nelson and Emma Hamilton had some racy bits in their letters, but they were very much the exception to the rule.' Something started to ring, and he lifted the handset on the landline phone beside him then immediately replaced it, cancelling the call. 'Sorry about that.' The phone rang again right away, and he scowled at it.

'Get it. It's fine,' she said.

He acquiesced with visible reluctance. 'Henry Inglis here? . . . It's not ideal timing, to be honest.' He listened again, then ground out, 'Very well. I'll be along shortly.'

'Where you gotta go?' she asked, as he hung up.

'The bursar called the Dean, who insists on hearing my full account immediately.'

'I need to continue packing, anyway. Henry? Only twelve days until we're together. Until then, my heart swells for you.'

'My heart swells for you too, Halley,'

She leaned into her laptop, giving him a sultry smile. 'Would that be your heart or your *heart*?' she asked huskily. Her expectation was that he'd laugh again, and hopefully blush some more.

Instead, he levelled a look at her that made her heart skip a beat, and her toes curl. 'God,' he said fervently. 'Both, sweetheart.'

* * *

Thursday, 16 January

From: Henry Inglis
Subject: 11 days . . .
To: Halley Hart

Good Morning, sweetheart,

I'm gutted I had to cut our date short like that. And interrupt it part way through. And that I worried you. The universe got retribution for you, in the form of the Dean making me scour CCTV footage to try to identify the miscreant. I'm not sure if she's angrier that he made it all the way up to the rooftop, or that he had the temerity to run across the grass when he was fleeing.

Hope the packing and presentation-prep are going OK?

Halley, are you driving to Chicago because money's too tight for the flight? If so, would you consider letting me pay for it?

With all devotion to the love of my life, (and all due credit to Lawrence Sedgwick!) *your ever true*, Henry xxx

* * *

Friday, 17 January

From: Halley Hart
Subject: 10 days!
To: Henry Inglis

Dear ever-true Henry,

I get that driving over two thousand miles cross-country sounds insane to you. But I can't accept your generous offer. I'm not letting you waste your savings. And if I did, I'd have to pay to get my boxes shipped to Chicago, and quickly sell my car here in California, rather than leaving it with Mom, who'll get a good price for it and send me the money.

I really appreciate your generosity in offering, and I'm sure I'll happily accept it when it comes to picking up restaurant checks, if you want us eating out anyplace fancy in the next half a year. *Half a year*, Henry — starting in 10 days!! And yes, Packing is DONE and my presentation's nearly there!

Did I tell you Mom won't even be there while I'm in Chicago? I'll have the house to myself, because she's on that wellness retreat again, and couldn't switch out the dates. I'm trying not to be offended that she hasn't just cancelled, since she swore never to go someplace where they enforce a digital detox ever again . . .

Love, your Halley

* * *

From: Henry Inglis
Subject: 9 days . . .
To: Halley Hart
Dear Halley,

You clearly have a lot of excellent reasons for embarking on that mammoth drive. Do me a favour, and execute it as competently as you do everything else? And please update me on your progress — I've just been to Blackwell's for a large map of the continental US, so I can follow your route.

Lawrence's last few letters have repeated his previous valedictions, so I've relied on my memory — and sub-par French translation skills — to take inspiration from one of Napoleon Bonaparte's letter endings to his wife, Josephine. Laurence Sedgwick's favourite phrase when writing to his brother is *death to Boney*, so he wouldn't at all approve!

Soon I will hold you in my arms and lavish you with a million kisses, Henry xxx

* * *

Halley

Angelie was holed up in their living room, with an entirely new group of collaborators — plus Ben, who was flat on his back on their couch, eating grapes right from the stalk, like some Roman Emperor.

Angelie glanced up from her laptop, which was balanced on the coffee table. 'Is it urgent?'

'Kinda time-sensitive,' Halley said. 'Given I, y'know, leave at dawn tomorrow.' Since Dan, Angelie had relented on communicating only via the refrigerator, but she'd also booked herself solid with start-up meetings.

'We'll be done in a few minutes,' Angelie said. 'I'll come find you.'

Halley had heard variations on that theme several times already, and Angelie had always had something more pressing arise before their conversation could commence.

'Cool,' Halley said. 'I'll wait.' She slid to the floor in the corner, her legs crossed.

'You gonna allow that?' one of the newbies asked.

Halley wondered the same thing, as Angelie stared at her.

'Just pretend she's not there,' Angelie said eventually. 'She signed a confidentiality agreement.'

Taken by surprise, Halley bit the inside of her cheeks to keep from laughing. Angelie had come up with the mythical legal contract to persuade her teams that her apartment was the safest place for them to meet, so she could minimize commuting time.

'It's not like we've got any intellectual property Halley could steal yet anyway,' Ben said, flicking the grape stalk into the trash before opening a bag of chips. 'Nor a mission statement. Not even a name.'

'We've got a unique concept,' a thin guy snapped. 'And is it worth the risk—'

'We're aiming to connect people who want to grow their own produce but don't have a backyard with small businesses with green space they're not using,' Angelie said, with impatience. 'What would Halley do with that?'

'Nothing,' Halley said. 'Even if I wanted to. Or your terrifyingly competent lawyer would sue me for a million bucks.'

That seemed to mollify the newbies, and it also made Angelie's mouth twitch. 'Let's get on with the name,' she said, calling everyone back to attention. 'Anyone got something better than Fruitful and Cherry-pick, or shall we vote between those?' She only allowed them two seconds, before steaming on. 'I say Cherry-pick, with the tagline of something like: *growing spaces exchanged for the fruits of your labour.*'

'Seconded,' Ben said.

Everyone else raised their hands in agreement with various levels of enthusiasm, and Angelie banged the coffee table as though she was holding a judge's gavel. 'Then dismissed. See you same time, same place, next weekend, Cherry-pickers.'

She didn't move as the others filtered out, so Halley joined her at the coffee table, opting to sit beside her, rather than opposite, and flipping open her notebook to her list. Almost everything was ticked off or crossed out.

'I don't have space in the car for my lamps, pans and dishes, and all my plants. I can leave them for you, or—'

'It's fine to leave them.'

Halley scored through *Go to Goodwill*. 'I'll dispose of my food this evening—'

'Don't bother. Ben can eat it.'

As Halley crossed off another chore, Angelie spun the notebook away. 'Can you stop that? We need to talk about the stuff that really matters.'

Halley retrieved it, but didn't open it again. 'Go ahead.'

Angelie's nostrils flared. 'I tried being angry about you leaving, to make it stop hurting. Then I went for replacing you, ditto. These past few days, I've been all but sticking my fingers in my ears and shouting loud, like a kid who doesn't want to hear bad news. But you're leaving anyway, and it still hurts.'

Halley shoved her hands into the pockets of her hoodie and made fists. 'I get that. I'm sorry.'

'I hate you for leaving, but I also love you,' Angelie said. 'You know that, right?'

It hurt to smile at her. 'I love you too.'

'But not as much as you love Henry.'

'I'm coming to suspect,' Halley said, in a voice that didn't sound quite like her own, 'that I'll never love anyone as much as I do Henry.'

Angelie rounded on her. 'You're giving up everything to be with a guy you spent considerably less than one day with, four months ago.'

'Yup.'

In response to her steady gaze, Angelie seemed to relent, and scooched in closer. 'You've only kissed him once. What if the chemistry's not there?'

Please sleep in my bed?

'I'm scared about a hell of a lot of things right now,' Halley said, entirely honestly. 'But not that one.'

* * *

Voice note from Viola for Henry:

Henry, Mum's on her way to hospital in an ambulance. Or maybe they're still waiting for it to arrive. Sorry, I don't . . . the carer was upset, and not very clear on the phone, except that she thought it was a stroke. Can you come? Straight to the hospital, probably. Or maybe one of us needs to go to Dad at home. I don't know. Fuck . . . I'm shaking. Just get on the next train. I'll be there in under an hour and I'll update you then.

* * *

Sunday, 19 January
Halley

A journey of 2161 miles began with a 1.7 mile hop. Halley undertook it pre-dawn, to avoid the traffic that would build up around San Francisco later in the morning. Once she merged onto the highway, the navigation was simple with the I-80 spanning the six states she had to cross to reach Illinois, and home.

'California,' she said into the silence. 'Nevada, Utah, Nebra— no, *Wyoming*, Nebraska, Iowa, Illinois.'

The only prior time she'd done this trip had been in her last car, and travelling in the opposite direction. She hadn't told Henry that Mom had accompanied her, and shared the driving, before flying home. Or that they'd taken a longer, more scenic route as a proper road trip, over the course of nearly two weeks, stopping off at multiple destinations. And she definitely hadn't confessed that she was nervous about it. If she'd admitted that, it would only have increased his worry. But the confidence she'd projected in her ability to complete the journey safely was genuine: it was the sheer monotony of it that concerned her.

On the scale of things to stress out about, however, a boring four day journey ranked pretty low. Topmost was the fact that in only eight days she'd be on the plane, readying herself to be reunited with Henry. And as he'd correctly pointed out, planes had it in for them. But she'd grit her teeth and put up with anything the journey threw at her to get safely into his arms. Then his sister's car, for the drive up the M40 to the Blue Moon — with Henry beside her, through it all. Picturing that cascade of upcoming events always triggered an entirely different sort of nerves in her.

But before that, there was the presentation to contend with. Her stomach writhed every time she thought about it. And this dumb journey on a boring highway didn't help. She indicated to overtake a truck, then moved back to the right, her eyes darting between her mirrors and the road ahead. Then, because nothing was more boring than thinking about boredom, she started some music, and sang along, out of tune, bothering no one's ears but her own.

* * *

Henry

Henry shifted on the plastic moulded seat in the waiting area, where he was sandwiched between Viola and his father. Dad was as immaculate as ever, in a three-piece suit, complete with silk pocket square, but every time anyone ventured down the corridor towards them he held hard onto his stick and levered himself to his feet, only sitting again when they didn't prove to be coming from intensive care, with news of his wife. During these bouts of parental distraction, Viola released soundless tears, which she caught with the edge of her sleeve, before dropping her arm to her side and turning her face slightly, as Dad sat down. He didn't approve of *snivelling*, as he tended to dub it.

Henry could bear the tension no longer, and jumped up. 'Can I get either of you a drink?'

'No, thank you,' Dad said stiffly.

'Sure,' Viola muttered, before biting her lip, probably against the threat of a sob.

'Tea, coffee, water?' he asked.

'Anything,' she breathed.

Dad was moving again, and Henry turned sharply to check the corridor. But no one was in sight, and Dad was reaching for his pocket square, rather than his stick. He shook it out and leaned over, wordlessly pressing it into Viola's hand.

* * *

Text messages between Mom and Halley:

> *Heading off on my retreat now, Junior. Drive safe, stay alert, and don't forget to bring your house key. Oh, and check out the deepfreeze for some batch cooking. Love you.*

> > *Love you too, Mom. Hope the retreat's more fun than last time! And don't worry about my key, it's in the car, along with everything else I own.*

* * *

Halley

Halley shifted her eyes to the clock on the dashboard, then away again, fist pumping internally. It was finally, *finally*, 10 a.m. — the self-imposed time before which she couldn't call

Henry. She wondered about drawing out her anticipation by waiting a little longer, then rejected the idea.

'Hey, Siri, call Henry,' she said.

'Calling Henry,' returned the disembodied voice of the digital assistant. It was replaced by a ringtone, which cut out after a split second.

'Halley?' he said, sounding like he was gasping for air. 'Is everything OK?'

'Of course it is. How about you — long day in the library?'

'Library?' he repeated. 'Didn't you get my message?'

'Umm . . . last I heard from you was an email yesterday?'

There was a rustling sound. 'Ugh, I see what happened. I wrote you a text last night, but it hasn't gone through. Rubbish connection in the . . .' He cleared his throat. 'I'd explained I might be a bit . . . tied up, so to message me rather than calling, unless it was an emergency. Which is why I panicked, when you called.'

'Definitely no emergency,' she said. 'I'm totally fine. What's come up to make you so busy?'

'Uh . . . long story, and I'm not somewhere that I can really talk. But there's nothing for you to worry about — focus on prepping for your drive.'

'You're behind the times. I'm about to pass Reno.'

'You're driving now?'

'Of course. Early starts are essential, because although it's eight hours a day, that's only the literal driving — breaks are on top of—'

'You shouldn't be on the phone while you're driving on a motorway!'

'Don't talk to me like I'm an idiot, Henry!' She inhaled slowly, then breathed out for three, not speaking again until she'd regained control. 'And rest assured, I'm on hands-free.'

'Talking's still a distraction!'

'Not so much as you being crabby!' Halley snapped back. There was silence.

'You're right,' Henry said eventually. 'And as I said, I can't really talk.' He sounded detached, rather than apologetic. 'So I'm hanging up now.'

And then he was gone. Before she could force out of him whatever he was reluctant to explain. And she couldn't even call back, now she knew he only wanted to hear about emergencies.

'Fucking hell,' Halley muttered.

'I didn't quite understand that,' Siri said.

'And you can fuck off, too,' Halley added viciously.

'Now, now,' Siri said.

PART THIRTEEN

Text messages from Henry to Halley:

*You called me crabby, and you were right, Halley.
I love you and am sorry. xxx*

*Halley, I shouldn't have got so angry. You probably
need to tick me off before you can consider forgiving
me, and that's fine. I'll keep an eye on messages xxx*

* * *

Monday, 20 January

Text messages between Halley and Henry:

*I didn't purposefully ignore your apology last night,
Henry. I read it, started figuring how to reply, then
fell asleep early. I'm setting off from my motel
now, but I'll check my messages at my first gas
stop. x*

> *So pleased to hear from you, sweetheart. Vid-call
> me when you stop for the night, however late? And
> drive safe. xxx*

238

That'll be at least 3 a.m. your time though? x

Not a problem. Stay safe! xxx

* * *

Henry

There was an insistent buzz. He was vaguely aware it meant something important, but he was knackered after forty-eight hours waiting at the hospital and—

He instantly threw back the duvet and sat up. Mum was in hospital, having suffered a stroke, and the intensive care team had promised to call with any updates.

Only, Viola's landline wasn't ringing. It was the alert for an incoming video call on his laptop. Which meant Halley.

He pressed to accept it, rubbing his eyes. Then he glanced at the screen, where Halley appeared to be upside down. He rubbed his eyes harder still, but she remained upside down, her hair trailing on a purple mat.

Her voice was muffled. 'Do you mind about this? I'm so stiff, if I don't do some stretches I'll be in agony in the morning.' He tilted his head, working out that her knees were in the foreground, with her head behind them. She had folded over from her hips, then, and flattened her soles and palms against the mat. 'I'm sorry we fell out,' she added. 'I know you've been anxious about my drive.'

'You've nothing to apologize for,' he said, recalling the good old days, when he was merely anxious about her drive. Since Mum's collapse, anxiety had strengthened into sheer terror — not helped by witnessing a paramedic running a comatose patient into A&E, yelling that her car had crashed with a lorry. 'My . . . heebie-jeebies aren't your problem, Halley.'

She squinted at him. 'Where are you?'

'Viola's sofa. I came down because Mum wasn't feeling great and stayed because Aron arrived to surprise Viola, but everything's under control now.' None of it was a lie — and

239

all a pale reflection of the truth. Halley had enough on her plate so he refused to add to her distractions.

'That's what you didn't want to tell me while I was driving? And you promise your mom's OK now?'

'I texted you about it almost immediately,' he said, deliberately only answering her first question. 'But I took the fact that the text didn't go through as a message from the cosmos, that it wasn't the moment to let you know.' Before she could ask for more details, he added quickly, 'Tell me about the drive?'

'It's boring,' she said, remaining upside down. 'And I'm only halfway there. Can I really not persuade you to chat while I drive? Pretend I'm not your Halley, if it helps. Just some random bored Halley.'

He laughed a little. 'The last thing I want to imagine is you being some random girl to me. You're the love of my life!'

She glowered at him. 'Dr Henry Inglis, why would you make a declaration like that *when I'm upside down*?'

'I'm sure I've told you that before?'

'Only as a sign-off in an email, quoting Lawrence Sedgwick,' she said, finally righting herself. Her face was rosy and her hair an insane mess.

'You're beautiful,' he said impulsively. 'And I've never told you anything I don't mean, even with borrowed valedictions.' Their eyes locked, and the intensity stretched between them. He was sure she was also thinking *a million kisses*. But he was on his sister's sofa, so he cleared his throat, as Halley dimpled at him, then resumed her stretching.

With her back straight, she reached to her right. 'There's something up with you . . . is your mom really—'

His heart thudding, he intervened. 'I had a nightmare about all the hazards of your journey.' It was true, as it happened.

Switching to stretch to her left, Halley rolled her eyes. 'Do you need me to list all my risk-mitigations? No — you list the hazards, and I'll answer with how I've mitigated against them.'

'Some idiot crashing into you, or your car breaking down in the middle of nowhere,' he blurted.

'I keep a large braking distance, and don't speed. Plus, I have a spare tyre, tools, and I changed my oil before I left. I've got plenty of bottled water to top up the radiator if the engine overheats. And I'm subscribed to the top-rated roadside assistance plan. Keep 'em coming . . .'

'Bad weather?'

She centred herself and swooped both arms up towards the ceiling, palms together and fingertips extended. 'I've got antifreeze, an ice scraper, and a small shovel, in case there's snow when I'm parked up overnight. But I'll stop if there's any sign of a storm, and wait it out in a motel.'

'I suppose tiredness is the other major hazard.'

'I've got cans of iced coffee for when I can't get the real stuff, and packets of hard candy. You know you can't fall asleep with something in your mouth? It's an instinct, to keep from choking.'

'I can't think of any more,' Henry said, feeling calmer. Halley had this.

'Well, I can,' she said indignantly. 'Risk, dazzle from the sun — then flip down the visor, and wear the sunglasses my boyfriend posted back to me. Risk, injury — I have a well-stocked first aid kit. Risk, getting too stiff to have good response times the next day — this yoga mat. Risk, not being near a gas station when I need to pee — I have a she-wee.'

Henry debated enquiring what a she-wee was, and got another flash of Halley's dimples. 'Ask Viola,' she said. 'Has all that made you feel better?'

Even as he assured her it had, he had another thought. 'How much can you do about personal safety, though?'

'Keep my doors locked. Avoid sketchy motels. Only give rides to hitchhikers with a kind demeanour and clean fingernails.'

'Halley!'

241

'Fine, sorry.' She switched her overhead light off and his screen became shades of grey and silver. 'Remember, I've been driving since I was fifteen, repairing cars since I was twelve, and absorbing street smarts since I was conscious of my surroundings in Chicago. Thanks to living in Stanford, I even know what to do if I encounter a mountain lion this trip — I read up about it, when they were sighted on the road to the observatory.'

He hadn't even known he needed to panic about mountain lions. But Halley missed his expression, turning away to pile pillows together. 'Update me on your mom?'

'I'd honestly rather talk about anything else,' he said gently. 'What about *your* mum? Were you genuinely upset she didn't cancel the retreat, to wave you off?'

She flopped onto the pillows. 'No. Or, maybe a little? It's complicated, because it ties in with something that's bothered me for a really long time.' She lowered her voice. 'Is there any risk at all that Viola can hear us?'

'She's not even here.'

'OK. Just . . . I've never told anyone this. When I was eighteen, I accidentally overheard Mom talking to a friend, who asked why she'd been single since my dad died. I knew I shouldn't continue listening, but I'd never known her even to casually date, and suddenly, like, desperately wanted to know the answer. Anyway, her friend pushed her a bit, and Mom said—' she broke off and bit her lower lip.

'You don't have to tell me,' Henry whispered

'I want to.' She inhaled slowly. 'She said, when Dad was dying, and she was facing raising me as a hard-up single Mom in an inner-city, she swore two things. To stay in college and get her nursing license, so she could provide for me. And to stay single, because . . . the biggest risk-factor for a kid — especially a fatherless girl — being like, groomed or whatever, was sharing a home with a man who wasn't a blood relative. Can you imagine how guilty I felt?'

Henry chose his words carefully. 'Some might say that was her choice, not something for you to carry.'

'I tried to tell myself that, but it didn't help. Especially as I'd already accepted the place nearby, at Northwestern, and during my four years there she still didn't date. So I applied to grad schools as far away from Illinois as possible . . . I didn't only choose Stanford because it was my furthest offer from home, but I didn't exactly not, either. I even broke up with someone in the process — he wanted me to go to Florida, where he was headed — but he was no loss.'

He remembered the text that had intrigued him, when he was rushing through the airport. 'Would that be that one ex we all regret?'

'Exactly. When he didn't get a Stanford offer and I did, he tried to talk me out of going by saying I wouldn't fit in.'

'What an absolute arsehole.'

'Yeah. Mom never liked him. The first time they met she told me he stole my light, and I should have listened . . . Anyway, I got to Stanford determined to be independent, and not go home too often, giving Mom the space to find some happiness, y'know? But she still doesn't date, and the only difference in her routine is the vacations she takes with Aunt Edie. I keep hoping she'll meet someone through one of those. So I certainly didn't want her to cancel a retreat in Arizona where she could meet a hot cowboy or something.' Her sudden levity ended as quickly as it had begun. 'Henry?'

'Yes, sweetheart?'

'That's haunted me my whole adult life. That Mom's lonely because of me. Have you had anything like that, that weighs on you when you try to sleep?'

He closed his eyes for a moment, unable to think of anything beyond what was happening at the hospital. But it wasn't exactly what she was asking. And if she was as upset by it as he suspected she would be, she'd be in no fit state for another two days solo driving. So he delved deeper, into the things he'd never expressed to anyone. 'For a long time,' he said eventually, in an undertone, 'I worried that I wasn't capable of the kind of love my parents share. There's this . . . indefinable strength to it that made them prioritize each other, over and over again. From the beginning, when Mum turned her back on music to live on seventeen different RAF barracks in twenty years, to . . . now, when Dad limps three flights of stairs to bring Mum her morning tea, because he thinks moving out of the bedroom she's known for twenty years would distress her.'

Halley shifted the phone as she rolled onto her side. 'Keep going. I'm listening.'

He inflated his lungs. 'All my relationships fizzled out, after one date or five or a dozen at most. It became a running joke during my Ph.D. years — *Henry specializes in such amicable break-ups that his exes end up dating his friends.* But I only managed that because I never felt deeply enough to be hurt that it was ending. And then I got to Oxford and it happened again, with Gabrielle and Julian, so I stopped dating. It didn't seem worth the hassle, when I wasn't capable of the kind of love that meant something.' He swallowed, and smiled. 'Until you.'

'So, not caring deeply enough isn't . . . uh . . .'

'Isn't something I've spent even a second worrying about with you, Halley. Do you doubt it?'

She met his smile, at that. 'I don't. Though I'm envious you've got rid of your haunting fear that triggers insomnia.'

'It was replaced by a new one,' he said wryly. 'Which is stupid and superstitious and I've already told you about — in an email after our abortive efforts to be reunited at Christmas.'

'The thing about Halley's comet being a once in a lifetime event? Because it's only my name. Nothing will stop me coming to you, I promise.'

'Logically, I know that.'

'Like I know that Mom's ultimately responsible for her own happiness,' Halley said, yawning. 'Which I can never quite believe, late at night . . .'

'Exactly,' he whispered, absorbing every detail of Halley's face. Her eyes started to close. Then they sprang open. 'Sleep,' he breathed. 'It's fine.' Her lids lowered again.

Please stay safe. Please come soon. Please don't be once in my lifetime. He wasn't sure if he was thinking it at her, or praying.

'Please don't be eaten by a mountain lion,' he whispered, for good measure, before he clicked to end the call.

* * *

Text message from Henry to Halley:

Sleep tight, my love.

* * *

Tuesday, 21 January

Text messages between Halley and Henry:

I can't believe you woke up in the middle of the night for me, and I fell asleep on you — so sorry!

>*Don't give it another thought — concentrate on driving safely!*

Always do! Stop worrying. You wanna know something?

>*Of course?*

Right before I left, I told Angelie I'm starting to think I'll never love anyone as much as I love you. Which I guess means you're probably the love of my life, too. x

>*That makes me so happy, sweetheart. How you feel, and that you and Angelie are talking again. I'll see you in six days! And please drive safely xxx*

You'll be asleep now, but I just arrived at motel #3 so it's the last night on the road, woohoo!

* * *

245

He opened the drinks cabinet and inspected the dusty bottles dubiously. 'Move these to a kitchen cupboard, you reckon?'

Viola glanced over. 'Hell, no. Empty them into the sink, then chuck them in the recycling bin. Dad said to get rid of everything we need to.'

'Of everything we need to, to get the dining room set up as a bedroom. There are space for these in—'

'He said anything can go, beyond some specific bits and bobs which I moved to the lounge before you got here.' Viola was using the tone that brooked no argument. 'Everything else we keep only makes it harder to downsize them once this place is sold. You know he's backtracking already, now Mum's turned the corner?'

'Seriously?' Henry paused with three bottles in each hand.

'Yup. Saying a bungalow will be perfect for them, when yesterday he was assuring us he knows it's time for sheltered accommodation.'

'Could we help him find a bungalow within some sort of sheltered housing complex?'

'Even so, the less stuff they have, the easier it'll be — so we're clearing this room out entirely.'

Henry wandered away to follow her instructions with the bottles. As Campari sloshed down the sink, he took the opportunity to check his phone, though Halley should still be asleep. There were no new messages, but he thumbed a quick one to her, requesting she let him know when she got to Chicago, however late.

When he returned to the dining room, Viola was removing glasses from the cupboard at the bottom of the drinks cabinet and rolling them in newspaper before setting them inside a cardboard box.

'Didn't they get those as wedding presents?' he asked.

Her sigh was pure exasperation. 'Only the Waterford tumblers, and I put those safely away already. The rest of it never gets used, so we're packing this box in my car, and you're dropping it off at the charity shop, along with the rug, the terrible painting and the pair of ceramic dogs, while I post photos of the furniture on Marketplace. Got a problem with that?'

'*Nooo,*' he said promptly, glancing at the box. 'Can I have the wine glasses and champagne flutes though? I've been meaning to buy some before Halley gets here. She had to toast with a mug at Christmas.'

She shrugged. 'Sure, if you take over packing them.' When they'd switched places, she posed the chairs around the table ready for photographs. 'So, Halley still arrives Monday evening?'

'Of course. Unless her flight's delayed, which knowing our luck it invariably will be.'

'You've been quieter about her, lately . . .'

Ever since Halley informed him that her mother was gossiping with Viola, he'd felt uncomfortable mentioning his girlfriend at all, for fear of fuelling it. But he couldn't address that when they were both raw from several days of teetering on the precipice of grief. So he made a noncommittal sound, and returned to wrapping glasses.

But he was aware that Viola's gaze remained on him, and eventually she spoke again. 'Also, when I came to think about it, I was a little surprised she didn't fly over sooner, to support you, when . . . y'know . . .'

When we thought Mum would die from that massive stroke, he thought grimly. 'That wasn't an option. She was in the middle of literally packing her whole life up to relocate over here — via Chicago, where she's speaking at a massive conference tomorrow.'

'I mean . . . it was pretty much impossible for Aron,' Viola said. 'He'd just touched down in Reykjavik, when I told him. But he rushed back anyway.'

'How long can he stay?' Henry asked cautiously. His right hand was still recovering from the enthusiastic wrenching the giant considered a handshake.

'At least a week. And on that . . . are you under pressure to rush back to work — I know term-time's tricky?'

'Thanks to that double teaching load last term, I'm pretty flexible at the moment.' When he emailed Rupert to explain his absence he'd copied in Hogshoo for good order, and even that old grump hadn't kicked up a fuss about a week's compassionate leave. 'Why don't you make the most of it, and sneak off with Aron until Monday?'

She looked torn. 'I'd worry about Mum.'

'I'll let you know if you're needed, but you've got to pace yourself.'

'I know. Fine — I'll make myself scarce with Aron, then take over here once you go back to Oxford. I can get Aron shifting their bedroom furniture down the stairs.'

'Excellent idea,' Henry said.

Viola stepped over and hugged him. 'You're really OK if I step back this week? I'll worry about you, too, without any support. I still don't understand Halley not coming early — and yes, I know she's got stuff on, but I can't imagine anything stopping you from flying out to her, if the tables were turned.'

Henry hesitated. He didn't want Viola to be offish with Halley when she arrived. And Halley Senior was on her digital-detox retreat, so Viola couldn't snitch to her at present. 'I haven't exactly told Halley how serious it was, yet.'

'*What?*'

'I couldn't risk upsetting her when she was on her road trip. And she's got this huge presentation to get through. The morning after that, I'll explain everything.'

Viola blinked. Then she blew out so heavily that a stray curl bounced. Finally, she folded her arms and regarded him like a recalcitrant schoolboy. 'You're going to be in *so much trouble*, little brother.'

* * *

Handwritten note from Mom:

SORRY NOT TO BE HERE TO GREET YOU, JUNIOR. HOPE THE PRESENTATION GOES WELL IN THE MORNING — I'LL BE THINKING OF YOU. AND CHECK OUT THE

DEEPFREEZE — THERE'S PLENTY OF FOOD!
LOVE MOM

* * *

Text messages between Halley and Henry:

I made it to Chicago — tired but all in one piece!
x

> *Thanks for letting me know, sweetheart! What are you up to this evening?*

Quelling my nerves for tomorrow with pizza! I've ordered enough for a family of 4, despite passive-aggressive reminders from Mom to help myself to her batch cooking . . . she must be on a new health kick.

> *Maybe she's left you something delicious? And it's natural to be nervous about presenting, but for what it's worth, I've never seen you unable to complete something you set out to do. Even that bloody drive. Sleep tight, and enjoy the pizza! xxx*

Thanks, babe. And hey — ONLY FIVE DAYS!

* * *

Thursday, 23 January
Halley

Halley had demolished leftover pizza for breakfast, and it had given her a stomach ache. It wasn't helpful, minutes away from presenting the work she'd dedicated five years of her life to. But her audience wouldn't be huge, with under three hundred people currently streaming into the auditorium for the first talk of the day. She just needed to calm herself down before going out there, with deep breathing exercises and sips of cold water and—

'Hailey?' a woman with a clipboard called. 'Hailey Hart?'

'*Halley* Hart? That's me.'

'You need to get miked up,' the woman said, advancing on her with a battery pack and a tiny microphone. As Halley clipped it to her shirt, the woman ran though instructions. 'This is how to switch it on, once you're up there. Once you do, please don't touch it, or it significantly affects sound quality for the remote delegates, and—'

'Sorry — remote delegates?'

'We get twice as many views for the livestream than attendances in person,' the woman said. 'Right, come this way . . . here's the controls for your presentation. Good luck!'

Halley found herself thrust onto the stage, and numbly walking to the glass lectern. She'd pictured this moment, with every eye in the audience boring into her, and utter silence as she opened her mouth.

The reality was a hundred times worse.

Beneath the banner declaring *The 27th International Conference on Developments in Astronomy & Cosmology*, delegates were talking to each other, or reading. Many were still holding coffee cups, and some hadn't bothered to take their seats yet.

The briefing document had stated that introductions wouldn't be made on stage — except for the professor giving the keynote after lunch — so each speaker should take a moment to confirm her or his name and institution before they began their presentation. It hadn't been stated that this would be necessary to gain the attention of the audience, who would otherwise ignore you. Then again, it also hadn't been stated that the entire thing was broadcast live around the world.

She checked over her shoulder. Her name was displayed on the large screen at the back of the stage, and thankfully correctly spelled. It might stick in potential employer's minds, if they happened to like her research. Though it was more likely, she thought, looking out over the sea of preoccupied people, that they wouldn't notice her or her name either way.

She cleared her throat. The hum of voices continued, and no heads turned.

She remembered her microphone, and flicked the on switch.

'Excuse me please.' Her nerves had caused her vocal cords to tighten, so her voice came out at a higher pitch than usual. And she'd spoken too loudly.

Now, everyone was looking. Halley flicked her eyes away from the multitude of faces, frantically wondering how she could ever have dismissed nearly three hundred people as *not many*. She focused instead on a red blinking light at the rear of the auditorium, as she inhaled slowly, to steady her racing heart. Was it the fire alarm system or — no, it was the camera, indicating that filming had begun. Her pulse sped up again, as she imagined a multitude of people watching on their computers at work, their feet propped on their desks, wondering why there was a woman gulping on the big stage in front of her memorably unusual name. Suddenly, she wished very hard that the organizers had misspelled it.

Halley opened her mouth again, but her throat was like sandpaper. Henry had been so certain that she had this. She couldn't imagine explaining how badly it had gone: especially since she may never be able to speak again. She imagined typing a description in an email . . . *So I crashed and burned in front of representatives of every academic astronomy department in the world* . . . After that disclosure, there was no way on earth she could face him. Not in four days from now. But her flight was transferable, so she could delay for a week, to try and get over it . . .

She stopped herself mid-spiral. Delaying seeing Henry was unthinkable. Facing Henry when she'd screwed this up was impossible. The only other option was to somehow . . . get it done.

She resolutely ignored the upturned faces and the blinking red light, and conjured up Henry, in an empty seat on the front row. The image triggered a memory: Mom's advice to keep from looking nervous — *smile*.

So she smiled. 'I'm Halley Hart,' she said, 'And I'm a fifth year doctoral student at Stanford University, about to head to the UK as a visiting student, where I shall be writing up the data that I present to you, in brief, now. Let's start with . . .'

* * *

Text messages between Halley and Henry:

It's over. Rough start but I think it might have gone OK after that.

> *It was brilliant! You were brilliant! Don't know what you mean about the start?*

Wait, what?

> *You walked out, glanced around, called for attention, then smiled like you belonged up there before nailing your presentation. I was so proud of you!*

Are you here???

> *Sweetheart, I was watching the livestream.*

What? What if it was a disaster — you'd have just sat there and witnessed my humiliation?! And how did everyone know there was a livestream but me??

> *That was never going to happen, Halley. And, I don't know . . . I read it on the website . . .*

There's a lot of people here . . . I think they're waiting to talk to me.

*So go and talk! And remember names, ready for
when you start applications! Love you, and see you
in four days* xxx

Cannot wait! x

* * *

Halley

Halley was hemmed in by a press of people. Some of them
wanted to speak to her, others merely to shake her hand, and
others to collar one of the people waiting to speak to her. She
scoured their lanyards for the names of their institutions, and
identified someone from Trinity College, Dublin.

A woman in her forties shouldered through the crowd,
'I'm in a hurry,' she said vaguely, in lieu of an apology to
those she was pushing past. 'Halley — I liked your talk.'

'Thank y—'

'I liked it, but I didn't love it,' the woman said, as though
clarification had been requested. 'A new denoising algorithm
always grabs my attention, but nine times out of ten it really
isn't novel at all, and the one time it is, the application's massively limited. Yours really is novel, but I'm not sure you've
given serious consideration to the applications.'

Halley's eyes flew to the woman's lanyard, which had
twisted, so she could only see the blank side. But to be in
attendance, this woman must be in academic astronomy, or
a closely aligned field, so she tempered her instinct to give a
cutting reply. 'I've got the data to prove I'm not overstating
my algorithm's usefulness,' she began.

'Of course you have,' the woman said. 'On an ocular telescope at a light-sky site. All of which is pointless, since it's dark
sky sites where we do serious astronomy, and radio telescopes
that suffer from the worst image noise. Yet you don't even seem
to have considered the application of your algorithm for us.'

'I'm sorry, but *you* being . . . I can't tell from your . . .'

The woman followed Halley's gaze to the twisted lanyard on her chest, and unfurled it. 'I head up this place,' she said pointlessly, because Halley could now see it: *Professor Helen Jansen, Department Chair — Astronomy & Astro-Engineering,* above a logo for the university hosting the symposium. 'And I'm on the organizing committee for this — I've had my eyes on you since your submission to present. I understand you're local?'

'I grew up in Chicago,' Halley admitted, wondering if she could wriggle free to grab the guy from Ireland. 'Before undergrad at Northwestern. Excuse me ple—'

The woman shot a hand out to pincer Halley's upper arm. 'Are your family still here? Interesting. *Then* five years in northern California and — why are you writing up in the UK?'

'Personal reasons,' Halley said. Realizing she sounded too standoffish, and the Irish guy could potentially hear, she rushed on. 'It's unrelated to my career, except that I'd like to work in Europe next.'

'Well that's no good,' the woman said, with growing impatience. 'And I'd urge you to come in to see us before you commit to anything. We'd probably meet any offer you're considering.'

This conversation was like hacking through ice with a toothpick. 'Offer . . . like, of *employment*?'

'Well I'd have to get you in front of our hiring committee first, but that's only a formality. Halley, our new project's the most significant my department's ever run. If we can even slightly denoise the images quickly and relatively cheaply — which amounts to your salary, plus the cost of getting you out there — it has the potential to improve—'

'Wait,' Halley said. Something was ringing in her ears. 'I'm really sorry to interrupt. But what project?'

The woman gestured at the conference programme in Halley's hand. 'You haven't read that? No matter — you'll hear the details during my keynote. My department's got three years access to the new radio-telescope at Antarctica.'

PART FOURTEEN

Henry pushed open the door, grimacing at the squeak of its hinges. But Mum was already awake, and propped up on pillows.

'*Henry*,' she said, and he relaxed a little. Awake *and* alert, unlike the day before, when she'd thought him a doctor, and told him wistfully that his eyes reminded her of her little boy's. He'd managed to hold it together until he was back in his bedroom at their house, the door locked against intrusions.

'I've brought your beau to visit you, Mum. He'll be through in a minute.'

Her speech was slurred, but discernible. 'He's . . . slow since he got . . . that stick.'

Seating himself, Henry didn't inform her how quickly Dad had scuttled through the corridor to catch up with her consultant, who he'd spied in the distance, calling back impatiently for Henry to tell his mother he was on his way.

There was a book on her over-bed table. 'Would you like me to read to you?'

She nodded. 'Chapter . . . three, please.'

As he read, he felt her eyes on him, until she closed them and raised her left hand off the sheets, tucking her thumb into her palm and arching her fingers, before beginning to lower her fingertips individually, as she mimicked pressing the strings on a violin.

He paused at the end of a section. 'What are you playing, Mum?'

She opened her eyes immediately, but then they clouded. 'I don't . . . recall.'

Lambasting himself internally, he was pleased when Dad rapped sharply, then entered. He sketched a salute to his wife, who stared at him impassively, then lowered one eyelid in a heavy wink. Henry had witnessed this exchange thousands of times — generally with mystification, not recognizing it until adulthood as a private joke between them. Mum hadn't ever yet forgotten the correct response, as far as he knew, and he dreaded the day it happened.

Henry rose, ceding the only chair to his father. 'I'll be back at the end of visiting hours,' he murmured, aware as he slipped out of the room that his parents hadn't even heard, already absorbed in each other's company.

He switched his phone back on as he strode through the ward, but there was no reception until several minutes later. When he reached the hospital lobby, his handset buzzed. He scrolled through the alerts, speeding his pace before he'd even finished counting: he had seven missed video calls from Halley.

As he got to the car park, he slowed again, thinking hard. It was the middle of the night in Chicago, but Halley was safely at her mother's home. And she was used to staying up all night. She was probably wired with the adrenaline of her presentation, or second-guessing it, and wanting a chat . . . Except . . . *seven* missed calls — it had to be something urgent.

He mused on options as he paid for parking, then unlocked Dad's car and hopped in. Noting the multiple signs around the car park showing him to be at Basingstoke

& North Hampshire Hospital, he pulled away. He'd park in a side street rather than alert Halley to the hospital this way. He'd provide her with a calm explanation at a perfectly appropriate time.

Unless . . . He groaned as he swung between the exit barriers. Somehow, Halley knew about Mum's stroke? Had Viola blabbed? And maybe Halley's mother's retreat wasn't as strict about removing phones this time.

He swore under his breath, then screeched to a halt an instant before running a red light. He considered getting in there first by telling Halley about his mum as soon as she answered, then discarded the idea. She wouldn't fall for it, and anyway, he didn't want to propagate his dishonesty further. He had to admit he'd kept the full extent of it from her, alongside assuring her that things were looking up now — Mum was making a decent recovery and Dad had agreed to downsize. And, without the massive distraction, Halley had executed her drive and her presentation.

And, next, she'd be executing *him*. Or worse, crying.

He turned left at the next street, but could only see resident parking. His phone buzzed with another incoming video call, so he manoeuvred into a space anyway, answering as he turned off the engine.

'I'm sorry, sweetheart,' he said, resting his phone on the dashboard and slipping on his glasses.

'It's OK. I don't expect you to be constantly available to accept my calls. I should have waited.' Her voice was thick with emotion and her face wan and streaked with tears, just as he'd feared. But her words weren't at all as he'd expected. 'I've got to tell you something really . . . really bad, and the longer I wait the more I hate myself for it.'

He shifted a little in the leather seat, reassessing. She didn't know about the stroke, then. Which meant, once he'd calmed her down, he must gently confess about Mum.

'What's wrong, Halley?'

'After . . .' she sniffed. 'After my presentation—' She broke off and buried her face in her hands.

'Your presentation went well,' he said. 'I watched it, remember?' Perhaps an error had been brought to her attention, or—

'It went too well,' she choked. 'I've been offered a job. With a three year contract.'

'But that's . . .' Henry bit back *fantastic*. Halley was crying about a job offer, which meant it wasn't the kind of job she wanted. Or, more likely, not in the location she wanted. 'Presumably . . . not in Europe?'

Mute, she shook her head.

'Is it in academic astronomy?'

She inclined her chin slightly. 'This woman introduced herself after my presentation yesterday, and she wants my algorithm for a new telescope in Antarctica—'

'It's a job in *Antarctica*?'

'Partly — but mainly Chicago. I was so flattered I agreed to visit her department after her keynote — I should have told you first but I really thought I'd be able to see it then reject them . . .' Her tears had intensified, warping her voice so much that he could barely understand her. 'She had me meet the hiring committee right away . . .'

He made soothing sounds until she calmed down. 'If you don't mind,' he then said, 'I'd really appreciate you starting from the beginning.'

She made a few false starts before she got going, pausing occasionally to dart looks at him before averting her eyes again, as she divulged the details. It wasn't difficult to keep his face serene — aware of the distinct possibility that she wouldn't get an enticing job in the UK, he'd focused instead on their imminent half-year together. If she wanted this job — and she was so wracked with guilt that presumably she did — then when she was awarded her Ph.D. and moved to Chicago to take it up, he'd find a way to go with her. He thought about Mum and Dad uneasily. Or travel to see her regularly. Or something.

When she got to the end and halted, he smiled at her. 'I always knew you were brilliant, Halley. Congratulations on the offer. Have you accepted already?'

'I wouldn't do that without speaking to you!'

'Oh Halley, I know you wanted to find something over here, but there were never any guarantees, and at least we get to be together until the summer. The dilemma of the longer term can wait—'

All colour had drained from her face. 'But it's not . . . Henry, it's not an offer for the fall. It's for now. Like, immediately now. They insist I write up here in Chicago, so we can start preparing my algorithm for Antarctica.'

Henry went numb. His hands had seized the steering wheel, and were gripping it so tightly his knuckles had blanched to the colour of bone. But he couldn't feel them, or take back control of his muscles and tendons. 'I don't . . . I don't understand.'

'I think Professor Jansen would have wanted me to leave for Antarctica right away and winter-over, if she'd met me a little earlier. But as it is I'll go in late August, when planes can get in and out, and stay for a few months of the summer season. Since it's the southern hemisphere, the seasons are the opposite to ours.'

'Halley,' he said unsteadily. 'You're not coming to England on Monday?'

She licked her lips. 'I mean,' she said, 'I am if I turn the job down.'

Their eyes met, and he read the same turmoil that he felt.

'Can you negotiate? Say you're busy until, say, May?'

'Already tried.' She scrubbed her face. 'I went back a month at a time, but she kept replying *unfortunately, that doesn't work for us*. Then I said I had a vacation booked, so the soonest I could return to Chicago is the last week in February. She said *absolutely not*, and bumped the salary by six thousand bucks.'

Henry didn't know whether to laugh or cry. 'They want you badly.' He gathered himself, and forced his mouth to turn up. 'Chicago's closer than California. And six thousand dollars pays for a return flight to England at least every other month.'

She didn't seem to be listening. 'I've been thinking of calling their bluff. Like, turn them down now and fly to you, keeping my fingers crossed that they'll renegotiate afterwards.' Her voice faltered. 'The problem comes if they won't, and I never get another opportunity like it. But then I wonder how I can even consider the job, with how much I love you and want to be with you.'

His eyes were stinging, but he knew what he had to say. 'I love you and want to be with you too, Halley. But we agreed on compromise, not sacrifice.'

'There isn't a compromise here. Only two different sacrifices! And I have no idea how to decide.'

Silence fell, and Henry's stomach plummeted with it. He couldn't think of a compromise, either. 'Have you considered the pros and cons?' he asked eventually, since something had to be said.

She scrubbed her face with both hands. 'If I reject the job, we'll be together. If I take it, we won't.'

'*But . . .*' he said, with insistence.

'*But*, I'd be earning immediately, rather than waiting until at least the fall, so I can rebuild my savings, and make rent in Stanford without a problem. And it's a great department, and headed up by a woman — that's still rare in astronomy.' She was touching her right index finger to each digit on her left hand, counting as she listed. It reminded him of Mum's habit of silently fingering an air violin, which she hadn't played in public since marrying Dad. 'And finally, I'll get to upgrade a telescope in Antarctica, which not only fulfils one of my biggest ambitions, but adds a lot of prestige to my résumé.' She tapped her ring finger several more times. 'That's all I can think of,' she said, sounding brighter. 'There's only three reasons to accept it.'

Henry reckoned it was more like five. But either way, there was only one reason for her to turn it down. And he'd never live with himself if she did so and her career never got off the ground. Then again, he also wasn't sure how he'd live without her. He clamped his teeth against verbalizing any of it. He refused to sway her. Including, he realized with a sinking feeling, by telling her about Mum. He didn't know if she'd instantly turn down the job and fly over, or take offence that he hadn't confided in her sooner, and accept the job without further thought. Maybe it wouldn't make any difference either way. But he wouldn't risk it.

'How long do you have to decide?'

She shrugged. 'I've asked for the weekend. So I guess by Monday I need to ' a muscle in her jaw flinched — 'sign the contract, or get on the plane, or . . . like, delay my flight and beg them — and you — for a little more time. I've requested they don't contact me further after sending the contract through. I don't want them talking me into it.'

He steeled himself. 'Taking some time without outside influences makes sense. I think . . . I think it's best if I give you some space too.'

She opened her mouth, and he thought he'd hear an objection, but then her shoulders slumped. 'Maybe you're right. But only if you promise you won't go nuts in the meantime?'

'I'll be fine,' he lied steadily.

'No quitting your job? You can't make this sacrifice to prevent me needing to.'

He raised his hands in surrender. Or maybe defeat. 'I promise I won't leave my job.' It was true, since it would do no good if he did — he couldn't move to America right now, anyway.

* * *

Saturday, 25 January

Voice note from Henry to Viola:

Hey Viola, quick update. Mum's vague today but was on good form yesterday. Also . . . uh . . . Halley has a situation going on. It's prevented me telling her about everything with Mum, but I honestly will as soon as I can, so please don't mention anything if you happen to hear

261

from anyone she knows. I mean it, Vi — we need some privacy. OK, bye — and say hullo to Aron for me.

* * *

Halley

She stared at the sheets of paper. The ink was slightly blurred from Mom's crappy printer, but the terms remained stark.

Ms Halley Hart was offered the role of salaried Research Associate while she wrote up her doctoral thesis, in return for full-time attendance at the department, to begin *within days*. As soon as Stanford confirmed the award of her Ph.D., Dr Halley Hart would be promoted to Senior Research Associate and her salary raised further. They additionally proposed a fully-funded summer season in Antarctica, to enable the upgrade of the new radio-telescope.

She'd placed a lidded case beside the contract, inside which was the fountain pen she'd received as a graduation gift from Aunt Edie. Its barrel was well-balanced, and engraved with her name, and the nib pleasingly smooth. She didn't even want to open it.

Halley pressed her palms against the orbits of her eyes, as if she could hold back the agony of indecision. If only it was a head versus heart dilemma. Following her heart, where Henry was concerned, had always been easy. But it was more like her heart itself was split in two. Half of it inhabited teenage Halley, who was whooping and hollering at the fulfilment of her biggest ambition. The other half belonged to the woman who was exclusively and officially dating Henry Inglis, and she was sobbing a protest.

* * *

Sunday, 26 January

Voice note from Viola to Henry:

I appreciate the update, Henry. But I don't know why you think I'd hear from anyone Halley knows. And what was that cryptic thing

262

about 'a situation' for Halley? If you mean she's got PMT, just say so. It's much worse for her than it is awkward for you. As for privacy, I've only told Aron about you keeping quiet about Mum's stroke. We'll be back first thing tomorrow, by the way, which is just as well because you sound exhausted.

* * *

Halley

Two and a half days with no contact from Henry, and she was desperate to speak to him. Instead, she scrolled rapidly through his emails, her eyes skimming the screen, not daring to read in any detail. His kisses brought a smile to her face even now, when she wanted to scratch her skin off in frustration at her predicament.

She should sign the contract and upgrade an Antarctic deep-sky telescope with her algorithm without a second thought. It was an achievement that would always be hers alone, separate from the successes of her namesake ancestor. It might even inspire little girls to learn to stargaze. But if she did so, she couldn't add her final few essentials to the suitcases beside the front door, and set out in the morning to spend six months with Henry. Who called her the love of his life, and who was almost certainly also hers.

Both. She wanted both.

Everyone who said that only children grew into selfish adults must be right, after all.

Her laptop chimed, and she glanced at it sharply. It was yet another email from her potential department. They'd taken little notice of her plea for a weekend without contact, and the subject lines had proved too enticing to ignore.

Women in Space-Science support group — weekly brunches.

Preparations for Antarctica, please see document attached.

Benefits package, pension plan & perks for H. Hart

The new one invited her to a lecture about the James Webb Space Telescope by a visiting speaker from Nasa, the following week. And to join Professor Jansen and the Nasa astronomer for lunch afterwards. It ended in the same way as all the others — with an assurance that the whole team were hoping to be working with her soon . . .

Recalled to herself when her stomach grumbled, she slammed her laptop shut. She didn't feel hungry, but couldn't recall eating anything since candy in bed the night before. She considered investigating whatever Mom had left her in the deepfreeze, but rejected it in favour of ordering an Italian beef sandwich from her favourite place, that used capers in the giardiniera. If anything could stimulate her appetite, it was that.

And maybe with some calories, her brain would engage properly, and cast a goddamn deciding vote between the warring halves of her heart.

* * *

From: Halley Hart
Subject: Delaying flight (I'm sorry) (I love you)
To: Henry Inglis
Dear Henry,

I love you, and I want to be with you. I need to say that upfront.

But I used to believe that I want to be with you more than anything . . . and that changed the moment I was offered a professional opportunity I'd never dreamed nor imagined could be mine.

The real truth is: I want to be with you *now* (and for six months) (and probably for a lifetime), *and* I want the job (and a salary) (and especially, to go upgrade a telescope in Antarctica). But getting all of that is impossible.

If I reject the job, we'll be together, and hopefully I'll get another job, given enough time. Is that fair on *me*? Is that fair on *you*?

If I take the job, we'll be apart, aside from short visits, for at least three years. Is that enough for *you*? Is it enough for *me*?

All this is to say, I'm going out of my mind with this decision, so have delayed my answer — and my flight — until Wednesday. Professor Jansen won't allow me any longer.

I appreciate you offering me space, Henry. I just need a little more of it. And I love you and miss you and am truly very sorry.

Your Halley x

* * *

Monday, 27 January
Henry

Viola would have taken one look at him, and forced him to explain what was wrong. Admitting that Halley had delayed would be unbearable, as would be the pity in his sister's eyes. So he'd avoided her entirely by informing Dad of a 9 a.m. meeting at St Jude's and setting out by train an hour before she and Aron were due.

Since the meeting was entirely fictitious, when he got to St Jude's he showed his face in the SCR, to ensure Geoffrey Hogshaw noticed he was back, before heading to the library. But the librarian who stored his archive box was engaged with a tearful student, and Henry abruptly turned and left. He couldn't face Lawrence Sedgwick today, anyway.

Instead he found himself striding along Oxford's high street, until he reached Queen's Lane which led into New College Lane. He didn't pause until he reached Edmond Halley's House, where he buffed the stone plaque with his coat sleeve. With a final glance at the golden comet depicted there, he resumed his walk, passing under the Bridge of Sighs. He only recognized his territorial instinct to reverse-trace the route of his tour with Halley as he cut down the side of the

Bod into Radcliffe Square. There he stood on the cobbles, at the place where he'd seen his Halley for the second time.

And then his phone buzzed. He wrestled it from his pocket: incoming call, from an international number he didn't recognize. His pulse sped — surely it was Halley, from her mom's house.

'Halley?'

'Henry — you're alive! Which means you purposely never got back to me about my podcast . . .'

Not Halley, but Halley-Anne. His shoulders slumped. 'I . . . uh . . . sorry about that.'

'Have you even talked to your Halley about whether she's up for coming on as a guest? Or can I at least put her name out there by sharing your email? Tell her my first three episodes went really well, and that the episode title for your one will be H(e)artless, with the e in brackets, so it's a pun on our surname, get it? Oh, and tell her to check out my ratings and reviews — and someone even said . . .'

There was nowhere to sit, but his legs were unsteady, and he bent instead, resting a hand on his leg as Halley-Anne raced on with anecdotes about her prior guests. It seemed an age before she ran out of steam. 'Henry? *If the man's hung up I'll*—'

'Still here,' he managed. 'Um . . . I had been discussing your podcast with Halley.' There was no point revealing that she'd asked him to give Halley-Anne her number. That was far from appropriate at this point. 'But things are . . . in a state of flux right now.'

'*Craaaaap* . . . you broke up . . .'

'No!' He gulped in a fortifying breath. Suddenly, explaining what was happening was no longer the worst thing in the world. It needed to be said, and quickly, to wipe away Halley-Anne's assumption. '*No*. But she's unexpectedly been offered a . . . life-changing career boost, in America, right as she was about to come here for six months. She can't do both.'

'Do you want her to pursue the career thing, or come over as planned?'

'I . . . don't want her to sacrifice the opportunity, and I want her here.'

'And what does she want?'

'Funnily enough, exactly the same.' He hadn't been surprised that Halley's email had expressed an identical reasoning to the one he felt. The only difference was that he could sincerely say that he wanted to be with her more than anything — but that was worthless, since it didn't release him from the ties that prevented him moving over there.

'So what are you going to do?'

'I have no idea.' He almost left it there. But now he'd started to talk, he couldn't stop. 'If every attempt to reunite hadn't ended in disaster, I think she'd—'

'Hang on — *every attempt to reunite*? You haven't seen each other since September?'

'Not . . . properly. It's been one mix-up after another. And now this . . . opportunity, from a source whose idea of negotiation is chucking more money at her, and who'll only allow her until Wednesday to decide. I don't know how she'll do it.'

He'd been speaking to himself, more than Halley-Anne, so he flinched when she whistled. 'Let me get this right . . . you haven't been together to confirm that whatever's between you actually exists? And then you've left her to make this massive decision totally on her own?'

'She asked for space and I'm respecting that.'

'Did she really?' Halley-Anne sounded doubtful in the extreme. When he didn't reply, she laughed. 'You suggested it, then? Jeez, I thought professors were meant to be clever! You told her she needs space to decide, then basically ignored her. But the other side won't be — you said yourself, they're even countering with more money — just as she feels like you've abandoned her.'

Henry considered that. 'You really think so?'

'Yes! Jump on a plane to show her how much you love her, you galah! I need you two together, or the pod episode won't be nearly so heart-warming!'

* * *

Voice note from Viola for Henry:

Henry, nothing to worry about — Mum's all right. Sorry to miss you this morning — Dad said you had some urgent meeting at College. Are you in trouble for the week off or something? Otherwise, I don't get why you didn't reschedule, so you could take my car back as planned. How will you pick up Halley later? And by the way, you forgot your new wine glasses, too. Have fun drinking champagne out of mugs!

* * *

Henry

With Halley-Anne's admonishments ringing in his skull, he thought hard as he meandered to the Blue Moon. He'd been convinced for a long time that Halley was it for him — looking back, he'd had some instinct about it even on the day they met. But she'd seemed to need to be reunited first, to be certain. That had never offended him, but he should have considered it, before suggesting leaving her alone to make such a momentous decision. And it had weighed on him that he hadn't told her about Mum's stroke. He'd feared it would influence her into turning the job down for the wrong reasons. But that betrayed a lack of trust in Halley's ability to weigh the evidence and come to whatever was the correct conclusion for her.

Arriving at his houseboat he booked a flight to Chicago departing early evening, paused only to throw a change of clothes, his laptop and passport in a bag, then locked up again before heading for the bus station.

By the time he alighted at Heathrow, he was second-guessing his impulse. Halley hadn't needed her arm twisted to accept the space to make her decision. She'd even thanked him for it, in her email. What if that meant he'd turn up and find his presence unwelcome? Well then, he thought grimly, at least that would make obvious the decision she should take. There was also their new year's resolution to consider. They'd sworn to give each other a head's up before hopping on a plane again, to workshop the logistics, as Halley had put it.

He reached the airport concourse. It was significantly less busy than when he'd last headed to America to surprise Halley, on Christmas Eve — or when he'd returned, a few days later, and their twelve hours together had drained down to zero. If he'd paused to tell her his plan before embarking on that journey, he'd have heard that she'd just arrived in England, and they'd have spent Christmas together in Oxford. That settled it, and he skirted the entrance of security screening in favour of a row of empty seats a short distance away, put on his glasses and pulled out his phone.

* * *

Text messages between Henry and Halley:

> *Thanks for your email yesterday. I love and miss you too, sweetheart. I know I urged you to take some space, but I think I was wrong. And there's something else it's essential I let you know. If you're awake, I'd appreciate a brief chat? xxx*

>> *If it's that your mom nearly died, don't bother. My mom told me an hour ago, when she called to say she's extended her retreat. I guess I'm literally the last person to know. I won't offer you the same disrespect: you're the first I'm telling that I signed the contract.*

PART FIFTEEN

Halley

The alert for an incoming video call appeared on her laptop so soon after she'd sent the text that she wondered if Henry had even received it yet. She was disabused of the notion within an instant of answering.

'Halley, I'm so—'

She cut in. 'I don't want to hear it. Just, tell me about your mom. Everything.'

He began with a voice note from his sister, which he remembered almost word-for-word, before recounting his hurried journey, and then a precis of each day, in short, clipped sentences. A witness might think he was the one who was angry with her, but she knew Henry, and this was—

She didn't know Henry, though. Not as well as she'd thought.

He came to a close after affirming that his mother's prognosis was now decent.

'Are you pissed at me?' Halley blurted.

His eyebrows shot up. 'Why would you even—' It seemed to take a palpable effort for him to break off the retort. 'No, Halley. I'm angry at myself.'

'I'm angry at you too. But I'm glad your mom pulled through.'

He nodded briefly. 'I know.' He didn't clarify which of her statements he was replying to. He was wearing earbuds and his reading glasses, which meant he'd called on his phone from someplace with background noise. And he was holding it in portrait, and close to his face, so she could only see him, and nothing of his location.

'Are you in public, Henry? We need privacy for this.'

'I'm . . . I can't be overheard,' he said. 'Can I ask you one thing about the contract? I'm not attempting to talk you out of your decision. Not at all. But I'm wondering if you'd already signed it, before you heard about Mum.'

She compressed her lips. 'No. After.'

He closed his eyes, and it was a few seconds before he reopened them. God, he had such pretty eyes. Even now, when they were so sad.

'For what it's worth,' he said, as tonelessly as she'd ever heard him, 'I was going to tell you at the first opportunity after your presentation.'

Halley sought to regulate her breathing. She'd figured it all out, after Mom's surprise call, asking sharply if Halley was at the airport as planned, or had gone to the UK early. When she'd confusedly asked what Mom meant, Mom had sighed. *You should have told me right before I left, Junior. Ischemic strokes are a bitch — I'd have advised you to get there quick-smart. As it is, Mrs Inglis got very lucky.* Speechless, Halley had stammered something, and Mom had assumed she was boarding the airplane, wished her a less tumultuous journey to Oxford than last time, and hung up.

'You were going to tell me *five days* after she had a stroke?'

'I . . .' he looked wretched. 'I texted you about it within an hour of arriving at the hospital. But then I had to turn my phone off, so missed that it failed to send until you called the next day. By then, you'd embarked on the road trip, and I didn't want to distract you.'

'Distract me,' she repeated, breathing harder. 'You thought your mom was dying — I *needed* to be distracted from my stupid drive so I could turn my car around!' Now her volume had risen, it was impossible to regain control. 'I'd have left everything back at my apartment and taken the next flight to England to support you.'

His slanted eyes were as wide as she'd ever seen them — like he was witnessing a UFO. 'But the symposium was—'

'You mattered more than that! Don't you get it? Wouldn't you have gotten the next plane if *my* mom was in a coma?'

He stared at her, then dropped his head, releasing a muffled groan. 'Nothing would have stopped me. Yet I stopped you, by not telling you. I get why that galvanized you into signing the contract.' He glanced up again, with a tight smile that nevertheless reached his eyes. 'Congratulations. You deserve it, and they're lucky to have you.'

All the anger drained out of her. 'Thanks, I guess.'

His smile remained. 'Look . . .' He stretched out his arm, or leaned back, because his head was taking up less and less of the screen. 'I said I had something to tell you? I'm at Heathrow. I'm coming to . . . well it was going to be to tell you about Mum, and support you through your decision. Now it'll be so you can be mad at me in person.'

'Don't joke.' She was shaking so hard she feared for a second that she might be having a seizure. 'Coming here's . . . not a good plan. And before you say it, I know you won't try to talk me out of taking the job. It's too late for that anyway,' she added, more because she needed the reminder, than for his benefit.

'Halley,' he said steadily. 'We haven't been together for over four months, and we're facing three more years of a sizeable geographic distance. We need to sit in the same room and discuss what that looks like. And if parting again is unbearable, we need to know that too, so I can think of a way—'

'You can't leave the UK — your family needs you! And even if you could, I won't let you give up your job for me.' *Not when I've given you up for a job.* She had a suspicion he could read on her face what she was leaving unsaid, so plunged on. 'I don't want you to come. It would only . . . make all this harder.'

He was so still that she thought he had perhaps even stopped breathing. 'Make what harder, Halley?'

Her face contorted with the threat of a sob, and she turned away, shuddering. Signing the contract had seemed the hardest thing she'd had to do in her entire life, but this entirely eclipsed it. 'Our . . . status . . .'

'Don't say it,' he said, as hoarse as she'd ever heard him. 'Not like this.'

'I have to.' Halley's voice rang hollow in her ears. That didn't feel incorrect: she had a curious sense that she'd hollowed herself out with this decision, in the hour between Mom's call and this one. 'We have to end it.'

'Not on a fucking video call!'

She was unaccustomed to hearing Henry curse, but it was the harshness of his tone that made her flinch.

'Halley,' he said, looking aghast. 'I'm . . . Halley, after everything, we can't do it like this. Tell me once I arrive, and I'll . . . I'll accept it, but I can't bear it to end before I even see you again.'

'But if we see each other first, it prolongs the . . .' Her throat caught on the word *pain*. Voicing it would trigger her tears, and that would be worse for both of them. 'Prolongs this whole thing. I-don't-want-you-to-come.'

'And you do want us to . . . break up.' It wasn't quite a question, but it also wasn't not a question.

And she owed him the answer, but her throat was a desert, and her tongue repeatedly stuck to the roof of her mouth. She grabbed her water bottle and swallowed. 'If I could have this professional opportunity *and* you, then . . . maybe it would be different. But I can't spend another three years like the past four months — continually torn between my life, and work, and friends — and you. Not if I want to make a success of my career, and rebuild a life in Chicago, and travel to Antarctica for months on end.'

She'd gone over and over it in her mind. Her feelings for Henry had almost made her sacrifice everything else, and that wasn't her. End it now, and she'd get over him someday. He'd get over her even sooner. The signs that he didn't need her as much as he claimed were already there.

'You're the love of my life,' he said, in a voice that wasn't his.

'You just think that,' she said dully. 'If I was, you'd have wanted — needed — me with you, when you thought your mom was dying.'

It was Henry's turn to flinch. 'I did, but I wanted you safe, more,' he said eventually, his eyes unbearably damp. 'Swee— *Halley*, you're really certain this is what you want?'

She hugged herself, her nails cutting crescents into the flesh of her upper arms. 'I am. And I have to go now.'

She couldn't entirely avoid sight of the screen, as she slammed her laptop shut. Henry's face was caving in on itself.

* * *

Tuesday, 28 January

> *From: Halley Hart*
> *Subject: About the apartment*
> *To: Angelie Lamdagan*
> Dear Angelie,
>
> My situation has changed and I've accepted a job here in Chicago. I don't want to go into the whole thing, but basically they want me here to write up, starting immediately. I'll be getting paid, so will have no problem with rent x2, and you can stop looking for a new roommate.
>
> Halley
> P.S. Please don't ask questions. I just can't.

* * *

From: Angelie Lamdagan
Subject: About the apartment
To: Halley Hart

I don't get it, Buddha.

And I don't know whether to congratulate you or say *oh shit*.

And I can't figure out what caused everything to change like that and what's going on with you and Henry.

You better not have done this out of guilt about the apartment!

There, no questions.

Answer your phone! I've tried, like five times.

Angelie

* * *

Wednesday, 29 January

To: Viola Inglis
Subject: Question
From: Angelie Lamdagan

Hey Viola,

I don't know if you'll remember me. We 'met' on a vid-chat a few months ago, via your brother, Henry, and my friend, Halley? I searched up your email address because I'm worried about Halley.

She contacted me yesterday to say she's in Chicago, not Oxford, and has a new job there. She wouldn't say more, didn't mention Henry, and hasn't answered any of my replies. Or her mobile. Or her mom's landline.

I was pissed at her for weeks about moving to England, so I guess I can't blame her for ignoring me now. But the guilt's killing me. She was so happy and excited a week ago! Do you happen to know if she and Henry are still together? If she broke up with him because of the dumb shit I said, or the pressure of making rent here or something, I need to put it right.

Best, Angelie

* * *

Thursday, 30 January

To: Angelie Lamdagan
Subject: Question
From: Viola Inglis
Dear Angelie,

Are you saying Halley isn't in England? I had no idea! I'd assumed the two of them were holed up together on Henry's boat.

Now I think about it, his behaviour on Monday morning was slightly odd. And he hasn't checked in for updates, however briefly, on a family matter — but I shouldn't say any more about that. I remember you well, and it's not that I mind you getting in touch — absolutely not — but lately Henry's had a bee in his bonnet about privacy.

I'd better not approach this all-guns-blazing, but I'll gently check-in with him, and let you know once I succeed. If you're able to do the same about any contact with Halley, that would be super.

Warmest, Viola x

* * *

Friday, 31 January

Voice note from Viola to Henry:

Can you give me a call, Henry? Nothing to stress about, just want to update you on the parentals.

* * *

Nothing helped. But people made it worse, and spare time, and talking. So he'd taken to running, as far and fast as he could through Oxford. Unfortunately, a storm cut short his evening run, and he returned to college, refusing to go aboard the Blue Moon until he was exhausted and yawning. Then he could trust himself to dash in and out of the shower room, averting his eyes from the bookshelves, before crawling onto the sofa bed to sleep. He hadn't ventured into the bedroom all week: she'd slept there.

He shook his head, hard, denying his brain the stream of consciousness it sought, and resumed his desultory search for a book offering the necessary level of absorption. Gale force winds howled outside, rattling the glass in the dormer window in his office.

Though . . . *that* was a particularly loud rattle . . . And it echoed in from further along his slanted ceiling than the window. Henry switched off his desk lamp, then eased open the casement, gasping at the sting of the wind and rain on his face. As his eyes adjusted to the darkness, he saw a figure hauling something along the pitch of the roof.

Henry hesitated for a split second, then moved to grab his phone. Hurtling out to the stairs, he pressed the bursar's contact.

It went to voicemail, so he rapidly tried the porter's lodge instead.

'Henry Inglis here — our climber's back . . .' he panted, taking the stairs three at a time. 'Yes, in *this* weather. I don't think he clocked that he's been seen — his back was to me. And he's slower than last time, distracted by something bulky. I'm sprinting around to where he exited before — can you circle to the other quad in case he takes a different route?'

Reaching the bottom of the staircase, he burst through the exit door into the rain, then darted to a vantage point in the shadows beneath a tree. The moon and stars were obliterated by clouds, so he could see nothing of vast swathes of the roof as he craned upwards. Nonetheless, he stood, silent and watchful, his eyes flicking between any windows that were alive with electric light.

After a few minutes, one of the lit casements was opened from the inside. Henry raised his phone, zooming in to record. He missed the person on the inside, who stepped back, before the figure slid in, pulling what appeared to be a sack.

Henry debated directing the porter to visit the room in question. But he wouldn't know precisely which one it was until he'd checked a plan, and he was certain it wasn't an unwelcome visit — the occupier had clearly opened the window for the climber. Besides, it was too risky to block the corridor and panic the idiots into hopping back out of the window and slipping to their deaths.

Without even a coat, Henry's teeth chattered and his fingers grew numb. He ended the recording and put his phone in the pocket of his joggers, then blew on his hands, his gaze never wavering from the window.

Then light spilled out of a door, and his eyes plunged down. It was a tall, thin figure, whose clothes were sopping wet, and his hair plastered to his face. The climber, who must have exited the room through the internal staircase. Henry froze as he loped away across the sacrosanct grass in the centre of the quad. He had no need to follow. Unfortunately, Henry recognized the climber.

* * *

Saturday, 1 February
Halley

She'd emptied the pantry of snacks. And the refrigerator. And the emergency-candy cupboard. Continuing to eat her feelings would involve leaving Mom's house. Or switching her phone on, to order online — but that was untenable with so many texts springing up from Angelie, some of them even mentioning . . . *him* by name.

The grocery store, then. She could get her boots and coat on and leave for the first time since Professor Jansen said she needn't start at the department until Monday. Ever since, she'd got used to dulling the waves of pain with sugar, motivation for anything else having drained away.

She made for the deepfreeze instead. She hadn't investigated it before, anticipating only Mom's healthy batch cooking. But maybe in the frosty depths she'd find a half-tub of ice-cream, leftover from the summer. She swung up the lid, revealing disposable foil containers with cardboard tops. But Mom froze things in Tupperware, she thought idly, reading a neat label.

Lasagne, love Henry.

Something stabbed her in the heart as she pulled out another.

Chocolate cheesecake, love Henry.

She grabbed the rest and sank onto the kitchen tiles.
Chicken Parmigiana. Sticky toffee pudding. Veggie chilli salad!

Love Henry. Love Henry. Love Henry.

She buried her head in her hands and wept, not heeding the distant noise from the hallway.

'Junior,' Mom called. 'I'm home! Where you at?'

Attempting to answer made her cry harder, so she waited for Mom to discover her, and gather her into her arms.

* * *

Sunday, 2 February

Voice note from Viola to Henry:

Hey little brother. The needs assessment is upcoming for whether Mum can come home. We need to catch up about that pretty urgently, so please call me today!

* * *

The knock on his office door was so faint he almost missed it.

'Come in,' he called.

The door swung open. Dexter looked as nervous as ever — but not shit-scared, like he should.

'You wanted to see me?'

Henry nodded at the chair he'd placed on the far side of the small room, limiting options for escape from the door — and the window. 'Sit down.' Once his instruction had been followed, he pinned the student with his eyes. 'Why have you been climbing into your girlfriend's bedroom?'

Mr Exactly's jaw all but unhinged.

'Is it something voyeuristic? A bet? A stupid attempt to impress her?'

The boy clamped his mouth shut.

'As yet, I haven't reported the matter,' Henry said. 'I'm prepared to hear the explanation before I decide whether I have to — and I may well have to.' He didn't add that Rupert's entreaty for him to keep an eye out for the under-graduate historians, and his own guilt that he hadn't man-aged to — even after his hackles were raised by them both remaining for Christmas — meant he'd really rather not report them for the potentially expellable offence. But he couldn't overlook something so dangerous.

'I . . . can't say,' the boy said. He looked like he was going to cry, and suddenly much younger. 'I promised.'

Henry stood up. 'Then I'll ask her.'

As a bluff, it failed — but it wasn't only a bluff, and he made his way down one staircase before skirting a small section of the quad, with Dexter at his heels as he re-entered the next staircase along, and sped up it.

'Wait,' Dexter said, as they reached the top. 'Let's go back, and I'll tell you.'

Henry clenched his teeth. He was here, now, and there were no guarantees he'd get the truth. So he turned and rapped. There was no reply.

'I've got your boyfriend here,' he called. 'Unless you let me in, I'm taking him directly to the Dean, and returning with the spare key.'

'Coming,' Olivia called back. 'It's just . . . I'm in the shower . . . Let me get dressed.'

Henry glanced at his phone. 'You have thirty seconds.'

Dexter slumped against the wall, his hands tight in his floppy hair.

'Three . . . two . . .' Henry called. The door sprang open. Olivia had a dressing gown tightly belted around her, but her hair was dry. He marched in, glancing around. 'Sit on the bed, both of you.'

'And you should sit on the desk chair,' Olivia squeaked. 'And . . . err . . . sorry for the mess.'

There was a mess, but not the usual student detritus of clothes and books and food wrappers. Instead, her belongings were organized, and rubbish was in the bin. She'd even separated her recycling. But there was a distinct whiff of something that he couldn't identify, a bucket of fresh vegetables on her desk, and stubby pieces of straw all over the carpet.

Straw had been found on this staircase the previous term. Students had been warned of mandatory room-checks by the housekeeping team, if it continued to be strewn around.

There was another squeaking sound. He looked sharply at the pair on the bed, but it had come from behind him. He spun, reaching the en-suite shower room an instant before the students could succeed in their attempt to block his way. He tore open the shower curtain. And saw a pig in a pink collar.

'I bought her the first week of term, when the Ox-pressure was starting to get to me,' Olivia wailed. 'She's my emotional support animal.'

Henry tried to process that. He supposed it would be unkind to ask how the emotional support was working out for her.

'She was tiny back then — the breeder promised she was a teacup-pig!'

'The breeder lied,' Henry said, eyeing the creature, which was hairy, and already the size of a cocker spaniel.

'Yeah. Persephone kept growing and growing, so now we can't even sneak her out for exercise anymore. And I can't find anywhere to rehome her where she won't be slaughtered for bacon!' She burst into tears, and Dexter wrapped her in his arms.

Henry moved his eyes away, blinking. *Persephone.* For the first time in what felt like forever, he was seized with the impulse to smile, and fought to keep his face stern. 'This is the only reason you were climbing, Dexter? Sneaking in straw?'

'Exactly,' he said.

'And other supplies,' Olivia said, sniffing. 'And taking out her dung, when it backed up the drains. He wasn't climbing for the fun of it.'

'Right,' Henry said, making a snap judgement. It made his already unpleasant week significantly worse, since it involved someone he'd been studiously avoiding. 'I suppose it . . . er . . . *Persephone* being an, uh . . . emotional support pig makes it a welfare issue. We need the chaplain.'

* * *

Halley

Mom often stated that one of her greatest strengths was tough love, and Halley could do without it.

'You haven't eaten a single one of Henry's meals,' Mom said, cornering Halley at the coffee machine that morning. 'I counted.'

'Not hungry,' Halley muttered, sacrificing a second mug of caffeine to escape.

An hour later, Mom waited for her outside her bathroom. 'Y'know, Henry spent two evenings in the kitchen at Christmas, purely because you were sad that he'd never cooked for you.'

Halley shouldered past, only grazing Mom, who backed away at the last second.

And now Mom had put on *Gilmore Girls*. It was a trap, Halley knew, but she couldn't resist, and slunk in to sit on the opposite end of the couch, cradling a cushion.

'Do you—' Mom began, and Halley flinched.

'I can't talk about it right now. I'm starting at the department in the morning, and I've got to get my head straight . . .' She trailed off, figuring something out. Or rather, attempting to, and drawing a blank. 'Wait, you don't even know about that? And Antarctica and everything?'

'I heard about an enticing job in Chicago,' Mom said. 'You'll have to fill me in on Antarctica.'

Halley stared at her. 'Who from?'

'Angelie got a hold of me. So I cut my trip short and drove home.'

'Drove? Hadn't you flown to Arizona?' Halley felt like she was looking through the wrong end of a telescope.

'Different retreat, this time,' Mom said. 'Have some M&M's in popcorn.'

Halley shrouded her face in the cushion. 'No. I ate that with . . .'

'*Henry*,' Mom finished for her. 'You may as well say it. We have to discuss what happened sooner or later.'

'There's nothing to discuss. It's . . .' She bit her lower lip hard. 'Over.'

'At whose instigation?'

Halley didn't answer.

'Halley,' Mom said so gently that she risked a glance over the cushion. 'You ended it, didn't you? Did you feel Henry wanted you to choose between him and the job?'

Halley scrunched her forehead. 'He wouldn't do that. He's made it clear I shouldn't sacrifice anything for him.'

Mom stood up, and wandered to the shelf of framed photos. 'And, it wasn't worth making the effort to hash all this out in person?'

She breathed through the burn in her lungs. 'He wanted to. I told him not to come . . .'

Mom swung back toward her. 'Why ever not?'

Halley felt her frustration rise. 'This is actually nothing to do with you!'

'My kid's been hurt,' Mom shot back. 'Just because you did it to yourself doesn't make it any less my business!' Halley curled up into a tighter ball, and Mom sat heavily beside her. 'I get that Henry's not in a position to move here, and that you've got a great opportunity in Chicago. Or in Antarctica. Or something.' She waved a hand. 'Those details can wait. It's splitting up from Henry that's making you miserable — and him too, by the way.'

Halley screwed her eyes shut. 'Angelie can't possibly know that.'

'Viola does, though.'

'I knew you were gossiping with her,' Halley hissed.

Mom ignored her. 'I still don't understand why you ended it. Long-distance isn't ideal, but—'

'Every relationship he's ever had has fizzled out. I recognized that we were starting to, and cut it off quickly. In the long run, it's far less . . . painful.'

There was silence. 'What were the signs of it fizzling out?'

'I only found out about his mom's stroke from you! So he couldn't need me nearly as much as he thinks he does.'

Mom frowned. 'He said that?'

'Kinda. He said, like, he wanted me safe more than he needed me there for him.'

'And you took that as . . .' Mom patted her head, like she was a toddler again. 'You know you need to ask Henry to fly over?'

'Shut. Up. Mom.'

'Listen, Ju—'

'Seriously, Mom — why would I listen to you on romantic relationships? You're even more screwed up than I am!'

An instant later, she wished she could grab the words back. But Mom looked more intrigued than hurt. 'What on earth do you mean by that?'

Halley shrugged. 'Don't worry about it.'

Mom examined her intently. 'I think you need to tell me. And I know I need to tell you about the gentleman I just vacationed with.'

* * *

Voice note from Viola to Henry:

Henry, you need to answer your phone, or call me back. The radio silence is making me worry. Please — we only need to chat briefly, but let me know you're OK.

* * *

Tuesday, 4 February

Voice note from Viola to Henry:

Henry, I don't want to pull rank, but I'm your older sister, and I need to talk to you. So call me back, or I'm driving to Oxford. I bloody mean it!

* * *

Henry

His feet pounded in time to his heart, as he ran south along the towpath, in the direction of the Blue Moon. It was still light, so hours earlier than usual, but Kwame and Ruth would be arriving soon, and their task was at least a three-person job.

The Blue Moon came into sight, and he experienced the familiar lurch. If only he'd immediately told her about Mum, she'd be there now, illuminating it with her brilliance—

He rejected the train of thought. If she'd done an Aron and got on the next flight, she wouldn't have been at the symposium to get the amazing career opportunity. He couldn't regret what he'd done. But dredging all that up only led to madness, so he stretched out his legs to increase his speed, puffing harder. The sky was bright blue, the air crisp, and the low winter sun caused the canal water to shine silver.

He steeled himself to focus on the Blue Moon, then scrunched his eyes up, straining to see . . . Ruth and Kwame had arrived — *no*, he let out a groan. There was only one figure on the deck, not two, and he recognized her long black puffer coat, even with her hood up — it was Viola, making good on her threat.

She was peering through the tiny window beside the door to the galley, so she hadn't seen him yet, and he slowed, considering running back the way he'd come. But she was unfolding his deckchair, clearly prepared to wait for as long as it took, as she sunk down onto it, taking her out of his sight.

He should have locked the boat up properly, with the chain and shutters, because only having secured the doors made his imminent return obvious. And he should have avoided this entirely by responding to Viola's messages, rather than continually putting off even a brief reply.

He mopped the sweat from his forehead with the long sleeve of his T-shirt, mentally rehearsing the spiel: *Halley and I are over. Now it's sunk in, I'm fine.* It had to be smooth, and he must maintain eye contact, and it would be hell, but he repeated it a few more times. As he paced the final few metres, he switched to deep breathing instead, preparing himself to smile and speak fluently.

Then he stepped aboard the deck and, even before he glanced over at her, some instinct hit him, and all the breath left his body.

Because the eyes colliding with his weren't his sister's.

The woman scrambling up from the deckchair, wringing her hands together was . . .

It was Halley. His Halley. In the flesh.

PART SIXTEEN

Halley

The air was vibrating. Or she was. Halley couldn't tell.

'I . . . I came to say I'm sorry.'

Her words unleashed whatever restraint Henry had been imposing on himself, and he swept forward to envelop her in his arms.

She revelled in the sensation of his warmth, and solidity and best of all this reception, which was much better than she deserved. But far too soon, he loosened his grasp on her. She didn't let him pull back far, instead stepping with him. For a moment she feared he'd insist on distance, but instead his arms flew back around her and she was once more tucked in close to him.

'How are you here?' he said, so softly that she felt the shape of it against her forehead more than she heard it.

'I remembered my promise,' she breathed. He didn't reply, and she wondered if she'd need to remind him of her vow when he'd shared his haunting fear — only ever seeing her once in his lifetime.

'But *how*, Halley? Your new department . . .' He attempted to step back again, and this time she let him. Happiness and unease were warring on his face.

'Uh . . . the explanation might take a while. Can we go inside?'

He tore his eyes from hers to regard the Blue Moon's door. 'It's just . . . A coffee shop might be better . . .'

He didn't want her in his personal space, then. 'Oh. Sure,' she said, attempting a nonchalant tone and turning away to the suitcases she'd heaved onto the deck. 'Should . . . could we lock these in there, for now? Or bring them—'

'*Halley*?' She met his gaze. 'I didn't mean you're not welcome inside. It's that . . .' He broke off, shaking his head helplessly. 'So be it.' He moved to unlock the door, then held it open for her. 'Come in. Please.'

She stepped into the galley, slipping off her gym shoes as she observed that the sofa bed was pulled out, and piled high with linen and pillows. Unsure where to sit, she glanced back at Henry, who was wheeling in her luggage. He caught up her hand, leading her to a seat at the wood-burner side of the table-come-desk.

'Are you cold?' he asked.

'Not at all.' An instant later she was aware of her error. If she'd said yes, he'd have moved away to build the fire, giving her vital seconds to fortify herself for what must be said. Instead he was sliding in opposite her, so close their knees touched.

'I saw you in the distance, but thought you were Viola,' he said, his voice not yet recovered. 'She has a similar coat.'

'Every woman who frequents places as cold as Chicago and Iceland has a coat like this,' Halley said, wondering why the hell they were discussing coats. 'Just . . . I need a moment.' She steepled her hands, rested her chin on them, and closed her eyes. Opening them, she caught a glimpse of something on Henry's face, before he shuttered it an instant later.

It had been fear, and she tensed, hating herself. Perhaps her first instinct had been right, after all, when she ended what was between them, rather than drawing out their agony.

'Halley?' he said unsteadily. 'You look like you're regretting coming. Please don't. I'm glad you're here . . . however short — or long — your stay.'

With his face only a foot from hers, it was impossible to miss the flicker of pain as he said *however short,* and his absolute agony when he added *or long,* and she suddenly knew what he was thinking, even clearer than she knew her own mind: it would be hell if she left — and even worse if she stayed, because of what she'd have had to sacrifice.

She held her hands out for his. He gave them to her, and she entwined their fingers. 'Henry, let me explain—'

'No,' he said, with surprising intensity. 'Let me . . . bask in this for a little longer, before everything else intrudes again.'

'Listen to me,' she whispered. 'I want us to be together.'

His brows drew together. 'But the job? And your dream — Antarctica?'

'Please listen,' she said again, and his hands tightened on hers in response. 'After Professor Jansen insisted, yesterday morning, that I tell her why I'd been planning on writing up over here, I confided . . . our situation. And then couldn't stop crying. For like, two hours. So she . . . well, she countered with a new offer. I think it's our compromise.'

The parallel lines appeared between Henry's brows. She wanted to smooth them out with her fingers. 'I don't understand.'

'They offered me the job in the first place because they wanted my input on their Antarctica telescope, right? Turns out, if I don't want the job, they still want my input.' Her throat ached, so even breathing hurt. 'They'll pay me to winter-over in Antarctica. Like, *this* winter. I can do the work on their telescope, and write up my thesis while I'm there. If I accept — if *we decide* I should accept,' she corrected, desperate for him to know she wouldn't make a unilateral decision again, 'I'd have to leave two weeks from now, and be gone for six months. Afterwards, I'll move here.'

She waited for his verdict, her stomach tight with trepidation. 'Six months in Antarctica,' he said slowly. 'But then . . . no job to return to.'

'Umm . . . Well, it's kind of prestigious, to be upgrading a telescope like that, right out of doctoral studies. Professor

289

Jansen alerted the London university who's partnering on the telescope. She says they'll . . . well, to quote her exactly, *snap me up.*'

Henry's face was inscrutable again. 'You're telling me that if we wait six months, you'll be here for good?'

'I mean . . . if we decide I should accept . . .'

Henry was laughing, as he leaned in so close that she felt his breath on her face. 'How could that ever be in question? You found our compromise, Halley! Only six months apart — when I've spent a week thinking it'll be at least three years before I'd be in a position to even try to win you back!'

'I'd have to fly to New Zealand on the eighteenth.' She didn't know what was wrong with her, listing objection after objection like this, when she'd spent the long journey here aching for him to agree to the compromise she'd found. 'The day before your birthday. I'll be flying the final leg by the nineteenth — I won't even be able to contact you.'

'So I'll get to spend my birthday knowing you're coming back to me,' he said, still smiling as he stood and drew her to her feet. He slipped his arms inside her coat and wrapped them around her waist.

She reached up to encircle his neck. 'But it's half a year apart, leaving in *fourteen days* — I'll miss you so bad!'

'I'll miss you too. Six months without physical proximity's rubbish, but we'd talk every day. And we're experts at virtual dates. We're good at that — we *started* like that.'

'We started with a kiss,' she said, her eyes flying to his soft lips. Instead of taking the hint, he made a demurring sound, and released her waist.

'We started with rain, and a queue. And your hair was just like this.' He touched the pencil she'd used to hold it up, then pulled it out, releasing her long hair. 'I've wanted to do that since September. And this.' He slid both hands from her neck into her hair, as she leaned in to meet his mouth halfway.

The memory of their first kiss had been seared into her lips for months, and every time she'd imagined being reunited with Henry, their kiss carried on from where that one had left off. But as good as it was, that kiss had been between near-strangers.

This one was instantly deeper, fuelled by the connection of their minds and depth of their love and the all-consuming desire to finally know each other in the one way that had been barred to them by distance.

When they eventually parted, she was grasping the round neck of Henry's top and he had a hand in her hair and the other spanning her shoulder blades. Neither of them released their hold enough for them to separate more than an inch, as she shifted her eyes in the direction of his bedroom.

'Shall we . . .' she began.

Henry pulled her close to him once more. 'Unfortunately, it's . . . occupied.'

'What?'

He was laughing soundlessly. She could feel the quake in his chest, and when she stepped back from him he only laughed harder, covering his face with his hands. 'Oh God. You'll think . . . I have no idea what you'll think . . .'

Giving up on an explanation, she turned to pace through the corridor, where she had to sidle past a double mattress, resting on its side against bookcases. The bedroom door was shut fast, and she knocked uncertainly before turning the handle. Inside was entirely bare, except for the bedframe and a large object, entirely covered by a blanket. She edged closer and lifted the fabric, exposing the mesh of an animal crate.

Inside was a pig in a pink collar, which snuffled at her.

* * *

Henry

As he and Kwame heaved the crate into the back of the van, Ruth was apologizing to Halley again. 'Henry didn't want the pig on the Blue Moon, but there was nowhere else,' she added, as if Halley might otherwise feel that he'd replaced her with a pig.

'And it was only for a few hours,' Henry said. 'After the vet appointment.'

'So you both keep saying,' Halley said, smiling as he returned to her side. He wanted to sling his arm around her shoulders, but wasn't quite sure whether it would be welcome, when he hadn't had a chance to change since his run.

Halley slid an arm around him, resting her hand on the waistband of his joggers, which effectively answered his question. He pulled her close and kissed the top of her head, inhaling the scent of her hair.

'I'd better get back to reassure the young fools that it's gone to the petting farm without any problem,' Ruth said, with a sigh.

'Don't say it like that to Olivia,' Kwame put in, slamming the van's back doors. 'She'll insist the creature's a her, not an it. You know she begged me to tell the petting farm that her name's Persephone OxPig?'

Ruth gawked at him. 'Don't you dare! I've spent forty-eight hours applying for the licenses to hold a pig, register a pig, and transport a pig, to legally enable the rehoming to go ahead, all alongside evading questions about where the creature came from and why it's been unlicensed until now. *Persephone OxPig* gives rather too much away, so she's become Perri.'

'Perri it is,' Kwame said. 'Mate, you ready?'

Henry wanted to say no, but it was his students who were being rescued from expulsion, and Ruth had already done more than enough. 'Sure,' he said, hugging Halley tight, before peeling himself away from her.

'Why don't you come back to St Jude's with me, Halley?' Ruth said. 'The boys will only be an hour, so they'll be with us by dinner.'

Halley glanced at him. 'Does dinner at college work?'

She'd made friends with his friends at Christmas, so it made sense that she was up for it. But he'd rather have her to himself tonight. 'If you want? Or a restaurant — or I could straighten the place up and cook?'

292

At the final option, her face lit up. 'I'd like that. And I'll get the Blue Moon straight while you're gone.'

Reluctantly, Henry got into the passenger seat of the van, then recalled what she'd need, and rolled down the window. 'Sweetheart?' He threw her the set of spare keys for the Blue Moon, and she caught them one-handed.

'Thanks, babe. See you in an hour.'

'A bit less,' he promised her, waving as Kwame pulled off, smirking. 'What?'

'You know Babe's a pig, right?'

'Maybe concentrate on speed, or I'll list all the ways Ruth's referred to you during sermons in chapel. My hubby-wubby—'

'All right — putting my foot down!'

* * *

Halley

After building up the log burner she'd hauled the double mattress through to the bedroom, before retrieving the linen and pillows from the sofa bed and making it neatly. Then she'd indulged in a long shower, re-dressed in knit lounge-wear, and sat crossed-legged in front of the fire, finger drying her hair.

It was still damp when there was a knock on the stern door, forty minutes after Henry had left.

'It's only me,' he called, his keys jangling.

'It's unbolted.' She smiled as he entered. '*Only me*? The love of my life isn't *only* anything. Come and kiss me.'

'The love of your life, eh?' He was smiling as he made his way toward her, but then paused and ran his hands through his hair rather ruefully. 'The love of your life stinks of a run and a pigsty, and you're all shiny and perfect. Give me ten minutes?'

'Five,' she said begrudgingly, but blew him a kiss as he passed her.

While she waited, she rubbed her hair vociferously with a towel. Twitchy for his return, she focused her mind on counting down silently, but it only increased her nerves. By the time he exited the shower room, she was trembling.

He wore a white T-shirt, and brushed cotton trousers that were probably pyjamas and, like her, had a towel round his neck. She wondered if her own expression was as serious, and intent.

He didn't sit beside her on the rug, but on the end of the sofa bed, from where he lowered his hands onto her shoulders. Her towel had become damp, and he unfurled it and set it aside, then replaced it with his own. 'Let me?'

Before she'd figured out what he was asking, he drew up the sides of the towel and started to rub her hair dry, much more gently than she'd been doing.

'I should buy a hairdryer,' he said, in little over a whisper.

His voice helped, and she found herself shifting back against his legs. 'I brought mine, but forgot a UK plug converter.'

He worked his way up from the lengths of her hair, and his hands lingered at her neck, parting her hair to stroke her skin. She closed her eyes and leaned back on his knees as his fingers rose again, rubbing circles into her scalp.

She was relaxing properly for the first time in days, and her nerves had dissipated entirely. As the tips of his fingers reached her forehead, she reopened her eyes, unsurprised to find Henry's blue-green gaze fixed down on her.

'I love you,' she breathed.

His eyes crinkled. 'I love you too, Halley.'

They had fourteen days, which left no time for shyness, so she stood up. 'Prove it.'

She thought he might blush, but instead he was instantly moving, and then she was flying, and laughing hard, as he scooped her into his arms. She held tight as he carried her into his bedroom and collapsed them onto his bed.

She'd landed on her back beside him, and rolling onto her side, Halley found herself nose to nose with Henry. She couldn't read his expression.

'Do you wanna do this?' she blurted.

His eyes went wide. 'Why, don't you?'

'Of course! I suggested it. I'm checking it's OK with you?'

'I think I'll cope,' he said solemnly, before he laughed again. 'You literally never need to ask. Just claim some of those million kisses I promised you.'

She was close to memorizing every valediction he'd used, but especially that one. '*Soon I will hold you in my arms and lavish you with a million kisses,*' she murmured, as Henry lifted her hand, and pressed a kiss to her palm.

'One,' he said.

'No,' she said, giggling because it tickled, and she was reunited with Henry, and she'd found their compromise. 'There were three earlier. That was number four.'

She could feel his smile against the sensitive skin of her wrist, before he kissed her there. 'Five.'

Before he'd even made his whole way up her left arm, it was her who'd lost count — and, she found, when she tried to point that out — the power of speech.

* * *

Wednesday, 5 February
Henry

Not only was Halley finally in his bed at the same time as him, but she was comfortable — and exhausted — enough to still be sleeping soundly. He tried not to rustle the covers as he got up and padded out of the bedroom, closing the door almost noiselessly behind him. He opened the wood burner and set a fire, then picked up the discarded towels from the floor, smiling.

Halley appeared before the kettle was even boiled, wearing his bathrobe.

'I forgot to thank you for the frozen meals,' she said, hugging tight around his chest. 'I had both the desserts on Monday, just after booking my flight, and they were delicious. And I know you claim I'm smart, but you must have reconsidered when I missed all the hints to check out the deepfreeze.'

'I claim you're *brilliant*, because you are — and soon there'll be an upgraded telescope in Antarctica to prove it to the rest of the planet.' For a moment he worried that he'd been wrong to mention it. Antarctica was why they only had two weeks together, for now.

But Halley smiled, before heaving a sigh. 'I've gotta cut down on coffee, ready for that.'

'Earl Grey then? Or herbal tea?'

'*Herbal*,' she repeated, imitating his pronunciation.

'It makes a lot more sense than '*erbal*.'

'No it doesn't. And I guess one coffee's OK.'

'And what would you like for breakfast?' he asked, spooning ground coffee into the cafetière. 'I might need to pop out for ingredients — I've run out of eggs.' He'd run out of almost everything. He couldn't even remember when he last bought groceries. Thankfully they'd both been too preoccupied for supper.

'Let's go out for breakfast? I'll bring a notebook so we can plan a schedule for the next thirteen days. I've got plenty to keep me busy whenever you've got to work, but I'll make sure I'm free whenever you are.'

'I've got very little on this week, and I booked next week off, remember? For our—' He caught himself. She'd leave the day before his birthday. 'For your birthday, and Valentine's.'

'You didn't cancel the leave, when I . . .'

'No,' he said, pouring boiling water. He darted a look at her. 'And I also didn't cancel something I'd booked as your birthday gift. Remember when we imagined what we'd do if we were together right at that moment — you suggested Antarctica, but then preferred my suggestion?'

'Stargazing in the Cairngorms,' she said, round-eyed.

'I booked that cabin we found. With a telescope beside the hot tub.'

'Oh my God!' She ignored the mug he pushed along the countertop, leaning up to kiss him instead. 'That's amazing! Though . . . I didn't bring a swimsuit.'

He waggled his eyebrows. 'Lucky me.'

Halley's smile was smug as he bent to return her kiss, but just as their lips met, his phone rang.

She pulled back. 'You're not getting that?'

'It'll only be Viola.'

Halley stepped back further. 'That reminds me. There's something I need to tell you.'

'Later,' he begged.

She shook her head. 'It's important. I falsely accused her of gossiping about us to my mom. It was never Viola. She and Angelie exchanged a few messages last week, and Angelie then talked to my mom, but that was all. Mom's informant was someone else entirely.'

Henry frowned. 'Who?'

'Rupert Peters! When Mom got your initial email, she decided to check it really came from the only Henry Inglis she could find in Oxford — on your college website. So she emailed your boss to confirm. He replied a few weeks later, and since then they've been emailing as much as us — maybe more!'

Speechless, Henry stared at her.

'Apparently Rupert mostly refused to discuss you, so useful things didn't get back to me — like when you were sick with flu. But when Mom planned my Christmas trip she got enough out of him to figure out where you were — or so she thought. And when you asked him about jobs in America, he freaked and told Mom to have me dissuade you. And they've just been on vacation together!' Halley winced. 'They booked it before they'd even met once! Mom refers to him as her silver fox, and tried to tell me all these things they've been up to . . .'

* * *

Thursday, 6 February

Voice note for Viola from Henry:

Hey Vi, your rubbish little brother here. Uh . . . as you'd surmised, I was having a rough week, but everything's fantastic now. How are

Mum and Dad — can I have an update? And . . . well . . . Halley's here, and wants to say hi — Hi Viola! Can I meet you really soon? And your parents too, if it won't confuse your mom too bad? — *So, yes, long story short, Halley's here for another twelve days, then in Antarctica for six months, then back here for good. And if it works for you, we'll come to Hampshire shortly, to introduce her to you all, and collect those wine glasses — let me know.*

* * *

Friday, 7 February
Halley

Henry was particularly cute in his reading glasses, but unfortunately, the middle of the Old Bod wasn't a place she could do anything about it. Except plot for later, so she made the most of sitting opposite each other, their feet tangled under the table, and surreptitiously opened instant messenger on her laptop.

> *Henry, wear those for me when we're alone and I'll make it worth your while . . .*

She knew when it appeared on his laptop screen, because he went pink. She also knew that he blushed because he was fair skinned, not because he was shy, so she was unsurprised when a reply flashed up.

> *Same, for the skimpy sparkly thing that's been winking at me from the wardrobe. xxx*

How about 8 p.m. tonight, your time (and mine)?

> *Make it 6 p.m., and you've got a deal. xxx*

It was hard to return her attention to her project after that, and she minimized it to reread their instant messages.

The xxx she'd loved when they couldn't actually kiss were such a pale reflection of the real thing. And it was all she'd get for half a year. She added another message.

When I'm away, don't message me xxx. We should wait for the real thing.

She was aware of Henry looking over at her, but kept her attention on her screen, and he got the hint.

Seriously?

She considered before replying.

Yeah. And none of the valedictions and I love yous in emails, either. Let's keep emails for practical stuff, and save the romance for video calls.

That's ludicrous, sweetheart.

It's not! All that feels like a step backwards — we don't need to hide between written communications anymore.

I'm unconvinced.

Well I'm not!

I'll think about it. Ready to go home?

Hell yes! But you had something important to check out?

Instead of a written reply, he was out of his seat, smiling at her. '*I'm done*,' he mouthed. They'd only brought one bag, and they both packed their things inside, before Henry shouldered it.

They exited into Radcliffe Square, and Henry spun to face her so quickly that for a split second she wondered if he was exasperated by her suggestion for their written communications. But he was grinning.

'I just found something I've been looking for since before I even met you.'

She paused from tucking her hair into her hood. 'What?'

'Information on Lawrence Sedgwick after he left the Royal Navy in 1815. There was no reference to him at all in the records from the Sedgwicks' local church, where the rest of the births, marriages and deaths were listed. I'd begun to fear that he died on the road after leaving his final ship.'

'Oh no, poor Christobel Mallory!'

'That would be Christobel Sedgwick,' he said, reaching for her hand. 'It's what I found — their marriage certificate, from that same day in 1815 — but in Portsmouth, where his ship had docked. She must have rushed there to be reunited with him, and they got married right away.'

'But what happened after that?'

He shrugged, and led her toward the canal, and home. 'Don't know yet. But I've got six months on my hands for digging around old parish records. I'll start with births registered in 1816, and go from there.'

'But they were reunited,' Halley said, as it sank in. 'All that love, in all those letters, through all that danger he faced, and they made it.'

'They made it,' Henry agreed, grasping her hand a little tighter.

* * *

Sunday, 9 February
Henry

He most liked everything that was impossible through screens. Examining all the tiny charms on Halley's necklace. Giving her tastes of food he was making. Touching,

touching, touching. And most recently, the romance of star-gazing — even though it turned out to mostly comprise of Halley's lectures on the night sky.

'So that's Mars and obviously, the moon,' Halley said, pointing into the sky with her finger, between the orange-red twinkle and the crescent moon nearby. 'Over the next few hours they're gonna make an even closer approach to each other. Not close enough that you'll be able to see them both at the same time through this telescope, but even with the naked eye it'll be cool.'

He bent to examine Mars in more detail through the telescope. 'How did I never realize it's so literally the red planet?'

'Because you're like most people, and don't look up,' Halley said, rolling her eyes. 'Don't ask me why.' She thumbed something into her phone. 'I'm checking which quadrant we should observe for the meteor shower — no promises, but we might see what's commonly known as a shooting star. Remember it's a meteor though — asteroids are too small to see, and comets are visible for days or weeks, not just a few seconds.' Her voice had grown distracted, and she sat abruptly on one of the dining chairs they'd carried out to the decking.

'Everything OK, sweetheart?'

'Would the drive home take us anywhere near Manchester?'

'It could do. You want to upgrade to a better footie team?'

She looked scandalized. 'Never! You can't change allegiance from Southampton, and we already agreed to support each other's teams — except for international competitions when we're UK versus USA all the way.'

'So why the interest in Manchester?' He wasn't used to seeing her look shy, and drew the other chair close to sit beside her. 'It's a great city, and we can definitely fit it in, whatever your reason . . .'

'I've got an email that means the news must be out about what I'll be doing in Antarctica. A professor in Manchester wants to show me around her department, because they've got a junior professorship opening up in September . . . I think I want to accept the offer in London, so I can commute from Oxford, but there's no harm checking it out, right?'

Headhunted for a junior professorship, right out of her Ph.D. He grinned at her. 'None at all. If you prefer the department, we'll live in the middle and both commute. If you don't, you can use it to negotiate your salary in London.'

* * *

Thursday, 13 February

Text messages between Angelie and Halley:

Happy Birthday, Buddha! Have you come up for air yet? And how's Project: Get-Henry-To-Watch-A-Whole-Ball-Game?

> *Thanks! And good — I recorded the Super Bowl and he sat with me!*

Did he watch it though?

> *It was more like I watched the game while he read, and rubbed my feet.*

Your 'feet' lol.

> *Yes my feet! We'd hiked twelve miles the day before.*

> *But yeah, OK, not just my feet! Everything good there?*

Very. Ben's joined all my businesses, so it's more efficient for him to move in. You don't need to bother paying half the rent anymore.

* * *

From: Halley Hart
Subject: Podcast
To: Halley A. Hart
Hi Halley-Anne,

This is Henry's Halley. I wanted to thank you for offering to help him find me, and for the great advice you've given him since.

He and I are very much together, but I have a long trip upcoming. I've been downloading episodes of your pod for the journey, and if you'd like me to call into a future recording then that should be possible. I'd like veto rights on the episode title, though!

Thanks again and take care,
Halley

* * *

Tuesday, 18 February
Halley

Neurologists recognized at least nine senses, but in the past week she'd discovered another, so distinct she was certain it deserved a name of its own — the sense of Henry's body next to hers.

She ran a hand down his sleeping form, and he turned immediately, putting his arms around her. Not sleeping, then.

'Last time sharing a bed for half a year,' she whispered, her eyes stinging. 'How will we bear it?'

'With email,' Henry breathed. 'And video calls and music and books and friends and family and the absorption of our work.'

She frowned. 'All that's a lot. But is it enough?'

'I wasn't finished,' Henry said, nuzzling closer. 'Most of all, with the knowledge that it is *only* six months. After that we've got at least another thirty-five years — because I refuse to believe we won't be together to witness your comet when it's next visible, in the 2060s.'

They'd discussed the second half of the year, and even the next few years, via which job Halley might take, and where they should live, and vacations they'd like to plan, but never specifically beyond that. So to hear suddenly that Henry's frame of reference was a minimum of thirty-five years made her load lighten. With decades ahead of them, they'd survive six months.

'You'll remember to only write me brief, factual emails though?' she said.

The vertical lines appeared between his eyebrows. 'I wish you hadn't talked me into that. Do you really insist?'

'Yes! I don't want to bawl every time I open my inbox. So we'll keep those practical, and save the sentimental stuff for video chats.'

Henry didn't look at all convinced, but she distracted him with a deep kiss, refusing to waste a single second more of these last few hours before they'd part at the airport.

* * *

Wednesday, 19 February

From: Henry Inglis
Subject: Are You My Halley Hart?
To: Halley Hart
Dear Halley,

After my encounter, back in September, with a woman I only knew as Halley Hart, I couldn't get her out of my head. I had no idea whether I stood any chance of finding her, nor, of course, of everything that lay ahead. Now, five months on, the reality is that the distance between me and 'my' Halley — you — is further than ever.

I know you'll recall that today's my birthday. I also know you won't be in touch. Maybe that's why I've been able to think about little but those early days, and why I've found myself compiling all the emails that resulted from my search. I've attached a copy for you. You've seen some of it before of course — indeed, you wrote parts of it.

I hope this doesn't make you feel worse about everything — that's far from my intention.

Henry

* * *

From: Halley Hart
Subject: OK you're right!
To: Henry Inglis

Henry!! I've landed an hour ahead of schedule so it's 11.52 p.m. in the UK and I'm officially in time to wish you a Happy Birthday after all — it's the first time an airplane has ever come through for us!

I hope you found the gift in the drawer by the bed? If not then go look, and don't read on until you do . . .

Do you see?! You've emailed me a document with all our correspondence, and I printed out and bound the same, for you! I've added in messages with Mom and Angelie, whereas you've included stuff with Viola and Rupert and other Halleys, so if we add it all together, it'll tell the whole story of us . . .

Babe, even from my first glimpse, it's so beautiful here. The landscape's really dramatic, and pristine — a real frozen paradise. And it's so cold out that the air almost — but not quite — tastes minty.

On a practical note, the professor in London asks if I have a spouse who also needs a placement or a visa. (I replied that I don't, I have a boyfriend and he's British.) (I didn't add that he's also gorgeous, and practically perfect for me, and I miss him already, but that's all true, too). But then I got to thinking, the whole double-placement double-visa thing will be a pain in the ass for as long as we're not married, so shouldn't we get on with that once I'm back? We don't need to make a big deal about it, if you'd rather not — though Mom and Aunt Edie might have other ideas.

I love you, birthday boy.

Your Halley x

P.S. Sorry! Clearly, you were right and I was wrong. I don't wanna exchange emails with you that are as stilted as business letters. So scrap everything I said before — I want kisses and valedictions and all the romance in every email!

* * *

From: *Henry Inglis*
Subject: *'On a practical note'*
To: *Halley Hart*

Halley my sweetheart, my future wife, my forever,

There's no need to apologize. I knew your rules wouldn't last — least of all, because you've never known the difference between romantic and practical messages. But proposing marriage under the guise of mere practicality really takes the biscuit, Halley. Having said that, YES, let's get married when you're back! And, like your mother and aunt, I probably consider it a pretty big deal . . .

I hadn't found that gift until your email and still can't believe we had the same idea, to compile our communications. I love the plan to merge it all, but even then our correspondence won't quite tell the entire story. Maybe on the long nights ahead, when we're especially missing each other, we could try joining the gaps by writing what we each experienced in between our messages?

I love you, Halley Hart.

Thine Henry xxx

THE END

ACKNOWLEDGEMENTS

This book's first reader was Rebecca Lewis, whose insights and encouragement never fail to help. Timoteo and Emily Rosal and their children inspired me to develop a Cebuano character, and I'm so grateful to them for hosting me in Cebu over the years, and the thoughtful feedback on Angelie at every stage. Thanks to Laura and Tim for their notes, Rach for advising on California and airports, and Sean Gourley who I quizzed at length on Stanford and start-ups. Many Oxford conventions — and the ensuing jargon — are centuries old, yet there are also changes every generation, so I'm indebted to current Jesus and Trinity students Hetty Nicholls and Genevieve McCauley for their assistance.

I'm always grateful for having my brilliant literary agent, Tanera Simons, in my corner, and also her fantastic colleague, Laura Heathfield. I'd like to thank my editor, Kate Lyall Grant, whose response to this story was beyond encouraging, and her colleagues at Joffe Books, including Sarah Tranter for the copyedits and Lahli Trevis, who rose to the unenviable challenge of formatting this with aplomb.

When working in Hong Kong, in my early twenties, I met a clever and lovely man in a bar. Within weeks he heard he was being transferred to London, and told me, 'Long distance is shit. Let's get engaged and move there together instead?' You had no idea what you were inspiring, Stephen — nor when you bought a telescope 'for our children'. (And sorry for Halley repeatedly using two sets of brackets in a row.) (Despite it annoying you.)

Finally, this wouldn't have happened without my wider family, in particular my parents, five children, and the six generations of women who've shared variations on my name, and passed down 'the Clara locket'.

THE JOFFE BOOKS STORY

We began in 2014 when Jasper agreed to publish his mum's much-rejected romance novel and it became a bestseller.

Since then we've grown into the largest independent publisher in the UK. We're extremely proud to publish some of the very best writers in the world, including Joy Ellis, Faith Martin, Caro Ramsay, Helen Forrester, Simon Brett and Robert Goddard. Everyone at Joffe Books loves reading and we never forget that it all begins with the magic of an author telling a story.

We are proud to publish talented first-time authors, as well as established writers whose books we love introducing to a new generation of readers.

We won Trade Publisher of the Year at the Independent Publishing Awards in 2023. We have been shortlisted for Independent Publisher of the Year at the British Book Awards for the last four years, and were shortlisted for the Diversity and Inclusivity Award at the 2022 Independent Publishing Awards. In 2023 we were shortlisted for Publisher of the Year at the RNA Industry Awards.

We built this company with your help, and we love to hear from you, so please email us about absolutely anything bookish at feedback@joffebooks.com

If you want to receive free books every Friday and hear about all our new releases, join our mailing list: www.joffebooks.com/contact

And when you tell your friends about us, just remember: it's pronounced Joffe as in coffee or toffee!

Milton Keynes UK
Ingram Content Group UK Ltd.
UKHW010337180724
445696UK00004B/135